Also by Robin Martinez Rice

Imperfecta

Hidden Within the Stones

Sisters in Pieces

Tales of the Elemental Goddesses

Day-of-the-Not-So-Dead and other Morbid Little Holiday Tales

THE BLUE CLAY POT

THE BLUE CLAY POT

ROBIN MARTINEZ RICE

RLMR

ISBN-10: 0692141871

ISBN-13: 978-0692141878 (Robin Martinez Rice)

Dedicated to Bella Dreizler, who invited me into the dance.

A WORD ABOUT HISTORIC FANTASY

This is a genre which is NOT based on historic fact. This is a work of fiction that takes place a long time ago. Everything is made up, although I have visited the ancient dwellings of New Mexico many times. The traditions of the ancient people, the language, the structure of the parks... all fiction. Yes, some things are based on reality, but they are manipulated to fit the story.

The story came to me six years ago, as I was hiking in Northwest New Mexico. It was one of those times when a character jumped into my head and insisted I speak for her. And that is how this tale came to be.

ONE

Martha needed REM sleep. She thought about this at two in the morning, willing herself not to sigh or open her eyes or turn over in yet another attempt to find a comfortable position. Going through all the cycles was necessary for a human to feel rested and she hadn't had the restful rapid eye movement cycle since they packed the new camper and left California. She tried to convince her husband that her wellbeing was sliding downhill.

"Glen."

"Hmm…" He kept his eyes on the road, which just happened to be as straight as if some giant had used an immense yardstick to draw a line. All the roads in Arizona and New Mexico seemed endless to Martha.

He could glance my way. Just for a second. "What do you think about staying in a motel tonight?"

Now his head swiveled. "What? Why would you say that?"

"I haven't had a full night of sleep in a week. I haven't had a single dream."

"Oh, Martha. You haven't had a full night's sleep in years."

This was true. Two years ago she got that CPAP machine. Don't ask her what those letters meant, she couldn't remember. Something about airways and pressure. Anyway, it did help with her sleep problems. For a while.

Glen and Martha hadn't shared a bedroom for a long time. Between her tossing, turning, and sighing and his snoring, there weren't any restful nights. She had moved into their daughter's old bedroom in an effort to sleep. Glen swore the CPAP machine, with its wheezing moan timed to her inhalations, didn't bother him, but it bothered her that he had to listen to it.

Glen had been out like a log for the last three nights, while Martha lay awake next to him on the thin mattress of the over-the-cab-bunk in the new camper. Their retirement dream purchase.

They weren't retired. Not yet. Granted, the last few years had been good to them, with no emergencies to suck away their savings, the kids all launched—although it was questionable if you could call Jack launched—and a fat end-of-year bonus from Glen's company. It was accidental that they were on this trip, a series of events tumbling like the dominos her children had set in long lines on the dining room floor. She was always called to come watch as each tile knocked into the next until the last one fell. If Glen's brother hadn't died at age sixty-two, if her husband hadn't grown tired of setting up the tent, if she hadn't been at loose ends since the children left home…those dominos had all fallen and Glen had decided that now was the time to buy the camper. Not ten years from now when they would be too old to enjoy it or dead like his brother.

She did like the camper. The tiny kitchen, with slim cupboards that had hidden latches to keep them from flying open while driving. Cooking while standing in one spot was so easy: swapping the cutting board for the strainer in a sink the size of a dishpan, reaching over to the two-burner stove to toss cut vegetables into the fry pan or stir the bubbling stew, twisting to get something out of the mini-refrigerator. And cleaning was more streamlined. She could dust and disinfect the whole place in ten minutes. When it was cold at night you could heat the space with the flip of a switch next to the bed. Sixty seconds later it was warm enough to venture to the tiny combined bathroom/shower/closet. And while there were those not-so-pleasant components of living on the road, such as emptying the dump tank and filling the propane cylinder, driving onto leveling blocks or adjusting the long steel legs to make sure their heads were above their hearts while they slept, Glen took care of those things.

She looked at her husband. "I'm really not sleeping well. Just one night."

Glen looked back at the road. "You are having dreams. I hear you talking in your sleep. You're just not remembering them. Isn't that a sign of REM?"

Martha tapped her finger on her knee and counted the telephone poles. She would know if she slept. She always remembered her dreams.

Lost in her thoughts she stared out the window as they zipped past red clay boulders forming strange stone figures along the highway. The scattered buildings gave clues to the names of some of the formations: Camel Rock Quick Stop, Little Bear Poker, Three Bulls Liquor.

She saw more than animals in the rocks. Ancient faces stared at her. Wise old eyes with an air of disgust. As if to say no one should build a highway here and rush by without stopping to share in the wisdom we hold in our ancient rock spirits.

"I think there are probably lots of those funky, retro motels in Los Alamos. It would be really fun to stay in one." Martha tried to come up with an idea Glen would buy into or at least one he would think was his own.

"We have reservations at the park. Do you remember how hard it was to get those?"

Martha sighed. Her husband—who constantly told her she needed to be more assertive and ask for what she needed—refused to listen. The story of her life.

What if she had a do-over? If she could go back to the very beginning and live her life again? Would she be more like Clarice, her daughter, always insisting on and getting what she wanted? Maybe she would be more like Jack, the baby of the family, completely free from anyone's expectations but her own. A smile touched the edges of her lips as she thought about her firstborn child. She was like Vince. More accurately, her son was like her.

Come to think of it, she would be a different kind of mother. Glen constantly bragged about what great parents they were, how their kids had turned out, ignoring the fights and bailouts with Jack, the stress when Clarice didn't come home on time, the…well…it was true there hadn't been much stress with Vince. But Martha would do things differently. She was sure that she'd had postpartum depression with Jack, such a fussy, rigid baby. She really hadn't bonded with him. That had to be the root of all his rebellion. And Clarice…Martha had pushed so hard to keep her from being a tomboy, surrounded by brothers, wanting to be like them and doing what they did. She had hoped to lure her daughter into the feminine world but she could see now that her intentions had backfired. Perhaps if she hadn't fought her daughter so much, Clarice wouldn't have resisted, and the pendulum wouldn't have swung so far in the opposite direction.

It seemed that by limiting her expectations—she simply wanted each of her children to be a good student, have nice friends and stay healthy—Martha had thought she would avoid disappointment. When it came to the kids, Glen always said "keep your eye on the prize" and he was able to float through colicky infants, broken collar bones and Clarice's tantrums. The river Martha floated on wasn't so smooth and deep, more like a sandy coffer dam, springing leaks with each new storm. She sighed and nodded off, listening to the hum of the wheels on the smooth highway.

That night at the coveted camp site, claiming she wasn't mad at him —although she was—Martha took a blanket and slept in the cab. She used the battery for her CPAP machine because there were no hook-ups at this park. Glen would have to find somewhere to charge it tomorrow.

The machine didn't help. Still no dreams because she never really fell asleep.

After a camper's breakfast of hot coffee, scrambled eggs, and oranges they drove down the narrow winding road into the canyon. The tiny Visitor Center held a museum, a book store and a theater. They visited the museum first, where Glen read every display: the descriptions of the early people, the timelines of those living in this canyon, so long ago, the year only 900. A year measured in only three digits seemed unimaginably far away and Martha was relieved when the timeline read 1100, 1200, 1300. The chart listed the reasons the ancestral Puebloans had left, the impact of weather and water on farming, and gave the explanation of the pumice which made up their walls. Martha skimmed through each plaque but was more interested in admiring the craftsmanship and beauty of the collections of pots, baskets, woven rugs and clothing. She was surprised by the cotton clothing. She would have guessed skins or nothing at all, but that was based on what she had learned back in elementary school. She took the time to read about how these ancient Puebloans had traded for cotton and in a few spots, grown it themselves.

Martha spent a long time looking at each of the clay pots, thinking about the hands that had formed these works of art a thousand years ago. Time was such a strange thing. If you were waiting for the news of an x-ray following your child's bike accident, a few moments felt like an eternity. Yet standing here studying the zig zag pattern of the painted clay, it felt like very little time had passed since this pot was created. She could almost feel the woman deciding which pattern to paint on the clay.

Glen pointed to a small sign on the wall. "They have a movie. Do you want to watch it?" Not waiting for her answer, he started off down the hall.

"Maybe we should hike before it gets too hot." Martha watched his retreating back. Oh well, the film couldn't be more than half an hour and it would be better to learn about the park before they hiked. She started after him but was distracted by a large model inside a glass case.

The whole canyon in miniature. She pressed the red button on the wall and a tinny recording explained that the area had housed people for thousands of years. The people of this area were farmers and grew maize, beans, and squash. There were lots of native plants which also supplied them with food, and they hunted deer, rabbits, birds, and other things to supplement their diets.

Half listening to the drone of information, she studied the intricate diorama which depicted life in the cliff dwellings more than a thousand years ago. Tiny figures with long, dark hair and clothing made from woven cotton and skins climbed to the caves. There was a round kiva in the middle of the valley, with a clay figure popping out of the hole in the roof. The huge complex of living quarters was open like the back of a dollhouse, and she bent forward to peer into the rooms. Women sat inside the clay walls working. Cooking and weaving baskets, she supposed, but the figures were so small it was hard to tell. Miniature children played next to them—arms and legs no bigger than pins.

Glen interrupted her examination of the ancient village. She must have stopped longer than she realized.

He waved a yellow sheet of paper at her. "I got a map. Let's go."

"What about the movie?"

"It started already. We should hike before it gets too hot. We can watch it later."

There were times Martha suspected Glen actually heard something she said, felt guilty for not responding and placated himself by returning and using the idea as his own. She had to be wrong. It was just a coincidence or even logical that he came up with her idea a few minutes later.

They hiked up the paved path, following the numbered signs placed at intervals throughout the ruins. Number 1: a view of the cliffs with an explanation of the early exploration of the canyon. Number 2: the volcanic geology of the plateau. Number 5: the kiva which was used for religious activities and educating boys and young men.

Martha paused. "So I thought they had a matriarchal society? Why were only boys educated here?"

"Huh?" Glen was fiddling with the camera.

"Nothing, just thinking out loud." Martha didn't want to get into any discussions right now and she regretted voicing the question. Once Glen got into lecture mode it was hard to turn him off.

Number 7: the entrance to the village. An apartment complex with four hundred rooms. She looked across the remnants of brick walls that were now only low stacks with weeds growing in between the stones. This was what was left of the building she had studied in the diorama.

Number 9: please use only the ladders to enter the caves. The ancient people used hand and footholds for all but the most difficult climbs.

Glen stood at the bottom of the ladder. "Are you going up?"

"Very funny."

"Here." He handed her the camera and his phone. "Take my picture once I'm up."

She watched him scramble up the smooth wooden ladder and squeeze his wide shoulders through the narrow opening. He turned and grinned, posing for the shot.

"Lean forward so your face is in the sun." She peered at the screen but with the sunlight so bright it was hard to see. She pressed the shutter a couple of times. "Okay."

"You took it already?"

She nodded.

"Take some more, on the phone, and this time warn me so I can smile."

With a sigh she lifted his phone and said "One, two, three…cheese."

Glen scrambled down. "Thanks. I wanted something to send to the kids."

"Good idea."

"Let me get one of you…if you stand right here, those yellow leaves along the creek make a great background."

Martha patiently posed while Glen adjusted settings and asked her to turn a little to the right. Hopefully the pictures she took of him had turned out fine.

After that, she quit reading the trail guide book. She was interested in history, but the sun was warm, the birds were singing and the sky was the brightest blue she had ever seen. It was a good time to enjoy the day without bothering to learn anything.

That night, Martha wasn't tired, in spite of the long day. "I'm going to read for a bit. Do you want me to use my headlamp?"

"Nope. I'm fine." Glen kissed her cheek and rolled away from her. She had decided to try the bed tonight after realizing the cab was too short for her to stretch her legs, and she hadn't slept anyway. They'd had lots of exercise with the hike and she had been careful with what she ate today. No chocolate or coffee after one o'clock. Surely she would sleep well tonight.

It wasn't until her eyes drooped and her book fell to her chest that she realized her CPAP machine battery wasn't charged. Glen was already asleep, his breath deep and steady. She slipped a bookmark into her spot and turned off the light. She would just have to sleep without her machine.

Seconds later, or maybe it was longer, because the air was cold, she felt a touch on her shoulder. *Oh Glen, don't wake me up, I'm sleeping so soundly.* She rolled over and pushed her face into the pillow. The cool smooth cotton soothed the allergies which plagued her constantly itching nose.

"Mar-tee-a."

This wasn't Glen's deep voice. This voice had nasal vowels and smooth, drawn out consonants.

"What?" Martha rolled over onto her back. "What are you saying?"

"Mar-tee-a." The voice repeated the phrase, as if by some chance saying the words over and over would turn them into something Martha could understand. "Mar-tee-a."

What a strange thing to dream, someone in the camper with them. Martha felt a laugh bubble up her throat. Dreams were so funny. This one must have come from the trip to the museum in the Visitor Center. Those buttons she had pressed on the exhibits and those first-person narratives at each display to bring the dioramas to life—these had slipped into her dream.

That explained the voice. But a woman in their bed? Was she fighting some subconscious jealousy?

"Mar-tee-a." The voice came again and a hand touched the back of her head, the gentle stroking of a mother comforting a child. She opened her eyes.

There really was a woman kneeling on the bed with her face close to Martha's. The outline of the visitor's head and shoulders was a silhouette in the faint light. A musky odor, leather and smoke, filled the camper.

Martha held her breath and pictured the turn and click of the deadbolt. She had locked the door last night before she climbed up into the bed. She looked over at Glen. He was asleep, the forest green comforter pulled up around his shoulders, his neck bent and tilting toward her. Sound asleep. This was definitely a dream. Her husband would have woken up if someone had come through the door and crawled up on the bed with them. She pressed her head into the pillow. REM sleep at last.

"Mar-tee-a, come please." The woman moved her hand under Martha's shoulder and rocked her forward.

Martha sat up, banging her head on the low ceiling.

In the dim light, it was impossible to make out much but there really was someone on the bed. Somehow, Martha didn't feel the urge to scream. Maybe because this wasn't real. A crazy dream. Glen would be yanked from sleep if she gave in to hysteria and then he would be grouchy all day.

"I can take care of this," she whispered and slipped the comforter off her shoulders. She scooted to the edge of the bed, slowly rolling onto her stomach, and slid off, waving her foot around to find the step. This was the part she hated.

With her feet firmly on the floor, Martha placed her hand on the edge of the counter for balance. Tugging her nightgown down from where it was stuck to her leggings, she slipped her feet into the sheepskin slippers next to the step.

The woman was illuminated by the dim light shining from the little adobe restroom building across the road, a thin shimmer through the tiny window in the camper. A dark braid wrapped with a strip of fabric hung over the woman's shoulder. Her nose was long, with a prominent bridge. Her skin was wrinkled and the glow of the irritating bathroom light reflected in her eyes like a cat in the headlights. Martha couldn't decide if this woman was old or merely weathered. Her hair might have had streaks of gray, but in the dim light it was impossible to tell.

"How did you get in here?" Martha whispered.

The woman shook her head and put a finger to her lips, then gestured for Martha to follow as she turned toward the door.

Martha's dreams had grown very strange over the last few years. So strange, in fact, that she had quit discussing them with the family. But never had a dream felt this real.

Glen and the children still held long conversations about the meaning of the unimaginable dreams they had. No one seemed to notice she wasn't comfortable with the interpretations of how people managed their lives, or the assumption that these dreams reflected psychological barriers in a person's past. Her life wasn't that exciting and it didn't hold all these mysteries. And if it did they were best kept hidden.

Have I ever had a dream in which I felt the cold of the early morning air? One in which I got up and followed someone out the door? Martha shook the thoughts from her head and recalled all the things she had heard about dreams. If you dream that you die, you really do die. Bathroom dreams, searching for the perfect toilet, but if you found it you would wet your bed. Premonition dreams, lucid dreams, dreams of your past lives.

If she followed this woman was she in danger?

On second thought, why couldn't it work out the other way? Instead of something bad—dying or wetting the bed—couldn't a dream bring something wonderful?

The woman motioned to her again. Martha felt a wave of pressure on the back of her head, pushing her forward. Feeling as if she had no choice in the matter, she climbed down the four metal steps, then pushed the door shut with a soft click.

A glowing sensation shimmered between her and the old woman, like a tether attaching her to the ghostly figure. Her chest, both warm and cold, held a glow that made her stomach churn. She knew this woman, as if she were a long-lost cousin or great-grandmother.

A spirit guide.

This was good. Spirit guides were important. The guardian angels of the ancient people. Martha had thumbed through a book at the Visitor Center yesterday, captivated by the idea that a guide could be an animal or even a plant. She was going to buy the book—the illustrations alone made it worth having—but the fifty dollar price tag changed her mind.

If you had a spirit guide you had someone to help you with life's complicated decisions. How wonderful would that be? No complaining to the women in her book club in an effort to gain clarity.

Martha had tried meditation once. She waited until the kids were at school and Glen had driven off in his truck each day. She used a CD borrowed from the library, carefully piling pillows on the living room floor and dutifully following the instructions. After a week of feeling very silly, she returned the CD. All this breathing and emptying one's mind might work for some people, but she couldn't help imagining what she looked like—legs folded, forefingers touching thumbs, hands perched on her knees, eyes closed. What if someone came home unexpectedly?

If I follow her I can find out what having a spirit guide really means.

She set off after the woman.

They crossed the campground and entered a thicket of trees that lined a narrow trail, winding slightly up a modest grade. The trees were tall, standing shoulder to shoulder. It was darker here and Martha kept her eyes forward—it wouldn't do to lose sight of her guide. Martha didn't have a particularly good sense of direction and she would soon be lost in this dark forest. After just a few minutes the trail led out of the thicket and onto the flat top of the mesa. The trees here were more like brush, small and bushy with sparse needles clustered at the ends of sharp branches. The moon, low in the sky as dawn approached, lit up the trail. This was a good thing, as there were rocks and boulders along the edges. At least she could see enough to avoid stumbling.

The woman turned and held up her hand, palm facing forward as she motioned ahead. They were at the edge of the canyon and the trail disappeared from sight, dropping over the steep edge.

Martha met the woman's eyes. "Where are we going?"

The woman didn't answer, just disappeared over the edge, as if she had stepped into vast nothingness.

If the trail went over the edge, there was a hill or a cliff. Martha turned and looked back the way she had come. It seemed darker in that direction and she could just make out the grove of trees.

Come on, dream. Take me back to my warm bed. She took three steps toward the campground. Pressure built around her, as if she were being pushed by hundreds of unseen hands. She stopped and took a deep breath. Something didn't want her to go back.

"Go on," she whispered. "Live a little." Drawing in another lungful of air, she followed the woman once more.

The sound of gravel crunching beneath her feet on the steep slope was very un-dreamlike. Martha thrust her arms out to the sides as the smooth soles of her slippers failed to gain traction, attempting to balance and searching for something to grab if she started to fall, sucked over some unseen edge that surely existed. The old woman's pace didn't slow and soon she was out of sight. Martha stopped and looked up. The sky was growing lighter as dawn crept up behind her. The bushes looked like short people standing with arms akimbo, reaching out and grabbing at her nightgown. Martha moved cautiously, sliding each foot forward and testing the path before shifting her weight. Her arthritic knee ached and she didn't want to risk it collapsing.

The trail curved sharply to the right. Martha still couldn't see the woman. Her dream had changed from a thrilling adventure to being lost in the wilderness. She longed for Glen's solid back, where she could curl into a spoon and smell his familiar warm french toast and peanut butter odor, with just a trace of his sweat thrown in.

She'd missed sleeping next to him these past few years. "I'm sorry," she whispered. "I shouldn't have blamed you for my insomnia." This must be a guilt dream, meant to show her all she was taking for granted. She stopped and squeezed her eyes shut.

She felt as if she had been running all night. Maybe she could change this upsetting event, use a half-waking state to rescue herself from the chase. She needed to guide this dream back to restfulness or she would be in terrible shape tomorrow.

She opened her eyes.

The right side of the path was bordered by a smooth stone wall and the left side curved out to a sharp drop. The entire trail was carved out of the earth, a slick expanse covered with fine gravel.

That's it. I'm going back. Martha turned around and stared at a black expanse. Where had this abyss come from? Hadn't she just walked down a winding trail?

This dream didn't allow for backtracking.

She turned and searched the dim landscape for any sign of the woman. Catching a glimpse of something that might have been her spirit guide, she placed one hand on the wall and secured her shoulder against the stone. She pressed her body close and slid along to keep from being sucked over the edge by the dark vacuum below. It was a good thing the light was dim, because if she could see the long drop she wouldn't be able to go on.

As she slid along the wall, the calls of the morning birds filled the air, the faint light their alarm clock. If she focused on the chirps and whistles maybe she would forget about the yawning space to her left. Behind the chattering birds another sound echoed off the rock walls—a rhythmic beat, like machinery. *Thump, thump, thump-a-thump*, repeated over and over.

Martha stopped to catch her breath and turned her head toward the sound. Goosebumps tingled between her shoulder blades as the tightness in her chest slipped away, and suddenly she was aware of the smell of sage blossoms. There was another odor, a smoky smell, not a campfire, but more the odor of meat cooking in Glen's black iron barbecue. She sniffed, like a dog with its nose in the air, as if that could give her a sense of what was happening. It was impossible to tell which direction the scent was coming from, and Martha knew that from where she perched on the edge of the wall of the canyon it could be below or above or anywhere at all.

It's a dream. Go find out what smells so good. She stepped forward.

The trail curved very sharply now. "Hairpin turns but I believe the real term is switchbacks." Martha coached herself along, speaking out loud as a distraction—her personal version of the "don't look down" rule. Eventually the trail flattened out, cutting across a wide ledge in the earth. It was light enough now to make out the rock wall on one side and the steep drop-off on the other and she was relieved to see that the trail cut right through the middle with at least six feet on either side. She could walk across this flat space without some evil spirit pulling at her, trying to convince her to jump. She could see ahead now and caught sight of the faint light reflecting off the woman's tunic. Martha tried to catch up, but after ten steps she was out of breath. At forty-eight years old she wasn't in terrible shape, but running was not in her repertoire of skills. However, if she didn't want to lose her guide again she would have to hurry.

When Martha reached the edge of the little plateau, a high white wall of rock rose in front of her, honeycombed with holes of varying sizes.

This was the pumice she had seen yesterday, Glen clambering up that ladder while she stood with her hand on the stair rail. Molten lava that had dried with lots of air bubbles, lending itself to the formation of caves.

The old woman waited in front of a narrow opening. She slipped inside and Martha followed. It felt like entering a bee cathedral and she smiled at the thought of a life-size queen bee seated on a throne at the end of this corridor.

The moon was gone and the small bit of light that penetrated the slot canyon was from the rising sun. The last of the stars had faded and the dark outline of the edges above her pressed down like stern soldiers guarding a castle. The walls were rough and full of holes. She reached out and touched them, like a blind woman making her way through the dim, winding rock tube.

"Ouch!" Martha sucked on her knuckle, the skin torn by the sharp rocks. She strained to see, and carefully touched the walls with just the tips of her fingers to avoid more injury. If her spirit guide would only slow down and be a bit more of a…well…a guide, it wouldn't be so hard to follow her.

The walls grew narrower still, barely wider than Martha's shoulders, closing in on her like a vise. Her breath froze as her lungs forgot how to exhale and a trembling began in her hands and moved up into her jaw. She was cold now. Her flannel nightgown was thick, but it wasn't warm enough to keep away the deep chill emanating off the rock walls.

I can't do this anymore. She sank down into a crouch and bit her lip. *Wake up, wake up.* She shut her eyes and repeated this mantra over and over.

She felt a sudden warmth on her face. The sun had made its way into the slot and a beam of light shone down between the constricting squeeze of the rocks. Her breath slowed and she forced her fingers to stretch out of the tight fists. She opened her eyes, sure that she would be back in the camper, sun streaking through the window, but she was not. All she could see was the white glow of the rock wall, sparkling in the sunlight. With a deep breath, Martha stood up.

She could still hear the thump, thump, thump-a-thump ahead, and she could see now, so she followed the vibrations.

"Mar-tee-a." The voice was soft, urging her forward. The beam of sunlight illuminated the woman's face.

Martha looked at the face, older than she had imagined. The woman's braid wasn't dark, as she had supposed in the dim light of the camper, but gray. Wrinkles radiated out from the edges of her lips, her eyes, her nose. Her brown cheeks sagged but were rosy, as if years of smiling had worn out the muscles but happiness still lived in her face. She wore a cotton dress. The weave of the fabric was loose and someone had sewn an intricate pattern of beads around the neck and across the shoulders.

She stared directly into Martha's eyes, unblinking.

The woman's deep pupils pulled at her and the world expanded, to a level that encompassed something endless. Mountains, skies, stars, people walking, sleeping, eating, laughing, smiling, crying. It was all there in one brief flash.

This woman was her spirit guide. How else to explain this strange sense of security in spite of the crazy hike they were on?

The woman turned and headed up the corridor and Martha followed.

Two

Glen Grimson kept his eyes shut and didn't move. One of the things he enjoyed about camping was waking up, breathing in the cool morning air and thinking. At home there was always the rush to make the coffee, feed the dog, watch the morning news, and get ready for the day of work. He listened to the quiet. His internal clock wasn't accurate when not in his own time zone, but based on the few birds twittering and the lack of human-produced sound outside the truck it was probably before six. Too early to get up, he decided, and pulled the comforter tight around his shoulders.

This vacation offered two weeks of practicing for a life of leisure after retirement, although he imagined permanent vacation would be very different from slipping out of town for a few days. He had always planned on working for as long as possible, following the advice of financial consultant Bart Collins, who Glen had first met when Vince was born and Glen felt the need to work out a plan that would take care of Martha and their son. It was his duty to keep up with the load their growing family placed on the bank account and he needed to build his pension fund to the maximum amount. As the family grew he continued to meet with Bart. With three children, one nearly right after the other, his focus was on their future.

Then his brother died. Mike hadn't bothered to take care of himself —he called the health movement the bowel movement—but still, no one expected him to drop dead while watching the Broncos beat the Raiders.

His brother died before he bought that fishing boat he always talked about. A Boston Whaler. Mike never lived his dreams.

Driving home from the funeral, Glen had recalculated. He still rolled off to his job at the plant each day, where he went through the same motions he had gone through for the last thirty years, but he met with a financial guy regularly. Not the same one—Bart had retired long ago, took his own advice apparently—now it was a younger man with computerized charts and graphs and projections. Glen had sat down with Martha and tried to explain what he needed.

"I don't think we should wait. Look—" he spread out the handwritten notes "—we can afford to do one thing now. Not a boat, I'm not sure I want that anymore, but a camper." He added the brochure to the presentation on the kitchen table. "I'll trade my truck in for this one and we can use it for the camper. And this rig, the Lance 850, it's smaller, just right for the two of us. We don't need to save my vacations anymore, we can use them." He didn't need much. Just a chance to explore this beautiful country.

Martha hadn't questioned his decision. There had been the issue of the ladder, but they had solved that.

"I can't climb it." His wife had frowned at the eager young salesman, then turned to glare at him. "You know I can't climb ladders."

"It's very strong, stable. See how it hooks into these holes here?" The young man had placed his hand on the ladder, rocking it back and forth.

Glen was a fix-it man; he had a garage workshop suited for a Mr. Handy television program. "Martha, I can build you a step, it's really not high and it won't take up much room here." He loved to modify things, making them just a little better than the original design. He was happy with his job, working as a quality assurance supervisor for nearly thirty years, because improving things was part of his day. Every day. He never dreamed of making millions or changing the world. Content with a fine home in the suburbs, two weeks off to take a vacation. Disney World or Santa Cruz—always something to make the kids happy. His one splurge was a new vehicle every five years or so, alternating between a truck for himself and a minivan for Martha. Once the kids reached the teen years he passed along the old vehicle to whoever had just turned sixteen. He never understood why they didn't want the minivans.

"You can camp in this van. Haul instruments. Take the dog crate," he had encouraged them. Vince and Clarice had passed up the offer, fighting over his old trucks, but when Jack was seventeen, and Martha decided a Honda Accord was her next vehicle, he took the Windstar.

Glen had built Martha her step up to the camper bed and now they were on vacation. No need for early rising today. He could spend the hour or so after waking lost in his thoughts or falling back to sleep for one more hour. A luxury.

There was something about not moving, letting his mind drift, as if a special kind of wave took over his brain, maybe those alpha waves Martha was always saying she needed. Last night he had slept deeply. She was always up two or three times a night and he hadn't woken at all. He felt a pang of guilt as he listened for the hum of her machine and heard nothing, suddenly reminded of yesterday's request.

His wife had asked him to recharge the battery for her CPAP machine, the little device that helped with her sleep apnea. It had to be charged off the solar panels because there were no hookups in the National Park campground.

"Sure," he had answered, then promptly been distracted and had forgotten.

When she started using the machine a year ago, she explained that all the getting up to empty her bladder was related to the closing down of her breathing during the night and the adrenaline burst that followed, causing the bladder to need to relieve itself.

"Lots of husbands and wives came to the class," she had told him. After the fact.

Glen hadn't thought about going to the sleep disorder class her doctor recommended—he had no trouble sleeping—but to be fair she hadn't invited him. It took him a while to get used to the noise of that machine, like a little fan tuned to the rhythms of Martha's breathing. In and out, in and out. She had quit getting up so much in the night, either because of sleeplessness or the bladder thing, and that had been nice. But she had moved into Clarice's old bedroom anyway, complaining that Glen's snoring kept her awake.

He lifted his ear off the pillow and listened for her breathing. No machine but she wasn't snoring. Martha's snores were usually fairly soft, but at times she gargled and snorted so loud that he would nudge her awake. This made her furious—her sleep took precedence over his, apparently. He lifted his head from the pillow and looked at her. She was sound asleep, lying on her back as still as death. He should film her with his phone to prove she did sleep in spite of her claims that it never happened. He did enjoy that new phone, what with its camera and all those apps. He was grateful that Clarice had told him to be sure the new truck had a bluetooth connection so his phone and his truck would have a happy marriage. His daughter had also downloaded lots of what she called "travelin' music" for him before they headed out. "You'll need it," she had said.

He turned away from Martha and considered another hour of sleep, his breath slow and his mind gone before he had a chance to complete the thought.

Glen woke again when the sun hit his face. Martha was still asleep next to him. With a loud yawn he rolled his neck. He moved his legs around, careful with the stretch so he didn't cause one of those damn leg cramps.

No one warned you about all the little physical problems which grabbed hold of you as you aged. He was a strong, athletic man, but he felt himself slowing down, in spite of his efforts to keep in shape. Instead of the daily five mile runs he had kept up for years, he walked every morning. Martha refused to go with him, even when he offered to go where she wanted, walk at a slower pace, change his routine to evenings instead of early morning. He had a membership to a gym he seldom used, but he lifted weights on the bench in the garage.

Last night at their campfire dinner, Martha had planned an early start for today. "Let's get up at six and do the long walk in the canyon." He was surprised she wasn't up and rumbling already.

"Hey lazy bones." He nudged Martha. She didn't move.

He pushed a little harder. "Thought we were getting up early." Martha remained still, her breathing soft. Glen leaned up on his elbow and looked at her face. The blanket was loose around her shoulders, her arms curled over the top. He could see her chest rise and fall slowly.

"Martha?" He reached out and put his hand on her shoulder, pushing firmly. Her face didn't change.

Calling her name louder, he pushed harder. He tried to sit up, bumped his head and leaned over his wife by twisting his torso and balancing on one elbow. Something wasn't right.

"Martha, wake up." Glen flipped up onto his knees and grasped both her shoulders and shook. Her body felt limp and cold. He placed his palms on her cheeks and called her name over and over, growing hoarse when she didn't respond.

THREE

Spirit guides lead you to where you are meant to be. Martha tried to remember what she had read in that book. Romantically, she had hoped her spirit guide would be a buffalo or pronghorn, but it seemed this old woman had been chosen by whatever power was living in these mountains. So she followed her through the slot canyon until they came to a large, cave-like room. Although the ceiling was open to the sky with its rosy hint of dawn, they were surrounded by the beehive walls on all sides. Free from the tight confines of the slot canyon, Martha's breathing slowed and her hands quit shaking.

Her attention was drawn to the center of the space and a large drum. Two men stood on either side and each held a club the size of a baseball bat, with the ends covered in leather. Thump, thump, thump-a-thump. The mysterious sound Martha had heard was the deep resonating beat on the drum as they raised their clubs high and brought them down with dramatic swoops, alternating in a well-choreographed dance, never getting in each other's way as they pounded out the beat. Her senses awoke and she felt the presence of more humans. She looked around and saw men and women pressed close to the edges of the cave, forming a circle around the drum. The people were quiet. She had walked into the middle of something, an intruder who didn't belong in this place. It was as if everyone had stopped talking, stopped enjoying themselves, stopped whatever they were doing, upon her entrance because every person in the room was silently staring at her.

I need to get out of here. She turned, hoping that this time the trail would be there, no more black holes behind her, no more weird air pushing her forward.

The old woman stood, her face grim. If Martha were to escape she would have to push her way past her spirit guide.

They aren't really here, they can't judge me. She turned back to examine the people.

There were men and women of all ages. They were dressed in simple woven cotton skirts and shirts. Some held small drums and others held sticks.

"Ha tu no." The old woman spoke loudly. The drummers stopped. A man walked toward them from across the circle. He was dressed in the skin of a deer, with two legs, complete with hooves, hanging down on each side of his chest. He wore pants made from a tanned hide which ended just below his knees. Beaded moccasins laced up the front of each leg, pulled tight around the end of the pants. He held a long wooden flute in one hand. The man walked straight at Martha and stopped with his toes nearly on top of hers. Martha pulled back and tried not to wrinkle her nose at the odor of old sweat, old leather, and old man.

His examination started with her face, frowning as he looked into her eyes. His gaze slid down her chin and ran over her body, his mouth curling to one side, as if puzzled by her appearance. He raised his head and met her eyes once more, a slight lift on the edges of his lips, almost a smile, but not quite.

"Mosinobu" he said, gesturing to himself.

She nodded and looked to the woman. But her spirit guide was not guiding at the moment. In fact, it seemed she wasn't even paying attention. Martha looked back at the man.

"Martha," she replied.

With a nod he raised the flute to his lips and started to play. The notes were soft, drawn out with breathy transitions from one tone to the next. Not a complicated song, but haunting as he began to play louder and the echo of the cave sent the music swirling. His music and his presence sent a wave over Martha, something akin to what she had felt looking into the woman's eyes. It was the feeling she had during particularly good sermons or when singing hymns, years ago watching

22

her children play together without fighting, or when a difficult recipe turned out just as planned. All those feelings in tandem, multiplied by a hundred swept her far away from all that she had known before, on the verge of something different. As if she were one of these people, this living history act she had fallen into.

Martha nodded back at him, smiled, then quickly tried to compose her face back into the serious expression he maintained. Blushing, she looked around for her guide.

The woman motioned. *Come further into the circle*, her gesture said. Martha took two steps forward and stopped. The old woman held out a smooth stick, about twelve inches long with bits of wood attached to the end with strips of leather. She shook it to demonstrate the sound it made, *chirr, chirr*, then held it out again. Martha took the rattle and looked around the circle. The drummers had started again. *Thump-a, thump-a, thump-a.* This beat was different; slower and very steady.

One by one the people began to walk with shuffling steps around the circle, shaking the rattles they held and striking small drums carried in one hand, the heel of the other sending out muffled thumps coordinated with the booms of the big drum. The old woman took hold of Martha's hand and pulled her into the line with the others.

"No, I can't..." Martha shook her head but the woman tugged her into the line. If she didn't move forward the people would back up behind her, like a bus stalled at an intersection, so she walked along with the others.

If a spirit guide took all this trouble to come to you in a dream and take you on a long hike and bring you to some sort of ceremony, you had to participate. Martha's cheeks flushed and she felt very foolish. She wasn't much of a dancer, mainly because she had no innate sense of rhythm. She never clapped along to music, knowing that her hands would come together just when no one else's did and everyone would turn to look at her with scorn.

Da, da, da-da, she counted, using silent words to keep in step with the others. Dust rose from the floor of the cave and she coughed once to clear her throat and squinted to protect her eyes. She followed the heels of the woman in front of her. She could feel her spirit guide behind her, the stare from those heavy eyes penetrating her body and pushing her forward.

This is a dream and that means I'm finally asleep. She imagined telling Glen about her adventure tomorrow—because she would tell him, she had to share this wonderful feeling with someone and who else was there? That world slipped away. The campground, the truck, and her husband, those things were the dream. She lifted the rattle and gave it a small shake, then blushed as the sound seemed to fill the short gap between the drum beats. Out of sync.

Staring back at the feet in front of her she noticed that this woman wasn't wearing beaded moccasins like the flute player. She had sandals made of thick leaves, but the back of her feet were heavily callused, as if she often went barefoot. Her ankles were dusty and covered with scratches.

Martha tried to match her own movements to the woman's shuffling steps. After three loops around the circle she felt something change, as if her heartbeat had taken on the rhythm. She looked up and glanced at those in line ahead of her unsuspecting teacher and found she kept the pace without so much concentration.

I'll try the rattle now. She raised the stick slowly and listened to the drums, jumping in with a shake just before the boom filled the cave. Good! She did it again, happy when the *chirr chirr* of the rattle kept her feet moving and she bobbed her head along as well.

The dance continued. The drums never paused, only changed beat. Some of the people sang out at times, a mournful wail, coming from deep within the throat. Her bad knee throbbed and her mouth was dry. No one else seemed tired, their steps never slowed. Finally, an old man left the circle. He walked slowly to the edge of the cave and squatted with his back against the rock wall. Sweat soaked the cotton of his shirt but his chin moved and his head dipped in the continued rhythm of the dance.

Martha was soaked with sweat as well. The tell-tale sharp pain of a pinched nerve moved down the back of her thigh, and she slipped out of the snaking mass of people. She leaned against the wall for a moment, then tried to squat. Totally uncomfortable. She looked around for somewhere to sit. She didn't want to get her nightgown dirty because this red clay dust stained everything. She had already learned that the day before, when she wore her white jeans.

Martha tried to get the attention of her spirit guide, but the never-ending beat and closed eyes were a barrier that she felt uncomfortable penetrating. She rubbed her sore thigh and knee. As she kneaded the aching muscles, the sting of the scrape on her knuckle burned, a reminder of her limits. Couldn't she dream away her pain? Maybe the scrape was symbolic of something important. She racked her mind for things about the right hand. *Seated at the right hand of the Lord* flashed through her head.

She attended church regularly but darned if she could come up with something when she needed it. Was it something to do with the last supper? Betrayal? Maybe the scrape on her knuckle meant the old woman was going to betray her. But that didn't make sense. If her dream was symbolic it had to be something to do with her real life.

Betrayal by Glen? Clarice? No, more likely Deborah. Her sister was always talking about her behind her back. Martha touched the red skin and winced. This had to be a dream, because what were the other options? Some elaborate living history arranged by the park docents? An episode of "This is Your Life?" How about an amazingly complex you-participate-with-the-actors, like the mystery dinners Glen loved, where the audience was drawn into the event, characters marching up to the table and sarcastically asking questions? Martha didn't like these dinners, she didn't like to be the center of attention. But Glen loved them, so she went along.

She sighed and studied the dancers as they circled in front of her. The faces were plain, not wearing makeup or painted. If this was a sham, these people wore clothes that had to have been carefully constructed to mimic the old ways of sewing. The weave of the cloth was coarse and the construction simple, but she could tell from here all the seams were sewn by hand.

In the center of the circle, the two drummers were as wet as if they had just stepped out from under a waterfall. She heard one of them breathe out with each beat, a strong *woof* as he put all his energy into the swing. She caught a tiny nod between the drummers and suddenly two new men took their places, moving in and grasping the drum sticks smoothly, never missing a beat.

Suddenly Martha's questions slipped away as if oiled. The top of her head felt light and her shoulders soft, the usual hard knots of tension so far removed from this world that it was as if they never existed.

Everything around her seemed to be floating and going on forever. At one point a young woman offered Martha some dried meat. The jerky was flavorful but tough. She had to clamp down tightly with her teeth and pull little bits off, sucking to soften them to a point where she could chew and swallow. Her mouth was parched and she longed for something, anything, to wash down the dry food. She licked her lips and tried to keep her throat moist. No one was drinking, there was no sign of anything that could actually hold water. She didn't see the skin bags or clay pots which had been on display in the museum.

Martha's eyes drooped, and she was mesmerized and tired. The cries of the people increased, now words were sung out as well as the a-yah sound coming deep from the throat. She felt a sound rising in her own throat when the drumming increased in volume, but she held it in. No way would she call out because she didn't know what the words meant.

The booms of the big drum echoed around the people, the tempo building to match the sound. The frenzy of the dancing increased and the old man clapped and swayed.

Suddenly everything stopped.

The drums were silent, the people stopped circling, no rattles shook, no voices cried out. They slowly filed out through an opening across from the narrow corridor where she had entered. Martha looked around and stood to follow, then felt a hand on her shoulder.

The old woman shook her head and tipped it toward the flute player, who sat on a rock.

The woman spoke to Martha. "You must sit also." She walked to the man and sat on the dirt.

FOUR

"Yeah. I don't think it's real nice either." Clarice spoke to the smartphone in her hand. The black case looked corporate, the image she wanted to achieve when she forked over the forty-five dollars. Only now it felt funereal, the angry words surrounded by a cute bubble, as if the conversation were a game at a child's party.

Are you really doing this by text? Keith followed his text with a puffy faced emoji, making the whole thing yet more ridiculous.

Of course Keith wasn't happy that she was breaking up with him via this social custom of avoiding human contact. *Of course* he didn't know she was actually answering him out loud because she wasn't typing, she was talking to her smartphone, dressed in its official business suit. She was surprised her voice-to-text app didn't speak out and remind her to use the video chat and make this a real conversation.

The screen stared at her: the nonjudgmental, silent screen, waiting for her answer.

She didn't have an answer. She was simply sitting and wondering what was wrong with her.

"I hope you understand. I just can't be your girlfriend right now." As she watched her words transform into letters on the screen, she knew Keith couldn't understand because he didn't know how messed up she was. And he never would because after today she was pretty sure this was the last text he would ever send to her. In all likelihood he was blocking her number right now.

She glanced at the top of the screen. Ten o'clock. The day had barely started and she'd managed to muck up three major areas of her life. This had to be a record, even for her. How many girls could boast that they broke up with their boyfriend, gave notice to their roommate, and changed their major—for the third time—all before church had actually started?

Not that she went to church. But she kept track because she lived across the street from Our Lady of Grace and Perpetual Traffic and on Sunday she called her mother just after twelve forty-five when the last of the cars had left the parking lot, the congregants duly filled with prayers, hymns, coffee, donuts, and gossip.

She punched in the speed dial for her mother. Talking to Mom didn't always help, but she had to do something. Everything was falling apart in spite of her careful planning. She felt incapable of making a smart decision, but she had to make up her mind about some things in life.

It had seemed so easy five years ago. Major in Economics because she wanted a job in a big firm managing money. Money meant power and a career choice like this would lead to a job with a great salary. The internship with the finance house had convinced her this kind of job was not the life she wanted. She didn't mind the expectation that she work a zillion hours a week while she was going to school—that was just a matter of time management—but it was the day she found out that the new intern was making nearly double her salary—that little piece of information had been the last straw in a long list of slights. What was with that? Was Darcy or Dacey, or whatever the perky little thing's name was, a niece to some bigwig? How was Clarice to have those kinds of connections growing up middle class with a father who worked contentedly at the same job for a lifetime and a mother who never worked at all? No chance of the contacts needed in today's world, so she quit the internship and the major on the same day. All it took was reviewing the courses the University offered to decide that she was better suited to a major in Environmental Studies, with a focus on Impact Assessment. After that, all it took was less than a semester to realize that a lifetime of staring at charts and graphs wasn't on her personal agenda.

That was yesterday. And last night when Keith couldn't keep focused on her decision to switch over to a World Studies major in January and kept changing the subject to his job interview and going on and on about how great it was to work at Google instead of helping her figure out how many units this change would add before she could graduate, well, that was when she realized she couldn't be anyone's girlfriend right now.

She probably should have told him then, and not waited until six in the morning to send him that text.

Mom wasn't answering her phone. Her parents were traveling, but Mom always made sure she was somewhere with cell service for their weekly calls. It was two hours later in New Mexico, so she should be answering. Or was it only one hour?

Clarice punched the end button when the phone asked her to leave a message. She stared out the window at the sun shining on the tops of cars waiting for the light to turn green. She had told Patricia that she would be moving, giving her roommate the required one month notice. This place was crazy and Patricia was turning into one of those needy roommates. Always trying to plan activities for the two of them. Clarice didn't want to sit in this apartment listening to the traffic for another minute and she didn't want to look at Patricia's sad eyes when she made excuses not to go to the movies or for a hike, but she really couldn't afford to bail on a whole month's rent. She had put up with it this long. What was four more weeks? Besides, she didn't have anywhere in mind to move and it really wasn't that easy to find a room close to school.

Where was Mom? With a shake of her head Clarice dialed her father's number.

He didn't answer, either. Just his businesslike "Leave a message."

"Hey Dad. Mom's not answering. Tell her I'm sorry I missed our phone date. Why aren't either one of you answering? I hope everything's okay. I really need to talk to you...well, Mom, so could one of you call me back? Thanks."

FIVE

"**I** am Kwe-in-ye. You have been chosen. You are here to perform a special task."

Martha rubbed her forehead and licked her dry lips. With all the people gone except these two, the cave was quiet.

"*Noshika pate bali du pahana.*" The flute player—Mosinobu? Was that his name?—scowled as he spoke.

Kwe-in-ye held up a finger and the man stopped speaking. "He says you must listen carefully."

"*Cha mo can tuk a pani. Do san ke pu te kepka so me la po.*"

"Our people are in trouble. We have prayed for help and you have been sent here. I do not know exactly what you will do, but I will help you to learn the ways of our people."

Martha's thoughts raced like some crazy production line conveyer belt—as quickly as one question came another rolled in and pushed it aside.

"How is it that you speak English?" The words left her mouth as if powered by someone else.

"I do not know. Three nights ago we asked for help, with many prayers and offerings. When I awoke the next morning my tongue was swollen and my lips were very dry. I walked up the canyon to what is left of the stream to drink. As I was swallowing the water a large coyote appeared across the stream from me. I opened my mouth to speak and strange words came out. At first I did not understand the words, but as I continued to speak with him, I began to understand. That night,

Mosinobu had a dream. In his dream there was a woman from another time and she spoke the language I was speaking. When he told the others about his dream, we came to the prayer circle to wait for you. When you entered, we knew you were the one who had been sent to help."

"That isn't what happened. I was camping and I woke up in the night." Martha shook her head and pointed at the old woman. "You were there, in the camper, you brought me here."

"Yes. Mosinobu saw this in his dream. You were in a strange world, very different from ours. You were in a cave, but not a cave. He sent my spirit to you."

Martha brought her palms to her eyes, and pressed. *So my guide is a spirit.* She felt her chest grow tight and her head continued to spin, unable to settle and focus on any one thought. *Concentrate, you have to concentrate.* Tears leaked from her eyes, yet she didn't feel the emotions which usually accompanied them. She wasn't sad or frightened, feelings which arose when she was confused. A dizzy, spinning sickness found her stomach and made it burn. *I'm going to throw up.* She opened her eyes and tried to stop the spinning by focusing on the flute Mosinobu held in his hand.

Kwe-in-ye stood and reached out a hand. Martha stared at it for a moment, then took hold. The woman's grasp was firm, her hand rough and warm. She pulled Martha up and led her to the opening through which the people had departed. As they came out of the gap in the rocks, Martha noticed that the sun hovered over the west wall of the canyon. It was late afternoon already. She had been in this dream all day.

The path narrowed and she had to let go of Kwe-in-ye's hand and follow her. She heard the flute player's soft steps behind her. They were headed downhill, clinging to the edge of the mountain, and Martha's pulse raced. She was near hysteria when the trail finally flattened out on the floor of the canyon.

Martha followed Kwe-in-ye as the trail wound along a stream bed with not much sign of water. A small trickle here and there and the stream occasionally opened up into small pools, but these were covered with a mucky film. Martha licked her parched lips, stopping to stare at the brown water. Kwe-in-ye didn't slow and she hurried to catch up. Maybe there was clean water where they were headed.

SIX

"**D**on't come all this way, son. She'll be out of the hospital before you can get here. I'm sure of it. We'll head for home right away once this nonsense is over with. Your mother will be fine."

His father's voice had been shaky, none of the usual Mr. Cool, when he told Vince that his mother was in a coma. Vince imagined that the trauma of waking up to find Mom unconscious had impacted Dad more than he let on. Calling 9-1-1, an air flight to Santa Fe for her, driving all that way on unfamiliar roads for him—this had to have been horrifying.

"But what is it Dad? What's wrong with her?"

"I don't know, son. They're running tests. Lots of tests."

"Dad, I'm coming. We'll figure it out. You shouldn't be alone." Vince punched the end button and dialed Sandra as he jumped in the car. The fact he had an old phone, no way to dial hands free, and two citations didn't stop him from talking as he drove. This was an emergency.

"Come on, answer already." Vince wanted Sandra to phone the airline for his ticket to save time. It shouldn't take long to get a flight from San Jose to New Mexico. Vince glanced at the clock. Two-thirty in the afternoon. He needed to get on a flight soon.

Flinging his phone onto the seat beside him, he pulled off the freeway and headed for the airport parking lot closest to the terminal.

Usually he insisted on putting the car in the distant long-term lot— saving five dollars whenever possible was how Vince managed to keep the family going. His salary as a new teacher was at the bottom of the pay scale. Sandra had stayed home for five years, first with Sara and then with Sam. They didn't like to leave the kids in day care at too young an age. Why have kids at all if you aren't going to raise them yourself? They did okay, but saving every penny was what it took. He hadn't complained when his wife announced she was going to find a job. Now that Sam was three and finally potty trained, Sandra had gone to work part-time in a real estate office and that helped.

Vince spotted a parking space close to the walkway into the airport. He rushed to the counter with the shortest line.

"Do you have any flights to Santa Fe today?"

The woman behind the counter did not, but she seemed to notice Vince's panicked expression.

"Let me see what else might be available. Santa Fe has a municipal airport, so the flights are expensive and there aren't too many. If you can fly to Albuquerque International it's only about an hour's drive and you'll save money." After some tapping and clicking she told him that another airline had an eight forty-five PM flight to Santa Fe. For over eight hundred dollars. But here was a flight at three thirty to Albuquerque for sixty-nine dollars. Was he interested?

"Yes. That one. It will be faster." And so much cheaper.

While Vince paced at the gate waiting for his flight to board, he dialed Sandra again.

"Hello?"

"Sandra, at last. I've been trying to get you. Dad called. There's been an accident...or...something. I'm not sure what happened, but my mother is in a coma."

"What? When? Oh Vince." Sandra stumbled for words. "Where is she? Where are you?"

"She's in a hospital in Santa Fe. I'm at the airport, I'm flying out."

"Do Clarice and Jack know?"

"No, Dad asked me if we could call them. He didn't want me to come, but Sandra, he sounded really...well...anxious or shaky or something. He sounded...old. I can't let him handle this alone."

"What about clothes?"

"I'm fine. I have an extra shirt that was in the car." He could hear Sandra's mind ticking away and he knew his wife was thinking *but what about underwear?* He was grateful when she didn't say it out loud.

"Do you want me to call them?"

"Yeah, that would be great. My flight is boarding in a few minutes." Vince paused. There was something else, but his mind refused to land where he directed it and he couldn't remember. "Oh, yeah, could you book me a rental car in Albuquerque? My flight arrives at five twenty-five."

"What hospital is your mother in?"

Had Dad told him the name? "I can't think of it right now. I'll call you when I get there."

The flight was on time and it wasn't long before Vince was landing next to the Sandia Mountains. He had been to Albuquerque once for a conference, but only to a hotel near the airport. His old phone didn't have GPS and for a minute he regretted his choice not to get a new one. He had a map from the car rental service and that would have to do.

He still had the drive to Santa Fe and after finding his way to the freeway he pulled out his phone. Six messages.

Sandra telling him the name of the hospital was St. Vincent's and that she had talked to Clarice, but Jack's number was not in service.

Clarice, asking why he hadn't called her immediately.

Clarice asking why Dad hadn't called her.

Sandra letting him know she had booked a room at a hotel near the hospital. It was a mini-suite with two rooms, so Dad and he could share space without being directly on top of each other.

Clarice screaming at him to call her back immediately.

Sandra letting him know she had talked to Dad, and Martha was stable, but still in a coma and that Glen hadn't got a room so the one she reserved was good. Also she had called the substitute line for him and left a message he wouldn't be at work tomorrow or the next day.

Before he returned Clarice's calls, Vince tried to think of a way he could convince his sister not to come to New Mexico, but he couldn't come up with a single valid reason she shouldn't. If he gave her the real reason—he didn't want her to fight with Mom, that is, when Mom woke up—she would be furious.

He was dialing his sister when the blue lights flashed beside him. He tossed the phone onto the passenger seat but it was too late. The state trooper was pointing to the off ramp and shaking his head.

After the three minutes it took for the officer to hand him the citation, along with the warning that the ticket would follow him to California, Vince called his sister. Might as well take advantage of being on the side of the road and give the policeman time to drive away.

"Clarice. It's me."

"What took you so long? How is she? Where is she? How is Dad? What the hell happened?"

"She's in a coma. I don't know any more than that. I'm half way to Santa Fe and I'll call you when I get to the hospital and find out more. Sandra called and explained, right?"

"Yes, she called, but you should have. She didn't know anything at all. And Dad isn't answering."

Vince shivered at the thought of poor Sandra phoning his sister. His wife felt that Clarice looked down on her because she had married him straight out of high school and stayed home with the kids. He tried to reassure Sandra that his sister wasn't doing so great with her own choices. At least he and Sandra had their house and their kids and he had his job. Lucky for him, teachers were in such short supply he could actually work on an emergency credential while he pursued his full credential with online courses.

"Hey Clarice." He interrupted her continued tirade. "Sandra said Jack's number wasn't in service. Do you know of any way to get ahold of him?"

"I'll try, but Vince, it can't be right. Mom can't be in a coma. Why would she be in a coma? You need to call me as soon as you know what's really going on. When you have the correct information, not some weird story." His sister hung up.

Vince was insulted but not surprised. Clarice used denial as a form of coping. She could insist black was white if needed, just to protect herself from emotions. He tucked his phone in his pocket so that he wouldn't be tempted to answer if it rang. He didn't want to talk to her again and he needed to get to Santa Fe. As he pulled back on to the freeway he realized, with a sigh of relief, that Clarice hadn't said a word about coming out.

SEVEN

Martha stopped to catch her breath. Her thirst and fatigue had reached the point where she couldn't follow Kwe-in-ye without a rest. The trail was well worn here—if she lost her guide it wouldn't be hard to find the way.

Unless there was a fork in the trail. With a deep sigh she started walking again and within a few minutes she reached an opening in the trees with a view of buildings near the walls of the canyon. In some places the rooms were two or three levels high. The walls were made of smooth mud and, where the mud had fallen away, she could see flat rocks stacked and mortared into place. The tops of the buildings were covered with logs and branches or mud.

I'm at the ruins. Only they aren't ruins, they're fine. Not just fine, fantastic. Nothing from touring this canyon yesterday could have prepared her for what lay before her. The stone walls above the tops of the buildings were painted with magnificent murals and designs. The wooden beams were polished smooth and stuck out of the walls like the legs of a giant caterpillar.

And the people. So many people. Men and women moved around the buildings and caves or on trails which forked across the floor of the canyon. They wore simple garments around their waists, woven cotton for the most part, although some were made from feathers or decorated with intricate beads. They didn't share the black, smooth hair depicted in the museum. Some had dark shiny hair, while others had wavy or kinky variations of brown, with red or golden hues shining in the sun. For a moment Martha supposed this really was a living history event and someone had pulled in lots of actors. If that was the case, they had rebuilt the ruins as well, and that didn't seem very likely. This was no Hollywood set.

As she passed people on the trail their eyes darted over her, scanning quickly and then flicking away. Martha glanced ahead. The chill of being an outsider made her clench her jaw and move a bit faster.

The trail forked. One branch turned sharply to the left, away from the stream bed, and wound up a hill. It led to one of the long two-story buildings snug against the canyon wall. Kwe-in-ye waited at the fork, and when she caught Martha's eye, waved her on to this path impatiently. Martha followed the old woman past several doorways, finally stopping in front of one about midway down the complex. Her guide slipped into a small opening. There was a piece of leather pulled to one side, probably used to keep the elements out when needed.

Although Martha had never considered herself tall at five foot six, she had to stoop to follow, taking care not to bump her head as the doorway was framed with rocks barely covered by mud. The room was dark and cool, and a mat made of woven plant material and feathers covered the floor. A large rug of dark fur was rolled up against the wall.

When Martha's eyes had adjusted to the dim room she saw two women seated near the wall. Both held things in their laps and it didn't take more than a second for her to realize they were sewing.

The first woman's almond eyes and square jaw were so similar to Kwe-in-ye that she had to be a daughter or sister. Her long hair was loose and didn't have any gray. She held a piece of the woven cotton that most of the clothing Martha had seen was made from. She was sewing beads on with a thick white needle. The second woman was much younger and she held a loom made from small sticks. Next to her was a basket filled with long strips of fiber.

Martha turned to Kwe-in-ye. "How do I greet people in your language?"

"*Ja pa.*"

She turned back to the women. "*Ja pa.*"

"*Ja pa.*" The two spoke in unison and laughed at the coincidence.

"I am Martha." She patted her own chest with the universal gesture. At least she supposed it was universal, she wasn't really an expert on falling back in time.

The older woman nodded. "*Yo-en-u Ta-a-ho.*"

"*Yo-en-u-ta-a-ho?*" Martha pointed to the woman's chest.

Kwe-in-ye stepped between them. "Yes, it is her name. Four Snakes, but we call her only *Yo-en-u*. And the other one is *Dam-po-nu*."

"Is Yo-en-u your sister?"

Kwe-in-ye hesitated. Her lips pursed and she nodded. "She is from my clan. I believe this is what you would call a sister."

"Can I look at what she is doing?"

The old woman nodded.

Martha knelt down next to the women. The white needle was made of bone or antler and tapered to a very sharp point. It was threaded with a thick fiber. The beads had holes large enough for the twine to slip through, but not the needle. Thus the work of sewing on each bead involved removing the needle after passing it through the fabric, threading the bead onto the fiber and then replacing the needle to punch through the fabric.

"Oh, I wish I could have brought you some needles." Martha smiled at the thought of showing these women her sewing tools. She turned back to Kwe-in-ye. "Do all the women sew?"

"Some people sew. There are many tasks in life. Tomorrow I will show you this and more, but now you must rest. There is much to do tonight and I think you are tired."

Martha wondered what she had to do tonight. But first things first. "Excuse me. Kwe-in-ye?" As if she were in a foreign country, Martha mimicked drinking a glass of water. "I'm very thirsty."

The old woman crossed the room and passed through another small door. When she returned she carried a small white clay jug, decorated with black zigzag stripes. She thrust the jug out in front of her, as if reluctant or angry that Martha would ask for something to drink.

The water was warm and it had a stale taste, but Martha drank it all, her dry throat soothed at last.

Kwe-in-ye shook her head. "There is not much water. You must drink as little as possible." She reached her hand out for the empty jug. "Come with me." She bent and walked through another small doorway.

Martha followed. This room looked just like the museum display. The walls were covered with a mud plaster, and the floor was made of smooth, flat stones embedded into the dirt. Tucked into shelves carved into the back wall were items she recognized: clay pots, the stones for grinding, and baskets of cloth. At the back of the room was the entrance to a cave, the opening only three feet high.

Kwe-in-ye motioned to it. "This is where you will sleep."

Martha crawled inside. A thick mat covered the floor and she lay down, curling into a fetal position on her side and tucking her hand under her cheek as a pillow.

Her hip pressed through the mat against the stone floor, so she turned onto her back. She tried to slow her breathing, willing sleep to take over. She looked back in to the room to see what Kwe-in-ye was doing, but the woman was gone.

Her eyes wouldn't close. Anxiety kept them open as if there were tiny toothpicks holding the lids. She focused on the door, expecting someone to come through it. Her thoughts had been curious and anxious during the dance and the hike, but now an edge of fear was growing stronger.

Time to think about something else. She pictured Kwe-in-ye's sister, Yo-en-u. Martha realized she hadn't actually seen her own sister in over a year. It wasn't because with all the new technology they communicated by other means—emailed or chatted or used one of those apps with a video feed and she had to brush her hair and put on a nice blouse before she made the call. She wasn't fond of those things and only used them when her children insisted. She really had very little contact with her sister at all. What would Deborah think of this place? Martha's thoughts cycled back to the canyon and the fear returned.

This wasn't a dream, this was real. It wasn't some sort of living history adventure. Martha was, somehow, somewhere in the past. Thoughts hammered through her head and the area above her right eye started to throb. Just what she needed, a migraine.

She turned and pressed her forehead against the rock floor, trying to squeeze the pain into a smaller area and searching for a cold spot. She turned over, then turned over again. Her shoulders and knee ached, and a sharp pain shot down the front of her leg as she tried to get more comfortable. *It's not real, this can't be real. Maybe if I sleep I'll wake up from this dream.* Martha squeezed her eyes so tight, the red of the back of her eyelids melted into a bright white flash.

A tear leaked from the corner of her eye and slipped over her cheek, pooling in her ear. It was followed by another and then another. Just as Martha was about to give in to the overwhelming urge to sob she heard a sniffling sound.

Her eyes shot open as she sat up and turned toward the doorway. A small brown head poked through the opening, the black shiny nostrils quivering and the bright eyes sparkling in the dim light.

A dog? It disappeared so fast she wasn't sure. She stared at the door and the sniffing sound resumed.

Martha whistled softly and the dog peered around the corner.

"Come here, don't be afraid." The dog studied her, nose twitching as the animal gathered information. She must smell very different from what this dog was used to.

"Come on." She tried again to coax it into the room.

The dog crouched and took tentative steps towards her outstretched hand. "That's it. Good pup."

"*Cho, cho.*" Kwe-in-ye waved her hands at the dog as she came in. The dog skittered out of the cave.

"If you are rested it is time to go."

EIGHT

Kwe-in-ye waited with such a sour look that Martha wouldn't have been surprised if the woman had tapped her wrist and pointed to the time, except, of course, no one had wrist watches here. Martha glanced down at her arm. She had her watch, but that didn't seem important right now. She didn't tell her guide that she hadn't rested and she had a headache and she wanted to pet the dog. But there was one thing she had to take care of before she followed the old woman to whatever was about to happen next.

What if Kwe-in-ye was taking her back to the campground? "I need..." Martha struggled for a way to tell the woman that her bladder was full to bursting, without sounding too needy. She crawled out of her little alcove and stood, her head nearly touching the ceiling, and pressed her hands against her abdomen. "I need to empty my bladder."

"Ah." Kwe-in-ye picked up a basket from a pile in the corner and turned. "Come."

The woman led the way to a spot among the trees, turned, and squatted to relieve herself. Martha was uncomfortable doing the same, yet feared she would lose her chance if she hesitated. Kwe-in-ye had merely pulled her dress to one side and bent her knees. She hadn't even set the basket down. Martha pulled up her nightgown and pulled down her leggings and underwear and squatted, supporting herself by grabbing onto a tree as her knee protested. Hot urine spattered around her feet.

Maybe this is a dream after all. And I just made it to the peeing part, so I must be wetting the bed. She needed to make up her mind. If it wasn't a dream then she could die or get hurt and it wouldn't be wise to take chances.

Darn it. She hadn't watched what Kwe-in-ye had done when she finished urinating, intent on doing this thing quickly. She stayed in the squatting position, bouncing a little in an attempt to shake off the final drips.

"You must come with me."

Martha slid her pants up and hurried after the old woman.

Kwe-in-ye led her to the center of the canyon, where many of the people from the dance were seated on logs or boulders placed around a ring of rocks. A fire pit, Martha guessed, but without a fire. More men and women were seated together on woven mats or animal skins, with children curled in front of them, snugly leaning against their parents' legs. She saw mothers gently rubbing a forehead and fathers placing a hand on the shoulder of a child. Everyone seemed connected and loving. It made her feel like even more of an outsider. As they joined the group Martha was aware of the sideways glances, especially from the children.

A stooped man stood in the center of the circle of people. His face was wrinkled and brown, like worn leather. His white hair fell down to his waist, the wisps so thin it gave the appearance of shadowy ghost-like creatures perched on each shoulder. His black eyes were surrounded by folds of skin, yet they opened wide as he spoke and his pupils reflected the glow of the setting sun. He slowly stepped around the fire pit, facing each of the children. As he spoke he waved his hands slowly in front of his chest. The children watched him closely, chins tilted up, eyes never leaving him, laughing in response to things he said.

"Sit here." Kwe-in-ye motioned to a mat on the ground in front of a boulder.

Martha sank down, curled her legs up under her nightgown, and looked around at the people. The families reminded her of her own children, back when they were young. She longed to stroke a small forehead, remembering how she could comfort them, smooth away any pain of the day at school. *Tom called me a name, Jessica wouldn't let me be first.* Touch would rid her child of fear—*Mom, I had a bad dream—* and soothe away the worries with long slow strokes.

Vince had loved to curl up next to her whenever he had a chance. Clarice had cuddled when it fit her own agenda, for comfort after a bad day, or when she wanted something. Jack was stiff, never wanting touch, pushing his mother away with his rigid, determined little body.

Kwe-in-ye returned with the small jug. The brown dog followed behind her, sniffing the ground. Martha took a tiny sip from the jug, conscious of the old woman's scrutiny. Then she held her palm out toward the dog.

"Come here, sweetie." She kept her voice soft. The long tail waved and the dog studied Martha without coming closer.

Kwe-in-ye settled next to her and pulled open a leather pouch. She ignored Martha's moves toward the dog and handed her more of the dried meat and some sort of root.

Martha broke off a small piece and placed it in her palm. "Come on, girl, you can do it."

The dog slunk down, bending its legs, belly on the ground, head low, ears forward, nose sniffing rapidly. Its eyes went to Kwe-in-ye and it didn't move.

"You should not give the dog your food. She can catch her own."

"Is she your dog? What's her name?"

"Dogs should not belong to people. They should not have names. In your place is this so?" Kwe-in-ye looked at Martha with a wrinkled brow and turned down mouth.

"Yes, dogs are pets. Family members really."

"Family members?"

"Not all dogs, but many dogs. I have a dog. Her name is Mandy."

Kwe-in-ye shrugged and shook her head. Martha stretched her arm closer to the wiggling black nose, the tiny piece of meat still sitting on her palm. The old woman looked at the dog with a "chaa" sound of disbelief. The dog inched forward.

"Come on, come on." Martha coaxed. The dog's head was only a few inches from her hand. It leaned slightly closer and reached a long pink tongue to snag the meat quickly, then sank back, moving only far enough to be out of the reach of human hands or feet.

Martha bit off a chunk of meat for herself. She considered giving the dog more, but felt Kwe-in-ye's disapproval, so she focused once more on the storyteller. He was tapping the heel of his hand on a small flat drum and moving around in the center of the circle. He sang now, a prayer or a lullaby, and the children snuggled closer to parents. She watched as fathers picked up sleeping toddlers and families moved off from the circle.

Martha leaned against the rock and looked up at the stars. Although the day had been warm, the night held the chill of Fall. The sounds of the storyteller's voice and his drum were hypnotic. This must be a lullaby. Her shoulders relaxed and her thoughts cleared. Just as her mind invited sleep to take over, she felt a warm furry body creep onto the mat and snuggle against her leg.

NINE

"Mom would have hated this." Clarice whispered, standing with her back to the wall of the room. She didn't approach her mother.

This couldn't be happening, her mother so still in the middle of the cold metal bed. Tubes ran into both arms, into her nose and out from under the blankets placed over her. Those thin blankets that only kept you warm when they were just brought in by a nurse, folded and cooked in some sort of giant blanket warmer. When they cooled they were not much better than a sheet, much too light to trap your own body heat.

Mom probably didn't have any body heat. When you were in a coma everything stopped, right?

Dad and Vince sat without a word and the steady beep of the machines filled the silence. It should have been comforting to listen to her mother's lungs continue to breath, her heart continue to beat, but all Clarice could do was wait for the sound of an alarm, so familiar from television shows, the signal for everyone to jump into action.

No one was doing anything for her mother. No heroic attempts to wake her up. She lay so still this would never be mistaken for sleep. The skin on her face sagged as gravity pulled her mother's flesh down. Mom looked so old.

Vince pulled the rolling stool close to Mom's bedside and reached for her hand. "The doctor said that for a person in a coma she has remarkable brain activity, as if she is having constant dreams."

"Of course she is." Clarice turned and glared at her brother. "She's dreaming of escaping the terrible place where she's trapped."

Her father didn't seem aware of their argument. He sat in a chair in the corner of the room, staring blankly at Mom.

Dad turned toward her. "Where is Jack?" Judging from the blank look in his eyes he had forgotten she was here. But why would he ask her about Jack? Wasn't Vince the one who took charge of everything? Before she could draw a breath to speak, her brother answered.

"Oh, Dad, you know Jack."

His answer bypassed the fact that no one could find their younger brother.

But her father's mind hadn't landed yet. He was off on another track. "I want to take her home now, today. I think things will get better if she's back there, in a familiar environment."

"Dad, the doctors said they would let us know today." Her brother had not left the hospital since arriving yesterday. Apparently he had convinced Dad to go to the hotel last night and get some sleep, but Vince was heavy into his role of the good son and hadn't left their mother's bedside.

Clarice had arrived this morning, finally able to make arrangements for missed classes. She didn't have a cheery little wife to arrange everything. Not only that, it had cost her over a hundred dollars to hire a ride from the airport. Damn rental car places wouldn't give her a car unless she paid outrageous fees. Too young. How ironic that someone who had been an adult for five years by every other standard couldn't rent a damn Hyundai.

Dad rubbed his hands along the tops of his legs, smoothing the brown corduroy of his pants. "Yes, home in her own bed, that's where she belongs."

"They're not going to let her go home, just to a hospital back home." Clarice didn't like seeing her father so confused. She stood up abruptly. "She has to have all those things hooked up to her. Don't you remember how she didn't ever want that?"

"I don't remember her ever talking about it." Vince looked at Dad. "Did she have anything in writing? A living will or a medical directive?"

"We were always going to get around to it."

"Did you talk about it? Do you actually know what she would want?" Clarice wasn't surprised her father had no idea. Actually she couldn't remember Mom ever talking about anything as negative as vegetative states or death, but she knew what most people thought and it wasn't this. Her mother avoided talking about things with deep emotions. It was one of the things that frustrated Clarice so much. She would try to engage Mom in a serious conversation and it always ended with a *whatever you say, dear* kind of statement. How was it a woman who grew up during the seventies and eighties could remain so un-liberated? Her brothers disagreed. They liked their mother just as she was.

Make that how she had been.

Clarice remembered the exact moment she realized her mother was not on her side. She had just turned eight years old and her father had planned an outing for the three kids. Mom wasn't going, probably wasn't invited. But it wasn't something she would have wanted to attend, anyway.

A baseball game. Thrilling to Clarice because she was nearly old enough to be on a team with all girls. She played with her brothers all the time and knew, just knew, she would be the best player on a girls' team. Every morning that week she had run to the kitchen as soon as she woke up, staring at the refrigerator where the four tickets were hanging beneath a leaping fish magnet. San Jose Municipal Stadium. Saturday, May 25, 2002. San Jose Giants. She was going to see Armando Rios in real life.

Then Beth Miller had invited Clarice to her birthday party. Two days before the party, which obviously meant Beth's mother had forced her to invite Clarice. The other girls had talked about the party for weeks, but she didn't care because she was going to the baseball game.

"How nice. A party. You can wear your new blue dress." Her mother had smiled and held the invitation up in the air like it was the golden ticket to the chocolate factory.

"I can't go, Mom. Baseball game."

"Oh, now, I think you would rather go to a fun party than out with your Dad and brothers."

She thought? How could she possibly know what Clarice wanted? Mom had been upset when Clarice refused a party to celebrate her own birthday, just two weeks earlier. After three days of arguments, bribes and tantrums, she had finally agreed that her mother could bring cupcakes to school for the whole class. No chance that Clarice would be forced to make a list of who to invite, knowing that her mother would want to include those kids she hated and possibly say no boys allowed.

"I'm going to the game. Beth is mean. I don't want to go to any dumb party."

Dad had walked in at just the right moment. Clarice knew he would be on her side.

"Hey Chickadee. Why the sad face?"

"Mom says I can't go to the game. I have to go to a stupid party and I'm not going."

Her father had looked at Mom, who continued to hold the invitation up.

"It's the Millers' girl. I'm sure there will be lots of fun things. A bouncy house or maybe a pony."

Obviously her mother didn't know Beth. She would never get dirty by touching an animal.

"Well, Martha. We did have this game planned for quite some time. And you know Clarice loves baseball." He grinned in her direction and she breathed a sigh of relief. It was going to be okay.

"Not this time. An invitation like this doesn't come along every day. There are baseball games every weekend. I'm sure one of the boys can take a friend and use the ticket." Mom had turned to her then, an awful smile plastered to her face. "I'm not going to argue about it, dear. Girls go to parties when they are invited."

Then Dad, her strong, tall father, her hero, had shrugged and patted her head. "I'll take you to the next game, sweetheart. That way you can do both."

Clarice had cried and stomped her feet and yelled, but the only thing that resulted from that was being sent to her room.

Mom always went along with the stuff Dad wanted. When Vince had begged to drop out of tennis lessons or Jack simply stopped going to his clarinet lessons Mom never argued. Why was it only when Clarice wanted something Mom would suddenly decide to be strong?

Clarice looked at her mother's motionless body. She wouldn't say she got along with her mother now, but she admitted when things went to hell in her life, Mom was who she called. They had fought so much over the years. There had been times when she screamed that she wished her mother was dead. All kids screamed that when they weren't being listened to, right? But that was a long time ago. Since she had grown up she only wished her mother would be more independent.

But this…she never wished for anything like this to happen.

TEN

Vince took advantage of Clarice's arrival to leave the hospital and head to the hotel for a nap. The next update on Mom's condition wouldn't be until late afternoon. He called Sandra to check in and was reassured that everything was fine at home. He dialed the number Clarice had given him for Jack and left another message. His sister swore the number led to a friend of Jack's and he would eventually get a message. His brother no longer had a phone.

"He knows Mom is here, in the hospital. I told Paige—that's the friend—and she promised to pass the message along," Clarice had explained.

"But you never actually spoke with him?" Vince wasn't as trusting as his sister. They couldn't be sure this woman had ever delivered the message to Jack.

"No. I didn't. If you're not satisfied with my performance, you call him."

So now he was left to carry the ball. If this Paige woman would at least answer the phone he could find out if she'd given Jack the message, but so far no one had answered. The voicemail was generic, no personalized greeting, and for a moment Vince wondered if his sister had given him the right number.

"Jack, you really need to call me back. Dad is insisting we bring Mom home as soon as the hospital will let us. I'm going to need your help with this. Quit avoiding me."

Vince punched the end button with his thumb. Damn his brother. He never had a sense of responsibility, only calling on the family when he needed something from them. Last time they spoke Jack had lost his job again and was about to lose his apartment because he hadn't paid the rent. Vince had loaned him some money, only to find out later that his father had also loaned Jack enough money for rent, but Jack was staying with friends anyway. Didn't sound like any of the borrowed money had made its way to a landlord.

Clarice blatantly refused to give Jack anything, vehemently stating that she had been burned too many times and calling the rest of the family enablers. And the weird thing was, Jack got along with Clarice better than with him. Reverse psychology or something. Vince wished he could refuse Jack, but his sense of family was too strong. Sandra supported him in this, but he was sure this was because she didn't want to run the chance of Jack moving in with them again. What a mess that had been, his wife having to clean up after his slob of a brother. It had sorely tested their marital relationship and it took months to recover after Jack finally moved on.

Vince untied his shoes and set them in the corner, then flopped onto the bed and let his head hit the pillow with a smooth whomp. He couldn't stop his mind from ticking off all the information from the last twenty-four hours. Transporting his mother home wouldn't be easy, whether they flew or took a ground ambulance. He would have to call the insurance company again today. The woman he spoke with yesterday seemed to think neither option would be covered. She informed him that "they"—the unobservable power—thought his mother should stay where she was. There was no consideration for the fact that Dad had a job and the whole family lived two states away. It seemed the insurance company expected his father to quit his job and stay with Mom. Or abandon her.

Vince tried to think of all the options. He was a new teacher on a temporary credential. There might be some sort of emergency leave he could take, but he doubted it was accompanied by a paycheck. There was no way they would ever hire him permanently if he took leave just over a month into his job. Clarice was missing class, a very temporary arrangement as she had let him know at least three times in the few hours they were together.

Jack. His brother could help if they ever found him, but the very thought of Jack actually being useful made Vince snort out loud. There really was no other choice but to convince the insurance company that it was vital his mother be moved to California.

Sleep finally came, but it didn't bring relief to his troubled mind. Vince fell into a confusing dream about his mother telling him to study history and art. "For me," she kept saying.

The jangle of his mobile phone woke Vince from the dream, just before his mother could explain why what he studied was so important.

"Hello?"

"Hey, Vince. Sorry I didn't get back to you, things have been kind of crazy around here."

Finally, Jack returning his call. "They're pretty crazy here, too."

"How's Mom doing?"

"Still in a coma. You got that message, right? The doctor is going to talk with us this afternoon and let us know when we can bring her back to California." Vince sat up and rubbed his head, trying to shake himself awake and out of the strange dream. "I'm working with the insurance company to figure out how to get her home. Not home, but to a closer hospital. When we get back I'm…we're going to need your help. Dad isn't handling this well. He's…well…he's confused or something. In shock, I guess."

"Here's the thing. I'm between jobs again. Trying to line something up here, and if it comes through, I have to take it."

Would it be a mistake to ask Jack to move home with Dad? The two of them didn't get along very well. Dad had a strong work ethic. A man should provide for the family and all that. Dad mentioned often enough that Jack had thrown everything back in his father's face although as far as Vince could see, Dad never failed to step up when Jack needed help.

His brother insisted that material things didn't matter much to him, but this just meant he didn't take care of things or save for the unexpected. Jack seemed surprised when his cars quit working, but even basic maintenance like oil changes weren't on his agenda. Jack's view that he didn't need a new car, just another junker, was his way of saying he wasn't materialistic, but he wasn't above asking for a loan when he needed transportation. Vince decided it would be best to talk to Dad about things before making any suggestions to his brother.

"Okay, but listen, you have to call me when I leave you a message."

Dr. Brown spoke directly to Glen, but he glanced at Vince occasionally. "The brain scan shows no visible damage. Her brain activity is high. In fact, we were concerned about seizures, but it seems steady, as if she were awake. All of her body functions are normal. However, we can't approve moving her until we figure out why she isn't waking up."

"When will she wake up?" His father asked the question again, for the third time in the last three minutes.

"We have no way of knowing that, Mr. Grimson. The prognosis is good. It could be any time, but there are a few more tests I'd like to run. We usually wait forty-eight hours before we order another MRI."

Clarice pointed to the machines connected to Martha. "What if she doesn't wake up? What about that feeding tube they're going to put in? I just know she wouldn't want this."

Before Vince could correct his sister, the doctor spoke.

"Actually, her swallow reflex is intact. She can eat if she is fed by hand, so the feeding tube isn't needed. Her medical condition is stable." The doctor turned once more to Glen. "Eventually, if she doesn't wake and remains stable, we will recommend moving her to a care facility. But I think she'll come out of this."

"Stable?" Clarice's tone was accusing. "She's in a coma. A convalescent hospital? Is that what you're talking about?" She turned to Dad. "Mom would hate that. She would never agree."

Vince stepped between his sister and his father. "Clarice, stop. What do you suggest we do? Lay her out in the desert for the coyotes? It hasn't even been two days. Why do you seem so set on no treatment for Mom?"

"What are you accusing me of? I love her as much as you do, Mr. Perfect. I just know she wouldn't want to be a vegetable. Who would?"

Dr. Brown glanced at the two of them, then he turned to address Glen again. "Mr. Grimson, Mrs. Conley from patient services will be glad to help with understanding the process." He handed Glen a white business card and headed for the door. "Let's give her some time." he said over his shoulder.

Clarice followed the doctor out of the room. Vince wondered what his sister had to say that she didn't want him to hear. Was she going to pester the doctor with more questions? It would have been better if she hadn't come to Santa Fe. By coming she was trying to take control, but Vince knew that everything would fall in his lap in the end. If they would just leave things to him from the beginning, life would be so much smoother.

ELEVEN

The shrill chirp ascended to a sharper note, penetrating Martha's sleep. The bird called once more and consciousness slowly heightened as the cold morning air touched her cheeks.

What a strange dream. Traveling to another time and meeting ancient people. She reached to pull the blankets up over her shoulders; the air was always cold in the morning when camping. When her hands didn't touch the cotton comforter, her eyes flew open. A dark skin covered her. She sat up and looked around. She was next to a rock near a fire pit that held no fire.

Martha rubbed her forehead. She felt rested and awake. In the past, she had experienced the strange state of waking and not waking. She had dreamed that she was having trouble waking up and dreamed she was awake, all while still asleep. Someone once told her this was called lucid dreaming, but she didn't know if that was true.

This was different. She felt perfectly awake and aware, just in a place that she had never been to before yesterday.

"Good morning." Kwe-in-ye carried a small clay bowl. "I brought you some food."

Hospitality was the same no matter what time you were in. Martha pulled herself up onto the flat red rock which had served as a seat the night before. Kwe-in-ye handed her the bowl.

"Did you sleep well?"

"Yes, I slept well. But am I awake? This must still be a dream."

"I know this is confusing for you. I have traveled to your time before, in a dream. People often are given messages and important information in dreams, messages sent from the spirit world. In my dream I saw that your people no longer believed. They no longer had such contact with the earth and the sky, or the spirits who guide."

"So this is a dream?"

"I do not believe this is a dream for you, Mar-tee-a. I believe you were sent to our world to help us."

"Me, help you? I think you've made a mistake. I'm nothing special. I have no special knowledge or power."

"I do not know the answers to your questions. I do know that you must learn about our people if you are to help us. You must learn to open your mind and believe what is around you. Today you will begin your lessons." Kwe-in-ye pointed to the bowl. "First lesson: eat your *pu-ti-yan*. Eat. *Iya-da.*

Martha looked at the warm gruel—the *pu-ti-yan*—which was in the bowl. She raised it to her face and sniffed. It smelled like the bulb food she sifted into the garden every fall when she thinned her bearded iris. There was no spoon, so she held the bowl up to her lips. The *pu-ti-yan* was slightly bitter and very thin, but she was extremely hungry and slurped it down. It tasted better than it smelled, kind of a nutty flavor.

The sun was shining down over the steep canyon wall, making its way across the narrow valley floor towards the circle of stones and the fire pit. Martha looked around as she ate, noticing that people were climbing down steep walls, coming out of caves in the sheer cliffs. The place was so big. In either direction, there were homes, gardens, people.

"Come Mar-tee-a, we will get started."

Martha stood and laid the skin on the rock. She looked at the empty bowl in her hand. "Should I clean this in some way?"

"That is a good place to start."

After Kwe-in-ye showed her how to wipe the bowl with leaves and put it, along with the mat and skin she had slept on, back into the room she had napped in yesterday, the woman led her across the canyon to the bank of the nearly dry creek bed. There she sat and motioned for Martha to sit as well. "You will listen."

Martha was beginning to understand the direct way this woman spoke. There was no *must* or *need to* in her language. The commands weren't bossy or pompous or manipulative—just direct. She was impressed with the method and thought about all the times in her life that such a technique would have been useful. If she were to say to Glen "you will listen," it would be labeled nagging, though it made perfect sense for her to ask—make that tell—him that she needed him to focus on her.

"Listen now." Kwe-in-ye repeated, as if aware that Martha's mind had wandered. "Today I will teach about the times that came before."

Kwe-in-ye lifted her chin slightly up to the cliffs, her eyes staring off as if she were reading the past from the high stone walls.

"Many years ago, when I was a very young woman, the people lived in a different place. This place was a special place...very...." she hesitated. "Very sacred, I think you would call it. The people were connected with the earth and grew all the plants we needed for our survival. The creek flowed all year and not far away was the big river. There were trees and rocks which were easy to chip and shape. The people grew lots of food and caught deer and bison and pronghorn to eat. They built fine shelters and kivas. Children were born, and dances and songs filled our hearts. The Raccoon people, the Redstone people, the Tallest Tree people, and my own family, the Sharp Beak Owl people."

Martha realized that the old woman was talking about the clans that had lived together. She nodded and shifted to get more comfortable. This was not going to be a short lesson.

Kwe-in-ye continued. "Over time the water began to disappear. There were not as many rains and the plants were small and sickly. The deer and antelope stayed, but the bison and elk went away. Our songs of joy were replaced with prayers. There were too many people. Suddenly, we felt crowded. You could not escape the noise of the voices or the smell of the bodies living so close together.

"One day a man appeared. We knew instantly that he had magical powers because he had three bodies, all the same. At least that is what we thought at first. We came to realize that although to our eyes there were three men all the same, they were not the same on the inside. The spirit of each one was different. I think that the gods had somehow divided one man into these three parts—good, evil and greed. These three men who were Man-With-Three-Spirits did not look like us. They stood tall and were as skinny as the egret but as furry as the bear with long whiskers on their faces. They wore heavy clothes and shoes that made lots of noise when they walked on the rocks.

"Man-With-Three-Spirits told us they were the grandsons of Spider Grandmother but we knew this could not be so. She had only two grandsons and they were protectors of our people. We listened to Man-With-Three-Spirits and they did not call the other spirits the names of Spider Grandmother's grandsons."

"What names did they use?"

"The good spirit was called *Sha-ar-lí,* the greedy one was *We-li-um* and the evil man was *Ba-ar-tun."*

Kwe-in-ye continued her story. "These spirits who were not our protectors told the people that we must believe in a different way. Man-With-Three-Spirits told of one god above all others. This god had many children and they were cruel and demanding. They told us if we did not pray to this god we would die and our bodies would go to dust, not to the spirit world. Some of the people did what Man-With-Three-Spirits demanded. They did the work that was needed, walking far away for more wood to build a large...*tewhá*...shelter, but very big, for the three men to live in, taking pots and skins to collect water and bring it to grow food for them. There was a river in this place where Man-With-Three-Spirits desired to live, but like all the others it did not have much water left. The people had to walk for many days to bring enough water for these plants. Man-With-Three-Spirits collected many things which were kept in the rooms of the shelter. They sent men to trade with other people in far away places. Man-With-Three-Spirits told the people that it was good to collect things, for these things could be traded for other things. The women were to make pots and baskets, the men to hunt and collect skins and bones. There was soon a group of boys and men who just made hunting weapons and tools and wove many mats to pile in a room, never to use for hunting or sleeping. No matter how many things the people gave to Man-With-Three-Spirits, they wanted more.

"The rains had stopped throughout the land. People from all the lands came to this sacred place, looking for somewhere that had food for them. They thought Man-With-Three-Spirits could save them, give them food and things from all these rooms that had been filled."

Kwe-in-ye stopped and looked at Martha. "You understand?"

Martha nodded.

"Man-With-Three-Spirits did give the people food and water, but to do this they sent them farther to collect. People were sick and many died. They said that it was good the people died after they prayed to the one god because they went to the spirit world and were happy in that place.

"Some of the people did not believe this. It is the way that one should not be near another when they die. This is because when the dead travel to the spirit world they do not want to be separated from their clan —they try to take the living with them. We have a special ceremony to protect from this, to send the spirit safely, but keep the living in this world. Many people who had gone to live with Man-With-Three-Spirits continued the old prayers in secret, and were silent during these new prayers that were demanded. They did not want to live in the new way."

Kwe-in-ye's eyes had filled with tears.

"My parents were of these people and one day this group decided to leave the sacred place. There was not enough food and water, the children were thin and sad, they did not laugh and play. My father and the other leaders of the group went to Man-With-Three-Spirits to tell them they wished to leave."

Kwe-in-ye paused. She licked her lips, dry from so much talking. She shifted and turned her face toward Martha.

"The spirits were not happy with this, especially *Ba-ar-tun,* the evil one. Man-With-Three-Spirits told my father and the people that they would not go to the spirit world, and that bad times would follow them, striking them down. *Your spirits will never rest*, they warned.

"My father and the people felt this was a chance they must take. They started packing some things for their journey. *Ba-ar-tun* came and said, "You cannot take those things, they belong to us." So the people left all the things and marched away with only the few belongings they could hide beneath their clothing.

61

"One man, *Ja-kwe*, said he knew of a place where the river was small, but good during the hot times. The people were able to find the way and they came to live here in *Tsankawi Owinge*. I lived here many years with my parents and the other people. We had many wonderful plants and fine shelter. The place was good."

"How many people came?" Martha was curious.

Kwe-in-ye thought for a moment. Although she did speak English with Martha, there were times when a concept seemed to be difficult to translate.

"I believe it would be five hundred."

So many! If this was considered a small group, then this sacred place Kwe-in-ye spoke of must have had thousands living there.

Martha pictured the canyon and the people she had seen. It seemed there were about eighty people gathered last night, but she didn't know if there were others.

"How many are here now? It seems like far fewer than five hundred."

"I will get to that part of the story." Kwe-in-ye was orderly and wouldn't give anything away in advance. She continued her lesson.

"I lived here and the times were good. The people kept to our old ways—we did not collect more than we needed. We did trade with others from time to time, usually the plants we were able to grow or the clay pots we made. But slowly, in this place too, the water began to fade. The creek continued, but became very small in the hot times. The deer and the antelope began to leave and the hunters fed us with rabbits and squirrels or small birds. We were called upon to eat animals we would have left alone, the raven and the snake."

"Why did you leave those animals alone? Isn't snake good to eat?"

"These animals have a special place in our prayers, they protect us and should not be eaten." Kwe-in-ye cast her eyes down, as if guilt plagued her. "Last summer the creek dried up completely. We did not have water here in the canyon. That is when some of the people decided that the curse of Man-With-Three-Spirits had found us. They felt that this place would no longer keep us happy and alive. The group packed up and returned to the sacred place, willing to do what Man-With-Three-Spirits asked."

Kwe-in-ye looked across the canyon toward the many houses built on the far wall and shook her head. "The rest of the people, the ones left here in the canyon, do not want to go back. We have prayed and prayed, but this summer the creek dried up again. We survive because we save water in pots, deep in the cool caves of the cliffs, and we walk to the big river and carry water to our village. We fear we will not make it through the hot times. Our plants have dried up and we do not have as many for the long cold times. We eat very carefully, just enough to keep our health. But the years keep passing and each summer is no better than the last."

Kwe-in-ye stood. She reached her hands out to Martha and pulled her up as well.

"Four nights ago all of the people gathered. We prayed and prayed, all of our special prayers, with dances and songs. We asked the earth to help us, to keep us safe from Man-With-Three-Spirits, to keep the old belief strong." Kwe-in-ye leaned closer to Martha and placed her palms on Martha's cheeks and looked directly into her eyes. "That night I had the dream. The dream of the woman from another place who came to us. When I awoke in the morning I met the coyote and I spoke a new tongue, although I did not understand the words yet." Kwe-in-ye drew in a huge breath.

"It is you, Mar-tee-a. You are the answer to the prayers and you will lift the curse."

TWELVE

Kwe-in-ye spent the rest of the day showing Martha around the village. On the floor of the valley there was a small stream, a bare trickle of water moving between the stones. Kwe-in-ye reminded Martha again that there was very little water here, as if her story hadn't brought that point home. The people were careful not to contaminate the river. She pointed to the stagnant pools buzzing with gnats under the shaded edges.

"This is no good for drinking," she said. "For drinking we keep the water up there." She pointed to the cool caves of the cliffs.

Martha wondered where the water in the clay pot came from if the water in the river was no good for drinking. She didn't want to get sick, but she really didn't have much choice as there wasn't anything else to drink.

With each fact Kwe-in-ye imparted, she glanced at Martha as if to reassure herself she hadn't summoned a demon by accident. Martha was frustrated by this whole you-save-us-but-I-don't-trust-you attitude.

In the center of this part of the canyon floor there was a kiva, a large round room dug into the earth with a roof made of tree limbs and branches. Kwe-in-ye walked by without a word of explanation. Martha remembered something from the trail guide—only men were allowed inside to take part in the ceremonies. But everything she had done so far included both men and women.

"What is this place? The kiva?"

Her spirit guide stopped. "Yes. It is our sacred place."

"Can women go in?"

"They can, when needed. Now come, you will learn more about this later."

Martha was frustrated that her tour and lessons were on this old woman's terms. Not only that, she was getting tired and that made her grouchy.

The fire pit was not the only area surrounded by stones which made for a good seat. Several other areas were scattered around the valley. These seemed to be work areas, where women sat and sewed or leaned over smooth stones grinding grains that looked like some type of corn. The men sat on the ground and formed tools, sharpening stones and sticks, binding things together with pieces of leather cording. Children ran everywhere and their laughter filled the air.

There were low stone walls in front of all the buildings. Inside these rectangular enclosures Martha could see a wide variety of plants: vegetables she recognized like squash, gourds, and beans, and many she didn't. There were also flowers and grasses growing both in and out of the stone gardens.

Martha listened to the soft hum coming from the group of women across the canyon. There was so much empty air here—air without the drone of freeway traffic or the sound of the neighbors watching reality television or someone two blocks away using their blower to clear leaves from their driveway. In this time, the sounds were all natural. The loudest thing she heard was the ringing of rock chipping against rock as a man worked on something in front of his doorway. A baby cried in one of the upper levels, his discomfort echoing off the rock walls and fading. She could hear the whoosh of someone sweeping and the hum from the women turned into a song. A chant really, with a rhythm similar to the drums they had danced to. The beat of their words continued and other women joined in, tossing the song back and forth like birds calling across a meadow. She would have liked to go sit with them, but Kwe-in-ye continued down the path.

Higher up the walls were more openings. Each cave had a narrow trail or a series of handholds carved into the stone. The entrances were covered with skins, hanging from wooden poles placed across the top of the doorways. Most of the doorways were small, but occasionally there was a larger cave with an arched roof rising up the canyon wall. Some of these caves held round kivas, while others held small buildings, windows facing outward.

"This, I know this place." Martha gasped in recognition when she saw a large cave with three separate openings. "I visited it, Glen climbed the ladder and I took his picture. Yesterday. We're in the same place." She stopped and thought. "No, the day before that."

"Kwe-in-ye? What of the other time?" Martha imagined Glen waking up and not finding her beside him. How long before he realized she was missing and not just wandering around camp or visiting the restroom? "What of my husband?"

"I wish that I could answer all of your questions, but I do not know this." Kwe-in-ye led her toward a group of men working in one of the little gardens.

Martha recognized one of the men as the older man who had grown tired at the dance.

"*Pa a sen wu kwee.*" Kwe-in-ye waved her hand toward Martha.

"*Ja pa,*" Martha greeted the old man.

He grinned and she cringed, her mouth painful in sympathy at the sight of his worn teeth.

"*Póetu,*" he said and patted his chest.

"*Ja pa, Póetu,*" Martha responded.

"*Katudu,*" one of the other men said. This one was young, with smooth skin and bright eyes. He gave a hop and slapped his chest.

"*Ja pa, Katudu.*" Martha was sure she would never remember all these names.

The third man stood up from his work and pounded his chest with both fists. "*Lu-te-na, Lu-te-na, Lu-te-na,*" he sang out as he turned in a complete circle while continuing his Tarzan-like chest pounding.

The men laughed and Martha smiled. She felt welcomed by these men and their playful antics.

"*Ja pa, Lu-te-na,*" she said.

But her tour guide wasn't stopping to chat. She set off up the path.

Martha followed Kwe-in-ye toward the huge complex of rooms which had the feel of an apartment building. They entered one of the rooms. Baskets lined the walls and furs and yucca mats were stacked in one corner. It took a minute for Martha's eyes to adjust to the dim light and notice a woman sitting in the corner sewing.

"*Ja pa, Yo-en-u.*"

The woman smiled, obviously happy Martha had remembered her. "*Ja pa Mar-tee-a.*"

Kwe-in-ye didn't bother with small talk. "*Se weta ba tumate.*"

Yo-en-u opened a basket and rummaged around. She pulled out a piece of cloth, then turned to the next basket and pulled out bunches of flat leaves.

"*Ba tomate a Mar-tee-a,*" she said, holding out the items.

Martha didn't know what she had said, but it was obvious Martha was meant to have the clothes. "Thank you." She turned to Kwe-in-ye. "I think that's something I need to learn how to say in your language. Everyone has to do so much for me."

"*Ah yi ee.*" said Kwe-in-ye.

Martha turned back to Yo-en-u. "*Ah yi ee.*"

She held the bundle to her chest and waited to see what Kwe-in-ye had planned next. She hoped it involved eating and drinking, and she really had to use the woods again. And this time for more than just urinating.

There was an awkward pause as the two women stood and stared at her.

"*Ah yi ee,*" she said again.

Just then two girls ducked in through the door. One was about seven, with wavy dark hair tied back from her face. She wore a cotton skirt, rolled at the waist and tied with a leather cord. Martha pictured an older sister, perhaps the second girl, passing along the clothing, just as Vince had passed things to Jack. Her youngest son could never wait until the clothes fit properly, and the old leather belt he would cinch around his waist to keep the pants up reminded her of this little girl and her skirt. The other girl was dressed in a simple woven dress. Both were barefoot.

"*Sha tu wu kee.*" the older girl said.

Kwe-in-ye scowled and shook her head, but Yo-en-u reached out and touched her sister's arm.

"No ken nu pas," she said.

The old woman shrugged and looked at Martha. "Try the clothes please. We need to know if they will do."

Martha realized that she was expected to undress in front of this group, which now included not only the two women, but these bright-eyed and staring children as well.

"Maybe I can go in another room?"

She realized her error solely by the raised eyebrows and bunched up lips Kwe-in-ye showed before she spoke.

"We must watch to see if they are right."

Martha turned toward the wall and set the bundle on the floor. There was complete silence in the room and she could feel the penetrating gazes of her audience. The woven cotton was a tunic or a skirt, she wasn't sure, too short for the first and too long for the other. The bundles of flat leaves were shoes—sandals really—although Martha had no clue how they were to stay on her feet.

With a glance over her shoulder she pulled off her nightgown and held the tunic out, trying to discover if she should slip it over her head or wrap it around herself.

But before she could figure it out she caught the glimpse of a figure moving toward her. The larger of the two girls, the one who seemed about nine, darted forward and rubbed a hand down Martha's thigh, feeling the fabric of her leggings.

"To-be-né, ban tay." Kwe-in-ye's obvious command barked out through the silence.

Martha clutched the tunic against her chest and turned. "It's okay. Really." She smiled at the child and tugged at the stretchy elastic of the waistband on her leggings. "Here, you can feel it."

With a giggle and a glance toward Kwe-in-ye, the girl reached out and tugged at the fabric waistband, pulling it away from Martha's body. Then she let go and it snapped back into place.

Martha flinched from surprise, as Kwe-in-ye scolded, but the look on the girl's face made Martha laugh. It made the younger girl laugh too, and soon Yo-en-u joined in. As their delighted giggles filled the room Martha flashed on how she would have been the one scolding, frowning and telling the boys that roughhousing was unnecessary for having fun and suggesting they play a board game. She hated how Kwe-in-ye stopped the fun, but lamented that she had done the same thing to her own children.

Yo-en-u stepped forward and reached for the waistband. Martha looked at the kind woman, who had laughed along with the children, and slipped off the pants, handing them to her.

The older girl now choked with laughter and pointed at Martha's underwear: white cotton with tiny purple lilacs.

"Ku yi ta wa."

"Yes, my underwear has flowers." Martha snapped the elastic waistband of her underwear. "And elastic."

The girls rolled on the ground with laughter, and the brown dog joined in, chasing her tail and yapping with excitement. Martha laughed until tears ran down her cheeks.

She expected at least a smile from Kwe-in-ye, but it was not to be. The old woman shooed the girls out of the room with the same "cha" she had used on the dog. With the children gone, she turned to Martha.

"Yo-en-u will help you with the clothing."

Martha nodded and handed the tunic over. Within seconds it was slipped over her torso—thankfully covering her breasts—and secured with the cord. She kicked off her slippers and Yo-en-u fastened the sandals to her feet by wrapping fronds between her toes and around her ankles.

Martha took a few steps around the room and shook her head. "I don't think I need these. I'll keep mine, if that's okay."

Kwe-in-ye picked up the sheepskin slippers and shook her head.

Martha pressed her lips together, Clarice's voice coming out of nowhere and settling in the back of her head. "Mom, don't be a pushover. She's stealing your shoes."

"I really think it's best if I keep those. I can't walk well in these, especially on the trails and the rocks." She stepped forward and reached out.

Kwe-in-ye didn't budge and Martha was sure she had committed some major *faux pas*. The slippers were probably considered payment for the clothes and food. She hesitated, but then felt the cold stone floor under the thin soles of the sandals.

"Sorry, I really need them," she said as she stepped forward and snatched the slippers. Then she scurried back and grabbed up her nightgown. With a sigh, she turned to Yo-en-u and motioned for the leggings. "I'm not trading."

She could hear Clarice saying "Good job, Mom."

THIRTEEN

Glen ran a hand over his chin and decided he could forego shaving this morning. He needed to get back to the hospital to be with Martha. He had been away from her all night and something might have changed. Vince had insisted he should get some sleep, but he hadn't slept much. At least some was better than nothing.

It was easy to pack up Vince's belongings. A simple plastic bag with the few items his son had purchased to get him through his stay. Toothbrush, underwear, and two shirts. Clarice wasn't messy either, most of her things still in her little blue carry-on bag. He picked up a green shower cap and a hairbrush and tucked them in the front pocket. He could carry this to the camper in one trip.

Glen stopped at the front desk and checked out of the hotel. He would tell the kids they had to go back to California. This whole fiasco was already costing every member of the family way too much money. He would have to pay the kids for their airline tickets and the rental car and of course Clarice hadn't stopped reminding everyone how much the hired car had cost. If there wasn't anywhere for them to stay, he could force them to leave.

Not that he didn't like having them here, but…actually, he didn't like having them here. Clarice with her endless disagreement of everything and Vince with his hovering.

"Martha, wake up today. If you could just do that for me." Glen spoke out loud as he looked around the parking lot for the truck. He had no recollection of where he had parked last night, not even recalling which entrance to the hotel he used. A camper should stand out, but he didn't see it. He pulled the fob from his pocket and pressed the unlock button until the faithful Ford answered him with a mellow beep, beep, from where it slept, tucked in the back corner of the lot next to the fence.

This was his fault. Insisting on buying this camper now, springing it on Martha with all those notes and brochures and then driving her directly to the dealership. She hadn't protested, but he should have known that she wouldn't. His wife went along with things. She told him she loved the tiny kitchen in the camper and didn't mind that she had to remove every single thing from the bathroom each time she showered, and she went along with climbing up into the bed each night once he added the steps. That should have been his first clue. At home she never even used a step-stool, waiting until someone tall was around if she needed something stored on the top shelf of the kitchen cabinets.

He had let his excitement get the best of him and ignored what she might want. The truth was, it hadn't been excitement that moved him to buy this camper. It was fear he would end up like his brother that drove him to act so impulsively. One night in a motel, that was all Martha had asked for. He leaned on the steering wheel and tried to hold in the sobs that squeezed his chest into a tight ball. He would sell the stupid thing, although it meant losing thousands of dollars. If she would just wake up, he would spend the rest of their lives treating her to luxury hotels.

When he reached St. Vincent's he found his son slumped in the armchair in the corner of Martha's room, an open-mouth snore gurgling from his lips. There was no sign of Clarice. Martha was still connected to all those machines, the rise and fall of her chest steady, her skin deathly white and her eyes closed like Vince's. Unlike his son's, hers didn't snap open when he spoke.

"Hey."

"Dad. You're here." Vince sat up straight and licked his lips. "Sleep okay?"

"Sure. What's the news? Has the doctor been by?"

Vince shook his head. "Not yet. Clarice…she's off to get some coffee."

"Okay." Glen pulled the other chair over to the edge of the bed. "Hey Martha…how are you today?"

His throat grew tight as he looked at her. It couldn't be just buying the camper. He'd been over and over everything, not only in his mind but with all the doctors and nurses, the kids, the insurance company, and Mrs. Conley, the woman who seemed to have all the answers. Martha had been fine. Tired, maybe, but only when it came to traveling. She had hiked all over the place and read and cooked spaghetti for their dinner.

But maybe he had caused this in another way. Maybe he hadn't listened to her enough when she said she couldn't sleep. A wave of guilt swept over him as he remembered thinking he would take a picture of her with his phone on the morning she didn't wake up. How heartless was that?

Glen shook his head and sighed. She was happy, he had heard her tell her sister that a million times. She didn't want anything more than being a mother and when the kids were grown she joined some of those clubs…the quilters and the knitters or some such thing. She was always meeting someone for lunch or shopping or on the phone. What had he missed? Had he failed to notice Martha because he was so focused on the kids? He had their children figured out. At least he thought he did.

Vince was all about facts, in spite of being the family artist when he was young. Come to think of it, his approach to art was scientific. Those colors he mixed, the precise edges and symmetry of his paintings.

Clarice, on the other hand, had been all about the whole picture. His daughter needed to know what everyone else was doing, where they would be while she was at Girl Scouts or school or anywhere at all. She even had to know what they were planning for dinner before she left each morning.

Jack had been the easiest to read, but the most difficult to understand. Jack told you what he thought you wanted to hear, then went off and did the opposite without so much as a glance back. How many times had he and Martha stayed up talking strategy in an effort to teach that boy what was important in life? Responsibility, truth, respect…the concepts never grew into anything visible with their youngest.

But his wife? Could he wrap up Martha as neatly as he did the kids?

Glen looked at her now. Someone had brushed her hair and clipped it back so her forehead seemed larger than usual. Her skin was pale as parchment and the dark circles under her eyes worried him. Surely someone in an unconscious state wasn't feeling emotions, but he couldn't shake the feeling she was closer than she seemed. The doctors—all of them—insisted there was no visible medical reason for her coma. In fact, they weren't calling it a coma, according to that lady doctor, the neurologist. What they were calling it, he couldn't say. When he asked, they referred to more tests they were running.

"Dad?"

Glen realized Vince was talking to him. "Sorry. I was just thinking… Go on."

"So, Clarice and I talked last night and you're right. We need to get Mom home. She'll do better and it's not selfish to realize we'll all do better, too."

Glen nodded. "As soon as the doctor says it's okay, we'll leave. I checked out of the hotel."

As he spoke Clarice walked in, two cups of coffee balanced on a cardboard tray. "What?" Coffee spilled, splattering her ankle. "Damn it!"

"Dad?" Vince jumped up and took the coffee from his sister. "Without a discussion? It's not like we can pop her in the camper and drive home."

Glen continued. "I'm going to stay here. I can nap in the camper."

"What about us?" Clarice grabbed the box of tissues off Martha's bedside table and wiped up the coffee.

"It's time you two go back. Your mother will…" Glen stopped.

"Right. Mom will what? We don't know the answer to that, do we? What if she takes a turn for the worse? And we're gone. I can't believe you didn't discuss this with us." Clarice slammed the tissues back on the table and turned to Vince. "Talk to him!"

Glen closed his eyes.

"Can we at least wait to hear what the doctor has to say?" Vince set the coffee on Martha's rolling tray.

Glen opened his eyes and looked at his children. Grown ups. Worried about their mother. "That's what I plan to do."

FOURTEEN

Martha stared at the palms of her hands, then flipped them over and looked at her chipped nails. She would have to find out how these ancient people filed and trimmed jagged fingernails. A minor problem compared to lifting a curse.

She had mulled over Kwe-in-ye's challenge all through a sleepless night. How could a housewife combat the man-who-was-really-three-men the old woman had described in her story? She certainly didn't have the athletic ability or physical strength to overpower someone, so it would have to be mental power. Maybe she wasn't supposed to confront them or have anything to do with them. Maybe she was here to invent some scientific way to deal with the drought. She smiled at that thought and shook her head. She wasn't a scientist either.

"You are awake." Kwe-in-ye came into the room next to the cave and rummaged through a pile of objects placed in the little shelf cut into the sandstone wall of the house. "I teach the children each day. You will come and help."

Martha crawled out from under the warm skin and reached for the edge of the cave to pull herself up. Kwe-in-ye watched and scowled. Her lips parted, then clamped shut with a snap. It was obvious the old woman had been about to chide her but changed her mind. Martha knew it was because last night she had changed back into her leggings and nightgown.

When Martha grabbed the wall, a small piece of the mud plaster broke off in her hand and she nearly fell. During yesterday's tour Kwe-in-ye told Martha that to use the wrong mud would mean building a house that would collapse during the hard rains. Most of the soil here was gritty sand, erosion from the volcanic cliffs made of pumice. The sticky mud needed as grout was claylike, used not only for the mortar but for making the clay pots used for cooking and water storage. This mud was collected down the canyon, by what the old woman had referred to as the big river.

That had to be the Rio Grande. Martha didn't know the course of the river but she and Glen had crossed it a long way back when driving to the park. It seemed quite far for these people to travel for building supplies. Or water.

Some of the rooms, like this one, were built along the lower edges of the cliffs, so that the back wall was actually the face of the rock. The walls of the canyon were fascinating; huge honeycombs of caves and nooks that looked like air pockets in lava that had dried quickly. The white rock was firm, yet if you rubbed it the stone soon melted away. This must be useful for enlarging and forming the caves. Some were living spaces, while others seemed to be for storage, high above the canyon floor, away from animals or other predators. During her tour yesterday Kwe-in-ye had explained that the deeper caves remained cool and dry, the perfect refrigeration units.

Martha shook out the skin she had slept under and rolled it against the wall. "Do I need to bring anything with me?"

"No, not now. The children will ask questions of your world and it will do for you to answer them."

Martha followed Kwe-in-ye out the tiny doorway and down the well-worn path to the area near the fire pit. She tried to picture her spirit guide, who was impatient, no-nonsense and terse, as the village teacher.

There was a sound behind her and she turned.

The brown dog stood waving its tail, her pink tongue hanging out in that happy grin dogs have.

"Hey girl. Are you coming?" Martha bent and the dog moved forward, tail pulled in and legs bent. Submissive or used to being kicked. Martha didn't have any food to give to the animal, but maybe she could pet her. "Come on. It's okay."

Full crawl now, the dog crept close enough for Martha to reach out and touch her head, but it was too much for the animal and she jumped up and ran.

Progress, but I need some sort of a treat if I'm really going to make a friend.

She could see children ahead, running around, jumping from rock to rock, laughing and chasing each other. When Kwe-in-ye and Martha approached, the children ran up to them.

"*Ja pa, ja pa.*" It was apparent to Martha that the words were not just a greeting but also an endearment and that the children adored Kwe-in-ye. As they flocked to the women, they held back from looking at Martha, their eyes flicking toward her to catch a glimpse and then darting away.

"*Ja pa, Mar-tee-ya.*" Martha recognized the girl who hadn't resisted the urge to tug the elastic. She smiled at the new pronunciation of her name. She hadn't thought it could be manipulated more than it already had, but the firm "ya" this child put at the end rhymed with the *Ja pa*, forming a delightful singsong greeting. Martha held out her hand and the young girl slid her hand over Martha's palm and then ran it down the flannel of Martha's nightgown. To-be-né was a curious child.

"It is not respectful for children to stare or to ask questions. This is why they ignore you. Once I have introduced you they will be different." Kwe-in-ye turned to Martha's little friend. "*Ja pa, To-be-né.*"

The old woman clucked her tongue in a sharp "*chu-chu*" and the children all gathered in front of her, sinking to the ground like any other group of children. Fussing over who sat where and next to who and in the front.

"*Pa a sen wu kwee. Mar-tee-a.*" Kwe-in-ye waved toward Martha as she spoke, and now all eyes turned to her. "*No pren gun a so?*"

"*Ta a won ma do no?*" one of the children asked.

"She would like to know if your hair was burned in a fire." The old woman smiled as she translated.

Martha smiled too, pleased to see that Kwe-in-ye might have a soft side after all. "No, it isn't natural though. I dye it." Apparently mahogany red wasn't something anyone in this place had ever seen.

Kwe-in-ye shook her head and frowned. "I do not know what this means. Your hair is dead? Why does it not fall out of your head?"

"Umm…." *How to explain?* "I have painted it this color."

The old woman nodded with understanding and spoke to the children.

"*Ta a tumate ku yi ta wa*?" asked a very small boy.

"He would like to know how you painted the flowers on your dress."

Martha looked down at the print on her nightgown. She needed a simple explanation. But these children did know about weaving. "When the fabric is woven the flowers are woven into it." Not a very good explanation as it could easily be construed to mean actual flowers were woven. "The threads are purple and green and the women weave the design into the fabric." Even Kwe-in-ye looked puzzled by her answer.

"*Ta a za pi too?*" asked an older boy.

"He would like to know what animal your shoes are made from."

"These are made from a sheep." Did they know what a sheep was? "Sort of like a fuzzy deer."

"*Ka wa ush.*"

"The children want to know about your bracelet."

"This is called a watch. It tells the time of day."

This time Kwe-in-ye shook her head. She didn't allow for any more questions and instead reached into the basket.

Kwe-in-ye's way of teaching was wonderful. She pulled objects such as spear heads, yucca plant fibers, and shaped rocks out of her basket. The children sat in a circle and passed each object around so that all could examine it. Sniffing, rubbing, and even licking items were encouraged. Martha had her turn with each of the objects, trying hard to listen to what Kwe-in-ye said, hoping that something would make sense. After each item had made the rounds the children would take turns speaking. It seemed to Martha they were telling stories about the objects or making guesses as to the use. Nothing about this language was familiar, but there were hand motions and intonations that Martha attempted to interpret.

When To-be-né held a bone needle, glanced at her, then met eyes with a boy about her age, a bit of doubt crept into the back of Martha's mind. Surely these children knew all about these objects?

Her doubt was confirmed when To-be-né smirked, made exaggerated sewing motions and spoke in a high-pitched voice, pausing between each word.

These very simple lessons were not for the students. They were for her. She flushed at the thought that this entire group of children was making fun of her.

When all the objects had been examined, Kwe-in-ye stood and motioned to her students. She pointed to a tall boy, one of the older children and said, "*Ten-pla, kepta bali.*"

Ten-pla strode off down the trail, with all the children following. The group chattered and skipped, picked up stones, and dragged sticks through the tough grass. A warm feeling swept through Martha as she realized children found joy, no matter when they lived.

Kwe-in-ye and Martha brought up the rear. To-be-né stopped by the side of the path, then turned and ran back. She took Martha's hand, walking beside her. The girl's smile was contagious and Martha felt a pulse in her heart as she thought about Clarice. She couldn't remember a time when her daughter had looked at her with so much happiness.

The group walked a short way to the creek where six women sat on mats like the one in Martha's room, woven from rigid leaves. Yucca plants were stacked in the center of their circle. Two of the women were stripping the leaves and rolling them, while others mashed the roots with the oblong pestle-like stones. The tall boy pointed to the women and offered an explanation to the group. It seemed the assignment was to find someone who was actually using one of the objects that Kwe-in-ye had passed around.

The children gathered around the women, who smiled and spoke with them. One of the women handed the children pieces of the yucca leaf and encouraged them to try their hand at the task. Aware that all of this was for her sake, Martha paid attention. In all likelihood she would be quizzed tonight and she didn't want any more tension between herself and Kwe-in-ye.

To-be-né pulled Martha forward.

"*Cha-pe*," she said and pointed.

Martha shook her head, trying to let the girl know she didn't understand.

To-be-né smiled and pointed to Martha. "*Mar-tee-ya.*" She pointed to herself. "*To-be-né,*" then turned and pointed back at the woman. "*Cha-pe.*"

Martha felt like a character in a western as she nodded and caught on. "Of course." She smiled at the woman. "*Ja pa, Cha-pe.*"

The woman—*Cha-pe*—smiled as To-be-né clapped her hands in delight.

Cha-pe handed Martha a piece of yucca. Martha thought that the task looked easy enough, dampening and rolling the fibers, but she soon realized this was one of those things that was more difficult when you tried it yourself. Her hands felt clumsy, as the fibers split and tangled rather than rolling into a single strong unit. Looking around at the children who were doing a much better job, a flush crept up her neck. Angry with herself, she stopped rolling the fiber. She was a weaver and a knitter, and she had made her own yarn from wool. This shouldn't be that hard. The warmth in her heart from the lesson and the friendly woman and the helpful little girl grew cold.

"It is harder than it looks." Kwe-in-ye took Martha's lump of yucca from her. "Do not become angry with yourself, Mar-tee-a. Everyone has to go through the lesson. You are as a young child in the ways of the people. It will take time, study and patience."

Kwe-in-ye splashed her hand into the bowl of water and rubbed the yucca, dampening it. "The yucca is a stubborn and particular friend. Each fiber prefers to be on its own—independent, not listening to the words of the others. Too much water and the fibers give up, drown in their need to be alike. Not enough water and the fibers run away, stand by themselves, refusing to become a part of the group." Kwe-in-ye gently rolled the yucca and continued. "The pressure of the hands must be comforting, give strength to each independent fiber." She handed the strand back to Martha.

Martha made another attempt, rolling the yucca between her palms, slowly, with a firm movement. The fibers seemed to listen to Kwe-in-ye's words—they started to bind with each other, forming a smooth, thick thread.

"*Za.*" To-be-né's soft cheer came from beside her. Her little friend was proud of her success.

After the students and Martha had spent the morning learning many things and the sun was high in the sky, Kwe-in-ye indicated that school was over. The children walked off in all directions, heading for home, Martha suspected. She was hungry but felt it impolite to ask Kwe-in-ye about lunch.

"*Pa tu chan.*" To-be-né tugged at Martha's hand. Martha looked to Kwe-in-ye for instruction.

"She wants you to go have food with her family."

"Are you coming too?"

Kwe-in-ye shook her head. "I have work to do."

Martha considered this a bit of a dismissal and thought about her options. She could wander around alone or spend time with this delightful child. Both options made her nervous because she had no way of communicating without Kwe-in-ye by her side.

"*Ta a no so.*" To-be-né tugged again and smiled with exaggerated emphasis. The girl knew how to communicate without sharing a language.

Martha did want to spend more time with this child. "I would like that, if it's okay?"

'Mar-tee-a, you do not have to ask an old woman for permission in this place. Each person goes the way that is needed."

"Do you need me for anything else today?"

"No, I think you had many lessons. Tonight Mosinobu has asked that you work with the people to teach them words of your language. I think it would be good for you to practice the words of our language, too."

Martha followed To-be-né. She had expected the smaller girl, Ha-ni, to join them, as the two seemed inseparable. She thought they might be sisters, but also knew that girls liked to pair up with a best friend. As they walked, To-be-né pointed out things to Martha: a smooth rock, an empty fire pit, a plant with bright red blossoms, and a chipmunk chattering from a high rock. She spoke non-stop, explaining each thing, her words one long string of sounds slipping into Martha's ears.

They came to one of the taller clusters of rooms, six levels high in some places. Handholds led up the walls, and there were a few doorways visible from the front of the complex. To-be-né stopped at the edge of the wall and let go of Martha's hand. She quickly climbed to the roof, then turned to sit with her legs dangling over the edge.

Martha shook her head. "Is that where you live? Maybe I cannot have lunch with you." It was silly to talk to this girl, but maybe her tone would send the message.

"*Pa tu chan*," To-be-né said. "*San o te omkasen.*"

Martha smiled. Here they were, one hesitant woman and one eager girl. Friends for less than a day and already they were arguing. This really did remind her of Clarice.

Clarice. All the time and energy Martha had spent on her daughter seemed to lead nowhere. No choice that Martha had ever made stood up to the critique of the strong young woman. Martha was proud of her daughter, she had accomplished so much, but she wished that they could get along. She respected her daughter's choices, so why couldn't Clarice respect hers? She must have done something wrong. Martha wished she knew the secret to raising a confident daughter who also had empathy for those around her.

Maybe she had been too serious with Clarice. Some parents played with their kids, although Martha had never felt comfortable doing this. She fell back on pretending that a good mother guided by example, adult behaviors demonstrated so that her children would have models of their future.

"Mar-tee-ya?"

Martha snapped back to the present. Or the dream or whatever this was. To-be-né motioned to her.

She glanced up. Maybe this was her chance. She couldn't make things right with her own daughter, but maybe To-be-né was in this dream so that Martha would see another means to an end. A symbol of her mothering skills, or lack of them. Something to point out her mistakes, but also to teach her something new.

"Okay, chickadee. I know what you want. I can try." She stood and stared up at the girl's legs, dangling over the edge of the roof. Such smooth skin and a strong, lean body. This child could never understand what it felt like to fear heights. Martha had no explanation for it herself. All she knew was that raising herself higher by stepping on the smallest stool made her dizzy and anxious. The blood would rush from her head and the earth would pull her down—as if her brain were made of steel and the ground was a huge magnet.

The roof was about six feet up. Martha could reach the top if she raised her arms. This was her chance to prove—once and for all—that she was strong enough to make changes in her life. She climbed, slipping her hands into the smooth indentations and curling her fingers tight over the slight bump, then pulling herself up while she tapped the toe of each slipper into the holes. This would probably be easier with bare feet, her slippers with their thick rubber soles were so much bigger than anything these people wore. When she reached the top, she had some trouble. The only way to clear that last portion seemed to be to heave herself up onto her stomach and roll to the flat surface.

"Made it." She grunted.

To-be-né grinned and immediately led Martha to the next wall This one was the same height, only about six feet, leading to the third level. Martha and To-be-né had a system now, and Martha made it up with more confidence this time.

She continued to listen to the girl's chatter as they made their way up to the fourth level. She glanced into the doorways of the rooms they passed. There didn't seem to be any other people in this building.

She wiped her dusty palms on her nightgown. "Your family would live on the top floor."

When they reached the top Martha looked around for where To-be-né lived. This level had not only doors into rooms, but cut-out entrances to the caves in the steep cliffs.

To-be-né turned and climbed back down to the level below.

"What?" Martha walked to the edge and looked down.

Big mistake. She instantly felt the pull of earthly force, just as she always had when she forgot to close her eyes. She sat down and put her hands over her face.

Why did I think I could be brave? Use this child to repair my real life mistakes? Time to wake up now, Martha.

She felt the soft touch of a small hand. Martha took her hands away from her face and her heart lurched. To-be-né's black eyes were mere inches from her own.

The girl nodded and turned, on hands and knees. She showed Martha how to crawl to the edge and turn her body, placing her feet on the second cut out and her hands on the first. Martha crawled to the edge and pressed her palms against the plastered roof as she felt around with her foot for the tiny ledge. After several attempts, she made her way down the wall.

To-be-né squeezed her hand when they had climbed down all the walls and had their feet firm on the ground. *"Za, za, d'ka lo pe."*

Martha nodded, just as the brown dog ran up to the girl. Not the submissive posture she had seen before. The dog's tail was wagging and she licked To-be-né's hand.

"Is this your dog?" Martha pointed to the girl and then the dog and raised her eyebrows.

"Pó-o-ko."

Martha pointed to the girl. "To-be-né." Then she pointed to herself "Martha." Finally she pointed the dog. "Pó-o-ko?"

To-be-né shook her head. She pointed to herself *"Wu na."* Then she pointed to Martha. *"Wu kwee."* Finally she pointed to the dog, *"Pó-o-ko."*

Not the dog's name. Perhaps it was the word that meant dog.

To-be-né grabbed her hand and tugged. Martha followed and called out to the dog. "Come on, you come with us."

As they walked Martha wondered why Kwe-in-ye had been so upset about her attempts to make friends with the dog. It was clear that animals were part of this child's life and that she had played with the dog. It seemed that learning about the ways of these ancient people was going to be complicated, especially if her spirit guide wasn't always on the same page as everyone else.

To-be-né led her away from the complex, toward the row of trees near the creek bed. They came to a group of three women and two babies. The women rose to their feet and moved to Martha, rubbing her nightgown with their hands and greeting her. One woman moved a flat stone closer to the group, motioning for Martha to be seated. She was served some dried meat and a chunk of some sort of plant. Martha tugged off a bite of the meat, letting it soften in her mouth while she watched what the others did with the plant. They bit off small pieces and ate them, so she followed suit. It tasted a bit like a turnip. The brown dog sat behind her, but she didn't dare give away any of the shared food.

She watched the faces and motions of the women as they talked and ate. She studied the babies, swaddled tightly to rigid boards. One of the babies appeared to be only a few months old, faint sucking movements on its face, as the baby dreamed of nursing. The other child was older, probably eight months, and his bright eyes followed the movements of the others as his mother occasionally placed a small amount of softened food into his mouth. He didn't seem to struggle in the swaddling although his arms were enclosed so that he couldn't reach for anything. Martha wished that she could ask his mother why he was restrained so. She would have to ask Kwe-in-ye. If she was going to help these people she needed to learn everything as quickly as possible.

How long did she have? Was she expected to lift the curse tonight? Kwe-in-ye acted as if this was going to be a long process, but nothing was as Martha expected in this place.

Go with the flow, she instructed herself. What else could she do?

FIFTEEN

"Thanks Paige. You've been swell."

"No problem, Jack. Your family seems wound pretty tight. Maybe you could tell them you aren't using my number anymore."

"Yep, I will." Paige was a great lady, fielding the hundred messages a day from Clarice and Vince. Not Dad, though. His father had never called.

His wonderful siblings. Doing what was right, what was expected. Jack tried to picture his mother lying in a hospital bed, devoted family at her side, but the whole image had such a soap opera quality he laughed. More than likely Clarice was out walking and Vince was in the parking lot on his cell phone dealing with some critical detail of life. With Vince everything was critical.

Dad. Dad would be sitting as close to Mom as he could get. Maybe lying beside her in the bed. No, there would be tubes and bells and whistles if she was in a coma.

Could she really be in a coma? No one could say, well not Clarice anyway, because she was the only one he had really talked to. The one time he had actually called Vince back, it was *Jack do this, Jack do that, Jack, don't forget I'm in charge*. Who needed that kind of conversation?

No, Clarice was strung tight, but in a different way.

"Mom is completely out of it and they have her hooked up to all these machines. It's worse than a movie. Things beep and whir and some nurse is always coming in to check and frowning, but they never really tell us anything." Clarice had asked him about conversations he might have had with Mom regarding what she wanted in a life-or-death kind of situation.

Jack couldn't help his sister much. "Mom and I never talked about philosophical kinds of stuff. She…she talked about muffins and book club and all her friends' kids I don't really remember."

"Are you sure? She didn't mention a medical power-of-attorney?" Clarice was a rat terrier when it came to answers she was determined to find.

"I'm sure. She's healthy, totally healthy." His mother didn't have high blood pressure or cholesterol or anything. She had mentioned that to him more than once. Usually followed by a lecture on drugs or smoking.

"Right. I guess she's not so healthy now."

"So did they do brain scans and stuff like that? Tests?"

"Yes, Jack. St. Vincent's is a regular hospital. Santa Fe is the capital of New Mexico, not some hole-in-the-wall."

"You're kidding, right?"

"Why would I kid about this?"

"No, I mean—" Jack choked back his laugh. "The hospital is called St. *Vincent's?*"

"Isn't that what I just—oh." He heard the smile in her voice as she caught on. "Yes, it is and he thinks he owns the place."

Now that he had his sister off her fast track to nowhere, he could ask his real questions.

"So when you guys get home, where are you taking her? To Stanford? Shouldn't we get a second opinion if they don't know what's wrong?"

"I don't know. They won't even discuss when we can bring her home. Dad is flip flopping all over the place. First he seems to think he's going to take care of her at the house. Like he could just move all the machines and this automatic bed into their bedroom." She paused just enough for Jack to know she was off in another direction. "What they say doesn't make sense to me. First they say she could wake up any minute and then they act like it's long term and she can't be moved."

"That's weird. Did you ask why?"

"I didn't get to ask anything because I wasn't allowed in on that particular conversation."

"Vince." They both said at once.

"Hey Clarice, let him know that you guys can't leave any more messages on the number I gave you. Paige is…well, just don't do it, okay? I'll call you every day for an update."

"I gotta go. Here comes Vince." His sister paused. "Unless you want to talk to him?"

"Nope. Not up to that just now. See ya, Sis."

After he said goodbye to his sister, Jack stared at the yellow sticky notes with the messages Paige had written down. None of them seemed important. In fact, they were all just the same. All from Clarice or Vince and nothing from the ten places he had left resumes and filled out applications.

He needed to do something for his parents. Vince and Clarice were out there supporting Dad, while he was stuck here. He would go make sure the house was okay. Mandy, his mom's beloved beagle, was there, so his parents had probably hired a pet sitter, but it wouldn't hurt to check on things.

He didn't have a key. His own fault. "Here you go, sir. I don't think I'm ready for this yet," he had told his father as he handed the key back after a dumb lecture on responsibility. His father had looked surprised, then angry.

Jack hitched a ride to Wesley Avenue, his parents' house, the house he grew up in. Some parents moved when the kids left home, but not Mom and Dad. They had gotten rid of furniture—his bed to be specific, although to be fair also Vince's bed—a clear statement that no child of theirs was ever going to move back home. There had been times when he'd really needed a place to crash, to the point that he would have put up with his father's lectures and disappointment rather than sleep behind some building. Not that he ever let them know when he was homeless and car-less, a bad combination. There were still so many times he wished he had Mom's old minivan, but that was long gone. It would have been way easier to sleep in the van than the tiny Honda Civic or the Ford Pinto with no back window.

Vince and Clarice had the easy lives. They never had a shortage of money—when they needed more they could walk into the bank or financial aid office and walk out with a loan. And they both had someone taking care of details—Sandra did it all for Vince and Clarice had the simple life of paying tuition and going to classes, all prescribed for her. Why couldn't his parents see that it wasn't that easy for him?

He was short now. Way short. Laid off again. Never fired. Well, almost never. But he just couldn't catch a break.

He rang the doorbell and knocked, listening to Mandy's crazed barking for a minute before moving around to the back of the house. The dog bounced against the gate and her bark melted into a whimper of recognition.

"Hey girl." He stroked the beagle's soft nose. "You look pretty lonely. Who's taking care of you?"

Jack jiggled the laundry room window until the latch came free. He hadn't ever told his father about this easy access to the house because you never knew when you might need it. Like when your mother was in a coma.

"You've been busy," he said to the dog, stooping to pick up a yogurt container, tell-tale teeth holes punched throughout. Mandy wagged her tail, no guilt at all. If people left good things around and left her alone… what was a dog to do?

He wandered through the house, climbing the stairs and moving from room to room, like a cat burglar. It had been a long time since he had been home. He stood at the door to the room he had shared with Vince, every trace that he had ever spent time here removed. Memories of how he plugged into his music, laying on the floor with his feet up on the bed, filled his mind. Listening to Sworn Enemy and Psycroptic on his generic portable MP3 player, which had been a gift from Aunt Deborah. Every kid needed a childless aunt to provide those things parents deemed an unnecessary extravagance.

He looked around the room. It was now painted a pale green, with new mini-blinds to match. Neat wooden shelves that looked like stacked kindergarten cubbies lined one entire wall. Plastic containers filled with fabric, yarn, and other colorful items formed an abstract design. A sewing machine stood on one of those fancy tables that went from high to low with the flip of a ratchet.

On one of the shelves was his mom's old rotary cutter. He'd tried that fancy round blade tool once, knowing full well it was one of those items no one was to borrow. A pain-of-death-if-you-break-this tool. At first he had cut long strips of binder paper, then moved on to cutting the sleeves off his t-shirts, mesmerized by the smooth lines and the way the tool glided through things. He had been about to try it out on his poster of Deaf Birds, thinking it would be cool if it had curved edges instead of the rectangle shape, when he sliced his thumb.

Jack held up his hand and looked at the thin white scar he still carried as a souvenir of his sin. He turned off the light and shut the door. The memories wouldn't be happy no matter what color the walls were and it was good his mother had her own room now.

The refrigerator was full of food so maybe there was a live-in pet sitter. Jack would have to listen for a car because he didn't want to scare someone into a heart attack. He fixed a sandwich and gave Mandy a piece of bologna. Standing at the counter to eat, he thumbed through the stack of mail.

"Mom sure gets a ton of catalogues," he said to the dog. He took the stack out onto the back deck and settled into the chaise lounge. A full stomach, the sunshine, the dog curled up in his lap…it only took six minutes for him to fall asleep.

The ringing doorbell woke Jack. He opened his eyes, confused by the sound. Where was he? By the time he sat up and remembered he was at his parents' house, heavy footsteps were crunching the gravel beside the house. He turned to see who had arrived.

"Stay where you are, son."

The tan uniform said it all. Jack lifted his hands, palms forward. "It's cool, man. I live here."

"Can you show me some identification?"

"It's in my wallet. Which is in my back pocket." Jack knew the drill.

"Fine. Get it out." The officer studied the driver's license, then tapped it. "This is expired. And it doesn't have a Wesley address on it."

"Yeah. I know. I'm not driving though. I don't have a car. And this is my parents' house. I'm staying here for a bit. My mom, she's in a coma. In New Mexico." Damn. The story sounded fake.

"We had a call from the house-sitter. No mention of anyone staying here."

At least the cop knew he was telling the truth about New Mexico. "Right. I wasn't. But things changed when my mom went into the hospital." Bad choice. If the police called Dad he would deny that Jack lived here.

"Let's just make a phone call and clear this up." The officer turned away and said something into the microphone attached to his collar. Then he held up Jack's expired license and read the numbers into the mike as well.

Could they arrest you for sleeping in the back yard at your parents' house? He thought about the mess in the kitchen, pretty sure he had left signs of the meal he had fixed. But those could belong to this mystery house-sitter, right? He would plead he hadn't actually entered the house. The minutes felt like hours as the officer stood and stared from five feet away. Jack remained silent. He had learned long ago the less he said the better.

"Got it." The officer must have had a reply through the earpiece. He turned to Jack and handed him his license. "Sorry for the misunderstanding. You might want to talk to the house-sitter and let her know you're staying here. Your father said it was his fault. In all the confusion with your mother's coma he forgot to let her know."

"Uh. Thanks. No problem." Jack slipped his wallet back into his pocket. "Do you know who it is?"

"Neighbor girl? Mindy?"

"Mindy Stanton?"

"That's the one."

Yeah, Jack would talk to Mindy, all right. The little twerp who had spied on him for years. She must be about seventeen now. Old enough to recognize him and know that calling the cops wasn't cool.

Thank God his father had caught on. And been able to fib to the cops, something Jack had a very hard time picturing.

SIXTEEN

When lunch was finished To-be-né once again took Martha's hand.

"*Ah yi ee*, Thank you, thank you for the food." Martha tried to use hand motions and tone to communicate her appreciation to the women, before allowing To-be-né to lead her away.

She was a bit surprised when the girl led her up the canyon. She was tired and hoped To-be-né was taking her back to her own…what should she call it? Cave? Room? Space?

The trail grew steeper and the walls of the canyon drew closer. It was interesting to travel with a child, a somewhat different route than Kwe-in-ye's tour yesterday.

"Wait." Martha stopped and looked at her watch, although this wasn't really what she was thinking. Habit, as if knowing if it was 12:30 or 1:00 made a difference.

To-be-né smiled and nodded and waved up the canyon.

"Right. We will go, but…" Martha stopped. How long had she had been here? Two days, but it would be easy to lose track. She would have to come up with a system—scratches on the wall next to her bed or something, like a prisoner in a cell.

To-be-né ducked between low bushes, climbed over rocks, and walked through the dry stream bed. Martha was out of breath when the girl stopped and motioned for Martha to sit.

"Thanks. I really do need to rest. I'm not as young as you." Martha sat on a smooth boulder and looked around. They were at the base of a wall of rock which stretched up to the top of the canyon. She twisted to take a look and saw footholds along one edge. Her gaze followed the indentations to the top of a ledge midway up the wall. She couldn't see any farther than that, as the rock sloped out slightly, blocking the view of anything above.

"I'm glad you don't live up there." Martha shook her head slightly as she spoke to To-be-né.

To-be-né turned and scampered straight up the wall. The girl was like a spider monkey, thin arms and legs moving with ease, and within a few seconds she was on the ledge.

She leaned over and called down. "*Pa chan.*"

"Great job, quite a climb." Martha called back, standing and turning so that she could see the girl.

"*Pa tu chan.*" To-be-né waved her hand, motioning for Martha to climb up.

"Oh, no, that's not what I meant. Fine for you, not for me." Martha shook her head.

"*Pa tu chan, pa tu chan.*"

Martha walked away from the wall, towards the middle of the canyon, craning her head back to see what was above the girl. As she watched, To-be-né turned and climbed along the outcropping.

"Oh my." Martha was shocked to see another set of indentations stretching up the cliff and ending in a large cave, the arched roof over fifty feet across. Taking several more steps back, she could see buildings tucked into the back of the cave and a kiva close to the outer edge. When To-be-né reached the top she waved once more.

"*Pa tu chan.*" Her voice was faint, she was so high.

What was this place? So far up the canyon, away from all the other homes. And so high, tucked into the cliffs, not really visible from anywhere. Martha studied the landscape across the canyon from the cave. It might be visible from over there, although with the turn in the wall just before the cave it seemed fairly well hidden. She didn't see or hear any other people, only the repeated cry of To-be-né, calling her to climb.

Martha thought about being here, in this other place. There was no explanation that made any sense. Had she really traveled through time or was this the most crazy, real dream she had ever had? With so much time passing, maybe it wasn't a dream. Maybe it was a hallucination. She had read about schizophrenia and people hearing voices. She had often felt that there was something near her, something out there that one couldn't see or touch, that no scientist could measure. Was she in that world now? A different dimension? A loop in time?

Oh come on, Martha. Time travel?

She rubbed the rough wall with her palm. This was real. She knew it was real. The way things felt, the smells, the people, and nothing dreamlike—like the weird way people turned into other people or the unrealistic leaps from place to place—had happened since Kwe-in-ye led her away from the camper.

Martha looked at the wall, rising so high above her head. What would happen if she was hurt out here, in this other world? What if she died?

Kwe-in-ye's words came back to her. At the end of her long story she had turned to Martha, her eyes imploring. "You must learn the ways of the people. These are different from your ways. I think that you are meant to help us to see our ways with new hearts. Our eyes have become dim with time and we can no longer see the details."

The indentations which formed the pathway were overwhelming. How could hands and feet grip such a surface? Yet, if she were to help these people—an idea she had yet to grasp—climbing was something she must learn. Access to nearly all the rooms and caves was either by steep path or small handholds in the rocks. This wall was very high, but really no different than the six foot walls she had practiced on earlier.

The girl had obviously had a plan all along. To-be-né might just be a very good teacher.

Martha took a deep breath and put both hands on the rock. She shook her head and pulled her hands back, holding them out and watching them shake.

"I can't." She sounded just like Jack when she tried to help him with math homework.

"*Pa tu chan. Ta a no so.*" To-be-né wasn't giving up on her.

She shouldn't give up on herself. She kicked off her slippers and put her hands back on the indentations in the rock. She climbed slowly and without looking down or to either side, keeping her eyes on the rough stone and feeling for each tiny hole, testing every grip of finger and toe twice. After some time she wanted to know how much farther she had to go, but she didn't dare look away from the space right in front of her nose. Suddenly the wall disappeared, giving way to rock several feet away. She was at the ledge.

The rock shelf was narrow, no safety bars here. She sat with her back pressed against the wall and her legs shaking. There was still more to go.

Maybe this was enough of a lesson, a test, for today. It had been a busy morning and mid-afternoon had always been her slow time. She was in the habit of taking a quick nap—lying down with a cranky toddler in the early years and later resting before the kids came home from school. Sweaty, noisy, hungry, and demanding children. It went without saying that she needed a boost of energy for the evening. She had never quit the pattern of the afternoon nap.

She would rest here for a bit and then climb down.

"Mar-tee-ya." To-be-né was beside her. The girl put her hand on Martha's shoulder and her face inches from her nose. "*Ts oe nana. Yi po cono.*"

Martha pulled her face back from the anxious girl. "I'm fine. It's just…this is far enough." She shook her head once more, although she wasn't sure this was very effective for communicating with this child. She patted the ledge to indicate that this is where she would be staying.

The gesture was misinterpreted. To-be-né sat very close to Martha, right on the spot she had patted. The girl hung her feet over the edge, swinging them back and forth, then leaned forward to look down.

"Careful." Martha grabbed To-be-né's arm, the words out of her mouth before she could stop them. How ridiculous was it for her to warn the girl in this situation? A situation where Martha was clearly not the expert. Children did not fall off cliffs here.

"That's it!" She pictured the toddlers strapped to the cradleboards. When they were little they would fall off the cliffs and the confinement kept them safe.

To-be-né stood and smiled. She obviously interpreted Martha's exclamation as an indication she was ready to climb again.

Martha looked up. From here the second half didn't look so bad. Not as steep as the first part because they were past the spot where the wall sloped out a bit.

Was she an infant strapped to a cradleboard or was she a grown-up woman ready for an adventure? She pressed herself close to the wall and moved along the ledge. To-be-né stayed just ahead of her and she watched where the girl placed each foot and hand and tried to do the same. In this manner they climbed the second section and within minutes they were in the cave.

To-be-né hopped up and down in excitement, while Martha sank to the ground, finally taking a look around. When she saw how close she was to the edge of the cliff, the opening of the cave sloping down, she scooted back several feet, then turned her gaze away from the perilous pull to study the buildings.

The construction of the rooms was similar to the other areas she had visited, rocks shaped and held together with mortar. The difference was that there were no windows and no footholds to the roofs of the rooms. The doors were filled with tightly stacked flat stones, not mortared closed, but blocked as if temporary, with the possibility of being opened when needed. On the cave walls, drawings were carved into the rock. The petroglyphs were clear, not yet worn by time. Perched on the edge of the cliff, toward the very front of the cave, was a small kiva.

"What is this place?" she asked To-be-né, knowing the girl wouldn't understand her question. "Are we supposed to be here?" Suddenly Martha thought about the wisdom in following wherever a child led her. Children were full of pranks and constantly pushing limits. Maybe To-be-né was showing off for Martha's sake.

There was an opening through the top of the kiva and she peered down into the dark room. To-be-né pulled her away and shook her head.

"Don't worry, I'm not going in. I don't think we're supposed to be here. What have you gotten me into, you little scamp?"

"Pa tu chan." To-be-né obviously thought that Martha knew what this meant. It seemed like it meant "come on, follow me wherever I take you, we'll only stay a minute and then we'll rush on to the next crazy

thing." Sure enough, To-be-né scurried over to the edge and started her scramble down.

Martha hurried after the girl. She wanted to place her hands and feet exactly where To-be-né placed hers. But the system didn't work going down because to watch To-be-né meant pulling her head away from the wall and twisting. An impossible action.

Martha was half way down when her knees started to shake. She had made it up, so she knew she could make it down. The wind's voice was loud. She heard it announce its arrival just before the gust hit her from the left. Her fingers slipped and Martha smashed her body as close and flat against the wall as possible, shutting her eyes tight. A second gust followed the first, and Martha cried out.

"Oh-Christ-oh-christ-do-not-let-me-fall-make-the-damn-wind-stop." Martha made up her own prayer. She clung to the wall, not moving a muscle.

"*Pa tu chan. Je mu sa.*"

To-be-né sounded miles away and the wind filled Martha's ears filtering out the sound of the girl's voice. Another gust hit and she sobbed as her fingers grew numb and her head pounded with pain and panic.

I must do this, I have to get down somehow. Martha willed herself to do something, but her body wouldn't obey and she stayed in one spot. As another gust pushed her to the left, her fingers slipped and she thought about Glen and the kids. She felt the scrape of the rough stone beneath her palms and she tried to find another spot to hold on to, but she was falling and then the world went black.

"*Ka n'ya.*" A soft voice whispered in her ear and a warm hand lay on her forehead.

Martha opened her eyes. A man was beside her and he wasn't Glen or anyone else she knew, so either this was the same dream or a new dream or…

She stared into his brown eyes and her whole body shook uncontrollably.

"*Ka n' ya. San tha poné.*" He repeated. He stroked her head, smoothing the hair off her forehead.

Her tremors stopped. She turned her head and saw the rock wall next to her. When she rolled her head in the opposite direction there was only empty space and the tops of trees. They were on the ledge, she and this man. Her temple hurt under his palm. At least the pain was a sign that she wasn't dead.

The warmth of his touch penetrated the soreness. She stared at him. She couldn't blink, couldn't look away, couldn't even breathe. She could see the entire history of the earth in his eyes.

If I don't breathe I'll faint and that will be it. I'll find out if this is a dream or not.

His palm moved to her cheek, a soft touch with callused fingers tracing down from her eye to her chin.

"*Pa te pe. Je me mu sa.*" He moved his hand down the back of her neck and under her shoulder, slowly lifting her to sitting. She could see To-be-né on the canyon floor below them, her little face pale.

The man placed her hand in his, cupping the back of it with his palm. "*Je mu phen yopenute.*" He turned onto his hands and knees and motioned her to do the same.

"I can't." She shook her head.

"*Ka n'ya*" he said, with a smile. He placed a hand on her lower back and urged her to shift her weight, then he shimmied over the ledge and stood so that the upper half of his body was still above the edge and took hold of her foot, gently moving it down until she felt her toe firmly in a foothold.

Martha drew in a deep breath. She had to get off this ledge somehow. Better to do it with help.

She made her way down the wall with him behind her, speaking to her softly, his chest pressed to her back. He placed her hands into the firm holes and used the tops of his feet to guide hers down until her toes could slip into the next indent.

Her entire focus was on his touch. When she reached the bottom and felt the firm dirt, first underneath one foot, then the other, she turned and crumpled, stretching out so that her entire front, arms and legs akimbo, was in contact with the earth.

Waves of emotions washed over her, crashing down on her flattened body, pounding her into the ground. A wave of fear, a wave of frustration, a wave of relief, a wave of loneliness. She wanted to close her eyes and open them back in her life, with Glen by her side. This world was too different, too strange. These people expected too much of her. She sobbed.

The sobs continued until they slowed to uncontrollable gasps and hiccups. Her chest was tight and the after-crying feeling moved up into her throat. She felt a small warm tongue lick her cheek and she opened her eyes. The dog. Doing what dogs do best. Trying to make her feel better.

To-be-né and the man were there. Just standing, eyes on her, hands at their sides.

The girl saw that Martha had opened her eyes and she pointed to the man. Then she pointed to the dog. "*Sope pó o ko.*"

Martha shook her head, not able to focus on what To-be-né was trying to tell her.

The man knelt down next to her, looking once again at her face. Martha turned away. She didn't want to meet his eyes. She felt different when she looked into those eyes, something she hadn't felt in a long time, something that scared her and made her feel good all at once.

She might have been more terrified than ever before, but in spite of all that, in spite of having clung to the side of a huge expanse of rock believing she was about to die, in spite of the idea that this was only a dream—a nightmare now—and knowing there was no way she had traveled back in time, Martha felt real.

SEVENTEEN

Clarice sat across from Vince in the hospital cafeteria. After the blow up with Dad she needed to get away from that room for a while. But her brother had found her. There was no escape. She was going to tell him about her conversation with Jack, but he jumped right in with his own agenda.

"I think Dad has a point." Vince said. "We can fly back to Santa Fe when she's ready to be moved. Or sooner if we need to."

She did need to go back to her classes. Changing majors didn't leave her open to abandon Earth Studies and Chemistry because the drop deadline was long past and her GPA was at risk.

"Do you think Mom is going to die?" It was times like these that Clarice wished she had a friend she could call, but there wasn't really anyone right now.

Friends. That had been another thing she and her mother couldn't agree on. All those parties and campouts and even Sunday School.

"Don't you have a friend you can invite?" Her mother would get that look of pity on her face, as if she thought her daughter wasn't capable of having any friends. Why couldn't Mom understand that Clarice didn't want to share things with some lame girl? Girls who didn't like to play baseball or sink into a good book, or explore the dark space under the porch or be silent and listen to things? When she did invite someone over —just to please her mother—all they wanted to do was spy on her brothers. She could tell these girls exactly what her brothers were doing at any given moment and it really wasn't that exciting.

"No. I don't think she's going to die. But…" Her brother shook his head.

"I get it. No clarity. No facts. All the things you use to make decisions."

"Don't take your frustration with Dad out on me."

"Sorry. But it's true. We need more facts. I'm going to find Dr. Patis."

"I'm going to go back to see how Dad's doing. When you find the doctor, will you bring her to the room so we can all hear what she has to say?"

But when Clarice tracked the elusive doctor down, she grilled her right then. What had the tests really shown? What was she not telling them? Were there more tests?

"I wish I could give you clear answers. I know this is hard. Your mother's brain activity isn't suggestive of a coma." Dr. Patis said. "It's normal and so is her breathing, her swallowing, and her reflexes. We've ruled out a lot of things."

"If it's not physical, could it be psychological?" Clarice thought about all the times she had faked being sick so she didn't have to go to some dance or party. Was Mom faking a coma?

"I suppose it could be." Dr. Patis glanced at her watch. "Was your mother under some sort of psychological strain? Your father didn't mention any mental disease."

"She wasn't ever diagnosed, if that's what you mean. But she's always been…extremely…well…passive. She never asks for what she wants. It's like she's the perfect Barbie mother. She just bakes and makes lunches and does laundry and claims it's all she ever wanted. That could be depression, right?"

The doctor smiled. "I suppose. But it sounds like your mother is just a little more old-fashioned than you like."

"That's pretty pompous of you. I thought you were different, but apparently not." That stopped the conversation between her and the good doctor.

"I've got to go." With no further explanation Dr. Patis hurried away.

Clarice knew she should be more...subtle? Polite? But damn it, she wanted clear answers. And now she didn't dare ask the doctor to come back and talk to Vince and Dad.

"So I found Dr. Patis. She didn't have much time, but she said that Mom isn't really in a coma."

Her father and Vince both spoke at once.

"Is she going to come talk to us?"

"Why didn't she come talk to me?"

Clarice looked away from the two angry faces. "I'm sure she'll be in."

"So what did she say? If Mom's not in a coma, why is she"—Vince motioned to the bed—"like this?"

"She couldn't say. She just said all the tests are normal. Her brain activity is normal, her swallowing, her reflexes." Clarice paused. How much did she want to get into with her Dad? "She asked if Mom had a history of anything mental."

Her father's face went white. "Mental? She thinks this is some sort of psychological state?"

Vince scowled at Clarice and laid his hand on Dad's shoulder. "Hey, how about you and I go find the doctor? I think we need our questions answered."

Clarice was relieved when the two left. She pulled the chair close to the bed.

The room hummed with the rhythmic beeps of the machines connected to her mother. Clarice stared at the screen, watching the waves of heart function dip and dive. The hospital was suddenly quiet and she could hear a symphony of beeps through the open door. Machines just like these in every room. Hooked to someone's mother, father, sister, brother, child. She shuddered at the thought of a parent sitting next to a child in the state her mother was in.

The sounds of the machines reminded her of the very start of a rainstorm, when the drops are still individual, each one plinking down to the earth, bouncing off the metal gutters, different notes combining to create a simple melody.

Blood pressure, oxygen saturation, pulse, cardiac waves. All that was left of Mom was on that screen. If her mother never woke up Clarice would be lost. She had been waiting for the time when she and Mom could relate as adults. A time when her mother would really listen to what she had to say, really see who she was. Not the girl who wore the party dress, but the girl who walked in her own direction. And in that process—the process of appreciating who Clarice was—her mom would discover herself. Clarice would rescue her from mediocrity.

Vince and Dad had sat for hours talking to Mom, but Clarice hadn't really touched her mother or talked to her. She picked up Mom's hand.

It was covered with scrapes.

"What happened?"

She reached over and grabbed her mother's other hand. This palm was scraped as well.

Vince and Glen returned just as Clarice was pulling the blankets off her mother and inspecting the rest of her body.

"What are you doing?" Her father rushed to the bed and pulled her away.

"Dad, don't. Look, look at these scrapes and bruises." She held up her mother's hand.

"Those weren't there before," Vince said. "I would have noticed. Are they some sort of drug reaction?" He reached up and pressed the call button.

"Look at this!" Clarice pushed the hair away from her mother's forehead. "It's a bruise, a big one."

Three hours later, both Dr. Patis and Dr. Brown sat across from the three of them in a small conference room.

They had examined her mother and run more tests.

"So you're saying the bruise has nothing to do with her being unconscious?" Clarice wanted to scream. "That doesn't make any sense."

"The bruise is…" Dr. Brown glanced at Dr. Patis. "Superficial."

"Wouldn't it have to have been a really deep bruise to take so long to show up?" Vince leaned forward and tapped his finger on the table, then turned to Dad. "She must have fallen and not told you about it."

"Wait a minute," Clarice interrupted, although her father didn't look like he was going to say anything to the doctors. "You're saying it's new. This is a new bruise. What the hell is going on in this place? My mother fell out of that bed, didn't she?"

"Miss Grimson, I can assure you that did not happen." Dr. Brown shook his head.

"What other explanation is there? Tell me that?" Clarice stood. "We have to get her out of here, Dad. She isn't safe here. They can't figure out what's wrong with her and now they're making it worse by...by... tossing her around."

"Now hold on a minute," Dr. Patis held up her hand, as if she could deflect Clarice's anger with a palm.

But it was Vince who took hold of his sister's arm. "Think about it. When could it have happened? She was never alone. We were here all night."

"Maybe we both fell asleep." Clarice turned and stared out the window. Nice view for a hospital, the peaks rising in the distance. Vince was right. Even if they both dozed off they wouldn't have slept through something as dramatic as staff dropping their mother on the floor.

"She spoke to me."

Everyone turned to stare at her father.

"Yesterday, just for a moment. She opened her eyes and asked me if this was a dream."

"Why didn't you tell us?" Clarice felt the anger that was already about to explode inside her leap and thrash in confusion.

Dad shrugged. "It was so fast, I thought...I thought I must have imagined it."

Could Mom have woken up and tried to get out of bed? Crept softly to the bathroom so as not to awaken them and fallen?

Not with all those tubes and machines connected to her.

Clarice's mind raced, searching for an explanation, refusing to settle on the one thought, the single idea that Dr. Patis had stated. That there was no explanation.

Eighteen

Every day there was a new job. Kwe-in-ye truly was making sure Martha learned the ways of the people. What might have seemed the simplest task wasn't simple at all. Martha learned to pull the dried corn from the cobs, store the cobs to feed the fires, grind the corn and prepare meals. She picked the corn and pulled weeds in the fields up on the mesa. She learned to treasure each drop of water, dribbling tiny amounts around the roots of each plant. Every element of life in the canyon involved many steps. At first Martha had been assigned to rather menial tasks like sweeping out her little room and shaking the woven mats, but now that she had been here longer the old woman was increasing the expectations.

Kwe-in-ye handed Martha a bowl. "Today you collect."

"Collect?"

The woman nodded. "Each member of the tribe must work to keep the food stores filled. I will show you what to look for. Come."

As Martha followed Kwe-in-ye up the trail she looked around for the dog. It would be nice to have a companion today, but she didn't see the animal.

At least they were headed into the trees. Martha's mouth was already dry and the day had barely started.

"You will look for these berries. But you must not pick the green ones, only the soft, blue ones. Hold each one in your fingers before you pull it free." The old woman pinched a berry and left it. "Too hard."

Kwe-in-ye pulled several berries from the branch and placed them in Martha's hand. "These are just right."

Martha reached up to the plant and quickly drew back her hand as the sharp juniper branches scratched her skin. "Ouch!"

"*Gagawan dagisid* does not give up her fruit easily."

Martha tried again, weaving her hand between the branches to the nest of berries and pinching each one. This was a slow process.

Kwe-in-ye watched her for several minutes, then nodded and left her to her task.

With a sigh, Martha looked around the forest. It was nice to be out here alone today. She had been in this place for almost two weeks according to her crosshatch scratches on the wall, though she often forgot to make a mark. She was always exhausted after the lessons and the tours and the work. She wasn't any closer to understanding the expectation that she was here to save these people. She didn't even know exactly what she was saving them from. The drought? The Man-With-Three-Spirits? Other than a rain dance or cloud seeding, she really didn't know anything about manipulating the weather. She sighed and looked up the trail. Today she would just relax and enjoy her berry picking.

She studied the red and yellow sand beneath her feet, the boulders that looked like a giant had rubbed the earth with his toe to stir things up a bit, and the honeycomb cliffs just visible beyond the trees. It was silent in the forest. She was far enough up the trail to be out of range of the sounds of the village. Up here everything seemed lazy. No squirrels flicked angry tails, no birds sang, and the shrinking pools of water in the creek did not gurgle as it wound its way under the stones, with just a hint of moisture visible here and there. Bugs buzzed and Martha swatted away the tiny mosquitos drawn to the back of her neck. She was covered with bites and itched like mad. Kwe-in-ye had given her a salve to rub into her skin, but it seemed a healing thing, not a repellent.

Her hands were soon covered with long scratches. She thought about the garden gloves Clarice had bought her for Mother's Day. A feminine floral print and delicate enough so that she could use her fingers, unlike Glen's thick work gloves which she usually used. Those new gloves would be wonderful for harvesting these berries. She wet the tip of her finger on her tongue and rubbed at the scratches on her hands. She had never seen anyone wearing gloves. What if she made some? They could be the kind with finger tips free, just a protectant layer for her hands and arms.

She had watched the women sew. Kwe-in-ye's sister, Yo-en-u, was in charge of the group who made clothes. They used bone needles and Martha was impressed with the beading and stitching. They made skirts and tunics and shawls. The women didn't make the sandals or the woven mats, though. There was an old man and a young one—likely an apprentice—who made three kinds of footwear. High leather moccasins that some of the men wore, sandals from yucca plants that nearly everyone else wore, and a kind of cross between the two she had only seen in the storerooms, never on anyone's feet.

"If I had some needles I could make gloves." Martha laughed. Here she was enjoying her day alone and already talking to herself. "Thread, too." Make that her whole sewing kit, complete with thimble and seam ripper. That would be better than just having the gloves…she would impress them with her ability to make all kinds of things.

Martha looked into her bowl. Only a thin layer of berries after so much time. She knew that Kwe-in-ye expected her to stay out here until the bowl was full and she was already tired and hungry and thirsty. A water bottle was another thing that would come in handy.

"I'm a weakling. I have to stop wishing for everything." Martha sighed. She didn't fit into this world.

Now that she thought about it, wasn't that what dreams were for? Dream Analysis 101 came to mind. She had read enough magazine articles to know a little about it. She ticked off the list of her weaknesses: she was a cold mother, a distant wife, afraid to climb ladders, and unwilling to take chances. This dream-or-not-dream had hit them all.

But she was a good cook. And she had a kind heart. Maybe the way she would save the people would be to use her strengths. Maybe this dream was meant to make her see them.

Or maybe she had to use her fears. Face up to them. Overcome them. Be strong.

Facing her fears hadn't turned out well at all. That disaster with To-be-né and the wall had set her back. She wouldn't be pushed by these people. It was dangerous. No, if she were to learn things it would be at her own pace. She would do what Clarice always advised: say no.

Martha wiped the sweat from her forehead with the back of her hand. Her fingers were sticky from the berries and because there was absolutely no other way to clean them, she licked the juice. It was that or rub it all through her hair and over her clothes and spread the blue dye everywhere else she happened to touch.

The juice tasted bitter and a bit like pine-scented cleaning solution. Not that she had ever tasted pine cleaner, but the smell was enough to leave a taste in her mouth. Maybe it was better if you ate the whole fruit. She popped a soft berry into her mouth and chewed. She wouldn't go out of her way to eat these, but they were better than the dry feeling the daily few drops of water left in her mouth. She walked up the trail, passing many bushes with the tiny blue berries too high on the branches. She would look for those within her reach and maybe her skin would survive her task.

Martha saw a loaded branch just above a flat boulder. She could stand there and pick enough to fill her bowl. She set the bowl up on the rock but decided she would empty her bladder before she made the climb. She walked to the other side of the trail. No reason to attract more bugs with her urine right in the spot she was going to work.

Martha had become an expert at squatting just so and allowing just enough time for things to drip-dry, which was shorter than usual because she didn't want any mosquito bites in that area of her anatomy. Just as she stood to adjust her clothing, a loud sound came from up the canyon. Something was running toward her. Tree branches and rocks cracked and clattered. Martha jumped off the trail and huddled by the boulder.

It was a deer. A young buck, she guessed, from the small size of his antlers. He saw her and stopped his flight, then took a staggering step toward her. She pressed herself back against the rock.

"Go away, get away. Yah, yah." She yelled at him, but he kept coming.

Martha scrambled up onto the boulder just as the deer fell to the ground.

A long stick hung from his neck. Blood ran from the wound.

"Oh no. You've been hurt." Not a stick—a spear, imbedded in the animal.

His breath was coming in loud gasps and he moved his front legs in rapid circles, sharp hooves sending rocks and dirt flying as he tried to stand. The buck's efforts were futile and it seemed he realized this, suddenly going still, with only his black eyes flickering as he watched her.

The animal opened his mouth and let out a high-pitched bleat. Martha's hand went to her chest as the sound sent a chill straight into her teeth, leaving her with that fingernails-on-chalkboard-feeling.

"I'm sorry, I'm so sorry, I wish…there's nothing…oh God." She covered her mouth with her palm, trying to hold in the despair that bubbled in her throat.

The deer's breath was coming in ragged gasps. His head turned and his ears flicked. Martha heard the sound of something else coming through the forest. She pushed her way behind the branches that hung over the stone, pressing her body down onto the smooth rock to escape being visible to whatever was making its way towards her.

It was a man dressed in leather leggings carrying a knife. Martha recognized him at once. It was the man who had rescued her from the wall. She began moving forward to call to him when he knelt by the deer.

"Ne satin nou wa ki ka wa ush. With a sudden movement he grabbed the buck's antler and twisted its head back. The knife flashed and penetrated the animal's neck. But this was no smooth slash; it caught and the man dug in deeper, grunting as he sawed through the flesh and finally hit what he was looking for.

The animal fell limp. Acid burned in the back of Martha's throat. She didn't move a muscle, not wanting this brutal man to see her. She watched him through the branches, the thick clusters of berries no longer important. There was a dog at his side. She pulled her chin up slightly, careful not to make a sound.

It was her dog, standing alert with ears pointed forward and tail held high. But she noticed something far worse. The man wore a cradleboard and there was a baby strapped to his back.

"Mu u yaw yiyi tonu piya." He pulled something from his pocket and laid it on the dead animal's chest. The man looked to the animal and then to the sky. Then he cupped his hand under the severed throat and filled it with the blood that flowed from the open wound. He raised his hand to his mouth and Martha gagged as he drank the blood.

He turned his head and stared straight at her.

Lunging to one side, she slid off the rock and ran, no longer trying to be silent, her only goal to put distance between herself and the gruesome scene.

She ran down the path, twisting and turning, unaware of the branches slapping her face, or the stones bruising her feet. All she could see was the life leaving the young buck's eyes and the blood on the man's lips.

Her chest was hot and her heart pounded louder than a crack of thunder. As she ran she could feel the shaking move down her legs and her hands grasped at the air as if she could catch onto something that would take her far away from this ghastly place. She was no longer on the path she had come up, and thick brush and boulders loomed in front of her. She ran anyway, her ankles banging against roots and stones, the sleeves of her nightgown catching and tearing on the sharp fingers of the branches. A fallen tree blocked her way and she threw her body on top of it and scrambled over, but her foot caught on a branch. As she lost her grip hot bile filled her throat. She turned her head and vomited. Her stomach contracted and her bowels spasmed.

She crouched next to the trunk of the fallen tree. She was covered from end to end in the filth of her body trying to expel the expression of the scared creature in its dying moment.

"Take me back, please take me back. I can't do this," she begged whatever force had brought her here. She wrapped her arms over her head and curled into a fetal position. She couldn't imagine any way out of this nightmare.

"Mar-tee-a." The voice was accompanied by a soft hand on her head which could only mean she was still alive and still in this terrible place.

"No, no." The words slipped from her lips in a desperate whisper. "I can't be here."

She felt something cool and wet wipe her forehead and she opened her eyes.

Kwe-in-ye knelt next to her. "You be still. I will take care of you."

Martha would be still because she couldn't imagine moving.

The old woman cleaned her. She turned Martha this way and that, slipping the soiled clothing from her and wiping her with a soft cloth. Martha was limp, allowing her body to be manipulated while she kept her eyes closed.

"Se weta ba tumate."

Martha heard the scampering of feet. Someone else was here, watching this terrible scene, her failure to control her bodily functions, her nakedness, her weakness. She didn't care. She hated it here so what did it matter?

"Mar-tee-a, what has happened?" Kwe-in-ye gathered Martha in her arms. "You are not hurt."

Martha stayed still, warm and supported by this woman who had been so harsh at times. She cautiously licked her lips and spoke. "No. Yes, I guess I am, but inside. The man...that man...he killed the deer. He's a monster, a vampire. He was drinking the blood. Oh my God." Martha choked and pulled away from Kwe-in-ye's grasp. She tried to stand, but there wasn't time. She turned her head and vomited again.

"What man?"

"The one who—" she wasn't going to say saved her. He was not a hero. "The man who helped me down from the cave."

"Sen-tshe." Kwe-in-ye reached out and took Martha's hand. She reached inside her vest and pulled out a bladder of water. "Drink, Mar-tee-a."

Martha took a sip and rinsed the water around in her mouth. It was tepid and tasted like it was straight out of the stagnant pond, but even so, it was better than the bitter remnants of vomit.

"Oh Kwe-in-ye. Why is he so brutal?"

"Hmm...I do not think Sen-tshe is brutal. He is a kind soul."

"Not only that, he had a baby on his back. In a cradleboard. The baby was watching it all." Martha gasped. "I think he was going to give the baby blood to drink."

"Mar-tee-a. I think you should lie down. To-be-né will be here soon with clothes for you and we will go to the cave."

"No! Kwe-in-ye. You have to tell me the truth. What's going on? Why won't you tell me everything?"

"Very well, but please, listen in here." Kwe-in-ye pressed her palm to Martha's chest. "Sen-tshe is a hunter. The hunt is important to the survival of the people. Did he not say a blessing as he drank the blood?"

Martha didn't want to relive the details of what had happened. "Yes. I think he was talking. I couldn't understand what he was saying, but it wasn't like he was talking to me. I...I was hiding." If he was such a great hunter surely he'd known she was there.

"Mar-tee-a, it is not brutal to drink the blood in a time of drought. It brings the hunter the strength of the animal who has been given to us. We must eat the animal to survive. You do not have a problem with that."

Martha's stomach burned and she felt the hot acid swell up her throat once more. She had eaten the jerky, but now that she had watched the fear in the buck's eyes, she wouldn't eat it anymore. Instantaneous vegan. It was true, what she had heard. If you had to see what those cows and pigs went through, you would never eat them.

"He could have warned me, motioned me away. Kwe-in-ye, he wanted me to see this, didn't he?" Martha felt a bit of guilt as she spoke. If he had seen her, maybe he wanted her to watch, but she couldn't say for certain if he had been aware of her.

"Sen-tshe is not a teacher. He is a hunter."

"He didn't have to be so brutal. He could have done it some other way." As she spit the words toward Kwe-in-ye, like throwing rocks to relieve her anger, Martha knew this wasn't true. How could there be a nice way to kill something?

Kwe-in-ye looked troubled. "Mar-tee-a, this is the way we do things. You must not judge. You must learn and understand."

"I don't understand. I don't want to understand. I don't want to be here. Can't you see that? I want to go back. I'm just some woman. I'm not a savior, I'm not strong. You were wrong to bring me here. Take me back!"

Kwe-in-ye reached for her, but Martha pulled away.

It hurt to pull away from the arms that had comforted her, but the words that would come from Kwe-in-ye's mouth would be placating, half-truths, and she really didn't want to listen.

NINETEEN

For two weeks Glen fought off guilt. He racked his brain to come up with some psychological reason Martha was unconscious. There was nothing about their life that could have led to this dire consequence—his wife retreating into a coma that wasn't a coma. He decided that once they were back home, surrounded by their nice furniture, manicured yard and friendly neighborhood everything would be fine.

All that was wishful thinking of the worst kind. There was no denying Martha was bad off. There just had to be a physical reason she was still not awake. All those tests with their pictures and numbers and the doctors still didn't seem to know anything. Nothing they did told the full story. What about that bruise?

Then the decision was taken out of his hands. After two weeks with no changes the hospital wasn't going to keep her. She needed to be transferred to a long-term care facility.

"I've arranged for an ambulance. Air travel isn't recommended." Glen had called Vince first, secretly hoping that he could escape the ordeal of talking to Clarice by getting his son to call her.

"I'll fly out, Dad. I can drive the truck home for you."

The ambulance would have multiple drivers so that they could travel straight from New Mexico to California without an overnight stop. It would be good to have two drivers for the truck, but Glen just couldn't let himself ask Vince to give up more time. "I appreciate your offer, son, but I'm not allowed in the ambulance. I'll follow behind in the truck. It's all set. We'll be home in less than two days." It was a long drive, but he would buy an extra thermos. With the one he already had there would be enough coffee to keep him going. "You'll let Jack and Clarice know?"

Martha started vomiting in Needles. The ambulance pulled over. He thought the driver and med tech were going to grab a hamburger. But when he approached, they were cleaning up his wife and calling the doctor. They gave her an injection and then were back on the road.

She had diarrhea in the middle of the Mojave desert. Glen paced around outside the ambulance, pulled off at a rest stop, while the technician cleaned up and wrapped Martha in a padded diaper. They let him hold her hand and kiss her before they set off again.

When they finally arrived at the hospital in Lindenville, the staff whisked her off and connected her to all their bells and whistles once more.

Glen called Clarice. "Hey, Sweetie. Mom's fine, we're here at Magnolia General. She had a rough trip. They want to watch her overnight, but tomorrow she's got to go to the convalescent hospital." The California doctor's opinion wasn't much different from the New Mexico crew.

"I'll be right over. Is Vince there?"

"No. He went home. I—" Glen stopped. "I was hoping you could call Jack for me. I think he's staying at the house."

"At your house?"

"Yes. You can try him there."

Clarice arrived with Jack in tow. His daughter rushed to Martha's bedside. "She doesn't look good. Did you ask them for tests? Maybe a second opinion?"

"They did some tests. It really was just some vomiting and diarrhea."

"Still?"

His daughter turned and looked at the door.

"No, Clarice. You don't need to find the doctor. There isn't anything else. I promise." Glen looked away and then turned back. "In fact, I think you should go home, get some rest. I'll need your help tomorrow." This wasn't especially true, but he needed to escape his daughter's accusing stare.

"Rest? You're the one that needs rest. One of us should stay here with Mom while you go home." Clarice looked at Jack. "You up for the first shift? I'll come back in a few hours."

"Sure. No problem. It's my turn, isn't it?" Jack saluted and Clarice frowned.

"Thanks. I'll just stay a bit longer." Glen waved his daughter toward the door. "I promise. I'll get some rest."

He managed to wait until Clarice left before he gave in to the sobs that had been caught in his chest. He had sent Jack to get coffee, but somehow his son was back already.

"Dad...I...are you..." Jack touched his arm.

Glen covered his face with his hands. "I did this to her. I didn't listen, I didn't use common sense and now...she's so sick now. Oh son, I'm sorry. I'm so sorry."

"Dad...you didn't do anything to Mom. They—those doctors—they said they don't know what caused this, right?" Jack hesitated. "I mean, I don't think you did. Or is there something you're not telling us?"

There was so much he wasn't telling them. But how do you explain to your grown children the relationship issues between their parents?

"I thought things were good between us, I really did. But she must not have. She must have been holding everything in and now she couldn't hold it in anymore so she ran away."

"That's crazy. Mom loves you. She's happy, she says it all the time."

After all the times he had scolded or rejected Jack, the boy—the man, now—didn't hold any of that against him. Or was this just his son trying to pretend that nothing was wrong?

Glen had a theory about his two boys. Vince was so perfect. As a baby he seldom left Martha's arms, where he would smile with contentment, fussing if she left him alone too long. Not that she'd ever left him alone. As a toddler Vince would play quietly next to Martha, no matter what she was doing; washing dishes, reading, watching television, or sewing. They both thought that all children were like this and marveled at how easy parenting was.

That perspective changed when Clarice came along two years later. She craved excitement. Glen would swing her up onto his shoulders, swooping her around as if she were flying, and she laughed with joy when he roughhoused with her. Martha had a hard time dealing with this kind of play, always worried that the baby would get hurt. Clarice was off on her own adventures as soon as she could crawl away. Martha had to set up a series of gates around the house to keep the baby where she put her, but even those couldn't stop the inquisitive child who could soon climb over the barricades.

Martha had her hands full with these two little ones, but with Vince just about to turn four and Clarice a busy two year old, Jack had unexpectedly made his appearance. Glen was thrilled. He loved his children and was never bothered by the noise or the mess. Having another infant to hold on his broad chest as he watched the evening news or the weekend football game was a feeling for which there were no words. Warm and eternal.

Martha had dealt with the new baby in her usual way, keeping busy with the household chores and never asking for help. Glen was surprised when Martha's younger sister Deborah had called him.

"She's not doing well with the baby. Have you thought about getting her some help?"

"Not doing well?"

"Whenever I call she's nearly hysterical, and yesterday she had to hang up quickly. I swear she was crying."

Glen had asked Martha how things were going. Her reply of "fine, fine, just fine" was typical, and he wanted to believe her. But Deborah had called again, persistent, so he had tried to take more of a role in helping with the children. As soon as he got home from work he would take them out to the park or for a walk, pushing Jack in the stroller while Vince walked slowly, finding bugs and rocks, and Clarice skipped circles around them all, singing loudly or chattering. On weekends he encouraged Martha to do things as a family, taking the kids to the zoo or the lake, with both of them along to manage the children. He had fixed up the yard, building a sturdy Clarice-proof fence, a playhouse, and a jungle gym with bars, swings, and slides.

He started to notice things. Martha would hold Vince in her lap, sitting at the kitchen table with him and patiently helping him learn to write his name. She brushed Clarice's hair into shiny braids, painted her toenails pink, and gave her blankets and pillows to build forts under the coffee table.

She was different with Jack. Most days she strapped him into his bouncy chair and set him at the edge of the action, or put him on a blanket in the middle of the living room, leaving him there while Vince and Clarice moved on into the kitchen. Jack grew into a silent, watchful baby. He didn't cry when he was left alone, just sucked on his tiny thumb and kept his green eyes open wide. Glen tried to hold Jack, but his son wiggled and pushed away. This baby was different from the other two. He looked different, with dark hair and almond eyes, a throw back to his Italian great-grandfather. Jack seemed content to be left alone, so that's generally what happened.

As the boys grew, Glen would catch Jack watching Vince, trying to do whatever Vince was doing at the time, but quietly, off on his own. He remembered Martha's surprise when Jack could ride a two-wheel bike. She marveled that he had been able to teach himself this skill. Glen wasn't surprised at all. He knew that Jack had spent hours alone, working on this feat before he was ready to show anyone.

Jack started high school just after Vince had graduated with honors, known and loved by all the teachers. At the same time Clarice was taking the school by storm, the star distance runner, diving champ, and pitcher, all while keeping up perfect grades. The teachers expected Jack to follow in his siblings' footsteps, but Jack had not. By the end of his freshman year Jack was smoking pot and drinking, although Glen and Martha didn't realize this until the following year. Three years later Martha and Glen had refinanced the house to send Jack to an intensive rehab facility.

And now his boys were men. Jack had fallen into a subservient role, pretending to go along with whatever Vince demanded. When Vince was angry Jack would apologize, over and over, without any intention of actually doing what his brother was asking. Vince often claimed—after yet another bad situation—that his younger brother was dumb, and had brain damage from all the drugs he had used. And yet, he gave Jack chance after chance, increasing the opportunity for his brother to snicker behind his back.

But Jack had completed the rehab program. He seemed to be keeping away from alcohol, keeping his life at a marginal steady sail. Glen suspected that his son still smoked pot. He had seen the pleased smile on Jack's face at certain times. To compound the problem, people liked Jack better when he was stoned. Even Glen himself liked the calm, funny man, rather than the sullen, withdrawn fellow. He hoped that his vision of his youngest son was clear enough that he wasn't being manipulated.

He looked over at his son, still recovering from witnessing his father's breakdown. No, Jack wasn't being insincere when he tried to help by insisting Martha loved him. Not this time. Not with his mother so ill. Glen dried the tears from his face and turned to his son.

He waved a hand toward Martha. "I'm not sure she was so happy. Deborah warned me."

"Aunt Deborah warned you?"

"Yes, it was just after you were born." Glen quickly added, "It wasn't you, but that's when it happened. When your aunt told me, I mean."

"I'm not surprised. You don't have to sugar coat it. But that was a really long time ago."

"I know. I tried to help her out. But lately, I've just been thinking about myself. That damn camper, that trip. I lost track of your mother over the years."

"I don't think that's what's going on with Mom. You'll see. They'll figure it out soon, or maybe she'll just wake up and we'll never know. But I know she's going to be fine."

"Son, I appreciate it. I really do. A positive attitude is a good thing. But I'm not so sure it'll happen if I just sit around and wait. I need to figure it out, do something to help her."

Jack looked out the window, drew in a breath and turned back to him. "Can I stay at the house for a while longer?"

"Oh, I don't need care-taking. I'll be all right."

His son shook his head. "The thing is, I'm between jobs. I've been looking around for something, but you know, there isn't much out there. It wouldn't be long."

He knew his son was lying. Clarice and Vince had explained weeks ago that Jack didn't have a phone, a job or a place to live. After that call from the police Glen meant to talk to his son, but there was just too much going on and he put it off. Better to let Jack squat at their house until they could work things out in person.

Glen took a seat in the chair opposite Jack. He glanced at Martha lying there in the hospital bed. She never had a hard time saying no to Jack, all those times he had come asking for help. But things had changed now, changed drastically.

Glen didn't need the help. He was a good cook, could push a vacuum around, and had handled the finances for the past thirty years. Mandy occasionally dug a hole under the fence, but nailing some boards and wire up didn't take much time or effort. Martha had done that in the past, but he could rebuild it and perhaps make something less patched-together.

He sat and considered his relationship with Jack. It was tarnished by the pulling back Jack had exhibited since infancy and the underlying rejection it signaled.

What if he could build a new relationship with Jack? As a man, not a detached infant or a sullen teenager. Maybe Jack was ready to accept his love, if he could give it to him in an unencumbered way.

"Jack, that would be great. I really need the help. I didn't ask before because it seemed…"

"Thanks Dad." Jack didn't wait for his father to complete the thought.

TWENTY

Martha shivered and pulled the thick skin tight around her neck, tucking her feet up closer to her body and wondering why no one had come to check on her. She expected Kwe-in-ye to come in and lecture her about her reaction to the murder of the deer. She would be told—once again—how important her role was here, that she had a purpose she must keep in mind, that hunting was natural, yada, yada, yada.

No one had come. Apparently one more thing about the ways of the ancient people was that they let you deal with your own issues in your own way. Still smarting from the whole event, she realized that sulking inside was only going to leave her hungry and depressed.

"Where is To-be-né?" Martha asked Kwe-in-ye as she emerged from her cocoon and looked around. She didn't see the girl anywhere. The dog was also missing but Martha realized now what To-be-né had meant the other day, with her pointing and her motions. Obviously the dog belonged to that man, no matter what Kwe-in-ye claimed about dogs having no owners. Martha would have to forget about her idea of making the animal her companion.

Something else was missing. "Where are my clothes?"

Kwe-in-ye never flinched as she answered Martha's first question while ignoring the second. "The girl is ashamed. She did not come out today. She is responsible for making sure these things do not happen."

"What do you mean, she is responsible? She's a child."

Kwe-in-ye shrugged.

Had they really given the little girl so much responsibility? Martha's well-being hanging heavy on To-be-né's shoulders? That wasn't right. "I need to go find her."

Kwe-in-ye grabbed her arm. "She will return in time. Let her sit through her trouble. It is good to think for a while when things have not turned out as one has planned."

Advice directed at her, no doubt. The old woman could pretend she wasn't mad at Martha, but it was obvious. And she had stolen the coveted slippers, as well as her clothes. Admittedly the soft shift was comfortable, but Martha wanted her things.

Thinking she would find the girl later, Martha followed Kwe-in-ye across the canyon and took her place beside the children.

Today's lesson was different. Kwe-in-ye had a long turkey feather, brown with golden tips. From the shaft of the feather hung leather cords, with knots tied and beads decorating the tassels. As she spoke to the children she also translated for Martha.

The lesson was about taking responsibility for one's actions. It was a moral lesson, stressing thoughtfulness rather than impulsivity. The lesson was also about being timid or being willing to take a risk. Martha knew that this lesson was pointed in her direction, like all the others. But somewhat stronger, following yesterday's catastrophe.

"*Ja pa, ja pa, Damé.*" The children jumped up and ran to greet Damé, the storyteller, and the flute player, Mosinobu. They stroked the old man's heavy cloak, made from the skin of an animal with the fur still intact, possibly a coyote or wolf. He ran his wrinkled hands over the tops of heads and smiled at them, greeting each one by name. Looking at his twisted knuckles and noting the likelihood of arthritis, Martha wondered how old he was. She had tried to ask Kwe-in-ye, but it seemed that the people used numbers and counting in a different way. They counted small amounts, such as needing three bowls of water for a cooking project, or the amount of roots to cut to feed those present. But there were other terms for the passage of time, a measure Martha didn't understand. Age was not tracked in years either, but more the passing of milestones. Kwe-in-ye had stated that she was born in the year of the rains and the raven and that Damé was born long before that.

The old man was stooped, unable to straighten his back fully, and usually walked with someone else supporting him. Martha had never seen him rise without the help of a strong person pulling carefully on his shoulders. He had black nubs of teeth, and he was always fed the thin gruel made of corn and squash. He could be sixty? Seventy? The lives of the people were so labor intensive, working to tend crops, cook, sew, hunt, harvest, and more. There was no dental care, and they didn't seem to do much to clean their teeth, other than poke at them with little sticks or sharp bones. She remembered something she had learned in the museum, when she and Glen had visited the ruins. The grinding of the corn on the stone metate produced a fine grit which was in their foods. The ingestion of this powdered rock was thought to have worn out their teeth.

Martha ran her tongue over her front teeth. She had been using her finger and little branches to try to keep her teeth clean and swishing her allotment of drinking water around before swallowing. How long before her teeth were as bad as Damé's? The thought of a toothache sent a shiver down her spine.

The children settled back down on the ground around the stone where Damé took a seat. Kwe-in-ye moved over to sit next to Martha.

"Damé will teach the children today. I will translate his words for you."

Although she couldn't understand his words, Martha was mesmerized by the story telling. Damé spoke in a soft low voice and the children were very quiet so as to hear him. His hands moved slowly through the air, with gestures for distance, surprise, impatience, all recognizable to Martha.

"Once the people did not live here. Only the star people were alive." Kwe-in-ye's soft whisper translated Damé's words.

"It was very dark, for the star people are bright and don't need lightness to see."

Damé covered his eyes with his hand. The children also covered their eyes.

"But one day, one of the stars stumbled down a steep slope and fell into the center of the earth."

Martha had the sense a lot was lost in translation. So much drama in the old man's telling, with the children gasping and laughing as his words wove around them.

"Now the people who were living below saw the light from the star man who had fallen into their world. They looked around at each other, other people they had lived with for so long but never really seen. Their eyes were opened now." Kwe-in-ye paused. "They could see the real world and not the world that was inside their heads and at the tips of their fingers."

Martha had the feeling Damé's visit was also for her benefit. But was she the star person or the one who had been living in darkness?

"Now the people could see the jackrabbits, the black tails of the deer and, when they looked up, they could see Páh-hee-oh in the sky."

Martha turned toward Kwe-in-ye. "What is Páh-hee-oh?"

"The moon spirit."

Damé leaned forward, his words a soft whisper that drew the children near.

"It is good to live with open eyes." Kwe-in-ye translated.

When the old man had finished his story the children walked with him to the gardens. Martha took advantage of the break to set out toward the big house to find To-be-né. She was proud of the girl for taking on the chore of teaching an old dog like her to do new things. If the child's assignment was to keep track of Martha, then she needed to let her know she was doing a good job. Although Martha had made up her mind she wouldn't be talked into moving faster than she wanted, she liked the fact that To-be-né was patient and didn't laugh at her efforts. Not too much, anyway. And that was laughter of encouragement, not shame. Martha knew she could grow from the relationship with this spunky child. So what if one of the lessons hadn't ended well?

Martha thought about the girl, alive in a world so long before her own life, and then Martha thought about her own daughter. There was something about To-be-né that reminded her of Clarice. Her daughter had been a spunky child as well, but things never worked out well between the two of them. When she tried to be involved in whatever Clarice was up to, her daughter was often frustrated or angry with her. "No, don't say that, say this." she would instruct. "Don't do it that way, do it this way." If only she had kept at it with Clarice, instead of making excuses to stay away.

Martha shook her head. Things had worked out, Clarice was extremely confident and accomplished. She was a leader in most everything she took on. Martha's heart grew tight in her chest and her breath caught in her throat. She missed her daughter.

"*Ja pa.*"

Martha stopped. It was that man, Sen-tshe. He stood in front of the kiva, a long, thick staff held in one hand. The staff was decorated with paint and feathers. The dog—his dog—stood at his side.

The man pointed at her. "Mar-tee-a." He pointed to himself. "Sen-tshe."

She should leave. Walk away from him right now. His eyes crinkled in a smile. He really had no idea what he had done to her. She bent and patted the dog.

The man laughed and she looked up.

"*Po-ko.*"

Martha shook her head and shrugged.

Sen-tshe tapped his chest. "Sen-tshe." He pointed to the dog. "Po-ko."

The dog had a name.

"She's a nice dog. You're lucky." She knew he didn't understand her but she couldn't keep from staring at him. She had always avoided the intensity of looking directly into someone's eyes. The emotion was too strong. It made her uncomfortable, as if she were lacking in some way, but with him she couldn't tear herself away.

A small gurgle came from his shoulder. She looked away from Sen-tshe's eyes to the bundle on his back. A tiny face peered out.

"Oh!" Martha gasped in shock. She expected this baby to look like its father or to look like the other children but it didn't. Yes, there was the same shock of dark hair, smooth skin, and round cheeks, but it was the eyes. Martha felt she was staring straight in to the face of her own baby. This child had Jack's green, almond-shaped eyes. The eyes Glen always claimed were Italian or some such thing.

Sen-tshe gestured to the baby. "*Wi-yen.*"

"Hi, little Wi-yen." Martha kept her eyes away from Sen-tshe now, mesmerized by this infant. Something strange was happening. Her arms and legs tingled, and her chest was warm. There was a surge of maternal instinct, almost like the feeling of milk letting down that she remembered from her days as a nursing mother. She could feel the baby's gaze on her skin. His soft odor, a kind of a nutty smell, filled her nose. She reached out and touched his cheek.

Her knees grew weak. Her hands shook and her mouth was dry. The baby cooed and smiled.

"Can I hold him?"

Of course Sen-tshe had no idea what she was asking. She tried to pantomime taking the baby off his back and out of the cradleboard, but the man didn't seem to understand what she wanted. He simply smiled, nodded and turned to walk away.

Martha watched them go. As surely as she had ever known anything, she knew this baby was the key. And she knew this was why she had been dragged into this world. She wasn't the one who would save these people. It was Wi-yen who would save them and she was only here to find out how.

Suddenly the man stopped and turned back. He looked at her from across the meadow, then turned to the dog at his side. She watched his lips move and saw his hand wave. Po-ko wagged her tail and turned, trotting back to Martha's side.

Martha knelt and patted the brown head, smiling her thanks back to Sen-tshe, but he had already continued down the trail.

TWENTY-ONE

"Say Dad, how about we tackle that bathroom today?" Jack set his empty cup in the sink, paused, then picked it up and put it in the dishwasher.

Good boy, thought Glen as he considered his son's suggestion.

Glen had promised Martha that retirement meant fixing up the house. "You'll get your fancy bathroom, but you have to wait a few more years," he told her.

Martha's idea of remodeling hadn't matched up with Glen's. She didn't understand how much they could save if she waited until he wasn't working and did it himself.

Now he had visions of her returning home, happy that it had been taken care of.

"Sounds good. Let me find those plans your mom drew up." Glen rummaged around in the third bedroom, the boys' old room, the one which had become his office and Martha's sewing room. Jack was staying in the room that had belonged to Clarice. Martha had kept that one as a guest room after the last child moved out. It had become her room when they quit sleeping together, but only for sleeping. She'd never moved any of her things in there.

Jack and Glen pored over the sketches and ideas Martha had collected. There really weren't any deep changes, just decorative things like a different vanity set up, new paint, and new lighting.

Jack looked up from the papers spread on the kitchen table. "What do you think about doing a little more than this? Maybe a new tub and shower, one that can work with a wheelchair?"

"A wheelchair?"

"Yeah. You never know, well...when she comes home, things could be...she could be..." Jack shrugged and looked at Glen. "She seems like she wants to wake up. Her eyes flick around so much, I just have this feeling any day now she's going to look at me and say, 'What the hell are *you* doing here?'"

A knot rose in Glen's throat. "A wheelchair?"

"I was thinking, you know, sometimes people's minds, their brains don't work one hundred percent after something like this."

This. They still didn't know what "this" was. He looked at Jack, so helpful, trying to think about doing the right thing for his mother.

His son shrugged and continued. "If she's in a wheelchair we should convert the dining room into a bedroom for her, and this bathroom could be accessed from there. That way everything will be on one floor."

Glen had been set on just taking one day at a time, and when he did imagine the future, Martha was back to the way she used to be. "Well, that sounds like a smart idea. I guess the thought hadn't really entered my mind."

"You never know, Dad."

"I try not to think about the future, Jack. I just feel overwhelmed when I do. It's only a few more years before I was going to retire. Your mom and me, we were going to travel some more. Long trips in that new camper. Now...well..."

"I guess there's some sort of happy medium, you know, think about the future a little bit, but take it day by day. When I'm with her I just see little things each time, like she's going to get better in tiny little steps. Maybe one of those steps will be coming home, instead of staying in that place."

Jack smiled but Glen noticed his eyes held a sense of hesitation.

"The hospital's not that bad. The girls are nice and they pay special attention to your mom all the time."

"They pay special attention to *you*. Mom gets good treatment, I know that, but it's just the daily routine. The staff there likes the fact that you're a nice guy. I've seen some of the relatives they have to deal with. You're a dream compared to them."

"I guess I should think about the future."

"Just a tiny bit. I don't want you turning into Vince. That would not be pleasant." Jack grinned and tapped the wall. "Should we get started on this teardown?"

The two men ripped out the tiles and removed the toilet and tub. The day was warm for mid-November, so after a few hours, a mid-day break seemed just the thing. Glen was surprised but pleased when Jack pulled out a soda instead of a beer. They settled on the back deck, feet up on the rail, no talk needed, enjoying the sun.

"What have we here?" Clarice spoke through the screen door, then slid it open and stepped out onto the porch. Glen watched her scope out his beer, then turn to see what Jack was drinking.

"Hey, Sis, grab yourself a soda, or a beer if the old man left any."

"No thanks, just stopped by to pick up that old wool coat of Mom's. I can have that, right?"

"Which coat is that?"

"You know, the black wool thing, double breasted with those pretty buttons? I think it belonged to Nonna or something. Mom doesn't wear it. I think with just a little bit of alteration it will be a cool winter coat for me."

Glen didn't answer.

"Dad, I'm not scoping in on her things or anything like that."

Glen actually hadn't been thinking along those lines. He had just been trying to remember where the coat might be.

"Clarice, don't be so defensive, girl. Give the man a chance to talk." Jack sipped his soda.

His son defending him; that was a new twist. Glen laughed and pulled his feet down from the rail.

"You go right ahead and take the coat, sweetheart. I'm sure your mother would want you to have it. I think it's in the front hall closet." He stood. "How about getting back to work, Jack, before this old man needs an afternoon nap."

Clarice trailed along as Jack and Glen headed back into the bathroom.

"What in the world are you doing?"

"Remodel."

"I'll say it's a remodel."

"We're fixing up a new shower and toilet, one that a wheelchair can roll into, for when Mom comes home." Jack pointed to the corner. "I think we might bring that wall out a bit, then the sink can fit right here, but extend over so that a wheelchair can roll under the counter, for brushing teeth and stuff."

"Mom's coming home? Why didn't anyone tell me?"

Jack shook his head. "We aren't keeping things from you. All I'm saying is someday she will be."

"She won't need a wheelchair if she comes home. She'll need a hospital bed."

"Maybe at first," Glen murmured.

"You're dreaming. That is not going to happen." Clarice turned and left without a goodbye.

A few days later the whole family gathered at East Park Convalescent. Sandra and Vince had insisted on a birthday celebration for Martha. Sandra baked a cake—Martha's favorite white cake with chocolate frosting—and Jack provided the chocolate chip ice cream. Glen's daughter-in-law served up slices for the family and little Sara helped out by carefully distributing the red plastic plates loaded with cake and ice cream. When she finished, she grabbed her plate and headed for his lap. Glen lifted her onto one knee and kissed his granddaughter's soft head.

"At least Vince didn't insist we sing happy birthday to her," he heard Clarice say as she settled next to Jack. Squeezing all these chairs into the small room hadn't been easy.

Clarice could make fun of Vince's insistence that they talk to Martha, but Glen hoped he was right. He played the role his son prescribed:

talking to Martha every day, updating her on the lives of friends, the morning news, the grandchildren, but he often ran out of things to say. There really wasn't much going on in his life between work and visiting Martha. Weekends he helped Jack with the remodel. Yesterday he found himself making up a story about Mandy chasing her tail because he couldn't think of anything to say to Martha's motionless body.

Sandra stood and collected the plates. Glen used the distraction to move Sara off his lap. "Let's say goodbye to Grandma."

Sara crawled up onto the bed next to Martha. Glen loved the fact that his granddaughter had gotten used to her grandmother's sleeping state. She took hold of Martha's hand and held it as if they were walking side by side.

Sara sat up and looked for her mother. "Momma, I think Grandma wants something."

Glen looked at Martha. Her lips were moving and she was squeezing Sara's hand. "She's waking up." He raced to her side and leaned close. "Martha, Martha. I'm here. We're all here."

Her lips kept moving.

"Shhh, shhhh, everyone be quiet." Clarice's sharp hiss covered the room and everyone stopped talking. "She's trying to say something."

They all stared at Martha.

"What Grandma? What do you need?" Sara leaned into her grandmother's face, one hand still clutched in Martha's, the other pressed onto Martha's chest.

A faint whisper escaped the moving lips. "Needles, needles and thread. I need to sew."

TWENTY-TWO

Martha had grown accustomed to the weather, but like any camping in winter, there was always that urge to dive back into the warmth of the bed, and she delayed rising until the sun had a chance to warm the air. The dog slept with her nearly every night, mutual warmth for both of them.

She had asked Kwe-in-ye about the dog and the man with the baby, but the old woman simply shrugged and shook her head.

There might not be any sun today. It had been snowing lightly when she went to bed last night, and there was that tell-tale hush. Martha listened for the usual birds singing, but they were missing from the morning sounds. She pulled a shawl from under the fur, where she had stuffed it last night so that it would be warm this morning.

Something caught on the fabric—a small, stiff rectangle of paper. Rising, she drew the shawl tight as she stooped out the door. She was intent on looking at the object in her hand and barely noticed the several inches of snow which crunched beneath her feet and coated the world with a pale frosting.

The packet held John James needles, all sizes. She had bought a pack like this to take with her to a sewing workshop, so that she would always have the right size and shape. Her favorite brand. Martha turned the packet over and over in her hands, puzzling how this could have come to be in her bed. She'd worked with the bone needle yesterday and her hands were sore from punching it through the thick leather. She had marveled that these women could do such fine decoration with their difficult tools, sewing not only the seams of the pants and dresses, but adding beads and decorative stitching. She had wished for needles, thinking about how impressed Yo-en-u would be with the fine steel sharps, slipping easily into the leather, or the curved needles, which made sewing two thick layers from one side—like a surgeon closing an incision—a dream. And she hadn't given up on her idea of protective gloves.

And now the needles were in in her hand. Martha paused. She had wished for thread too. Rushing back inside she pulled up the fur blanket, sank to her knees and patted around with her hands. Yes, here were two spools of thread. One black and one white.

This time when Martha left her room she did notice the snow. Two inches covered everything. The morning was cold and gray, clouds threatening more cold weather to come. Winter was here.

Martha wished she had kept track of the days like she had started out to do, but she hadn't. In the beginning it had been easy to think, I've been here for one day, two days, seven days, and to make scratches on the wall. But in the midst of so much happening she had lost track. Once she lost track it didn't make sense to count anymore.

If there was snow it must be December, although it really didn't seem like two months had passed. Her birthday had likely come and gone. She hadn't been there to get those funny cards reserved for turning forty-nine. Maybe she would be home for the important birthday, fifty, a special cause for celebration. Martha laughed. Things that seemed so important in the other world had very little meaning here. These people were grateful to be alive each day, to be blessed with the presence of the elders, to kiss their children each morning. Her heart grew heavy as she thought about her family and longed for another chance to kiss them and touch them and tell them she loved them.

There was nothing she could do about it and when she let her mind go there, she felt terrible all day. Glancing down at the needles and thread she held, she went in search of Yo-en-u.

She ran into Kwe-in-ye just outside the door.

"Come, Mar-tee-a. It is time for the ceremony."

"What?" Martha envisioned some terrible ritual they were now going to put her through. She should have known better than to relax and think things were settled. "I'm not ready. You have to tell me what's happening before you expose me to these things."

"Not you. Pat-o-le-si died yesterday."

She tried to think of who Pat-o-le-si was. An old woman, she thought. She was usually sitting down near the group of potters. Martha was pretty sure the woman was blind. But she turned her head for the smallest sound, so her hearing had been keen.

Kwe-in-ye explained that the woman's death brought great sorrow to the people. "The dead one is heading to the other world, but she doesn't want to go. She doesn't want to leave her loved ones. It is important to keep a distance, for she will try to take them with her to the other world. But those who love her don't want to say goodbye from a great distance or she will forget them and their love. She needs this ceremony to help her prepare for the next world."

The needles would have to wait.

Kwe-in-ye led Martha down the canyon, with Po-ko following at a safe distance. Although the dog usually walked close to Martha, when the old woman was around she hung back, just out of scolding range.

As they walked, Martha was surprised at the distance. She hadn't been in this direction much. The canyon grew narrow, then wide again, then very narrow between tall cliffs. They finally stopped on the edge of a drop. She could see that when the creek was full this was a waterfall. There was a crowd of people here and all were facing Damé, who stood very close to the edge of the precipice.

Martha spotted To-be-né with her mother and aunts.

"Hell-o," Cha-pe grinned at her. "Hell-o."

"Hello, Cha-pe." Martha smiled at the pride the woman showed in her English greeting, then quickly dropped her face back into a solemn expression. She didn't want to insult the family of Pat-o-le-si.

Martha looked around. Póetu stood with Ka-a-poo, leaning on his walking stick. Those two were always together. Martha wondered about the relationship as neither had a family. The handsome young Katudu was off to one edge of the crowd, his attention directed toward Dam-po-nu, who stood next to her mother, Yo-en-u, who in turn was staring back at Katudu as if considering the young man's attention to her daughter.

Martha didn't see a body anywhere. Maybe this was more a memorial service than a burial.

Damé spoke in a soft chant. The people grew silent and lifted their hands, palms facing the sky, and repeated his prayer.

Now the storyteller raised his hands high, his voice growing in volume and pitch. Three men came down the trail, carrying a rolled mat.

Here was poor Pat-o-le-si. With a skip of her heart, Martha wondered if they were going to throw her off the cliff.

They set her in front of Damé. He pulled something—cornmeal, Martha thought—out of a pouch on his side and sprinkled it over the body. Two women knelt, wailing and crying, and rubbed their hands in the cornmeal, wiping the powder onto their own cheeks. A low moan started from the people. As the moan grew louder everyone started backing away in small, shuffling steps. Those closest to the trail backed along it. The crowd grew thin as more people slowly stepped along the trail, never turning or taking their eyes off Damé and the rolled mat.

The sorrow spread and Martha felt a wave of sadness flow through her. She pressed her lips together and a tear slipped down one cheek. Was she a hypocrite for crying? She didn't really know this woman, wouldn't miss her, but surrounded by those who grieved the loss—Pat-o-le-si's children, her family, her friends—Martha couldn't stop her tears. She looked down at her hands and turned her palms toward the sky.

"Lord, I don't know what your plan is, but bless these people. They are good and they are sad," she whispered, suddenly feeling very silly.

That feeling was instantly replaced by a thought that slammed into her chest and took her breath away.

Was she dead?

On the walk back to their rooms Martha considered her question. Her thoughts circled but always landed back in the same spot. There were only a few choices: she was dreaming, she had time traveled, or she was dead. Or she had lost her mind, but that didn't seem right. She hurried inside and picked up the sewing supplies. She would take them to Yo-en-u and quit thinking about these things that had no answer.

The needles improved her status with the group. Yo-en-u loved them. Martha fell asleep that night thinking of her collection of seed beads and how nice they looked sewed in designs. But the next day, when three tubes of beads showed up next to Martha's bed, she realized that there might be a better way to use the treasure.

"See? Nice, right?" She held out the tubes and let Yo-en-u examine them, then curled her fist closed over the shiny colors. "Now where are my clothes?" She pointed to her dress and her legs and her feet, then waved her hands around.

Yo-en-u turned away for a moment and Martha watched the wheels turning in her friend's head.

The woman held up a finger—wait—and then slipped away. She returned in less than five minutes with Martha's nightgown and leggings, carefully folded.

"What about my slippers?" Martha pointed to her feet. "And my underwear."

She mimicked snapping elastic at her waist, but the woman just shook her head and held out the clothes.

Something was better than nothing. Either Yo-en-u didn't know where the slippers and underwear were or she was too scared of her sister to hand those things over. Martha swapped the beads for her clothes.

She had to hand it to Kwe-in-ye. Her spirit guide didn't blink an eyelash when she saw Martha dressed in her nightgown and leggings. They had been washed and repaired and Martha felt a bit guilty about the whole thing. She was used to the dress the women had given her. Donning her own clothes was more of a power shift than anything else. Did she really need to exert herself over Kwe-in-ye?

Three days later the decision became easy. Yo-en-u walked up to her and held out one of the simple cotton dresses. But this one had been transformed into a creation of beauty. The bodice and neck were covered with an intricate design of stitching and beads.

Never in her life had Martha received a gift that held so much honor. She examined the garment, impressed with the embellishments, but more impressive was the fact that this dress had set in sleeves. Clearly Yo-en-u had studied the construction of her nightgown and somehow recreated the pattern.

"Is this for me?" Martha was cautious about taking gifts. There were times when the people presented her with things to show them to her, taking them back after she had examined and commented.

Yo-en-u nodded and motioned for Martha to go change into the dress. When she returned, the perfect fit and soft fabric made her feel like a queen. She spun in front of the group of women and knew she would never wear her nightgown and leggings again.

The thing Martha loved most was learning to make the beautiful clay pots. There were several types: plain ones used for cooking and carrying water and more elaborate art pots used for trade. She had finally gained the trust of the women who worked down at the edge of the creek every day making them. Even without the flowing water, the shade of the cottonwood trees kept the women comfortable and they had access to the water they needed from one of the small pools. Martha begged off her daily responsibilities of teaching language, eager for a chance to join the potters.

Ta-kan, a woman who Martha guessed was about her age, was in charge. "*Pan a cre so no,*" she instructed. Making pots required patience.

Martha soon found out just what this woman meant. The clay was in the form of solid chunks. An all-day hike was required to gather the proper materials. When they returned, Ta-kan showed her how to dig a hole in the cool dirt under the trees and line it with leaves. With sign language accompanying words Martha was beginning to understand, she learned that only certain leaves would work. These leaves kept the water in the hole for the next step. The chunks of clay were placed in the hole and some of their precious water was poured over the top. Then more leaves and finally a layer of dirt.

Ta-kan sent Martha back to her students, holding up two fingers. When Martha returned in two hours, the woman shook her head and said "*Yi po connu tan.*" She drew an arch with her hand across the sky from east to west, then waved it again.

Two days.

The process continued from there. Massaging and kneading the clay, adding a bit of some other dried clay Ta-kan had stored in a pot, filtering out all the little stones in much the same way they ground the corn, making a slurry and then letting that sit in a cool cave for several days.

It was a week before she finally made a pot.

The clay was smooth and cool and forgiving. If she pressed too hard and the whole thing leaned to one side, she could simply add some water and start over. As Martha grew to understand the nature of the soft mud, she was able to correct her mistakes with a little finesse and didn't have to go all the way back to the first step every time. She sat on the yucca mat next to the other women and a sense of belonging washed over her like a warm shower on a cool day. Her doubts drained away and her mind was fresh.

Her pot was small, Ta-kan hadn't given her much clay. Valuable stuff, the clay. With so much work involved, Martha wasn't surprised.

The pots were placed in a covered pit, this time filled with the moist leaves of a different plant, and Martha thought she would soon be eating out of her creation. She was wrong. There were still many steps to go.

After the pots slowly dried in their cool holes, Ta-kan showed her how to sand the sides with a soft piece of wood. Then the old woman took her into the woods to gather plants and bark which they used to mix the paint. A kind of wild spinach grew up on the mesa and this produced the near-black used for the intricate designs. Thin fibers of the yucca, carefully shredded at one end, were their paintbrushes.

Martha watched the women paint starbursts and zig zags and interlocking triangles. Ta-kan had modified her yucca more than the others so that she could paint the thinnest of lines with a single strand. Her designs were more complex, with thick lines and thin lines intertwining around the bowl. Her pottery was never for everyday use, but kept for ceremony or trading.

Most surprising was that Kwe-in-ye joined the women on the day they painted. Dam-po-nu offered the old woman one of her pots and a brush and Kwe-in-ye settled in to paint the small bowl. Martha watched as Kwe-in-ye carefully turned the pot while keeping the brush still, resulting in a perfect line all the way around, just a few centimeters from the edge.

Martha didn't want to copy what the other women were doing. She had to come up with her own design. She stirred the paint with a small stick and considered the blank canvas of her pot. She had taken a water color class last year but didn't think a black apple or tulip was what she wanted. With her skill level, simplicity might be best. She finally settled on a zig zag border along the top edge. If she put it on the inside as well, her pot would be distinguished from the others. As she held the pot in her lap and carefully dipped her brush into the black mixture, the thin green strands of the brush bent and a huge blob interrupted her careful line.

"If only I had my brushes!"

"You must not wish for things, Mar-tee-a."

Surprised, she turned to Kwe-in-ye. "But I only wish for things we need."

The woman shook her head. "We do not need these things, Mar-tee-a. You need them. But that is not so. You only think you need them."

Ta-kan looked over and reached for Martha's pot. She wiped the black blob away and used the sanding wood to smooth out the dark smear. When she handed it back to Martha she smiled and nodded. Encouragement in the face of any adversity. Martha suspected Ta-kan was trying to stop the tense conversation between her and Kwe-in-ye.

Martha pressed her lips together and stared at her pot. It wouldn't do to argue with Kwe-in-ye. The woman was her guide and there was always a reason for what she said. It was just that the reasons weren't always apparent and every time their conversations got tense, Martha couldn't shake the idea that there were things Kwe-in-ye wasn't telling her.

"You confuse me. You want me to be magical in some way, yet you tell me not to wish for the things that might be just what I need to…" Martha didn't want to use the word save. She still didn't think this was her purpose. "If I am to be normal then you have to let me be normal."

"It is not that simple." Kwe-in-ye stood, handed her finished pot to Ta-kan and walked away.

"That's what we call passive-aggressive," Martha mumbled to the old woman's retreating back, then turned back to her work.

She lifted her pot and dipped the brush back into the paint, tossing aside Kwe-in-ye's warning and thinking about her black canvas case filled with every size and shape of paint brush. She wanted the tiny, firm tipped one she treated with the utmost care, cleaning it with a soft touch each time she used it. It would be perfect for this kind of design.

And she wouldn't say no to some turquoise paint. That would show Kwe-in-ye that her wishes were not bad things at all.

TWENTY-THREE

"Hey, Clarice. I need your help today."

She hadn't heard from Vince in days and now he didn't wait for her to say hello before he asked for something.

"What?"

"Mom asked for some blue paint and brushes. I don't have time, meetings after work. Can you go by the house and get them? Dad said they're in one of those containers in her sewing room."

"You mean she mumbled some more? Did Dad ever follow up on what this means?" Clarice, and everyone else, had been sure Mom was going to wake up when she started talking. But it was only another weird not-a-coma behavior that puzzled them all.

"I think so. The doctors have no clue, according to Jack. Anyway, can you take the paint to her?"

Clarice glanced at the clock. If she gulped her coffee and left now she would have time to go by the house. She was planning on visiting her mother today anyway. But if she agreed without an argument, then her brother would be calling every day for favors.

Don't fight. She heard a voice from the sky drift down. Maybe her conscience was alive and kicking after all.

"Sure. I can do that."

"Thanks. I owe you."

Right. Like Vince ever felt he owed anyone something. Her brother's tally of how much he did was carved in ancient glacial ice and floated just below the surface of every conversation. No one would ever save up enough favors to tip the balance in their direction.

Clarice let herself into the house because Dad's car was gone and if Jack was around, he seldom heard the bell. Only Mandy was there, wagging her tail and trying to jump up for a pat.

"Stay off." Clarice hurried up the stairs to the sewing room. It didn't take long to spot the plastic container holding her mother's paints. Tubes of acrylic neatly lined up in rainbow order.

Which shade of blue? Mom had three choices: turquoise, cobalt and aquamarine. The turquoise was obviously the favorite, the tube squeezed down—neatly, of course— to nearly nothing. Clarice picked up that one. If she was going to leave something in a basket next to her mother's bed it might as well be something useless. What if someone took it? She looked for brushes but couldn't find any. Mom would just have to do without.

But as she opened the front door, pushing Mandy aside with her leg, Clarice felt a flush of guilt. Who knows what it meant that Mom mumbled these crazy requests every few days? Vince had taken on the job of bringing the things she asked for and he was always very exact in his choices. If he saw the empty tube of paint and no sign of brushes he would complain and accuse her of not caring about Mom. She walked back upstairs and snatched the full cobalt tube. This time she noticed a black canvas case, filled with brushes. She picked out two, one thick and one tiny, and slipped them into her purse.

"Okay Mom, here's the stuff you asked for. Going to paint us a marvelous blue picture tonight? The sky, I bet. You sure you don't need paper too?" Clarice straightened the bed-sheet, pulling it taut and tucking it under her mother's arms.

Clarice set the paint and brushes in the basket next to the needles, pocket knife, thread, glasses, yarn, crochet hooks, and coffee. When they tried to remove things from the bedside, her mother started mumbling and moving her hands a lot. Clarice thought it might actually be good for Mom to get upset. It certainly led to more movement. But she hadn't been able to share this idea with her father. He wouldn't agree and he was in charge. Besides, she had given up making suggestions weeks ago. Now she just went along with whatever Dad said because anytime she contradicted him he reacted and she didn't want him to have a heart attack.

One of the nurses had suggested a container for all the requested items to make things a bit tidier. The basket stood as a sentinel to the mystery of why her mother wanted these particular things.

A young woman entered the room. "Hello. You must be Mrs. Grimson's daughter." She had dark shiny hair and skin the color of walnut. Clarice half expected dark eyes, but the woman looked at her through hazel eyes. The kind Mom claimed changed color depending on mood. Very similar to Jack's eyes, although his were a more brilliant green. The woman smiled and held out her hand.

Clarice took the outstretched hand. The nurse squeezed slightly while giving a shake.

"I'm Naomi, your mother's new nurse."

"Good to meet you, Naomi."

"If you need anything special or have any questions, please let me know."

"I will, thanks." Clarice felt uneasy and wondered why this woman sent chills up her spine.

"There is something I would like to ask of you."

Of course, that was it. The nurse had bad news.

"What is it?" Clarice prepared herself for the latest bombshell.

"I like to get to know my patients. It would help me a lot if you could tell me about your mother. I mean, before this situation."

"Like what?" Nosy nurse. What was she after?

"Things about her personality. Was she quiet or the life of the party? I want to treat her in the way she liked to be treated. Patients respond better…I don't want to be soft spoken if she likes action and excitement. But I don't want to be too loud for someone who likes it calm."

Clarice relaxed. Just a bit. It was nice that Naomi thought about this. Maybe the nurse saw her mother as a person, not a body in a bed.

Unlike Clarice, who couldn't shake the feeling she would never talk to her mother again.

"Okay. Let's see. My mom." She paused. "She was a good mother, very un-liberated. What I mean is, she liked—likes—to take care of everyone. She was always cooking or sewing or cleaning." Clarice pointed at the basket of items. "Knitting, crocheting, painting. She was... is... pleasant, always pleasant. Mom never really argued, argues..." Clarice didn't want to talk about Mom in the past tense, as if she were dead.

"Let's include your mother in the conversation, shall we?" Naomi reached out and held Martha's hand. "Martha, Clarice is going to tell me some stories about the past, special things she remembers. This will help me when I take care of you." Turning back, Naomi explained. "I already introduced myself to your mother. I've told her about me so I don't think she'll mind if you tell me about her."

Clarice nodded and tried to think of something that would illustrate what her mother was like. "Okay. Mom, do you remember when you rescued me from that brutal first grade teacher? The one who only liked needy kids? She wouldn't believe me when I said I lost my reading card. She accused me of being careless. I was devastated, I had worked hard to get lots of stamps on my card." She turned to Naomi. "You got one each time you read a book to the teacher. When you filled your card she would take you across the street to the mini mart for an ice cream bar. My card was missing and she told me it was my own fault and I would have to start again." She turned back to Martha. "You marched into that classroom and talked with the teacher. I wasn't there, but I've always had a hard time imagining you angry. You probably just explained things in that way you have. Calm. Careful."

Clarice stopped. That was her mother. Calm and careful, but there was something else. "Powerful. My mother was powerful when she had to be. She might not always stand up for herself, but she always stood up for her children."

Naomi listened with great concentration, her eyes moving from Clarice to Martha, including both in the conversation. Clarice told several more stories. She talked until Mrs. Harris, the head nurse *harrumphed* from the doorway.

"Naomi, it's time for medication rounds."

Naomi jumped up, moving the chair back to its place by the wall.

"I'm sorry Mrs. Harris, the time got away from us. I'll just finish up here."

Mrs. Harris nodded and left.

"Clarice? I just want to mention something to you. Please don't take this the wrong way."

Clarice clenched her jaw. What now? There had to be some ulterior motive, she knew it. She stared at Naomi.

"I asked you to tell me stories about your mother, and, it's just...you told me stories about yourself. Maybe tomorrow you can think of some stories about *her*. Things she liked, what she did for fun, her hobbies, her dreams."

A wave of guilt left Clarice clenching her jaw even tighter. She could barely open her mouth to speak. "I'm...you're...it..." She shrugged, angry at the truth in the accusation.

"Great. I'll see you tomorrow." Naomi flashed a smile and left the room.

"Hey, what do you think of that hot new nurse Mom has?" Leave it to Jack to focus on Naomi's beauty. "Is she native or something? I mean, those eyes, wow, I can fall for miles in those eyes."

Of course you could. Clarice wasn't surprised her brother had been impressed with the nurse, but she was surprised to run into both Jack and Dad visiting Mom at this time of day.

"Dad? You're not at work?"

"Day off." Glen didn't elaborate. "I met Naomi the other day. I like the way she's taking the time to get to know your mother by asking for stories."

"Yeah? Me too." Jack laughed as if this was some kind of inside joke. "She asked me to tell her some stories about Mom. I thought it was just an excuse to get me to stay and talk, you know. I felt something there. Now you have to go and pop my bubble."

"Did she scold you for not telling her what she was after?" Clarice paced the room.

"Scold me? No. Why would she do that?"

Dad walked over to the bed, then turned and made his way to the window. Clarice had never seen him so unsettled. He usually pulled up a chair and sat next to Mom. Held her hand. Brushed the hair off her forehead.

"She's a nice girl. She asked me to tell her about when your mother and I first met. I heard her singing to your mother the other day. I believe she's Native American. The song was like a chant of some sort. I swear your mother lights up when that nurse comes into the room."

"She seems young to be a nurse." Clarice glanced at her mother. Suddenly everyone was more in the know than she was. She couldn't help it if her life kept her out of the loop. Dad was enthralled with the nurse, enthralled with Jack, and ignoring Mom.

"She is young to be a nurse, only twenty-one, but she graduated high school when she was fifteen. A very smart girl."

"How did you find out so much about her?" Clarice was not only out of the loop, but on a different planet.

"Tit for tat, I told her. If I told her my stories then she had to tell me hers." Dad shrugged.

Jack drummed the foot of the bed with his palms. Clarice wished he wouldn't do that, Mom's feet were under there. He'd give her bedsores. "Why didn't I think of that? Would have been a good way to get my foot in the door. What do you think? Should I ask her out?"

Clarice snorted. Dad could go on about how her brother had changed but that was only because Jack was staying with him. Sure, he was helping with the remodel but what about finding a job? What girl would date a guy with the prospects of a turnip? Obviously Jack didn't see things that way.

"That's a terrible idea." Clarice snapped. "You shouldn't put her in that position. You should be the one to see that it's not right to mix business with pleasure. There's a name for it. Dual relationship, that's it. It's against the law for doctors or nurses to date their patients."

"Excuse me, dear sister. You seem to be forgetting, I'm not the patient."

Clarice wasn't going to argue with Jack over this. Not right now.

"Mom asked for paint, blue paint and brushes. I brought them."

"Your mother does love to paint, all those little jars and such. Wonder what she has in mind this time?"

Clarice stood by the basket, picking up things and setting them down again. "I keep thinking that she'll say something else, ask us something or, I don't know, tell us why she needs all these things."

"Gee Clarice, I think maybe you ought to spend the night down here. I think she probably gets up in the wee hours and uses the stuff." Jack tapped his hand on his forehead, then circled it around. Was her brother referring to her or Dad?

"I asked Dr. Braundo—" Dad stopped and rubbed his forehead and she noticed her father's hand was trembling. "She's so close and I want to know why she's not...not...back yet. Martha's not in a coma, she's in a catatonic state and I want the doctor's opinion. He's ordered some more tests. Wednesday."

"Dad, why didn't you tell me sooner? I have class on Wednesday." Clarice couldn't believe her father didn't realize the sooner the better on these things.

"Sweetie." Dad looked down at his hands. "Not this time."

"What?"

"I'll be with her. Just your mother and I. The transport company takes her and there's only room for one family member."

"I'll meet you there, Dad. It's really not a problem."

"No. I...I want this to be just your mom and I."

Clarice looked at Jack. He shrugged, as if he had no idea what was going on.

Great. Just fantastic. All Jack had to do was pound a few nails and Dad forgot everything Clarice had done for them. No way she was going to leave her mother's future in their hands.

TWENTY-FOUR

Martha pointed to each item as she instructed the children. Spring had arrived but she was still using the dried food pulled from storage for her lessons. At least they were outdoors. The five long months of winter had been hard on everyone.

"Corn. Squash. Yucca." She paused at the fourth item. The green leafy plant had been on a poster when she and Glen visited the museum, but for the life of her she couldn't recall its name. Something that made her smile. Pigsfoot? Pigweed? Or was it goatweed?

She enjoyed teaching the children and each day they brought her small gifts. Initially she thought this was the way families paid her, but then she noticed that the children didn't bring things to Damé or Kwe-in-ye. She was worried that the people had an elevated view of her status.

"Thank you, but no more gifts," she told Ha-ni. She handed the small basket back to the girl.

Ha-ni held the basket, a puzzled look on her face.

Martha turned to Ten-pla and shook her head, clasping her hands behind her back so the tall boy couldn't give her the dried meat he held. "Nothing, you don't have to bring me things."

"Mar-tee-ya, why do you not want our gifts?" To-be-né was her star pupil when it came to English. All the hours spent with Martha outside of class accounted for her expertise. "You make Ha-ni sad."

Martha thought about her own children and the times they had brought her gifts. Not just the bunches of wildflowers or the drawings which she dutifully stuck on the refrigerator. She always framed one or two from each child and allowed them permanent status on a wall, somewhere out of the way, but still prominent enough to stroke each budding artist's ego. It was the events they put together she thought about now. Breakfast on Mother's Day or a lengthy talent show, prepared during the long summer hours between swimming lessons, ballet, soccer camp, and the skateboard park.

Had she hurt their feelings, too? Not making enough of their efforts, polite applause before telling them it was almost time for dinner and they had to deconstruct the stage they had made by hanging sheets from the ceiling?

"I'm sorry, but I worry that they're bringing me things...too much." She didn't want to accuse the children of stealing from their families, but she knew that a basket was no small item.

When the adults started to join the class she discovered that they presented her with gifts as well. Her cave wasn't big enough to keep all the things her grateful students brought to her. Kwe-in-ye relented and gave her some storage space in the main room of their dwelling.

The group repeated the words slowly, the sounds different from the words that fell so smoothly off their tongues. Her language probably puzzled them like theirs confused her: one long string of sounds with no idea where the breaks were. She noticed some consistencies which helped, such as the *ja* in the *ja pa* greeting. Initially she had equated it to the "good" in good morning, but now she suspected the greeting had more of a religious twist, like a "God's blessings be with you" kind of thing. She had recognized the same *ja* in the prayer that Damé often spoke when the group gathered around the fire in the evening. She discovered that being surrounded by language all day, every day, made the process of learning different. Suddenly she was aware of what people were saying without knowing individual words.

It was easier to learn from the children. Following the lead of To-be-né, they liked to take her by the hand around the canyon, pointing out things and listening to her speak. They, in turn would label items and talk to her slowly, using hand gestures and pantomime to help her to understand. To-be-né remained her constant companion, although she didn't appear jealous of the attention Martha gave to the other children.

Martha continued to find things she wished for in her bed. She had tried to control what was coming by speaking out loud, imagining life with a picture book, some shampoo, her nice hair brush, but that didn't seem to work. She adapted her morning ritual to cleaning up without water and, after watching the mothers work at wiping off their children's gritty hands and filing their nails, using the tiny bone awls to clean the dirt from under them, she realized wishing for shampoo or soap was useless because she couldn't waste the water needed to use these things.

Items that actually showed up were things she thought about, but usually in some vague way. Tweezers, her multi-function pocket knife, a comb. Once a pack of gum showed up and she was torn between passing it out to the children or saving it for repairs. It was as if God or the great creator or whoever was orchestrating this whole drama was sending her items that should have some meaning and guide her to her destiny. But the teddy bear she imagined showing Wi-yen hadn't appeared.

The baby had changed more than anyone in these past months. Of course, the jump from six months to almost a year old was significant in all babies. She listened to his jabbering and helped him to say words in his language as well as hers. He would grow up bilingual. Was that why she had the overwhelming sense he was the key to solving their problems?

She shook her head. No, others were speaking her language now, and Kwe-in-ye had been fluent all along. She didn't want to imagine that she was here for a task that relied on Wi-yen being grown up enough to speak English. Surely she would go home sooner than that.

"Spinach, root, stone." She pointed to some more items and her diligent students repeated the words. What if she wished for pen and paper? She could teach them how to read and write. Chalkboard and slates, maybe, like an old-fashioned schoolmarm.

The needles had proven to be the key to improving her social status. When Yo-en-u used them to make a feathered shawl the whole village gathered to admire her work. To-be-né loved the paint, although she was still learning that her choice of surface was important. Martha wasn't so sure about Damé and the reading glasses she had dreamed up and presented to the old man. The fact that he carried them everywhere and waved them around, but seldom put them on his face, led her to believe they did not improve his vision.

Kwe-in-ye had assigned Martha the job as teacher, reducing her other obligations. Even when Martha showed her the protective coverings she had made for her arms—long fingerless leather gloves—the old woman didn't send her back out to look for berries. Martha liked teaching, but she wanted more chances to explore the other things in the village.

"Grinder, cornmeal, pot." She pointed to three more items. For some reason this last one brought smiles to the faces of the adults and giggles to the children. Martha looked around.

"Okay, what's so funny about a pot?" She pointed again. Now the adults laughed too.

"Mar-tee-ya," To-be-né jumped up and pointed to her rump. "This, this is my *pot*."

Teaching language was filled with lessons.

Mosinobu and Sen-tshe were her most diligent adult students when it came to learning to speak English and not just memorizing nouns. She could actually carry on short conversations with them, using a mixture of their language and English. Sen-tshe sought out Martha several times each day, Wi-yen always strapped to his back. Martha was still cautious around him but she wanted—needed—to be close to Wi-yen. She hadn't told Kwe-in-ye about her epiphany that the baby was key to saving the village because she didn't really have anything more than a feeling.

"Mar-tee-a, hungry?" Sen-tshe approached with a pouch in hand. Sitting down next to Martha he presented her with pine nuts, a slice of some green plant and some corn paste.

She looked at his eyes. Kwe-in-ye must have told him she refused jerky. His expression was serious, but there was a hint of something else. Was he making fun of her?

She had learned to take any food offered. She didn't have permission to go into the stores and meals were not formal things in this world. "Yes, thank you." Martha took a handful of the nuts and one of the slices. Cactus of some type, she guessed. She reached out and playfully popped a piece in Wi-yen's mouth.

"When does he get to be out of the pouch?" Martha was amazed that this baby, who seemed to be nearly a year old, remained so placid strapped to the backboard. At least his arms were free today.

"When the snow melt." Sen-tshe seemed to want to say more, pinching his mouth to one side and looking up, the expression Martha had come to recognize as him searching for words she would understand.

"Only Sen-tshe to watch."

So that was it. He was worried about watching over Wi-yen when the child was free to move about. Martha knew that the tribe was upset at Sen-tshe for keeping Wi-yen when his wife had died in childbirth. It would have been customary for one of her sisters to take on the child, sort of a god-parent thing. Kwe-in-ye had explained that the elders held a special meeting and ordered Sen-tshe to give the baby to Lo-nun, his sister-in-law. The night after hearing those orders he had disappeared with the infant. He was gone for nearly two months, returning with the baby strapped to his back and never saying a word to anyone. But he hadn't moved back into his rooms. He spent his days in the village, but each night he disappeared down the canyon. No one had enforced the mandate that the child go to live with relatives and Sen-tshe worked in the fields, hunted and even danced with the child on his back. No one had ever cared for the baby other than Sen-tshe.

Two days later when Martha crawled out of her sleeping cave Kwe-in-ye stopped her from gathering the basket she kept for carrying things out to teach.

"Today we go to the big river. You will not be teaching."

"But I promised the children we would—"

The old woman didn't let her finish. "The children go too. Everyone except those who cannot walk will go."

Thirty minutes later they were walking in a long line down a narrow trail. People carried every possible container—clay jugs, pouches of tightly sewn skins, baskets—strapped to backs and hips and looped over shoulders. Martha realized that they were headed down to the Rio Grande.

The sun had yet to reach the trail and frost covered the rocks. Although spring was approaching—she could see the tops of new plants breaking through the soil—Martha shivered and stepped cautiously, grateful that the large group moved slowly. Within a few minutes she could see the tops of trees below them. If this approach was as steep as what she could see, the last part of this journey was going to be quite a test.

The trip didn't take as long as she thought it would. Less than two hours, according to her watch. She hadn't been able to give up her habit of checking the time, but one of these days her battery would fail and she would have to adjust. But on a day like today she wanted to know how long it took them to get to the river because it would give her an idea of how long it would take to get back.

As they reached the small beach next to the swiftly moving water, Martha felt a surge of doubt. Surely this river didn't dry up during the summer? If they could walk here today, why couldn't they come for water at the end of summer?

"Mar-tee-ya." To-be-né ran to her. "Come, come. We…" The girl stopped and tugged on Martha's sleeve. A smile burst on to her lips. "We wash."

Sure enough, the men and women were stepping into the eddies along the shore where the current was slower. They splashed and called out from the cold, quickly dunking their heads and rinsing their hair. Children were carried into the water, squealing and laughing as parents stripped off their clothes and washed those as well.

As Martha followed To-be-né she noticed that once the children were bathed, the men and women removed their own clothes and washed those too. When everything was clean they spread their clothing to dry in the sun. She was surprised by their nakedness because no one had walked around in a state of undress in all the months she had been here. Yet on this day it seemed natural to them. They went about the tasks of filling all the pots and leather bags with water, feeding snacks to the children, and lying on the banks of the river.

I'm not stripping. She would bathe in her clothes and let them dry on her body. But after she had joined To-be-né, rubbing the girl's hair as well as her own, Martha had to reconsider. The water was very cold and she was in and out as quickly as possible. Her dress sagged and clung to her body, the wet cotton completely transparent. Shivering from the wet cloth, she realized modesty had no place in this world.

"Let's go over there to dry." She pointed off to the edge of the group at a small clearing surrounded by bushes. To-be-né followed her and they removed their dresses and draped them over the branches of the brush. There were tiny thorns on the bushes and Martha was careful not to snag her dress. She found a smooth boulder and lay down on her stomach, folding her arms under her head and closing her eyes. She smiled at the ridiculous feeling that if she couldn't see anyone, they couldn't see her.

Something tickled her cheek and Martha reached up to brush away her unwanted guest. "Po-ko, you scamp."

"Hel-lo, Mar-tee-a."

She turned at the sound of Sen-tshe's voice, forgetting her nakedness as she sat up. He was sans clothing, and her face was level with his—

"Oh!" Martha twisted and grabbed her dress from the bush. "Oh no," she cried out as the branches snagged at the loose cotton. Ignoring the man the best she could Martha stood and carefully lifted the garment off the bush, then slipped it over her head and tugged it down around her hips. Only then did she turn back to Sen-tshe.

He stood without shame, Wi-yen balanced on his hip. Although she usually avoided looking directly into his eyes, this was different. She locked her gaze on his face.

"You startled me."

"Star-told?" He raised his eyebrows.

"Yes. It means you surprised me. Not scared, not frightened."

He shook his head.

"Pa." Wi-yen grabbed his father's ear.

Sen-tshe grinned. "Wi-yen, he…" He pinched his lips together and one side of his mouth curled down as he searched for the word. With a shrug he backed up several steps and set the baby on the grass, holding his shoulders and balancing him.

Martha glanced at the baby, then looked back at Sen-tshe's face.

This was only the third man she had seen naked. Glen had been the second. He had been her first sexual encounter. But when she was twelve years old, selling Girl Scout cookies to unwilling neighbors, Mr. Barstow had answered her knock completely nude. She had run home, gasping out her devastation to her mother.

"He's a drunk. Don't go there again." That had been her mother's only response.

Two naked men and now a third.

"Mar-tee-ya, look, look." To-be-né clapped her hands.

Martha kept her gaze high, avoiding looking anywhere near Sen-tshe's hips, but a movement near the ground caught her attention. "He's walking!" she cried out just as Wi-yen fell back onto his plump bottom.

To-be-né ran to the baby and stood him up. His wide grin showed off three teeth and he toddled toward Martha. She crouched and held out her arms. When he made it to her she scooped him up and hugged him.

"Wi-yen walking." Sen-tshe smiled and nodded.

Martha smiled back and was suddenly overcome with emotion. This was the moment usually shared between parents and this man had come to her. He not only didn't have a wife at his side to care for his child, he had no family to fill in. The way these people banished him for not following the council's directives wasn't fair.

"Shall we have some lunch?" She motioned toward the small pouch sitting on the rock.

"Yes, Mar-tee-a. I will bring my food." He turned and walked back toward the river.

She watched him walk away, wondering why it didn't feel as invasive to admire the smooth skin of his buttocks. Maybe he would get dressed before he returned. Her dress was still quite damp and a bit uncomfortable. She held Wi-yen and watched his father pick up the cradleboard and a drawstring pouch, then turn and make his way back to them.

She turned to To-be-né. "Let's set up our picnic on this rock." If they sat, maybe it would be easier to avoid looking directly at Sen-tshe.

Her plan halfway worked. He sat and held Wi-yen in his lap, feeding the baby small bits of soft food. To-be-né stayed for a few minutes, ate quickly, then ran off to join the other children. They were warm enough now to go back into the water for games, splashing and laughing.

"Sen-tshe, why don't the people get water from this river when they run out?"

"We get water here." He nodded and pointed to the large collection of clay pots.

"Yes. And during the hot times, summer, do you come for water?"

He shook his head. "It is small."

"This big river dries up?"

"No. The part we carry. It is not big. For the hot times, we need more water for the people and the plants."

She was pleased with his effort to speak to her and impressed with his skill.

"So, it is not enough water?"

Wi-yen had fallen asleep in his father's lap, effectively blocking the view. As they talked she studied Sen-tshe's chest. He did not have much body hair and his muscles were clearly defined. Lean, but muscular. A tiny scar streaked across his chest like the tail of a shooting star.

A tingling sensation which started on the roof of her mouth traveled over her tongue and onto her lips. With a flush of shame, Martha realized she wanted to kiss him. The feeling dropped from her mouth down to her breasts and quickly dove to a warmth between her legs: she was completely aroused.

Their conversation had stopped. She stared into his eyes, unable to move or pull her gaze away or think of anything other than the way his odor was filling her head. He raised his hand to touch her cheek, and all she could think about was his face coming closer and his lips on hers.

"Mar-tee-a." Kwe-in-ye's voice shattered the moment as if she had physically slapped Martha.

Sen-tshe jumped up, scooping the sleeping baby with such a jerk that Wi-yen awoke with a cry. Without a word he grabbed the cradleboard and his pack and rushed away.

Martha watched him go, unwilling to break the spell of the moment. But Kwe-in-ye wasn't about to let her have this gift.

"Mar-tee-a, you must not do this thing." Then the old woman turned and walked away, as if her word was law and a simple sentence would drive the warmth from Martha forever.

Not this time.

TWENTY-FIVE

"**D**ad. You're not looking, Dad. I made it for Grandma." Sara's insistent voice pierced through Vince's thoughts.

"Nice. She'll love it."

"But she can't really see it, can she?"

"She knows, Sara. She knows you're there." Reassuring himself as he reassured his daughter.

Did his mother know? She had seemed ready to wake up, with her mumblings and moving and asking for things. But so much time had passed and even with the new tests Dad requested all the doctor would say was that he couldn't find a reason for the state she was in. Not anything as understandable as catatonia or a fugue state.

"Are you going for a bike ride today?" Sandra held Sam, who was squirming and hollering.

Vince reached out for the boy. "Why is my sister insisting that Mom should die? That's what I want to know."

Sandra frowned and shook her head, rolling her eyes toward Sara.

"Sorry." He lifted Sam up in the air and smiled. "What's with all this ruckus?"

"How about a snack for these two?" His wife turned to him, that knowing look on her face.

"A-okay, right?" He scooped up Sara with his other arm—not easy because these two were getting big—and headed to the kitchen.

When the kids were seated just outside the slider on the deck, crunchy carrot sticks and hummus dip the focus of their attention, Sandra motioned to the kitchen table.

Vince hugged his wife and slid into the chair. "Thanks. I'm just anxious today, I guess. I keep thinking about my mother and how Clarice is behaving. I just don't get this thing about acting like we can pull the plug. Doesn't my sister get that there is no plug? She thinks because we lift a spoon to Mom's mouth, that's life support. As if we should just let her starve to death."

Sandra nodded. "I think…it's complicated. Clarice and Martha… their relationship isn't like yours Vince."

"I know that, but no one can say that my mother wasn't a good parent. In this day and age? A mother that stayed home and made sure we had everything?"

"But that's just it. Clarice wants to be—she is—a strong woman. She views Martha as weak for staying home."

"Mom has told her a million times that she's happy with her life."

"I know that. But from what I've heard—what you have told me— things weren't easy for Clarice. You know, Vince, it sounds weird, but you really are your mother's favorite. I don't think Clarice or Jack had it so easy."

"That's just not true."

Sandra gave him the did-you-just-speak-without-thinking look she had.

He stopped and thought about his mother. Mom had read to him, set up science projects, taken him to parades, parks, zoos, museums, and made sure he invited friends over to play several times a week. She had dressed him with care and never fussed when his jeans were torn from an adventure. She had done the same for Clarice and Jack.

Hadn't she?

More memories came to mind. Clarice slamming doors and screaming. Dresses pressed and ready for a party or a dance, flung out into the hall. Shiny patent leather shoes hurled out the back door, Clarice shouting that she wasn't going to whatever event Martha had planned. His sister had been a bit of a tomboy—she trailed after him and tried to do everything he did—and his mother had worked hard to make sure Clarice remembered she was a girl.

"Mom was just trying to do what was best for Clarice, you know. Make sure she had a bit of a feminine side. And friends. My sister didn't want any friends and Mom knew that would be a bad thing."

"Hmm…I'm not sure Clarice would see it that way. She had friends, just not the ones your mother wanted her to have."

"Come on, you know how my sister is…she isn't even friends with you."

"We talk. She's come around. I think now that we've been married so long she thinks she can help me. You know, to not turn out like Martha. Not be just a 'stay-at-home' mother." Sandra grinned.

Vince tried to smile in return, but he wasn't up to his wife's gentle teasing. "It's not just Clarice. It's Dad too. He's still so depressed. I thought Jack being there would help—and I have to say it is keeping him busy. But the two of them? All that remodeling? I can't think that Mom is going to be happy that her house was torn apart while she was…gone for a while."

"I'm kind of worried about that, too. Moving the bed and making the bathroom bigger was one thing. But the rest of it? They do seem a bit out of control." Sandra reached for his hand. "Is the anxiety bad again?"

Vince shook his head. "Not too bad. But I can feel it coming. I sleep, but I don't wake up rested. And my heart seems to be on overdrive all the time."

"Let's make time for what you need. I don't want this taking over."

He heard the silent "again" at the end of her sentence. He didn't want that either. Panic attacks were no joke. Sandra had been through it with him right after Sara was born. At a time when he should have been helping her, she was helping him. She went with him to the therapy sessions—nursing baby in tow—and listened to everything the psychologist suggested. Sandra downloaded the meditation tapes and made sure he practiced every day. His wife's calm presence had been what cured him, of that he was sure.

"I don't have time for this crap." Vince sighed and dropped his head.

"We'll make time. I know you think you have to visit Martha every day, but just for now, how about making some time for what you need? A bike ride? Weren't you going to go today?"

"I was, but then I decided to go visit Mom instead and I'm thinking you might have asked me to watch the kids this morning?" A wave of guilt flashed over him as he realized he couldn't remember just what Sandra had planned. "I'm sorry. I know you get pushed to the end of the line and that's not fair. It's not fair or right."

She squeezed his hand. "I'm okay. I know it's only temporary."

"I'll watch the kids so you can—" he shrugged, "you can go to the..."

Sandra laughed. "I was just going to go get my hair cut. No biggie. I think this is the perfect morning for a bike ride."

As Vince pedaled hard up the incline near the river, he thought about his life. If his anxiety returned he wouldn't be of any help to anyone. The kids were old enough now that seeing their father have a panic attack would impact them. He wouldn't let his kids witness this kind of weakness.

He rose from the seat and pushed down hard on the pedals, racing uphill as if his life depended on it.

TWENTY-SIX

Glen scooped up the thin gruel and held it to Martha's lips. There was no response. His hand shook and the gruel spilled onto the cotton bib he had placed over her chest.

Martha was getting worse. For months she had seemed so close to waking up. Her mumbled requests, her chewing and swallowing the food —they brought her favorites—and her rapidly moving eyes and hands, these were the things that kept him and the kids optimistic. *She'll be coming home soon* was the unspoken mantra that ran through his head.

All that, then suddenly she had gone away again. Since February his wife had been very still. She didn't open her mouth, her eyes barely moved, and she never spoke. Not even a mumble to ask for more things.

Dr. Braundo's latest report was depressing. "Mr. Grimson, I'm sorry but if she doesn't improve we are going to have to move her to a more intensive placement. She'll need supplemental nutrition if she can't eat."

Clarice had told the story of Martha not wanting any artificial life support so many times that Glen had begun to believe it. How could he refuse the nasal tube when he knew Martha was still in there? All her mumbled requests had been for the things she loved to do the best: sewing, painting, her glasses. She probably had found something good to read wherever she was.

"Morning Mr. Grimson. Doesn't look like Martha's with us this morning." He hadn't heard Naomi enter and her voice startled him. He tipped the bowl and the entire contents slopped over the edge, splattering down onto Martha's chest.

"Damn!"

"I'm sorry. I caught you by surprise. Here, no problem, these bibs work great." Naomi set down the papers and a book she was holding, grabbed the corners of the bib and folded it into a neat container for the spilled gruel. She smoothed Martha's gown, checking for any damp spots, then pulled the sheet up and tucked it under Martha's arms. She lifted each limp hand gently, as if judging what a comfortable position would be, then placed them over Martha's stomach, the right atop the left.

"I'm worried."

"I'm worried, too." Naomi paused and pulled up the other chair next to Glen, resting her hand on Martha's arm. "In fact, I want to talk to you about something."

Glen had grown to know Naomi. She never seemed in a hurry like the other nurses, always taking time to talk and sing to Martha and spending many hours talking with Glen. While he shared stories of his life with Martha, Naomi shared stories of her past. Glen knew that she had grown up on the *Po-Woh-Geh-Owingeh* pueblo in New Mexico. Not all times had been easy, but her parents valued education, so Naomi had been encouraged to pick a career path at a young age. She had accelerated her education with online study, graduating from high school at age fifteen. She had known from a young age that she wanted to go into the medical profession, and had considered being a doctor. Once she started working with people, though, she knew that nursing was her calling, because she liked the personal relationships she could establish with each person, coming to see them day after day. If she had been a doctor she would have been unable to deliver this kind of ongoing care.

"What I have to say is going to take…some trust, I guess. You trust me, right?"

Glen did trust this kind-hearted young woman. "Go ahead."

"My family still follows many old beliefs. There is a rich heritage of rituals for everything—growing crops, rain, healing, birth, marriage, death. From the first time I met Martha I felt a deep connection. I have listened to her mumbling and I swear, at times she's speaking in the language of my pueblo. It's not exactly like mine, but there are strong similarities." Naomi reached for his hand and clasped it between her palms. "There are ancient stories which tell of people who came from another place to help my ancestors in times of crisis. I know this sounds kind of crazy, but what if Martha is one of those people? What if she is on a journey to ancient times?"

Glen considered this theory. It didn't sit well with him at all. Some sort of hocus pocus, native or not. It was as if Naomi had become a member of the family by being so attached to Martha. She needed a theory now too, something to explain why Martha wouldn't snap out of this unconscious state. Glen sighed. He already had to take care of Vince and Clarice and their constantly changing emotions. Jack was easier, but still...he had moved in. Add Naomi to the list of people looking for answers.

That wasn't fair. She was trying to help. He squeezed her hands between his own.

"I know you care for Martha deeply," he started.

Naomi interrupted. "Look at what she has asked for: glasses, needles, thread, pliers, aspirin. All of them useful things for survival, yes, but paint? Blue paint? And beads?"

Naomi pulled her hands away from his, stood and walked over to the dresser where she had set down the papers and the book. She returned to the chair, opened the book to a page marked with a yellow sticky note.

"I found this. These are pictures of the petroglyphs found in the ruins near my home." She turned the book toward him.

There were photos of rock walls covered with familiar spirals and simple figures. Glen recognized a turkey and a pronghorn.

Naomi tapped the picture in the lower right hand corner of the page. "Look at this one."

This ancient drawing was completely different from the others. A strip of squares held a series of figures, like a comic strip.

Naomi tapped again. "Look at this one. This is a woman with a dress and boots, fingers on her hands and little stars or flowers or something decorating her dress. Like a print fabric." She slid her finger to the next box. "And this one, three men, they look angry."

Glen examined the photo. He didn't see what Naomi described. The pictures were faint and her imagination was strong.

"But this one, it's the one. Look at this. It's something from the sky. It's taking the baby up and the people are sad."

He shook his head. "So what does that have to do with Martha?"

"I think these people are traveling to another place."

He looked over at his wife, then back at Naomi. "I don't understand."

"There's more." Naomi turned to the next sticky note and held out the book.

This page had photos of clothing. Glen saw the loosely woven skirts —loincloths, he guessed—and other clothing he had seen in the Visitor's Center and museums in New Mexico.

Naomi pointed to the photo in the center of the page. "Listen to this." She turned the book back and read aloud. *"In 1952 archeologists discovered a sealed Kiva in Area 3. It had been buried under a rockslide in what appeared to be a ceremonial cave. This find was considered the decade's most valuable discovery because the items within the kiva were well preserved, most likely due to the dry, sealed nature of the kiva. Among the tools and pottery was a collection of clothing incomparable to any other. The cotton dresses had set-in sleeves and finely embroidered designs which included tiny glass beads."* She paused and Glen shook his head. *"Scientific methods for dating these items were unclear. Although it appeared they were of the archaic time period, they were unlike anything ever discovered previously. 'It's almost as if some time traveler brought these things as a gift,' Dr. Baker said, when questioned about the provenance."*

Naomi lowered the book and raised her eyebrows.

"You can't believe that Martha traveled back in time. To this exact place, no less." Glen turned away, unable to meet the hopeful stare of the young woman.

"This place, these ruins, they are close to my home. The same ruins which you were visiting when Martha...went away. The ruins where these paintings were in a cave and this clothing was found." Naomi sat perfectly still, but Glen noticed her hands were trembling. They were both silent.

"It couldn't be, it just couldn't be." His voice came out in a whisper.

"Here's what I want to do. Just listen to me." She jumped up from the chair, leaving Glen holding the book. She paced, waving her hands around.

"There is an ancient healing ceremony. It was used for people who were very ill, going to die, but the goal was to bring them back by reminding them of all they had in this world. The theory was they were being called to the other world by the departed, a strong call if they had loved ones who had died. It was kind of a contest—we love you more so stay with us." She stood in front of him. "What if we perform that ceremony with Martha? Convince her that there is more for her here than in this other world? She's slipping into that world. The way she was talking to us? Only asking for things she needed there. Now that she has them, she's staying there and we need to keep her from remaining there for good. What could it hurt, Mr. Grimson? What could it hurt?"

This was so far-fetched. Crazy as could be. The only ceremony that would be happening for Martha was her memorial service.

Oh God, why did he think that? Wasn't it better to have a ceremony now, something that made the family and this caring nurse feel like he was willing to do everything for his wife?

"What is the ceremony?"

"We need everyone in the family to participate. My uncle will come, he knows the words to the chant. He knows it in Tewa, it's similar to the ancient words. It involves drumming and dancing, some symbolic feathers and beads. Family members will need to have her favorite objects to offer. I think the grandkids will be especially strong, so have them bring something that represents a good moment they had with Martha."

"The hospital won't mind all of this?"

She was silent and for once her gaze didn't meet his. She turned her head to the window and licked her lips.

"I can't ask for it. I already do things differently than this hospital likes."

"But if I ask for it?"

"Would you? I know it's a risk for you, getting the family to do it. Their reaction might be…less than positive."

"What risk? I'm an old man now, and without Martha I'm even older. It's time to change how this family operates."

TWENTY-SEVEN

Kwe-in-ye was using the not-subtle-at-all strategy of keeping Martha too busy to seek out Sen-tshe. Since the trip to the river the old woman had sent Martha up to the mesa to help with the planting, kept her inside one of the rooftop apartments to learn to make sandals, and taken her on an overnight trip to a nearby village. All these things were fascinating, but Martha missed Sen-tshe and, admittedly like a teenager with a crush, she couldn't stop thinking about him. The two of them had hiked back from the river side by side that day, trailing the slowest people. Sen-tshe had done his best to point out landmarks, to explain how hunting had changed with the drought, to talk of the times in his grandfather's life that there had been excess rain and his hope that this type of weather would return, although flooding presented its own problems. He asked her about her life. As they chatted she was able to look at him in a different light. Any vestiges of the brutal killing of the deer disappeared as she learned he truly had a gentle spirit.

This morning, Martha was barely out of bed when Kwe-in-ye started in. "Today we climb to the second kiva. It will take all day so bring food and water." Kwe-in-ye looked at Po-ko. "Don't bring the dog."

"Where is the second kiva?" Martha remembered the high cave and the closed-off buildings. There had been the small, walled off kiva there. Although she could climb to the doorways and caves now, she really had no desire to return to that particular cave again.

"On the second mesa." Kwe-in-ye pointed to the southern wall of the canyon, the side with no living quarters because it faced north and held the snow and shade much longer than the other wall.

Martha collected what she needed and joined the old woman. She wished for her sheepskin slippers, but in spite of many attempts to find them, their whereabouts remained a mystery. She tightened her sandals around her ankles and considered asking for some of the deerskin moccasins she had seen Mosinobu wear. She had never seen a woman wearing them and hadn't yet figured out who had the status for such footwear.

Kwe-in-ye led her to the edge of a landslide with boulders that ranged from the size of a meatloaf to the size of a Volkswagen. The old woman climbed straight up the tumble of rocks, hand over hand. Martha followed but was soon out of breath. She stopped and sat on a midsize rock, wiping her palms on her dress and allowing herself a tiny sip of water from the leather bag she carried. She looked at the mountain and realized they were not even a quarter of the way to the top. She rose and caught up with Kwe-in-ye, who had also stopped to rest.

"So tell me the truth. Is the second kiva really important to my lessons or are you doing this to keep me away from Sen-tshe? Because if you are, number one, it won't work and number two, this climb is too hard without a very good reason."

Kwe-in-ye stared across the canyon. They were above the tops of the trees, looking straight into the caves above their rooms. She licked her lips and mumbled something, then turned to Martha. "It is important for you to visit the second kiva and the second mesa, and also I do not want you to be with Sen-tshe."

"Why?"

"These are places the people used to live, but no longer can we live there. I want you to see what will happen to all of us before long. The end of this corn season, I think."

"Fine, but that's not what I was asking. Why don't you want me to be with Sen-tshe?"

"He is a distraction. With your mind on a man you will not move toward your goals."

Don't you mean your goals? Martha thought. She didn't want to fight with Kwe-in-ye, but she wasn't going to give in so easily.

"There is something we have learned in my time, something I think would be useful for you to know. When people are happy they do better. They work more efficiently and they reach their goals sooner." Martha reached out and touched Kwe-in-ye's wrist. "I promise you that my friendship with anyone—To-be-né, Yo-en-u, or Sen-tshe, will not distract me from my job here. In fact, there is something that tells me I need to be near Wi-yen. I felt it the first time I met him."

"The baby? How does the baby fit in?"

"I don't know, but I will find out." Martha smiled. "So you see, it won't do for you to put all these obstacles in my way. That will keep me from making progress more than anything."

"I will think about what you have told me, Mar-tee-a." Her guide nodded slightly and stood. "But we still have to climb to the second mesa."

The two women walked through the ruined farmlands and abandoned houses, with Kwe-in-ye pointing out the grave sites surrounding the kiva, explaining how first the oldest had died, then the babies as their mothers no longer had milk, then the men who had double the workload, hauling water from the big river to save the dried crops, until finally the small group had asked if they could move into the canyon. This is what was happening to people all over the region, the old woman explained. This was why Martha must help them.

A boom of thunder shook the earth.

"Rain!" Martha looked up at the dark sky. "It's going to rain."

Kwe-in-ye shook her head and pointed north. "The thunder gods are trying but the earth pushes them away."

Martha looked toward the mountains surrounding their canyon. She could see the slanting pale lines of rain against the black clouds. They didn't seem that far away.

She recognized this storm, like those she and Glen had seen during their drive from Arizona to New Mexico. Rain that vaporized in the hot air high above the desert. Rain that never reached the ground. For a moment she had been thrilled, thinking the weather had changed and she was released from her obligation of figuring out how to save the people. But that hope evaporated, just like the moisture that would never find its way to the people.

The next day Kwe-in-ye must have considered Martha's plea because she sent her back to the fire circle to work on language with the children. When the lessons were completed Martha slipped away to search for Sen-tshe. Po-ko was basking near the upper trail.

"Hey girl. Come here." She snapped her fingers.

The dog ran to her, jumping with the joy of finding a long lost friend.

"Where's your master?"

With a yip the dog turned and ran up the trail. Martha was astonished the dog knew what she wanted and started after her.

Po-ko picked up a stick and ran back to her, dropping the prize at her feet.

"Oh. Good girl, but that's not what I wanted."

Po-ko wagged her tail harder.

"Mar-tee-a. You are here."

She turned and there he was, Wi-yen strapped to his back, both faces smiling and her heart pounding at the sight. She nodded, speechless because all she wanted to do was throw her arms around them. She took a step forward and reached out, imagining the warmth of his embrace.

He took her hand in both of his and clasped it out in front of his body, effectively keeping her at a distance.

Had she misunderstood? Doubts swarmed like angry bees. Was it all in her imagination? The interrupted kiss, the sensual aura, the look on his face?

She should be angry with him, but she knew that there was something between them—there had been from that very first day.

She was lonely. She had come to believe that life in this canyon was no longer temporary—this *was* her life now. She still thought about Glen and the kids, missed them tremendously, but there were times when days passed without a thought of them at all.

Sen-tshe let go of her hand and touched her cheek. Martha opened her eyes and met his gaze. When she sat close to him she could make out the pupils, but his eyes were so dark they pulled her into a space she could only describe as spiritual. As if there were a whole different world in the mind of this man, tucked behind that gaze.

Suddenly he reached up and pulled the cradleboard off his back. He untied the leather straps and pulled the baby from the frame.

Martha reached out and the boy wrapped his arms around her neck and nuzzled her cheek. She kissed his dark hair, warm from the sun, and smiled at Sen-tshe.

Sen-tshe leaned forward and wrapped his arms around the two of them. The embrace was not the one she had imagined. It wasn't the rapture of a lover, it held only the stability of a friend.

What had she been thinking?

"Sen-tshe." She pulled away from his hug.

"Mar-tee-a. You come with me." He took Wi-yen and slipped the boy back onto the cradleboard, hoisted him onto his back and took her hand.

Martha didn't know where Sen-tshe lived. He always melted away as silently as the coyotes and bobcats she had chanced to glimpse. Kwe-in-ye said he lived down the canyon, but she knew there weren't any of the stone shelters farther down that way and the only cave she had seen was high on the cliff.

Sen-tshe led her down the trail toward the big river. They passed the cave she had seen before, then turned and walked straight into a high wall. What she hadn't been able to see was a narrow canyon, merely a slot between the walls. The path diminished, and the walls of the canyon were close. Just beyond the bend Sen-tshe stopped. He pointed to her feet and then his own, then turned and stepped on stones which seemed natural on first glance. As she followed Martha realized he was purposefully keeping from bending grass or plants.

Keeping the entrance to his home hidden.

Very hidden, because when they reached the wall of rock on the edge of the canyon he stepped up on a tree that had fallen against the wall at an angle, the top hidden behind the branches of the trees which grew thick here. He turned and reached for her hand.

Climbing. Again. Although she had grown used to going up and down the small walls of the long house and the storage caves, it still required total focus and a deep breath.

"Mar-tee-a, you do this." Sen-tshe tugged at her hand. "Please."

Martha stood below the log and thought about this man. She liked watching him work, always completely absorbed in what he was doing. While most of the men gathered in groups, he set off alone. It seemed to her that he avoided interaction with the people, except for the time he spent with the children. They in turn, followed him around, talking to Wi-yen and making him laugh with their antics. She saw a man who grieved for his wife, stood up against the elders, and was starting to enjoy life again. She had come to accept the killing of the deer as necessary, although she still pushed it from her mind.

Now he stood, gazing at her without blinking. She kept her eyes on his, not turning away, although she did blush. Her mouth and lips were dry and she licked them before she spoke.

"I mean, it's no problem. I like children, I raised three of my own. I know how to watch a baby." Sen-tshe must see her as an old aunt or something, caring for her because he worried she couldn't take care of herself.

He reached out and ran his finger from her ear to her chin. "Come."

Martha nodded and pulled herself up onto the log. He tried to turn and help her by holding her hand, but this felt unstable so she pulled away and held onto the bark and small branches. Sen-tshe nodded and moved up.

When they reached the part of the tree that was too small to support their weight he turned back to her and smiled. Then he pointed higher. Martha could see the tiny hand and foot holds that served the best climbers. She looked back down to the spot where Po-ko stood, her tail waving.

He went slowly, showing her where to place her hands, how to shift her weight and how to keep her center of gravity parallel to the wall. When her hands trembled he spoke to her softly, in his language, not hers. But the words comforted her and soon the tremors subsided. It really wasn't far to the cave hidden in this wall of stone.

He untied the leather straps holding the cradleboard to his back. He swung the board around and set it on the floor. Wi-yen held his arms out to his father. Sen-tshe loosened the swaddling and lifted the boy out.

Wi-yen settled onto the ground in a placid sitting position. He gurgled and jabbered. "*Pa pa pa pa.*"

Martha liked the sounds he was making, happy as his bright eyes watched his father walk away.

"Mar-tee-a. I will be back when the sun is setting."

TWENTY-EIGHT

Jack looked down the hall before slipping into his mother's room and shutting the door. He knew that Dad and the others wouldn't visit at ten o'clock in the morning and he was pretty sure Naomi was on night shift this week. He took off his jacket and hung it on the hook by the bathroom, then scooted the ugly vinyl chair over to the right side of the bed. The left side was by the window and he always felt like he would just be a silhouette against the bright sun if Mom should happen to open her eyes while he was here.

"Hey Mom, how's it going today?" He lifted her hand from its limp position next to her thigh and held it between his palms. So cold. Even with the temperature high in the care home the lack of movement left her with no circulation. His mother got a medical massage every day, but Naomi had shown the family how they could help. He gently rubbed each of her fingers, starting at the tip and working toward her palm.

He eyed the door once more before he started talking.

"So this has been a pretty good week, Mom. No super stress, no urges, no setbacks. Dad and I finished the bathroom and we started on the kitchen." Jack laughed. "I hope Dad knows what he's doing. I was okay with the bathroom, that's pretty generic, but the kitchen? I hope you like Neapolitan. Not the ice cream, the style."

Mom never moved and her hand felt colder. Jack sighed and looked away from his mother's face. If only he had been a better son. If the two of them could have talked in real life maybe he would be able to think of more to say to her now.

"I'm sorry. I know I wasn't the easiest kid. But it's all good now." Would she think all the money she and Dad had spent on his rehab and the interventions and the unpaid loans was worth it? He wasn't ever going to be a Vince or a Clarice, no way he wanted to be like them, but he knew that being under the influence of, well, all the things he had been under the influence of, wasn't the way to go. That last time had been the worst and his parents didn't know about that one. Thank goodness Paige had been around to scrape him up and put him back together.

"All that stuff, Mom, it wasn't wasted, I promise. I know you didn't want to do it, but I'm glad you know how to do the right thing, no matter how big a screw up your kid is." He remembered the look on her face the first time she had to come to the police station—not the first time he was arrested, just the first time no one could get in touch with Dad. Jack had always suspected he was the least-favored child, but the pale, quivering grimace she wore as she signed the paperwork and passed over the bail check was the first time he realized she hated him.

"I learned about love at the last place, Mom. About how we're just biological beings and sometimes we can't control how we feel, but we can control how we react. It was a good thing for me to learn because, you know…because of how you feel about me." Jack dropped her hand and jumped out of the chair. What a fucking idiot he was. Having a heart-to-heart with his mother's body. Telling her things he hadn't told the therapists he respected or liked. He paced across the room and stared out the window.

Breathe, brother, breathe. You can't afford to let yourself get into any kind of state. He had to remember he wasn't here for himself, he was here for his mother. He walked back over to the chair and sat. The harsh complaint of the vinyl reminded him of every hospital waiting room he had ever been in. And there had been plenty.

"Okay, sorry Mom. Just a little backslide. Let's talk about something else, shall we? How about the weather? Or maybe those Astros…what a season." He kept his eyes focused on the tented blankets raised above her feet. He had watched Naomi carefully place the contraption over Martha's lower legs and pull the clean sheet over it. Apparently the sheet touching those immobile toes caused bed sores. He shifted and the little notebook in his pocket brushed against his hip.

"You'll like this, Mom. I write poetry now. And I keep a journal, just like Clarice did with that blue diary. You remember? I read it. Did you? Were you the kind of mother who snooped on all her children or just the bad kid?" Jack imagined Clarice's reaction if she had caught Mom reading her diary. Not that there was ever anything very exciting in it. No, it wasn't likely that his mother had invaded his sister's privacy. And Mom probably hadn't wanted to search his room, but what choice did she have? He wasn't remorseful when he got caught and she knew he would sneak pot into the house whenever he could.

"So, Mom. I'll read you something I wrote." He slipped the notebook out and flipped through the pages.

"Dark. Crimson. Colors don't tell the story. I want to write you the novel of my life but I can't remember how to spell the words. Tell me your story using sign language." He looked at his mother's face.

"Nice, right? Do you want to hear another one? No? Not right now? You have a headache? Jack, just be quiet for a little while? That poem sucks? Clarice would write a better one?"

Fuck. He had gone from whining to harsh sarcasm. Nice going, dude.

"I'm sorry, Mom. I really am. How about this? You'll never have to do anything for me again, not one little thing. And I'll do things for you, lots of things. I'm grown up now and it's my turn to take charge. No more doing just because I'm your kid, I'll do because you're my mother. But for this deal to work you have to open your eyes. You have to wake up from wherever you are." He slapped the notebook against the palm of his hand, as if the noise would rouse his mother. "Right. Tell you what, I'll leave this here and you can write down your answer. You know, in the night when you wake up and use all those things you ask for." He slipped the notebook into the bottom of the basket that held the needles, the glasses, the blue paint, beads, aspirin, a compass—that one made sense if she was lost—and a stack of drawings from Sara.

He reached back into the basket and took out his book. Flipping to the end he pulled a pen out of his shirt pocket. He wrote in the book, then closed it, and clipped the pen tab over a few pages to hold it in place. He reached over and patted his mother's hand.

"I'll put this pen in with it, you know, because you'll probably need that too."

TWENTY-NINE

Wi-yen stirred next to her. If she didn't get up soon the warm urine of the now-awake baby would soak through the cloth she had wrapped tightly around him last night. The mornings were warmer now that it was spring. She chided herself once more for not keeping track of time. The corn plants were over a foot tall and tender green shoots poked up through the loose dirt under the trees in the sunny parts of the canyon, but that didn't tell her much, other than the general idea that winter was finally ending. New plants grew later in the higher elevations, and fool that she was, she didn't even know how high she was situated. The high desert...that much she knew. But how high?

"Hey little Wi. How are you today? Ready to brave the cold?" She touched the boy's soft cheek and stretched her legs.

She no longer felt strange waking up in Sen-tshe's cave. Kwe-in-ye had been very unhappy when she told her she was moving.

"You must convince him to give the baby to Lo-nun. She will watch him. She has three children of her own."

"You don't understand. I...need to do this. I..." How did she explain to Kwe-in-ye that holding this baby made her feel better than she had in years?

Martha knew that holding Wi-yen was her chance to make up for setting Jack down whenever he fussed.

"It is too far. I need you here. The time will come when you must follow the directions of the spirits. I can feel it. Each night the coyote comes to me and whispers that this is true."

How could she convince Kwe-in-ye, stubborn old woman, that she really wasn't the one to save them?

"Okay. I'll move there and then I'll convince him we must come back here, to these rooms." Martha pointed to the long row of rooms built at the base of the cliff. "Not with you, but near you. There are some empty spots."

Kwe-in-ye scowled. "You are wrong to do this."

"Why? Why is it so wrong?"

"The people are not happy with Sen-tshe. They still work to forgive him. They will see you as a bad spirit if you go to him."

"Yet they know it is just for the baby. Remind them I have a husband and I'm old enough to be Sen-tshe's mother." Martha didn't really believe she was old enough to be his mother, since she had no clue how old he was. He seemed older than Vince, and she had been only twenty-three when she had her first child.

She had been living here for weeks and hadn't even tried to convince Sen-tshe to move. Kwe-in-ye reminded her whenever she had a chance, growing more impatient with Martha's delays.

Today, with spring here and new buds and the sun moving higher in the sky, leaving its southerly sweep, this would be the day she would bring it up to him.

She pushed herself to her knees and moved Wi-yen out from under the warm skins that covered the two of them. As she unwound the cloth from the baby she glanced over to where his father slept each night. She didn't expect him to be there, as Sen-tshe was always out before the sun had reached the cave.

Martha wasn't exactly sure what he did every day. His role in the village was hunter, she knew that. But he also walked the trails and the empty south rim for hours. Sometimes he invited her to come with him, strapping the cradleboard to his own back and keeping his pace slow so that she could follow him. Whenever he stopped for her to rest he scanned the walls of the canyon opposite or peered down the long valley. It was as if he would outwardly pretend all was well, but he sensed danger coming.

As Martha straightened the sleeping mat and skins she was surprised to see a small green notebook next to the mat. She hadn't dreamed or wished for things since moving in with Sen-tshe. When she picked up the book a pen fell out.

"What have we here?" she jabbered to Wi-yen. His green eyes watched her every move, but she knew he was just waiting for the chance to run away from her. She scooped him onto her lap while she looked at the book.

Inside the front cover was the cramped squiggle of her youngest son. This book belonged to Jack. She read the first entry.

Time. Races. Stands still. Runs out.
Now is the time.
Time's up.
When will you have time for me?

The second page was slightly wrinkled, with a brown stain in the corner. Her son must have written this poem while drinking coffee. There were no dates but the content suggested he had started this journal around the time he finished the in-patient program at that rehab center.

"Ba..." Wi-yen squirmed.

"Okay, okay. I know you're hungry and wet and we need to get moving." She flipped to the end of the journal where there were only blank pages. She would have to read the rest later.

Sen-tshe returned just as she had finished cleaning the baby and herself. It wasn't much of a bath, but she used soft cotton dipped in a small bowl of water to wipe her face and neck. Later in the day she would go to the tiny spring he had shown her and rinse the cloth and give herself a sponge bath. She was only allowed this luxury once a week, but that felt normal to her now. She had grown used to the odors of the people, as well as the odors of her own body. She could actually identify some people: Kwe-in-ye with the smell of yucca and pine, Damé's old-man smell of skin that has been covered with dust and clothes that haven't been washed, To-be-né's sweet odor, her breath usually filled with the spicy mallow scent and rose blossoms she loved to chew. And then there was Sen-tshe, with his faint odor of saltbush and lambsquarter. At first the odor had brought to mind smelly socks and Martha was happy she didn't sleep right next to him. But over time the odor had come to represent safety and comfort. He supplied her with more food and water than Kwe-in-ye had ever allowed.

Of course Martha knew this was because his son was involved. He expected her to care for the child in the best way possible, keeping him smiling, clean, and fed.

She picked up the boy and pressed him against her cheek. Turning her nose she inhaled. Wi-yen smelled of the tender four o'clock branches his father brought for him to chew and soothe his aching gums.

He smiled at her. "Ma."

"Yes," she whispered. "Mama."

Po-ko stretched and licked Wi-yen's tiny hand, then walked to the front of the cave, her tail wagging. With a flush of guilt Martha turned and watched Sen-tshe climb into the cave. Part of the deal she had made with him when she convinced him Po-ko could live in the cave was that she would carry the dog down to the valley floor each morning.

"*Ja pa, Sen.*"

"Good morning, Mar-tee-ya." He set a large rabbit down in the corner and reached for his son, who had toddled to his father. He glanced at the dog and smiled, the shake of his head barely perceptible.

"He's walking all the time now." Martha glanced toward the front of the cave. "I'm worried about that edge."

"He will not fall."

"How can you know that?"

Sen-tshe sighed. "Mar-tee-ya, this is the way it is. He has had more freedom than other children, removed from the cradleboard before his time. He doesn't crawl over the edge."

"True." Her heart beat hard against her ribs. "But I worry about him and that is wearing me out. I can't take my eyes off him for a moment."

Sen-tshe raised his eyebrows and waited. This was his way when he suspected she had more to tell him. It seemed he always knew when there was something else on her mind, as if he could read her face or her nervous hands clenching tight or waving for emphasis.

"I think we should move to the village. There is a place near my old room, on the bottom level. Wi-yen would be safe and each day I could take him to be with the other children."

"Do you not go each day to see them?"

"Yes, but…" How could she make her argument stronger?

Sen-tshe took a step closer and reached out, laying his broad palm upon her arm. "Mart-ee-a, I know that Kwe-in-ye has put pressure on you and I know she guides you."

"I don't understand why she keeps insisting I stay with her. She wants me to know your ways, but she can be so controlling."

"She is wise. Often the things she does do not have…" Sen-tshe paused. "A man cannot see the whole mountain at one time. It is like the way she makes you teach Ing-lish to us. Do you not wonder why we need to know your language?"

"I…guess…it's always good to learn another language?" Martha felt stupid because she had never asked herself why Kwe-in-ye started the language classes.

"I first thought it was so that you would become a part of our people fast. Also so you would learn our language as we learned yours. But now? I think there is perhaps more. The hidden waterfall on the far side of the mountain that a man cannot see until he has followed a long path." He smiled and his eyes crinkled at the corners. "If you must go back then that is fine. Wi-yen and I will be fine."

"No!" The word sprang out much too loud. Wi-yen's eyes grew wide and Po-ko jumped up with ears perked forward. "I don't want to leave, that isn't what I meant."

She dropped her chin and pressed her lips together.

He slid his hand up her arm and under her chin, tipping her head up so that she looked into his dark eyes. "I am happy you don't want to leave."

The air between them was charged with something. Martha felt like she was twenty years old, her mouth and tongue tingled and the few inches between their lips seemed at once miles and no distance at all.

This was all in her mind, he was so young, he didn't see her in a romantic way, she was a pervert, a married woman, absolutely crazy... and yet ever since that day at the river...

He kissed her. Somewhat awkwardly, as Wi-Yen was wedged between them, but not the kiss of a son or a friend or anything other than a lover. His hand moved from her chin to the back of her neck, as if to keep her from escaping, but she had no thought of escaping, opening her lips and then pressing them further into his. She felt the warmth of his touch moving down her body, into her heart, yes, but more surprisingly into her stomach and down to her core, down to the part of her that hadn't felt so much desire and so alive for twenty years.

He pulled his lips away, but not far. "I don't want you to leave. I want you to stay, but I want you to stay as my wife."

She leaned back, as if to escape his words, but he wouldn't let her go. "That's crazy, Sen-tshe. I am much too old."

He slid his hand down to her chest. "You are not old, Mar-tee-a. You are warm and kind and smart. I would not have asked you to be here with me if I did not mean what I say."

"Except...." She had a husband. A man who believed in her promises.

"Are you worried about what the others will say?" He smiled. "They already say it."

This time she did pull away, turning and walking to her fur rug. She sank down and put her head into her hands. He rushed to her and sat as well, setting Wi-yen beside them. The boy immediately crawled over to the corner and pulled a stick from Po-ko's mouth, putting it into his own and growling at the dog.

"I did not mean to make you sad, Mar-tee-a."

She shook her head and spoke without uncovering her eyes. "You have not. I have to think, that's all."

She did need to think. She needed to think about her old life and this new one and how much time had passed and what things would be like in her future and so much more.

Was infidelity so terrible? Hurtful, yes, but it really meant one partner had needs so heavy that the feelings of the other lost the critical mass needed to keep a relationship together through tough times. Cheating was minor compared to so many other things that could happen. You could have a stroke, or worse yet, a child could die. Terrible, terrible things. She knew she was trying to justify the decision she wanted to make. Glen isn't here, is he? He won't be hurt because this isn't his world.

All she could think about was Sen-tshe's lips on hers. She uncovered her eyes and stared at him. He stared back, unblinking. Waiting.

She leaned forward and touched his smooth jaw. "I will live here with you, Sen-tshe. I will love you and—" she blushed "—make love to you and be as if I am your wife. But I am already married to another man, so I cannot truly be your wife."

A smile broke over his face. "That is fine, Mar-tee-a. That is very fine." He turned and called to Wi-yen. "Do you hear that? Come to us, little one."

An ugly bit of doubt sat inside Martha, right next to the image of Glen.

THIRTY

Martha awoke to the sound of Sen-tshe rising. She reached out her hand to touch him, but he had moved away, dressing in the corner. "Why must you get up?" she whispered. "Wi-yen still sleeps. We could…" She blushed, not totally comfortable asking Sen-tshe to come back under the skins and make love, even after a month of such mornings.

He turned and touched her cheek, then shook his head. "Póetu has been here. Kwe-in-ye has sent word that the warriors are going to arrive today."

"Póetu here? How did he find us?" And how did the old man make the climb to their hidden cave?

The corners of Sen-tshe's lips crept up and he sucked in his cheeks to maintain his serious frown. "Póetu may be old, but he is strong and quite a good tracker." He glanced out of the cave and down the canyon.

Martha followed his glance, suddenly aware that no matter how hard she had tried to keep the approach to the cave hidden, her daily treks to and from the village had left a clear trail.

"What does that mean, what warriors? Are we being attacked?" Martha sat up, tucking the blanket around the baby.

"They are coming to collect the share of our seeds and pots which we must pay to Man-With-Three-Spirits. We won't have as much as they expect, so there could be trouble." He moved the rock that covered a small storage space, picked up his knife and placed it into his belt where a loop kept it securely tucked out of view. "You stay here today, Mar-tee-a. You and Wi-yen."

"Hide?"

"That is one way of looking at it. Another is that you are protecting the child."

"She cannot hide." At the sound of Kwe-in-ye's voice, Martha let out a cry.

The old woman heaved herself up onto the lip of the cave and stood. "This is what she was called here to do. After so many months the time for her to act has arrived."

"How can you know this?" Sen-tshe scowled. "She must stay safe. We don't know what will happen nor do we know what her purpose is."

"She is here to keep us safe and this is not what one does by hiding." Turning to Martha Kwe-in-ye continued. "I brought you this to wear." She handed Martha a robe. "The women are waiting to help you dress."

Martha shook out the robe and examined it. The garment was made of cotton and skins—rabbit skins it seemed. There were many fine bone beads and cedar seeds, painted blue and sewn in an intricate pattern over the shoulders and flowing down the back. Feathers were stitched across the shoulders, and she recognized Yo-e-nu's fine needle work. If she put this on she would look like a phoenix rising from the ashes.

"What are you planning?" Sen-tshe was not ready to concede to Kwe-in-ye's plan.

"The council will meet with the men when they arrive. We shall present them with many fine pots filled with corn seed and piñon, also a small amount of dried meat."

"They won't be happy. That is not enough."

'No, they won't be happy and surely they will demand more. We will then bring Mar-tee-a in. She will stand tall and stern. She will instruct them to take what we offer and return to the sacred place. A little threatening tone won't hurt," she added turning to Martha.

"If they continue to refuse, you will give them the needles and glasses, and tell them to take these things. This will show the great magic you hold."

Martha didn't want to face these men. She longed to do as Sen-tshe said and keep Wi-yen safe. In fact she wanted to bring all the children to their cave, away from these warriors.

But that wasn't what was meant to happen in this world. If she avoided these warriors she would never move forward. She had been sent here for something, some way to help the people. What if everyone died because she shirked her duty? How would she care for Wi-yen and To-be-né? The only way to keep the children safe was to do what Kwe-in-ye asked.

"Of course I will do this."

Sen-tshe grabbed her arm. "You are sure?" He was nervous, but she saw a glimmer of pride in his face.

"I'm sure. And now you two get out so I have room to dress. Here, take this silly little boy with you." She nudged Wi-yen to his father.

Kwe-in-ye shook her head. "We must go to the village to prepare. The women wait for you." The old woman turned back to Sen-tshe. "You stay here with your son. The people do not need to be reminded of what you have done. They need to see Mar-tee-a as strong."

"I will not. This is not safe for her and I will be there to protect her."

"Protect her at what cost? If the village does not survive then no one will be safe."

Martha watched the two face off. "Please, don't argue." She didn't know what solution to offer. She could see the logic in Kwe-in-ye's request. People had not looked upon her living as Sen-tshe's wife with favor. There were rules and ceremonies for such things and she had broken them all. But she was scared of what was to happen and she needed Sen-tshe there to keep her safe. Even if there was no physical attack, she needed the solidity of his love.

"For now, let's all go down." She didn't care if people saw her with Sen-tshe. And if it wasn't safe he could take the baby and leave.

They climbed down the tree and headed into the village. Once there Sen-tshe went over to where Póetu and Katudu were standing, glancing back at Martha with a tiny nod.

She followed Kwe-in-ye to her house where the old woman pulled out a basket of clothing. She dressed Martha in a fine doeskin gown and leggings, carefully wrapping the intricate laces and smoothing the beads. Next she gave her a pair of soft moccasins. Not the tall, beaded boots that

Mosinobu wore, but delicate, low slippers. Finally she draped the magnificent robe over her shoulders.

"It is important that you remember the stories of Damé."

So many stories she had heard the old man tell. "Is there any in particular you have in mind?"

"The stories that tell of those who move forward with great bravery, into unfamiliar situations. If you imagine yourself to be brave, you will be brave."

"Do you think these men will hurt me?"

Kwe-in-ye shook her head. "No, and you will not be alone. Mosinobu would never let them hurt you." She adjusted the neckline of the dress. "But they will try to intimidate you, particularly since you are a woman. It has been the way of Man-With-Three-Spirits to treat women like squirrels…bothersome and necessary but hardly worth any attention. Think of how Damé moves when he tells the stories, how his body sends the message of the star people or the fire people. Use your body to send the message to these men, as well as your words. You will feel the strength of all of us behind you if you do this."

"I'll try my best."

Kwe-in-ye led her out the door where four women waited. They gathered around her, not saying a word. Dam-po-nu wove feathers into Martha's hair and bound it tightly with leather cords. Cha-pe used Martha's paint and brushes to create a design on her cheeks and forehead. Martha tried to follow the strokes of the brush to guess what her friend was drawing, but could not. She used her reading glasses to see a reflection, but they made a poor mirror. Some sort of powerful zig zag across her forehead and circles on her cheeks.

I'll just have to be who I am now, instead of my reflection. She looked into the eyes of the women. They were serious about the job, yet she was reassured by their nodding heads and the slight upturn of their lips.

When the women had finished with her, Cha-pe pushed on her shoulders reminding her to stand straight. She was taller than them and she thrust her chin up and out, practicing her stern look on them. The women nodded, approving of this new Martha.

Feeling prepared, she walked slowly across the canyon to the kiva. A faint curl of smoke slipped out of the vent and deep, slow voices rumbled through the opening. She couldn't make out what they were saying.

Her shoulders slumped down and her breath grew shallow. Then a warm nose nudged her balled-up fist. Po-ko wagged her tail and thrust her head under Martha's hand.

Martha uncurled her fingers, then straightened her spine and looked across the clearing. Sen-tshe stood with Póetu and Lu-te-na. Her lover's face was firm and serious, but the slight nod he gave her when their eyes met reminded her of all she had.

Be brave, be brave, you can do it. Act brave and you will be brave. She nodded back to her lover and turned to where Kwe-in-ye crouched near the side vent, her ear pressed close.

A pile of baskets, pots, and skins were next to the old woman. Months of hard work about to be handed over to these criminals. From what Mosinobu and Póetu had said these men were no more than the mafia, demanding payment or they would kill and maim the people. Though the people of this canyon had left the sacred place, trying to get away from the demands of the three strangers, the commands had followed. These warriors were the enforcers, insisting that they were being good by allowing the people to move away and practice the old religion, and that payment was needed in return.

Kwe-in-ye's head popped up like a prairie dog. "Now, we need you now."

"Are you coming in with me?"

Kwe-in-ye stood beside Martha. "No, it is enough that one woman enter the kiva, two and everyone would think we are completely crazy. Do you remember what you are to do?"

"Yes." Martha held up her hand, ticking off on her fingers. "First offer my favorite pot, filled with the best corn. Next be stern and god-like, telling them they are instructed to leave, then the needles and glasses, finally anger."

Kwe-in-ye's eyes were wide, her lips pursed and the wrinkles on her face even more apparent than usual. She nodded and reached behind a rock. "Give them these." She thrust Martha's missing slippers to her.

Martha reached out and took the sheepskin slippers, shaking her head in disbelief. She didn't have time to dwell on Kwe-in-ye's deception, as she stooped and descended into the kiva. She had to hitch up her skirt and tuck her slippers under her arm while she crawled down the narrow opening.

Her feet touched the stone floor of the kiva. It was hard to appear powerful on your hands and knees, so she stood quickly, lifting her chin and throwing her shoulders back as she turned and faced the men.

"*Ja pa.*"

"*Ja pa,*" Mosinobu and Damé greeted her.

The two strange men with them stared. Martha studied them while they looked her over. They were dressed in heavy leather, armored with many shells and curved wooden breast plates. They held tall, thick spears at their sides, the heavy stone points too big for hunting. Their heads were covered with helmets made of bone, not just functional for protection from attack but threatening, the skulls of animals placed to make these men into monsters.

One of the men spoke to Mosinobu in a language Martha did not recognize. He thrust his hand in the air and waved it with a sharp jerk. Her throat clenched and she bit her lower lip. This was the gesture her father had used when he was dismissing her. Not a friendly wave, but a hostile dismissal that said you are not important enough for my time. She felt pressure in her veins as her blood boiled and the shaking in her legs gave way to a tensing of her fists. Drawing herself taller she stepped directly in front of the man and glared.

She could play this game too. She moved her glance to Mosinobu for a split second, then back to the man. "What did he say?"

"They are offended that a woman has entered the kiva during the negotiations."

"Did you tell them who I am? The spirit from the stars?"

Mosinobu faced the men and spoke. They shook their heads.

"Tell them I give them these things, which I have brought with me from the stars. They are for their leaders." She frowned and held out the needles and a pocket knife. Was she actually offering them a weapon? As she held out the items she realized that in her agitated state, she had forgotten to start with the pot of corn. "Make it sound a bit more mystical, please."

Mosinobu translated. The warrior shook his head and did not step forward to take the things from her.

Be brave. She didn't want to be brave. She didn't want to be here at all. Her hands shook and she started to close her eyes, wishing to escape this responsibility. She never signed up for this. She was just a California housewife, a good wife and mother.

Images of Sen-tshe's soft touch, his kisses, their love-making filled her head.

She wasn't a good wife. Or mother. She had betrayed her family, forgotten them. Guilt replaced fear. She had to make things right and since she couldn't make things right with her family, at least she could make things right with these people.

Be brave.

She flung the needles and knife on to the ground in front of the man, grabbed the slippers from under her arm and threw them down as well. Reaching into her pocket for her glasses, she changed her mind. She really needed them and wasn't going to give them away.

"Tell him I wish him to take these to the leader."

The man stood firm, scowling and shaking his head.

Martha turned and picked up one of the pots filled with corn. She threw the pot with all her might against the stones of the fire ring. It shattered, the white clay and painted shards striking against the legs of the warriors. They jumped, swinging their spears towards her.

"You will not insult me like this. You will go to your leader with the things I have offered and tell him that this is it, no more. You will never return to this place. We are no longer going to give you this ransom you demand." She waved her arms in big circles, saliva flying from her mouth, and her cape making swooping noises as she shot the words out toward the men. She barely noticed the spears aimed at her, stepping closer and adding "Do you understand?"

She maintained her position, arm up and fist clenched.

Mosinobu stepped up next to her and spoke to the men. Martha tried to get a sense of his translation through his face and hands, but his face remained still and his eyes flat. Hopefully his words held more fire. When he had finished she turned and crawled up through the tunnel, not a very dignified exit, not at all in keeping with her attempt at portraying the all-powerful goddess, but she had to get out of the kiva.

She heard Mosinobu speak to Damé as she made her way out.

"What happened?" Kwe-in-ye jumped forward and held on to Martha's arm. But they were interrupted by Damé exiting the kiva.

"Go, *nupe le gran po*." Damé instructed, pushing her up the trail.

Martha hurried to the little rise on the edge of the village. This was a good spot to see down the canyon. She knew how one could look standing here, like a scout or a saint. She stood tall, tossing the cape so it flew out in the wind, staring down the canyon, not turning when she heard the warriors climb out of the kiva. She continued to stand while the warriors placed the stacks of items into large leather packs and strapped them to their backs. She listened while they talked to Mosinobu and Damé, then left the canyon. Although her legs ached and her shoulders were filled with cramps, she didn't move until Mosinobu approached and took her hand, leading her back to the kiva.

The room was filled with members of the council. Kwe-in-ye was also present. Everyone sat in the circle while Damé spoke. Although Martha had learned to follow much of what the ancient people said, his lecture was complex and fast. She turned to Kwe-in-ye and motioned for translation.

Kwe-in-ye whispered next to her. "We have averted disaster today, for this moment only. By giving what we did to the men we have depleted our supply of seed and food for the winter. There are no rains. The spirits of the earth remain angry that the people who turned away from the old ways, became greedy and did not respect the earth. It is not enough that we have tried to go back, there are too many others who continue to take more than they need. We shall surely starve this winter."

Póetu had another worry on his mind. Kwe-in-ye told Martha what he said. "We will be attacked soon, not only by these men from the holy leaders, but by others like ourselves, those who do not have enough to eat. I spoke with the brothers who were with the warriors. There is famine in all of the land. Many have left the sacred canyon, but now they have returned to Man-With-Three-Spirits. These leaders have food stored, enough for all. They offer work to those who are hungry, building more storage and roads."

One of the younger men asked a question.

"He wants to know if they would work for the Man-With-Three-Spirits and then get food in return."

There was mumbling among the council members.

Damé cleared his throat and all hushed.

Kwe-in-ye translated the old man's important words. "I believe this to be true, that we could work and receive food. But to do this is to give up the old ways, we would not be allowed to pray to our spirits or to perform our ceremonies. The holy leaders have a different belief, and their belief does not allow for the old ways."

Another man spoke up. "*An tapo chu co in pe. Man to fe pe lone cros le gran sotepos.*" He thoughtfully turned to Kwe-in-ye and Martha and waited for the old woman to translate.

"It's not just that we cannot pray, they think we are evil. They say that our spirits will burn in the underworld." She shook her head. "I do not understand why the underworld has become evil since Man-With-Three-Spirits arrived."

"May I speak?" Martha whispered.

"Mar-tee-a would like to speak." Kwe-in-ye announced. The men of the council nodded.

"What is this religion, this belief that they have? Do they have a name for it?"

Kwe-in-ye translated Martha's question.

Mosinobu answered, speaking directly to Martha in English. "The new way. That is what they call it. They speak many languages and they sent men out very far to bring back people from all places. They said it was good that we built such storage houses, but that we should build more and fill them with not only food, but pottery, tools and weapons. We should repeat the prayers as they said them, down on our knees, with faces to the ground."

Damé continued. After a lengthy diatribe he paused, his face sober and his mouth turned down while Kwe-in-ye translated. "We did what they said, but when we tried to have a rain dance to prepare for the spring planting, they were angry. 'Do not do this anymore,' they demanded. If you do this again you shall go to a fire place, deep in the earth. Your skin shall burn into blisters and peel from your body with great pain. When I asked them, *what of the spirit?* they told me the spirit would be trapped also, not able to go up to the star people or return to the earth."

Damé resumed speaking, his voice angry. Kwe-in-ye's words held the same fury as she efficiently translated not only what he had said, but his outrage. "I do not believe this. I think these men are tricksters. Since the people have begun following their ways the earth has been angry. The rain no longer comes, or it comes with a fierce mind, slashing the earth and destroying the plants, washing the seeds far away. The plants do not grow, the corn is small and hard, too hard to grind. The animals who provided us with meat are gone, no antelope spring through the valley, no deer hide by the river. The mice and squirrels do not come. These strangers have filled the storage areas, yet they ask for more. The people have nothing to eat. Why would they fill the storage areas before they would fill their stomachs?"

Martha tried to picture what the men were saying. Where had these holy men come from? What they described was not what she read in the museum. There was religious unrest, but she was pretty sure it had been the Katchina movement that accounted for the wars. What these men described sounded like something else…more like Christianity than anything ancient.

Suddenly Martha knew why she was here. "If we go to the sacred place, would I be allowed to talk to these men?"

"I think so. They have some respect for Kwe-in-ye. When one of them was very sick, Kwe-in-ye was able to improve him. If she asks to see them I feel they will do this." Mosinobu looked around at the others.

"If some men want to go and others don't, shouldn't you vote?" Martha didn't think the younger men knew what they would be getting themselves into.

"Vote?" This concept was not one which the men understood.

"Each person will say if they want to go or stay. Then we will count. What the most people want wins." Blank stares all around. "You do what the majority, the most people, choose." She turned to the old woman. "They don't understand. Will you explain?"

Kwe-in-ye frowned at her. "Mar-tee-a, I know that you have taught us many new ways, but this way does not make sense to us. It is not the way of the people."

Mosinobu nodded at Kwe-in-ye and turned to Martha. "Mar-tee-a, this sounds like a thing that might work sometimes, but our decision must be made. The council will decide."

Kwe-in-ye rose and went to the tunnel, speaking over her shoulder, "Mar-tee-a, we must leave now, while the council prays and makes a decision."

THIRTY-ONE

"You're kidding, right? An ancient ceremony? Dad has really lost it now." Clarice sprang from the kitchen chair and paced back and forth. "This family needs an intervention, not some hocus-pocus. Can't you see, Vince? Dad has flipped. There's a law or something. Elder abuse? Power-of-attorney? We need to take some steps. We can't let him make all the decisions. He's not rational. There must be some sort of legal action we can take."

"Legal action? Are you talking about suing Dad or something? And what's with this "we" business? This is your opinion." Vince glanced at his wife.

Clarice watched as Sandra pulled Sam from his high chair and took hold of Sara's hand, leading her out of the room, promising something with a whisper into her ear. It must have been something good, because Sara left without protesting.

"You mean you agree with Dad? That we should perform some primitive ceremony on Mom? What's next? Fly to China for special acupuncture?"

"If I thought that would help, I would do it."

Clarice had expected Jack to agree with Dad's pronouncement that he was letting the miracle nurse cast a spell on her mother, but she had been sure Vince would see reason.

"Even if there's no harm to Mom in whatever hoodoo you want, what about Dad? Can't you see what this is doing to him?"

"I think it's a comfort to him."

"What makes you say that?"

"He's calm. I think in part that's thanks to Naomi."

Agh. Naomi, Naomi, Naomi. Clarice was so tired of hearing about the wonders of Naomi.

Vince continued. "And strangely enough, I think the other part is because of Jack."

"Jack? When has Jack ever been anything but a headache to anyone?"

Why do I argue when he's right? Clarice couldn't stop the words from flowing in to her head. Truth was she had stopped by Mom and Dad's house a few times and Jack had been busy. The remodel now extended beyond the bathroom to the kitchen and dining room.

Vince must have read her mind. "Jack has changed. He's been a big help to Dad. I think Dad's kind of sad Jack got a job. He likes having him there. I think our brother actually knows more than we think about building." Vince paused and shrugged. "I don't know. It's hard to put into words, but Jack and Dad seem to click. Dad is relaxed, full of energy."

"Great, relaxed and full of energy and forgetting that his wife of over twenty-five years is a vegetable."

"You think he should be miserable?"

Clarice hesitated, sat back down at the table, and fiddled with the fork next to her plate. "No, I don't think he should be miserable. I just don't think he should forget."

"He isn't forgetting. How could any of us forget? He still visits her twice a day. How often do you visit?"

"I visit when I can, okay. But it's not the visiting I'm talking about. It's doing something active, finding out what's keeping her this way or letting her go, not this in between thing, this purgatory."

"Isn't having the ceremony doing something active?"

"Something medical, that's what I'm talking about. Tests or something. Treatments." Clarice's voice was loud, with a high pitch. "Am I the only one in this family that hasn't gone off the deep end?"

Sara came in and crawled into Vince's lap. "Daddy, Mommy says it's time for dessert."

"Okay, sweetie, it just might be that time."

Sandra served pie and ice cream and the conversation turned to child-safe topics like kittens, vacations, and jokes about frogs. Clarice aimlessly spooned the sweet mess into her mouth.

She realized that she and Mom had balanced out the energy produced by Dad, Vince and Jack. It was too sexist to imagine it was male vs female. It was just that all of them saw things in a set way and only Mom could convince them to look at another point of view. It seemed obvious this ceremony was going to happen no matter what tactics Clarice used to convince them it was a ridiculous idea. Without Mom to back her up she had no influence at all.

"Fine. I'll go along with this, but you owe me." This time her brother really did owe her. She would cash in this chit with Vince when she moved forward with the power-of-attorney. Her mother needed rescuing, a practical solution, not with bells and whistles.

And certainly not with drums and rattles.

THIRTY-TWO

Sen-tshe paced back and forth. He stopped and shook his head, then paced again. Martha and Wi-yen watched him in silence.

There was so much she wanted to say to him. Although he had caught on to speaking English and she was able to converse quite well in the ancient language, there were still times when words couldn't communicate all that was needed.

"It is a dangerous trip, Mar-tee-a. Children are not going." He waved toward the toddler. "He cannot walk far and the journey takes many nights."

"I know." She looked down at her hands. Chipped nails and calluses. Funny how she thought she worked hard in her old life, but her hands had been soft and her nails filed to perfect ovals, covered each week with a new layer of shiny polish.

If someone said to her "You can go back, now. Just click your heels together three times" what would she do?

She stopped, the right lower corner of her lip caught under her teeth as she chewed on the idea of leaving Sen-tshe and Wi-yen behind. She loved Sen-tshe. She loved everything about him. His thoughtful ways, his kindness toward children, and his way of staying calm. To an outsider, sleeping with Sen-tshe might be seen as cheating on Glen, but that wasn't the case. Modern people divorced or separated, they abandoned their spouse and children without so much as a backward glance. But there was the tiny thorn in her heart, like those tiny burrs that get into your sock and irritate your heel with each step you take. What she tried to tell herself, to pluck that nasty thorn, was that she had been deserted by circumstances and she needed—deserved—love.

She and Sen-tshe had been talking for hours, ever since the council had announced their plan.

A select group of people would travel to the sacred place. Martha would meet with the Man-With-Three-Spirits and…and what? Have a tantrum like she did with the warriors? She didn't want to face this task without Sen-tshe by her side. Not only that but she couldn't shake the feeling that Wi-yen needed to be there.

And that was what she couldn't tell Sen-tshe.

Not in her words or his.

The next morning the small group gathered, prepared for the journey. Sen-tshe had helped her pack what she needed. A skin strapped to her back would serve as her bed for the journey, a small bag filled with dried meat—she couldn't convince him she didn't want it and he insisted she would be happy to have it—and some roots and vegetables was strapped to her waist. She carried another bag with the items that continued to appear magically from somewhere: aspirin, her glasses, tweezers, another Swiss Army knife, three large yellow rubber bands, a small magnifying glass, a pack of gum, one of those tiny black barber's combs, and three emery boards.

She held Sen-tshe's hand and squeezed it as Mosinobu addressed the group of travelers. Kwe-in-ye, of course, and her sister, Yo-en-u. Ka-a-poo. Póetu stood next to Cha-pe. The sons of Pat-o-le-si, the woman who had died, were also present. Four young men, barely out of their teens, with many items tied to their backs. Two more men, a bit older than the teens, carried large jugs strapped to their backs. Ta-kan, the woman who made the wonderful pots, stood next to a large dog harnessed to a travois covered with skins and mats. Martha was glad to see that funny young man Lu-te-na was here. It would be good to have someone who liked to make her laugh along on the trip.

All the people of the village arrived. The crowd gathered around the travelers was solemn, standing and sitting wherever there was space. Martha was sure that this was the largest group she had seen since her arrival. It had to include everyone, even the farmers who stayed up on the mesa.

Some unheard signal must have swept through the crowd because everyone turned and walked up the canyon.

"What's happening?" Martha asked Sen-tshe.

"You will start your journey with a prayer. We take you to the prayer circle cave."

Martha had not been back to this cave in all her months in the canyon. The place where this life had started for her with drumming and dancing. But she was happy that she got to walk with Sen-tshe and Wi-yen.

The crowd stopped at the fork in the trail and the travelers walked up the steep trail to the cave. The council members, Sen-tshe, and families of the travelers came to the cave as well.

Lu-te-na held Damé's elbow and escorted the old man up the trail.

There were no drummers, no dancing, just the long prayer Damé recited. Martha could understand some of what he said. Wishing them safety, success, and wisdom. She opened her heart and let the old man's words sink deep inside her. She would need the help of the gods if she was to succeed.

When the prayers were over, it only took a few minutes for Mosinobu to get things moving. The group moved back down to the canyon, then turned up the narrow gorge. Martha embraced Sen-tshe, kissed Wi-yen and quickly followed the group up the trail, her face turned from his so that he couldn't see the tears streaming down her cheeks. She felt the small brush of Po-ko's tongue on her hand and looked down.

"Sorry girl. You have to go back. *Nupe.*" She waved her hand and the dog trotted back to the village. As much as she wanted her friend by her side she had no idea what this journey would bring. Better the animal stay with Sen-tshe or To-be-né.

As they traveled up the canyon the trail grew narrow and steep. Several men lifted the travois onto their shoulders and she wondered about bringing such a thing on a journey like this. She soon quit thinking about anything other than putting one foot in front of the other, focused on avoiding the sharp rocks on this trail that was less traveled than those around the village.

Mosinobu called to the group and everyone slipped the burdens from their backs. Cha-pe walked around with a jug of water and the people took small sips. Barely enough to wet her lips or soothe her dry throat, Martha suppressed the urge to chug the whole thing.

Above them mountain after mountain seemed to loom in the distance, each taller than the last. But they didn't actually climb any of these peaks. Instead the group wound around the base of each mountain, sticking to the dry creek beds. It was the second day before she realized this was because there were occasional small pools and springs where they could refresh their water supply.

Each time they rested Martha grew more desolate. It was as if Sen-tshe and Wi-yen were phantom limbs. She could hear the boy's babbling, smell Sen-tshe's sweat and feel his soft touch. Finally she approached Kwe-in-ye, who had been avoiding her.

"This is crazy. I can't do this. This is a job for the council, for you or Mosinobu. You're the ones who should talk to these men. You know that."

"It might seem that way, but that is not what the gods have to say."

"When did you ask them? Why won't you listen to what the gods say to me? They say this is a woman who doesn't know a thing about us and she can't save you."

"Mar-tee-a, I know that you yearn for Sen-tshe. What I ask myself is why you did not yearn for your own husband this way?"

"That's not fair," Martha glared at Kwe-in-ye. "You don't know how I feel."

Of course, Kwe-in-ye had struck a cord and that thorn was right back in Martha's heel.

On the third day they crested a swale and the group stopped, voices chattering. Martha felt a spring wind blowing over her tired body. She raised her head and gasped.

Before them lay an endless meadow. It was a huge bowl, with trees and peaks surrounding every side. A small herd of elk was grazing on the new grass that spread like a fog of pale green across the broad expanse.

This world was big. Since she had come here she had thought only of the canyon, the village, the stone houses, and the caves. Even the trip to the Rio Grande for water had slipped from her mind. Was she always so narrow in her view of things? She felt energized looking at the sky and the grass and the distant mountains. Surely she was doing the right thing, traveling with this group who had only the best interest of those left behind as their goal.

"We camp here so that the hunters can go after the elk." Kwe-in-ye pointed back into the trees. "But don't set up yet. We must be quiet so as not to send the animals away."

Martha was happy for the chance to rest. Later that night, in spite of her resolution to be a vegetarian, she appreciated the fresh meat. The men put chunks of elk on sharp skewers and roasted them over the fire. It was the best thing she had tasted since coming to this place.

It took two days to walk across the bowl, which Martha suspected was the inside of a volcano. Thinking back to Glen planning their trip, which was like thinking of something so out of touch it didn't seem real, she recalled him talking about visiting a caldron. And this place did look like a soup pot.

She thought they would be able to walk more quickly across the huge meadow, but it only looked smooth from a distance. Up close the ground was uneven beneath the thick blades of grass. The new spring growth came up between cracks in rigid chunks of dried mud and each step required balance and effort. The landscape slowed them down. What had been beautiful with first glimpse quickly became exhausting. Her thighs ached from lifting each leg high before setting her foot down and testing the ground for enough solidity to hold her weight without sinking down into the crumbling dirt.

At night she lay and looked at the stars. She was determined to dream up a water bottle, a map, some socks, and hiking boots. Nothing appeared and she realized the map would be completely useless because she had no idea where she was. The boots would be fabulous. During the brief rest stops Martha read Jack's journal. Filled with sad, strange poems, it made her heart ache. She knew only the sulky, defiant boy, but now she peered into his sadness. He felt so hopeless! Had she really compared him to the others so much that he felt he was no one at all? Her tears splattered the pages of the little book.

When she reached the last page she was stunned.

Hey Mom, If you are reading this then I know you really do have a use for all those things you ask for. Maybe you can write some poems and that will bring you back to us. Love, Jack.

What did this mean? A message from her son. How did he know where she was? More questions flew like starlings around her and she looked around for Kwe-in-ye. Before she found the old woman she reconsidered. Did she really want to bring this up now? It wasn't likely to lead to any answers.

Martha looked at the pen. She pulled it off the edge of the notebook and clicked its tip into place. Then she wrote.

Once the travelers made it across the expanse of meadows, things got better. To Martha's surprise they came to a broad road, about fifteen feet wide. And not just some track made by people walking the same path. The road was banked, with berms built to keep it level and very straight. Unlike any highway she was used to, this road didn't curve around the terrain. It seemed the terrain had been modified to fit the road.

The people walked side by side now, clustered in groups, but there was little talking. No smiles or jokes, not even Lu-te-na laughed. They continued down another set of mountains, although these were smaller than those surrounding their canyon. When they traveled through the narrow gorges the road was very steep. In some places steps had been carved into the rocks. The others were able to walk down these carrying loads, balancing and agile, but Martha slipped often and needed a hand to steady herself.

By the seventh day she wondered if she would make it all the way to the spiritual place. She had to ask the others to stop and let her rest and she could see the distant look on many faces. Thankfully they were soon out of the mountains and began to cross a broad plain. There were still many washes to climb down and back up, but these were small compared to the deep canyons and gullies they had been through. Far in the distance Martha saw more mountains, but directly in front of them was sandy earth. It was packed hard in many places, yet soft and more difficult to walk on in others. There were a wide variety of plants, from spiny broad leaf cacti to long, spindly, snake-like plants and sparse bunches of sharp grass. Martha saw new growth here and there, but many dead plants lined the road.

The plains went on and on. Martha lost track of the days, but she felt sure they had been walking for well over a week. Sen-tshe had told her it was a two-week journey, shorter with a small group like theirs. Each day was hotter than the one before and she was soaked in sweat before she had rolled up her sleeping mat and gathered her belongings in the morning. They no longer built a fire at night and there was no fresh food to be had.

She was exhausted. And it was this fatigue that distracted her so that she stumbled and slid on a spot in the road which was nearly flat. The smooth red rock of this part of the country was different than the white rock of the canyon. There was a fine layer of gritty sand covering it, and her weight was slightly forward when her sandal failed to grip and slid out from under her.

Her right leg twisted to the side in front of her, while the bulk of her weight shifted out over it, just before she lurched across the road and landed on her side. The light pouch she carried, the others having relieved her of most of her load when they saw the trouble she was having, flew from her hands, and bounced down into a small gully next to the trail. "Oh no!" Martha clutched her knee as pain zapped through the joint and up to her hip.

"Mar-tee-a!" Kwe-in-ye ran back toward Martha. Mosinobu waved his hand and everyone came to a stop.

Ka-a-poo dashed to her side and knelt, his hand upon her shoulder. "Stay."

Martha looked at him and nodded, her teeth grinding to keep from crying.

Kwe-in-ye laid her hand on Martha's knee. "Is it this part?"

"I think so. I might have scraped my elbow too, but I really tweaked my knee." Martha bent her arm to look at the blood dripping from her elbow. Ka-a-poo quickly pulled a strip of soft leather from his pouch and pressed it to the wound.

Kwe-in-ye placed her palms on either side of Martha's leg, applying firm pressure while pulling it gently toward her.

"Ahhh." Martha squeezed her eyes shut and hunched forward as a wave of nausea swept over her.

Kwe-in-ye stopped pulling. She rotated her hands around Martha's knee, placing one on top, cupping the knee cap, and one underneath. She applied pressure from both sides.

"Better." Martha choked out.

"You have just stretched your knee in a way that it should not be made to stretch, but you have not damaged it." Kwe-in-ye called out to Mosinobu and the others. Yo-e-nu brought a long smooth piece of deer hide and some leather laces. Kwe-in-ye expertly wrapped Martha's knee.

Póetu brought his sturdy walking stick, curved at the top with a spot for Martha to grasp and lean upon.

"I can't take this from you."

The old man shook his head and smiled, then took three dancing steps and refused to take the cane back.

With Martha up and hobbling, Mosinobu gave the command for the group to walk on. Martha leaned on the stick and had walked a fair distance when she remembered her pouch.

"Kwe-in-ye, my pouch, I left my pouch in the gully."

Kwe-in-ye wrinkled her brow and the corners of her mouth turned down. Martha had not witnessed a scowl from her guide in quite some time but now the stress that the people were under was high, and she only seemed to add problems.

"I will send Lu-te-na back for it. He moves quickly on light feet."

"Thank you, it has the things I will need when we get to the sacred place." Although what she would do with these things she still hadn't a clue.

Martha's thoughts were interrupted by a gruff tone from Mosinobu. He had stopped by the side of the trail as the others moved on. He spoke rapidly with Kwe-in-ye. Martha could understand enough of what he was saying to realize that he was not happy that the pace had slowed so much on account of her injury. The group would be without water for too long.

"You take the others on, I will walk with Mar-tee-a. Lu-te-na will catch up with us soon and he will accompany us." Kwe-in-ye motioned up the road. "I have what we need and we are less than two days walk from the valley."

That was a relief. Two days.

"The splitting of groups is never a good idea. We are so few...if there should be any trouble." Mosinobu shook his head.

Martha knew he was trying to figure out what to do about her. If they had been in the forest still, she had no doubt he would have constructed some sort of litter to pull her along, but this part of the land offered nothing more than the scrub brush and clay soil.

"Go. There is no need for the whole group to be thirsty." Kwe-in-ye clucked her tongue and Mosinobu joined the line of slowly moving people.

There must not be a source of water close by. Martha really didn't want to be a danger to the entire group, but on the other hand wasn't her presence the whole reason they were making this journey?

Good Lord, when did she get so full of herself? Martha sighed and watched Mosinobu walk quickly, speaking to those he passed, and the pace of the group increased.

She tried to keep her own pace steady, but the pain in her knee kept her at a slow, shuffling gait. Within minutes the rest of the group was out of sight. Yo-en-u walked slowly, staying with her and Kwe-in-ye.

When the sun set she begged Kwe-in-ye to stop. She couldn't bear to put any more weight on her leg. The pains shot straight up and into her clenched teeth. The old woman nodded and they moved to the side of the road. Yo-en-u cleared a small space by pulling up some of the plants with a sharp stick. The two women gathered enough brush for a small fire, which Kwe-in-ye lit while Yo-en-u spread out the three sleeping mats.

There was no sign of Lu-te-na and her missing pouch. Martha hoped he would show up because there were aspirin in that pouch and she surely needed them now.

The women didn't speak. Many days together had depleted them of anything to say. Martha didn't want to ask any questions because she sensed the underlying frustration of her guide. She wouldn't be surprised if Kwe-in-ye was having significant regrets about this whole message-from-the-gods story.

Martha stared into the flames of the small fire and wondered why the old woman had built it. They hadn't cooked anything and it wasn't cold. When a coyote howled, joined by its mates, she shivered and realized that the fire was meant to keep the predators away. A huge moon—full and a brilliant red—rose over the mountains to the east.

Are you looking at the moon too, my love? She pictured Sen-tshe sitting at the edge of the cave, holding the sleeping Wi-yen. *Give me a sign, let me feel you, here in my heart.*

This was that same moon. The same stars. She had looked at the sky a thousand times and it was exactly the same when she sat with her children or Glen and pointed up into the sky as it was for Sen-tshe and Wi-yen. But it was so far away, you couldn't really see the details. Would it be unchanged in her time? It had to be a thousand years later, didn't it? Maybe she wasn't looking at the same thing at all.

A large yellow moth flew over the fire. *No, not that, don't fly into the flame.* Her heart clenched as she held her breath, willing the insect to change direction.

Like a moth to a flame. The old saying jumped into her mind. She hadn't ever thought about what it really meant. Something so attractive that the insect ignored the peril. Was the moment of death ecstatic instead of horrible? Was she walking toward the flame or was Sen-tshe the flame and now she was making the right choice, to leave him behind?

Stop this. Negative thinking will only make it worse. She tried for a pep talk. Not a flame, an opportunity. That's what this was. Martha couldn't remember the last time she had pushed herself into an uncomfortable situation. Before she came here, anyway. There had been unlimited uncomfortable situations in this time, but in her old life? She couldn't think of a single one. Not that every situation in her life had been comfortable. She wasn't complaining, she really had been happy with her life, but once in a while the sameness of each day, the repetition, settled on her like a heavy blanket and she wanted something else. Why was it that life in the canyon, filled with the daily tasks of living, never left her yearning for some unknown thing?

Martha rubbed her throbbing knee. Maybe it was because it wasn't really a thing she wished for. It was an emotion. But what? Happiness? Love? She'd had those things her entire life. How could she make a change if she didn't know what to wish for?

When the fire had burned down, with Kwe-in-ye and Yo-en-u long asleep, Martha considered looking for more brush, but even the thought of rising caused her to feel light-headed with pain. She limped to her mat and lay on top of it—the night was so warm she didn't need to curl up under it. But the coyotes howled and their yips sounded so close. She spread her skin over her and pulled her head underneath. This land was endless and filled with danger. Opportunity? Now she wasn't so sure.

The big mystery of what she was going to do kept her awake. Not that it mattered. She couldn't just go back to her own time and Kwe-in-ye wasn't about to let her go back to the canyon without completing her task.

She didn't think she would ever sleep, her mind still spinning and the coyotes still letting out the occasional yip and howl, but she was awakened by Kwe-in-ye shifting and coughing. The morning sun had replaced the full moon. Martha stretched her leg and flexed her knee. It didn't hurt as much as last night, but it was still very sore.

Yo-en-u was sitting quietly, ready to go. No one spoke, not even a morning greeting, and Martha felt like she was in church, in the middle of some sort of religious rite, as if people were in silent prayer or showing their respect to some deity. She rolled up her blanket silently, and was tying it to her back when Kwe-in-ye motioned to a rock.

"Wait, I must check your knee."

Martha sat. When the bandaging was removed she noted that her knee was bruised and swollen. Kwe-in-ye rubbed a salve over the area and wrapped it tightly. Today she placed two small sticks on either side for added support. This made it more difficult to walk, as Martha had to swing her leg out to one side, but it greatly relieved the pain.

The small group trudged on, stopping to rest whenever Martha called for it. The road soon became smooth and level, much easier to traverse. The landscape flattened more, the washes now broad and flat, no longer steep gullies. Martha was surprised to see small farms with some plants growing, but many dried and dead. When the road passed close to the stone buildings, scattered like cow pies randomly across the land, the families came out to watch them. Occasionally someone called a greeting, but many of the people merely stared. The children were thin and hollow-eyed. These people were also suffering from the drought and lack of food. A large number of the buildings and pit houses were empty, the fields near them bare and dusty.

As the road curved along a dry river bed, the land changed. Rock walls started off small but grew taller along each side until they walked in the middle of a wide low canyon. The road did not drop down off the mesa into a canyon but rather the mesa stayed flat, with the cliffs rising gradually on each side. There were people everywhere, many setting up camps on spots close to the rock walls, but others simply stopping and spreading their belongings on the dry river bed.

"There it is." Kwe-in-ye pointed ahead.

The sun was sinking behind the red cliffs and it took a minute for Martha to see what was in front of the orange glow. As her eyes adjusted she saw a huge stone building, four stories high in some spots. It was built close to the red wall of rock, as if it were a part of the canyon itself, and the upper levels reached the mesa. The whole thing emerged in a sort of strange morph from the rock, growing like sugar crystals in a jar. The brickwork was smooth and even, not the crudely chipped rocks of the farms they had passed or their own canyon homes. There were logs for support, their bark stripped and the wood polished to a glass-like shine. The entire front of this grand building was a curved wall. There were no windows or doors, no openings at all. A line of men, holding sticks and spears, stood shoulder to shoulder.

"Guards?"

"Yes, that is something new. As is the wall. There has been much added since my last visit." Kwe-in-ye started walking again.

"Is it a fort?"

"It was a storage building, and I heard it became a home to the Man-With-Three-Spirits, but now, who knows?"

As the group walked past the front of the huge building, it brought to mind a castle. Martha saw more guards perched up high, in towers built on the tops of the highest walls. The walls must be thick, with room to stand, such as in medieval times, as the guards walked back and forth, watching over the valley. There was a single doorway, visible now that they were moving closer to the front of the curved wall.

Kwe-in-ye moved on and although Martha's knee begged her to stop, she was glad when they left the grim soldiers and hulking monolith behind.

They walked past several smaller versions of the castle, and more groups of people in crude camps.

There must be over a thousand people here, maybe two thousand. Martha was amazed, but the pain of her knee and her fatigue kept her from having any deep thoughts. She wanted to take some aspirin but Lu-te-na had never arrived. She wanted her pouch, but she worried about the young man. What had happened to him?

At last she saw Póetu approaching. He led them to where the others were camped. They had a prime spot behind a building in some large rocks near the base of the wall, the rocks providing shelter as skins had been stretched for roofs. Martha sank down on to a mat, extending her knee out in front of her with a sigh.

She looked around at her people, all sitting quietly and seriously with no words of greeting.

These people—her people—sat as if awaiting execution.

THIRTY-THREE

The frightened stares around her brought a wave of despair flowing into every part of her body. Instantly, her knee ached, her stomach clenched, and her head pounded.

Then the soft notes of Mosinobu's flute filled the air. Martha saw the leader standing next to the fire pit, filled and crackling with bright flames. Three of the young men rose and began to move around the fire, their shuffling steps accompanied by a soft chant.

"A blessing," she whispered. It was what they all needed.

Ka-a-poo pulled out a small drum and set the beat.

The tones of the flute flowed around like the sparks on the wind and she let them carry her away. Martha's imagination took her beyond the rock walls to a place high enough to look east to the mountains. Back across the vast caldera, all the way to the canyon—her canyon. She saw Sen-tshe holding Wi-yen, calming the boy in preparation for the night's sleep.

"I am with you," she whispered, hoping he could hear.

A voice broke through Martha's reverie. "*Ha-hi-ya, o-pa-tu-a.*"

The others picked up the chant.

"*Ha-hi-ya, o-pa-tu-a. Ha-hi-ya, o-pa-tu-a.*"

Martha recognized the song. The women chanted these words when one of the young girls was in labor, about to deliver a new spirit into this world. The men sang the tune when someone had been injured in the hunt. The children held hands and sang as they circled around a friend who had failed at an attempt to try something new.

It was a prayer for someone who needed the love and support of the people around them.

"Ha-hi-ya, o-pa-tu-a."

She joined the circling people and her heart filled with the words these people were singing for her.

When she had circled once, her feet responded to the beat and soon her breath, her head, and her heart were all in sync, even while dragging her sore leg. She was part of something organic, alive, as if she were a corpuscle flowing through the bloodstream of a sleeping dragon. As she circled, Martha moved deeper into this strange world. This dance, this music, these people, she had known them all her life. She let her thoughts come, no longer trying to fight what filled her mind. Tomorrow she had to confront three very powerful and, if the stories were accurate, brutal men. She didn't have her pouch, no tricks up her sleeve. If something had happened to Lu-te-na it was her fault. She tipped her head back and let her breath flow out her nose. *Help me now, God or someone. Whoever is out there, help me now.*

Martha danced. She felt the drum beat as if it were her own beating heart. The flute became her spirit, her soul, the very life energy which flowed through her veins. The beat grew stronger and more people joined the circle. Martha danced and soon her mind cleared of all thoughts. Her body moved without direction, her physical self taking on a life of its own. She didn't need her mind to guide her, and her troubled thoughts had disappeared as if they were never there at all.

She felt her body. Movements flowed down her arms and into her fingertips. She snaked her spine, each tiny crackle releasing something that had lived inside her and kept her tight. All constrictions left her. There was no more pain, just sensation as her legs and feet pounded and kicked. Free, free, free.

Voices joined the sound of the flute, not chanting, but humming all around her. Were these the voices of the gods? The ancient spirits who had listened to the prayers and come to help? Martha rolled her head, lifting her face to the sky, welcoming the spirits.

She felt a warm sensation on her hand and sensed something very close to her leg. She opened her eyes and looked down.

Po-ko wagged her tail and licked Martha's hand again. Martha knelt and wrapped her arms around the dog, letting the soft tongue lick the salt of her tears from her cheeks. The dog must have followed them, tracking them all the way from the canyon to the sacred place.

"Ha-hi-ya. O-pa-tu-a," came a whisper from behind her. The voice was close, just over her shoulder, soft in her ear. She held her breath.

"Ha-hi-ya. O-pa-tu-a."

Tears streamed down her cheeks as she stood and fell into Sen-tshe's arms.

Later, after she had choked and cried and clung to him, wrapping her arms around his body and the cradleboard that held the squirming Wi-yen, he told her what had happened.

"Mar-tee-a, just one day after you left, a group of people arrived. They were from a village far to the south. They were very thin, near starvation, and they told how they were driven out of their village by warriors from the sacred place. Although they had been promised safety when they had given the yearly payment, it was a surprise attack. This was when the strongest men were away on a hunt and the warriors were brutal. They didn't kill people, they tortured them. Broken legs, smashed fingers, even the old, the children, those who could not defend themselves. These cruel warriors took all the stores and destroyed what they could not carry." Sen-tshe shook his head. "This story scared us. There were many in our village who hadn't agreed with the council's decision to send so few to the sacred place. What if those warriors attacked us? What if they had attacked you and you never made it to this place? It was decided that we should hide our stores and send more people after you in the hope that we could avoid the terrible fate of the village from the south."

Sen-tshe handed Martha her pouch.

"How—?"

"We met Lu-te-na on the trail. He told us what happened. We insisted he travel with us. It is not safe for a man to travel alone in this place."

Martha strapped the pouch to her waist. This might help, although she didn't know how. But she would worry about that tomorrow. Right now all she wanted was to tuck her body as close as possible to Sen-tshe and hold Wi-yen in her arms. She reached up and loosened the straps on the cradleboard. Sen-tshe bent his knees so that she could reach the boy and pull him out.

"Ma!" Wi-yen grabbed her ear and giggled. She smiled at his twinkling eyes and the special look he had only for her.

Martha pushed her nose into the crease of his neck and inhaled his warm odor. Something had brought Sen-tshe and Wi-yen here, some power she couldn't describe. How was this little boy tied to saving the people? She had the pouch, the boy, the people…what she didn't have was any idea how all this was going to work.

The sun was just casting its first rays on the valley when Martha heard Kwe-in-ye talking to her sister.

"You stay here. Get everyone up and start the prayers. Come to the outside of the storehouse as soon as you have gathered all the people."

Lifting Sen-tshe's arm from her shoulder, Martha carefully moved Wi-yen into the spoon of his father's body. When Sen-tshe opened his eyes, she shook her head and held one finger to her lips. He nodded and held the boy, watching as she rose and walked to where Kwe-in-ye stood.

It was time.

Mosinobu came from around the boulders and held out his hands palms up. Martha stepped forward and took his hands. He didn't say a word, just tightened his grip. She heard his silent prayer and stood for a moment.

Kwe-in-ye interrupted the prayer. "Come now. If we are to see Man-With-Three-Spirits today it must be now."

She turned and moved rapidly down the rocky trail to the main road, waving her hand over her shoulder so that Martha and Mosinobu would hurry. Kwe-in-ye was practically running and Martha's knee gave a tiny pinch, but she could jog at a steady pace. Her spirit guide pushed past others walking up the road, reaching out with her hand and gently moving them to one side. When people saw who it was, they moved to the edge of the road, and watched the threesome as they ran toward the huge storehouse. Martha wondered how they knew who she was, then realized she was still very different looking from anyone else here.

He is only a man, this is only a dream. Martha's mantra fell into the rhythm of her racing feet. The road led them to a small doorway and after a brief conversation between a guard and Kwe-in-ye, they were led into the storehouse. It was dark inside and Martha paused for a moment to let her eyes adjust. There were no windows in this small room, but another doorway was directly across and the three followed the guard as he ducked into the next room. This room was as small and dark as the first, with nothing in it but a dirt floor. The rooms and doorways continued, sometimes turning off to the right or the left.

Martha was soon completely lost, the rooms and doorways forming a crazy maze. She fell behind the others, the stepping up and down through the doorways was making her knee ache, and her hands were shaking. She needed a minute to clear her mind, but she didn't want to lose the others.

Kwe-in-ye, Mosinobu and the guard moved so silently that all at once she found herself alone in a room with no doorway other than the one she had come through. She went back out and stared at the empty hallway.

Breathe. Be brave. Listen.

She walked in the direction she hoped was correct, peering into doorways and looking for signs that this was the way she should go. All the rooms were empty. What about the great stores of food these leaders had promised? The entire valley was filled with people from all over the land. When their crops had failed and their water dried up, they had traveled here in expectation of being fed and cared for. The hairs on the back of Martha's neck stood up and she shook her head as doubt spread through her mind and down to her heart.

"This way," Kwe-in-ye whispered, her head poking out through a door. "Don't get lost."

"I'm trying not to, but this place is crazy."

"Shhh. You should not talk in here."

Martha followed silently, wondering why she shouldn't talk. At last she could see sunlight ahead, and as she stepped through the doorway into a courtyard, she saw the others waiting.

They were in an open space, with curved walls forming the perimeter. The guard turned and squeezed into a narrow passage between two of the walls. There was a steep stairway leading up between the stones.

More twists and turns, narrow passageways and stairways, dark tiny rooms—all empty—and doorways. The group followed the guard silently, footsteps barely making a sound.

"*Chotena*," the guard ordered, holding up the palm of his hand to stop them. Wait. He disappeared around a corner.

"Kwe-in-ye, I don't have any ideas yet, I don't know what to do. I'm sorry." Martha shook her head and laid her hand on Kwe-in-ye's arm.

The old woman placed her hand over Martha's. "It will happen, I know it will. I have...trust. No...I have faith."

Was faith going to be enough? Martha ticked through a list in her mind. What did she know about history? Religious persecution? Why hadn't she paid more attention in that world studies class she'd taken in college? All she could think of were the movies she had watched, gory massacres, the only salvation coming from assassination of the cruel leaders. But how was she to kill this man? She couldn't find her way out of this building if she did do something so brutal.

"*Pa tu chan*." The guard was back and he beckoned for the group to follow again.

The final stairway led them into an open room on the top of the building. From the outside Martha had been able to count four stories, but now it seemed they were even higher, perched just under the giant red rocks of the cliffs. This room was round and a tall wall curved around the perimeter. Guards stood up above them. The brilliant blue sky behind them would have made a beautiful sight if their weapons hadn't been held at waist level, silently pointing down at her. This was the wall she had seen yesterday, thick like a castle or fortress. These must be the guards she had seen when they first arrived—atop the walls with a view of the whole valley.

At the far end of the room were two thrones, constructed from stone and wood and covered with smooth hides. In each of the chairs sat a man, the long thin faces and white hair of each identical.

Twins. But what about the third spirit? Kwe-in-ye called these men Man-With-Three-Spirits.

They were lanky and long, unlike the short, tight build of the ancient people. These men were of a different race, bore the features of another part of the world. Their long, narrow noses had sharp points, their foreheads were straight, not sloping, and their eyes were the blue of a Siamese cat, startling against their suntanned skin. Their brows matched their bright white hair. Pale lips were pressed into tight lines and gray stubble grew on their jaws.

Martha glanced around the room and even behind her back, not trusting anything about this situation. She leaned toward Kwe-in-ye. "What of the third man?"

Kwe-in-ye shook her head and walked slowly up to the men. She knelt, placing her hands on the floor, muttering something. Mosinobu knelt to one side of Kwe-in-ye and started muttering also, his forehead nearly touching the floor. Martha stood and watched.

"*Shabish.*" The guard pushed Martha forward toward the others.

Martha fell to her knees next to Mosinobu, not taking her eyes off the men. Although her initial thought had been that they were identical in every way, even the vests made of horn and bone and decorated with turquoise and other stones, she detected a slight difference in the faces. One had a harsh look, angry, with forehead wrinkles and thin lips a straight tight line, turned down on the ends. The other was softer, his mouth relaxed. His eyes met hers with a slight raising of the left eyebrow, amused and interested.

Soft-twin raised his hand and moved it in a circle, beckoning to Kwe-in-ye. She did not stand, but crawled closer to him, keeping her eyes down. Martha was shocked at this behavior. Though she had heard the stories of the control these men had over the people, this was disgusting. Subservient, not in keeping with the pride and strength of this woman.

The man spoke to Kwe-in-ye in a language different from that of the people, and Martha did not know what he said.

Kwe-in-ye answered in this same language, her voice soft and direct. Scowling-twin's mouth turned down even more as she spoke, his lower jaw jutting forward and his shoulders arching back as he leaned toward her. He waved toward Martha, and whatever he said had a questioning tone.

"He wants to speak with you. I will have to translate because he does not speak the language of the people."

"What do I say?"

"Just follow your heart."

Although Kwe-in-ye had remained kneeling when talking to the twins, Martha did not feel that she could hold a powerful conversation in this subservient position. Taking a chance, she slowly stood up. She kept her eyes on Soft-twin's face. She would speak to him, a more receptive audience.

"I am Martha. I came here from a different world." She stopped and waited.

"*Cosupa* Martha. *Vendina sobay cha na tempe.*" Kwe-in-ye did not look at either of the twins as she translated Martha's words, still keeping her eyes focused on the floor.

"*Va tempe?*" Soft-twin asked.

"What world?" Kwe-in-ye translated.

Martha glanced at Kwe-in-ye, but her eyes met only with the side of the old woman's head.

"This world, but at a different time, many suns and moons in the future. The land is not the same. The world is very different."

Kwe-in-ye translated, while Martha watched Soft-twin's face. He glanced over at Scowling-twin, but it was a look of knowing or conspiracy, not a questioning look.

A loud crack of lightning, followed closely by a boom of thunder interrupted her thoughts. Everyone in the room looked up. A black cloud had pushed the brilliant blue aside.

Martha had an idea. If it rained she had to make it seem like it was because of her magic. Of course if this was another of those frustrating dry thunder storms, she would turn it around and claim that the evil men had driven the rain away before it had a chance to hit the ground.

In the silence that followed the echo of thunder Martha could hear the muffled sound of the people singing.

"I would like to talk to you about the…the problems of the drought. And also about the way you have stolen hope from these people."

Scowling-twin smiled, an evil grin.

He understood what she said.

Martha felt her back straighten and her chest rise. Just like that, she knew. She knew without a doubt.

"You're from a different time, too." She didn't ask the question of the twins, but made the statement directly to them. She took a step toward them. "You understand everything I'm saying, because you speak English, don't you?"

Soft-twin glanced at Scowling-twin. "I think we've let her make enough of a fool out of herself, haven't we?"

When Soft-twin spoke in English Kwe-in-ye's head jerked up as she turned and stared at Martha, her eyes grew wide, her mouth fell open and a burst of air puffed out.

And in that look Martha knew. *Not Sha-ar-lí, We-lí-um* and *Ba-ar-tun. The names Kwe-in-ye had explained to her so many months ago. Speaking of the good, the evil, the greedy spirits.*

Charlie, William, and Barton.

"You're Charlie. Where are you from?" Martha had no doubt this was the man Kwe-in-ye had said was good. Was Scowling-twin William or Barton? She would much rather deal with a greedy man than an evil one.

Charlie smiled and shook his head. "So wise for a simple woman. The year 1857, but it was long ago that we came here. More than twenty years."

"And what about the third man? Your brother?"

Charlie's face grew hard. "Never mind that. Where did you come from?"

Martha didn't answer his question, considering the fact that these men were from the future. Well, her past, but the future for the people. There must be a way she could use this knowledge.

Have faith. Be brave.

"Why do you make these people your slaves? Persecute them? Make them give up their religion?"

Scowling-twin answered. "They are heathens. Their religion is primitive, as are their ways. We didn't ask to come here. We're trapped here so why not make the best of it?"

"The best for you, but not the best for them." Martha thought about the slaves she had seen carrying loads of turquoise, and the pots and skins and food and baskets the people had paid in response to the extortion of these men. "What about this place? The rooms are empty. What happened to all the things you stole from these people?"

"No more questions! You answer us." Scowling-twin stood and reached for the staff leaning against the side of his throne.

Martha instinctively moved back. As she did, her pouch swung against her hip. She smoothed her palms down the side of her tunic, as if wiping sweat from her palms, trying to rub her hand over the pouch and figure out what it was trying to tell her.

"What do you want? Why did you come here?" Charlie remained seated.

"I want to help these people. I want you to leave them alone and let them be who they are."

"Why do you care so much about them?"

So many things filled her head in response to his question. *They are my family. They have taught me so much about life, about the ways to be happy. More than I ever learned in the other world.*

"They are people. Isn't that enough?"

"And the drought? What about that? Are you willing to starve with these people?" Charlie held his hands up at the question. "We didn't bring that with us."

Scowling-twin sat down abruptly, but kept his staff in his hand, pounding the floor with the end as he spoke. "We feed them, don't you see that? They are better off following what we tell them to do. They would all die if we weren't here."

"You feed them, but you make them work so hard for it. They are nothing more than slaves to you. You only feed them so they can work, not because you care about them."

A sudden darkness fell over the group. They all looked up at the sky. No hint of blue remained, simply the black cloud looming above them. The strange cloud moved slowly around in a counter-clockwise spiral. A tornado was forming.

Scowling-twin laughed, his hand flipping backwards through the air. "Just how do you plan on saving them?"

Martha's whole body tightened, her hands immediately gripping into tight fists. A dark wave of anger filled her mind. This waving of the hand, again, brushing off her words as if they weren't important. She might not have been as liberated as she should have been, but no one had ever treated her as if she had no value.

A soft touch brushed against her clenched fist. "Follow the way of the people." Kwe-in-ye whispered.

Scowling-twin's scoffing tone continued. "Follow the way of the people? What way is that? Lie down and starve?"

Martha was an expert at holding in her screams. What mother got through life without the desire to bellow her rage, shout her directions, or shriek her impatience? Sounds that were swallowed down into a throat burning with duty and a stomach filled with acid. She fought the blackness in her head. She took a deep breath. She could do this, she could. She just had to open her mind. The answer was there.

It had to be.

THIRTY-FOUR

Naomi flushed with excitement as she escorted Uncle Roy and her cousins to Martha's room. He wore his feathered headdress, the blue and red feathers nearly touching the low florescent lights that lined the ceiling of the hallway. The shells sewed to his leather leggings and vest clicked together softly, already starting the beat they would use for the ceremony. Her cousins, Jeff and Mark, followed behind him, carrying small drums. She hadn't been able to convince them to wear the traditional garb. Mark looked straight out of the sixties in a buckskin jacket with fringed sleeves and Jeff simply wore a white t-shirt and blue jeans. But nine-year-old Simone had come through. Her mother must have borrowed this dress from a museum. It was woven cotton with a beaded belt. Her cousin's long dark hair hung loose, with tiny feathers braided into one skinny piece of hair that hung near her left ear.

Normally her cousins would be toting a huge drum which they played with long beaters. The brothers had impeccable timing, swinging the sticks in powerful arcs to land on the big drum. Not for this ceremony.

"It won't be noisy, will it?" Mrs. Harris had lectured. "I'm saying yes to this because Mr. Grimson is so dedicated. But Naomi, I'm warning you, don't get so involved with the families. Your heart is in the right place, but you'll become the target when things don't go right. I speak from experience." Her supervisor had sighed. "Just keep it subtle. I don't want the residents disturbed."

It would have been better if they could have had the ceremony somewhere else, but Glen Grimson was extremely fearful about moving his wife. Naomi had compromised by instructing her cousins to bring their small drums.

Simone trailed behind the group, her eyes wide as she peered into the rooms with open doors. She was a vision and Naomi smiled at the thought of the bed-bound patients catching a glimpse of her beautiful ancient spirit peeking in at them.

The family was gathered in Martha's room, and they had moved all the furniture against the walls as Naomi had instructed.

"Mr. Grimson, thanks. This is my uncle Roy, and these two are my cousins, Mark and Jeff. And this magical spirit is Simone."

The men shook hands and Glen smiled at the young girl.

"Thank you, thank you. I hope Naomi told you I'm happy to pay you."

Naomi shook her head. She had talked this over with Glen and told him not to bring it up. He didn't seem to get that he had just insulted her family.

"Don't even think about it. We're happy to help." Thank goodness Uncle Roy was not old-fashioned, although he did practice very traditional ways.

She caught sight of a shy Sara watching Simone and tugging on her mother's arm.

"Mommy, I want to take my shoes off."

"I don't think…" Sandra looked at Naomi.

"It's not necessary but for some people it increases the connection with the earth."

Sandra looked down at the worn linoleum. "Keep your socks on," she said to her daughter.

"We're just waiting on Clarice." Glen paced back and forth.

Naomi wasn't surprised his daughter was late. Clarice hadn't agreed with the idea of the ceremony, going along only because of something Vince said to her. The nurse was glad to see Glen moving to Martha, who was propped in a recliner, pillows holding her in place. Her body was floppy, and she couldn't sit alone or hold up her head. He stroked her cheek and adjusted her hands, anchoring them in the center of her stomach with a towel.

Naomi set a shopping bag on the foot of the bed and removed ziplock bags with different herbs, bones, and other objects. She wore a simple leather dress with tiny beads sewn to the bodice. There was a fringe at the bottom, with beads tied to every third strand. Her hair was smoothed into two long braids, each with a red ribbon woven in. Her face was clean of any makeup. She kicked off her sandals.

She glanced at her watch. It was important to the ceremony and the family that everyone was here, but if they didn't start soon there wouldn't be time to finish. Uncle Roy had taken a couple hours off work, but he had to be there by one o'clock.

"Mr. Grimson, maybe we should get started, I'm sure Clarice will be here any minute."

Glen nodded.

"Okay, let's gather in a circle around Martha. We'll start off slow and as you feel ready to join in do so. When you pass Martha, place your item onto her lap and tell her why it has meaning."

Jeff and Mark started off with a soft beat of the hand-held drums. Uncle Roy circled around Martha with a slow, shuffling step. Naomi stepped up behind him, holding a string of jet black beads.

Jack was the first of the family to join, falling in behind Naomi, shuffling his feet and keeping his eyes down. She nodded her approval and continued the dance. As she passed in front of Martha, she placed the beads on the woman's lap.

"Martha, you are so powerful. I give you these beads which belonged to another strong woman because I know how strong you are."

The group circled again. Simone stopped near Sara and held out her hand. The little girl smiled and took it. Sara wore one of Martha's aprons. Her mother had tied a knot in the neck and folded the waistband, just as Martha would do when her granddaughter helped her cook. As the two girls danced along behind Naomi, Sara placed a large wooden spoon next to the beads.

"I miss you Grandma," she whispered. "Come back so we can bake cookies."

Jack pulled a dog collar out of his back pocket, the tags jingling. He set his gift on his mother's lap and spoke.

"Mom, we all miss you, but there is someone who can't be here who really misses you. She waits by the door for you every day. She knows how to show her love, and maybe I don't, but I love you…" Jack choked and shook his head. He stepped back and followed Roy around the circle.

Naomi saw Vince turn as the hinges of the door squeaked and Clarice slipped through the narrow opening. Martha's daughter stood very still, watching the circling dancers. She held a small brown paper bag in her hand.

Glen stood. His hands were shaking and he never took his eyes from Martha's face. He didn't attempt to move in the slow shuffling dance step, just walked slowly in the circle. When he came to Martha he reached in his pocket and pulled out her wedding ring. Yesterday he had explained to Naomi that when the hospital had told him she couldn't wear it, he had kept it at home. Each day he had looked at the gold band sitting in a tiny, flat bowl Martha had for it on her dresser, and felt the pain of it not being on his wife's finger.

He brought the ring to his lips, kissed it and slid it onto her finger. She was so thin that it slid on with ease, and he rearranged the towel to prop her hand up on her ribs to keep the ring from sliding off. He walked once more around the circle, then stepped over to the window. His gaze was intent as he stared through the glass, but Naomi guessed he looked at nothing at all.

One by one the other family members joined the circle. Sandra placed an embroidered handkerchief on the pile. "Thank you Martha, for teaching me how to sew." Vince placed a box of crayons. "Mom, all those hours helping me color outside the lines. It was good. I thank you for it and for putting my pictures on the refrigerator." He lifted Sam, who placed a plush stuffed raccoon on Martha's lap. "Memaw…Coonie for you," the little boy said.

The group continued to dance in the circle, Naomi and Roy sang a repetitive chant. *"Pa-tu-ne-so-wen, go-po-ca-tu-se, ja-pa-mot-en-tu."* The drum beat increased in tempo.

"Now you all sing. Follow what we are saying. This part is easy." Naomi didn't stop moving as she delivered instructions. "*Ha-hi-ya, o-pa-tu-a. Ha-hi-ya, o-pa-tu-a.*"

The family joined in. "*Ha-hi-ya, o-pa-tu-a.*"

Clarice remained near the door, her back pressed to the wall, her knuckles white from squeezing the paper sack.

Naomi moved to Clarice. She put her hand on the young woman's shoulder and spoke in a soft whisper. "You can do it, it's time."

Clarice looked up and nodded, then walked straight to Martha's side. The family slowed and all eyes were on Clarice as she opened the brown bag, took out a small glass horse, and placed it in her mother's hand, careful not to disturb the wedding ring her father had left. She kept her hand over her mother's to hold the horse in place.

"I love you Mom. Please come back to us." Clarice spoke in a loud voice, not a whisper as the others had.

A collective gasp filled the room when Martha's hand shot out and grabbed Clarice, the wedding ring and glass horse tipping down into her lap.

Clarice screamed and pulled back, but Martha's grip was tight.

Roy stopped drumming and the room was silent, as they all waited.

"I need my cell phone right away." Martha's voice was strong.

With the words floating like a day-old balloon, Martha's arm fell back to her lap.

Clarice jumped away. "That's it? That's all we get for this ridiculous ceremony?"

"Where is her phone?" Glen mumbled, and Naomi was a bit worried about the confused way the man was patting his pockets. "I haven't seen it…well…since…since…I don't know when."

The family all looked back and forth at each other, accusatory. Naomi had been through Martha's things a million times and knew there was no phone here.

"I have it." Jack pulled a phone from his pocket. Everyone turned to him. A few jaws dropped.

"You have it?" Vince was the first to speak.

Jack nodded and set the phone in Martha's lap.

THIRTY-FIVE

Martha opened her eyes and looked at Scowling-twin. "Are you William or Barton?"

He laughed, a wicked *ha ha, ha,* out of an old time horror movie. Shades of Vincent Price—and Martha knew this was Barton. Not greedy, evil.

"The way of the people is to believe in the best. To believe that the world is good." She turned to Kwe-in-ye and Mosinobu, still crouched on the floor. "Stand up. Stand and pray."

"You pray to a god that doesn't exist. Some corn spirit that has no power over me." Barton struck his staff against the floor once more. "You're wasting my time. Leave now."

Martha looked at Kwe-in-ye and Mosinobu. "Pray."

Suddenly she felt something bump her hip. She reached down and touched the pouch, then slipped her hand inside.

Her cell phone. That didn't seem useful and she hadn't wished for it. But it was here, so it must be a sign. She pulled it out and pressed the power button. This was crazy. It wouldn't work here.

She prayed that airplane mode worked with time travel, although she hoped Kwe-in-ye and Mosinobu were praying to their gods for a different kind of help. The happy little tune Clarice had programed into the phone for her jingled away. Power.

Barton stepped forward. "What is that? What do you have?"

"I have a tool, a tool from the future. This is the key to our freedom."

Charlie stepped closer as well. "Our freedom? You have something that can take us back?"

"A tool of magic, for magic exists in the future. I am from long after 1857, many hundreds of years."

"Give it to me."

"No, it is no use to you. Only one trained in magic can use it." Martha tapped the camera application. "First I must capture your spirit with the magic tool."

"Capture our spirit? How can that be a good thing? I will not let a witch like you capture my spirit." Barton took a step back.

"I don't need your permission." Holding the phone up, Martha took a picture and the phone let out the little *bing-bong* click sound of a photo being shot.

"What have you done?"

Martha turned the phone toward Barton.

"Your spirit is now captured." Martha looked toward Charlie. As she raised the phone to take his picture, he smiled.

"I know a daguerreotype when I see one, no matter how small and different."

His words hit her like a boulder.

What now, what now, what now? Martha lowered the phone. Fumbling with it by her side, she listened to Kwe-in-ye and Mosinobu pray and their soft words grew louder.

"I can do this, I can save them, I am powerful," she whispered as Kwe-in-ye started to circle and chant. The old woman moved to the edge of the room and Mosinobu followed. The sound of the crowd outside the walls was louder and another boom of thunder interrupted her thoughts.

The black cloud had grown, a swirling giant overhead.

Barton spoke. "You wish you were powerful, but you are weak. You are a woman, maybe a bit of a magician, but there is no magic in this place." He laughed. "What a thought, that you could overpower us."

The black cloud continued to form into a spiral, yet Martha felt no wind at all.

She looked at the phone in her hand, the colorful icons lined up like soldiers. She pressed the application button for music.

A song she had never heard exploded from the phone. It was bold and strong and as Martha punched up the volume, it was loud.

Charlie laughed.

Martha swiped the volume to full and moved her feet. She waved her arms and swung her hips. Barton frowned and the smile dropped off of Charlie's face.

Martha was filled with immense energy at the thought that she had shocked them. She could do this. This would be her prayer dance.

She kicked her feet high and twirled across the room. The music wasn't anything she had ever heard, nothing loaded onto her phone's music library. This evil man was wrong, so wrong. There was magic, lots and lots of magic.

She let the sound take over, the pounding in her heart reminiscent of watching Sen-tshe kill the deer. She felt the spirit of the dying animal travel over all the months and all the miles and enter her. She was afraid of these men, she was afraid of dying and her fear was growing. But she wouldn't let them know. She would dance out her fear.

She didn't notice the guards drop their staffs and spears, joining into a circle with Kwe-in-ye and Mosinobu. She didn't notice that they no longer prayed, but followed her rapid movements, with flailing arms and stomping feet. She didn't notice that the shocked expression on the evil twin's face wasn't focused on her, but on the sky above them. She felt only her dance, the strength of her movements. It was as Kwe-in-ye promised—when she used her body she felt the strength of all the people, not just the people who had traveled here with her, but everyone, in this place, in her canyon, in the past and in the future. The strength of all of them filled her. The thunder claps grew stronger, the crashing booms closer together, as if timed with her music, her dance, her prayer. With each crash she stomped her feet hard and twirled, then jumped to land and stomp with the next boom. The sound filled every crevice of the room and echoed off walls.

When the shout of one of the guards atop the wall broke through the music from her phone, they all stopped. Three guards motioned and yelled to the people gathered below.

Martha watched as people crowded their way onto the top of the wall. They moved around the wide edge that surrounded the open throne room, standing shoulder to shoulder, circling above like a ring of angels.

She looked up to the heavens, to the black cloud that twisted and spiraled through the sky. Whatever it was, she needed it. That much she knew. She felt it deep within every part of her being. The parts that lived here, the parts that lived in the other time, and the parts that held all the dreams and wishes of her ancestors. The next song on the phone started. Another unfamiliar tune, with drums and loud guitars and power.

Without hesitation Martha resumed her dance. She whirled and sang, stomped and flung her arms about her. She sent her message up into the sky, the black cloud responding, swirling faster and opening up into a great funnel.

Kwe-in-ye let out a cry. Martha looked to her friend and saw her staring up into the cloud. The figure of a woman, six times larger than life, stood in the opening of the vortex. She was dressed in a long green gown and the hat on her head reminded Martha of the Statue of Liberty, with spikes of sunlight radiating out around her face. She beckoned to the people on the wall, motioning them forward.

"Grandmother," Kwe-in-ye whispered.

Lightning cracked above them and everyone in the throne room cringed. The hairs on Martha's arms and neck and legs stood on end and she stopped dancing, sure they were all about to be electrocuted by the strange buzz that filled the air.

The black cloud swirled faster, reached down to the top of the wall, the point of this whirling tornado forming the vortex that stopped just above the people crowding closer. The goddess motioned to them again.

People stepped into the vortex. Although it whirled like a tornado, they were not sucked into it, but moved as if alighting into a gently rocking boat. Martha watched as the lines of people walked toward the woman in green, into the vortex that would save them, that she had called forth with her dance or that the people had summoned with their prayers.

Two guards ran into the room with a tall wooden ladder. They leaned it against the wall and climbed.

"Stop them," Barton yelled. He stood next to the wall, his staff still in his hand, an extension of his power that he waved around from his spot of safety.

"No!" Martha ran toward the ladder, determined not to let these warriors prevent the people from their escape. The top of the wall was crowded with people and it would take some time for all of them to go through the vortex.

Charlie grabbed her arm. "Is this it? Is this the way home?"

Martha looked into the man's desperate eyes. "Where is your brother? William?"

"Stop them, stop them." Barton ordered the guards as he ran toward the ladder, waving his staff like a battering ram.

Charlie and Martha turned and saw that the guards were not climbing the ladder to keep the people from entering the vortex. They had thrown down their weapons and they were pushing through the crowd on the wall.

Making their way to the front of the line, the fleeing guards stepped into the swirling cloud.

She turned back to Charlie. "Where is he?"

Charlie shook his head and ran after Barton. His brother had already started up the ladder and Charlie was quick to follow.

"Help me," Martha called to Kwe-in-ye and Mosinobu. She ran and grabbed the base of the ladder, pulling it toward her and pushing it to one side.

It didn't budge.

But when the others joined her the three of them managed to shift the top of the ladder away from where it leaned on the wall and the whole thing fell to one side. The two brothers fell with the ladder. Charlie was low enough to jump away and land on his feet.

Barton was not so fortunate. Martha watched as he clung to the falling ladder. He hit the floor with a loud thunk and he might have been okay if the back of his head had not struck a rock, the ladder landing on top of him.

"What have you done?" Charlie ran to his brother and knelt. "William, it's okay, brother. Wake up."

He slipped his legs under his brother's body and cradled his head. "Come on, Willy. We can go home now. Back. We can find Charlie."

Charlie?

The man, whoever he was, turned to Martha. "You bitch. You fix this now or you will be sliced to bits in front of your friends and then I will slice them as well."

She stared at him and shook her head. How could she have been so wrong? She saw the evil gleam in his eye and she knew that true evil had hidden from her. It had worn the disguise of something soft and warm. How was a person to get along in a world where the bad blended with the good and there was no way of telling which was which?

"*Mar-tee-a, pachinta.* Come quickly."

She looked up to see Sen-tshe at the top of the wall. He waved down to her and motioned to the ladder, then the vortex.

It was smaller now and there were only a few people on top of the wall. She could see that the woman in green still stood and guided them into the gate.

"Come on. We need to go up." She waved to Kwe-in-ye and Mosinobu and they ran to lift the heavy ladder.

Surely this evil man would stop them.

But Barton, for that is who he must be, was busy with his brother. William. Martha could see that the greedy brother's eyes were fluttering.

"Hurry." She knew the warning was unworthy of her friends, as they knew the danger they were in. The ladder was in place and Kwe-in-ye started climbing. Mosinobu motioned for Martha to go ahead of him and she quickly followed the old woman. He was right behind her. She couldn't stop herself from glancing over her shoulder.

Barton was helping William stand.

"Faster, Mar-tee-a," Sen-tshe called.

She looked up. The vortex was now a tiny thing, not more than three feet wide. "Go through, go through. I'll be there. You must save Wi-yen."

Sen-tshe shook his head. Kwe-in-ye reached the top of the wall and Martha stepped off the last rung of the ladder.

Once she was standing on the wide ledge she had a view of the entire valley and stared at the amazing sight before her. Black cloud vortices were everywhere. Lines of people curved like giant snakes, all quickly disappearing into the gateways. The people had dropped whatever they were doing, cooking fires left unattended, stones and logs dropped by the sides of the roads. All the guards had thrown down their spears. Martha could see their empty arms—except for women holding babies, no one had stopped to gather their belongings. It was clear to the people that the days of prayer had been answered. The spirit figures who stood at the mouth of each vortex welcomed the people.

"Come, Mar-tee-a." Sen-tshe touched Martha's shoulder. He was holding Wi-yen. The toddler reached toward Martha and she took him and squeezed him to her chest. He wrapped his arms around her and pushed his face deep into her neck. Martha kissed his warm hair and followed Sen-tshe.

He reached the opening and turned back to Martha, holding out his hand to help her through. She turned back for one last glance at this place, only to see that Barton and William had made it to the top of the ladder.

"We can't let them through," she said.

But what if that was wrong? Was it right to leave these men trapped in this place where they had done such evil? There were still people here —all the farms she had passed, those who had stayed in the canyon, and many more in places she knew existed. Maybe it was the destiny of these men to return to their own time.

"Don't worry about that. Just come with me." Sen-tshe took her hand.

Martha turned to follow, but Kwe-in-ye pushed between them and pulled Wi-yen from her arms. She practically threw the boy toward his father, who was quick enough to grab the toddler. Then Kwe-in-ye grabbed Martha's arm and pulled her away from them.

"You cannot go. It is not how things are meant to be."

Martha twisted and tried to pull her arm away. "Let go of me, you don't know anything. Let go." It was too much and Martha started to cry.

The green woman stepped between her and the vortex and held up her hand. The spirit looked at Martha and slowly shook her head.

Sen-tshe stepped back. "What does this mean?"

Kwe-in-ye tightened her grip and spoke. "It means she must stay and you must go. That is how it is to be if she is to save our people. I saw it."

Suddenly Martha knew what her spirit guide had been hiding all these months. She knew that Martha was to be trapped in this failing world while the rest of them made it to safety. Martha gazed into the eyes of the spirit figure. This ghostly woman was a guardian or a god or something beyond any world she knew. In the woman's deep, dark pupils Martha saw the canyon. Damé and the others, the old and young who had stayed behind, were gathered around the firestones. Their faces were clear to Martha, thin and thirsty.

She turned to Sen-tshe. "It means I cannot go with you. My work isn't quite finished." She looked away and her heart drew into a tight clench. "As much as we have tried, we both know I am not truly one of the people."

"I will not go, either."

"You must go." Martha rubbed her cheek against the top of Wi-yen's head. "And Wi must go with you."

"No, Mar-tee-a. You and I...we...are married forever, that is what my spirit guide tells me." Sen-tshe shook his head as he spoke. Tears trailed through the dust on his cheeks.

Martha stepped toward him, and holding Wi-yen in between them, she wrapped her arms around them both. She held him tightly, feeling the love for these two and wishing for a way to make things easier. No words came to mind that could bring any comfort to either one of them.

A loud boom of thunder accompanied the crack of lighting that struck the red cliffs just above them, breaking off a chunk of rock and sending it crashing down. Martha pulled away from Sen-tshe.

She wanted to say something wise, something comforting, but her throat was tight and she couldn't speak. With tears streaming down her face, she pushed him toward the vortex. Sen-tshe stood, not moving, not turning, keeping his eyes on her face.

The spirit ran her hand over Sen-tshe's back, then placed her palm on his head. She whispered something and a smile came to his face. With one more look at Martha, he turned and walked toward the passageway. Kwe-in-ye hurried after him.

Suddenly, Sen-tshe turned back and pushed past the old woman. He rushed to Martha and grabbed her hand. He pressed something into her palm then turned and slipped through the vortex.

A tidal wave of dismay swept over Martha as she watched him disappear. She slumped forward, hands covering her face. Why wasn't she allowed to go with the people? Although she thought of Glen and the kids at times, it was as if they were the dream now. Kwe-in-ye, Sen-tshe, Wi-yen, Mosinobu, To-be-né, they were her family. At the thought of this loss, Martha's knees gave out and she slumped to the stones which covered the top of the wall. As she curled up in pain, clasping her arms around her knees, she felt a sudden warmth in the palm of her hand. She opened it and stared down at the raven totem Sen-tshe had pressed to her as a final sign of his love. Opening her eyes and lifting her head, she stared into the eyes of the spirit. A breeze, cool and warm at the same time, permeated her skin, filled her body. The spirit woman reached out and took Martha's arm. She lifted her to her feet, then bent low and looked into her eyes.

"Finish it."

THIRTY-SIX

Martha stared directly into Barton's evil eyes. He pushed her aside and headed toward the vortex. Finish it, the green woman had said. That must mean that she had to keep these men from going through. William had regained consciousness, although he leaned heavily on his brother's arm and his eyes were glassy.

"No!" She grabbed Barton's arm.

He twisted and pushed her to the edge of the wall with one arm, holding his brother up with the other. She scrambled on hands and knees out of reach, just as he lifted his foot to send her over the edge.

"You won't stop us."

She would. She had to. This was what she was here for. Ten feet away lay a spear, dropped by one of the fleeing guards. She crawled toward it, trying to rise to her feet as she moved.

Barton dropped his brother and rushed after her. He jumped on her back and flattened her against the rough stones.

Martha looked up to the green woman for help, but the spirit had faded, a shimmering mist all that remained.

The vortex had faded as well. Martha covered the back of her neck with her hands and lay still, as if Barton was a black bear and she could fool him into thinking she was dead. The black cloud lifted, swirling upward into the crystal blue sky. Her sudden surrender got through to him and he looked over his shoulder.

"No! No!" He leaped up and ran toward the spot where the vortex had been. Martha watched as the distraught man flung himself toward the gateway that he had dreamed of for so long.

Barton fell the four stories to the sharp rocks below without a sound. It was William's cry that echoed through the canyon, as the greedy twin watched his brother die.

Martha scrambled up and ran to the ladder. She climbed down as fast as she could. William would surely seek revenge when he realized there was nothing he could do for his brother, and she had to get away while she could.

Martha didn't see anyone at all as she ran down the road along the wash. Everyone must have escaped through the strange vortices. She cried as she ran. What kind of terrible thing had she fallen into? Everything and everyone, both old and new, was gone.

William found her. She was back in the camp trying to figure out what she would do next when he appeared, as silent as a fox.

"He's dead."

Spinning around at the sound of his voice, Martha clutched the knife she had found among the things left by the people.

He held up a hand. "Don't worry. I'm not going to hurt you."

Like she believed a tyrant. She tensed, ready for his attack.

"It was the way out, wasn't it? Why didn't you go?"

"It wasn't the way out for me." She tightened her grip on the weapon. "Or you," she added.

"Why do you say that?"

"Where is Charlie?"

William shrugged. "We don't know. He was gone one day. He never stopped trying to figure it out—how we got here and how we could go back."

"Why are all the rooms empty? What did you do with all the things you stole from the people?"

"Gone. We filled those rooms, over and over. I think...I think Charlie figured out a way to take things. They started disappearing after he left."

"Wasn't he the good one?"

"What?" William scrunched his eyebrows.

"You're the greedy one."

"I'm not sure what you're talking about, but..." He looked down, then turned his head toward the valley, licking his lips. Finally he turned back to her. "We were all greedy. When we came here...we were out in this place looking for things to sell. We knew that there had been discoveries and we wanted to get to them first. Museums, archeologists, all those folks wanted a piece of the action."

"How did it happen? How did you..." Martha hesitated. "Time travel. That's what this is, right?"

William rubbed his hand over his forehead, wiping away the beads of sweat that had gathered. "I thought you knew. What with your magic and calling up all those spirits."

She shook her head.

"So we were here—in our time, I mean—climbing into one of those caves and the whole thing collapsed. Next thing we knew someone was digging us out. It was these people and we were not where we had been."

"So they saved you and you turned around and ruined their lives."

"Hold on. Maybe we were greedy, but the drought ruined their lives, not us."

"Not the drought. The theft of their spirits...what did you think would happen when you took away what they believed in? You made them hopeless...that is worse than starving them."

"You're wrong, there, missy. We gave them hope. A god to pray to who would save them in death. If they died with those primitive beliefs they would burn in hell." William seem to puff up as he spoke, filled with the importance of his words.

Martha eased back a step. She didn't need to confront this crazy man. The people were gone and she doubted he would have any influence over anyone left. For all she knew the black clouds had sent down pathways to the next world all over the land. Maybe there was no one left at all except for William and herself.

"It doesn't matter." She took another step back.

"No, I guess it doesn't. But the way I figure it there has to be another way out. Charlie found it and I aim to find it too." With that William turned and headed west. He leaned on his staff, dragging one leg, but never looked back.

She hoped he was right, that this way would lead him back to where he wanted to be. She hated him but couldn't keep from feeling that his circumstances had put him in this world and he had done what he was driven to do. Hadn't she done the same? Slowly forgotten about her other life, her family, her husband, children, responsibilities? He had been punished with the death of his brother, but this didn't restore what the people had lost because of these evil men. Still, maybe he had learned something. Maybe there was some bigger scheme and the three brothers had been sent, just as she had. Shaking the doubt out of her head she turned and stared at the empty buildings.

She was the only one in the valley. Everyone had gone through the vortex. Martha was alone and she had no idea what she should do next.

Damé flashed into her mind. They had left the old man behind and she had seen in the spirit's eyes that he was in trouble. It was two weeks of travel to get back to the canyon, and she didn't know if she could actually find her way back. She didn't have any choice, really.

Martha walked a short distance and realized she wasn't prepared for travel. She returned to the camp and gathered what she felt would be most important for the journey—a blanket and something to carry water, her cane in case her knee acted up again, a small pouch of food she had hidden in case one of the people had taken ill and couldn't do without nutrition. But this really wasn't enough food for two week's journey.

She wouldn't be able to hunt. She could gather fresh greens once she made it to the mountains but if she had a bit more dried meat the journey might work. The last thing she wanted was to die alone out there on the plain or in the middle of the vast caldera.

Martha searched the camp for more food, but the people didn't have much and it seemed everyone was smart enough to take it with them. Staring at the huge fort, thinking about the maze of empty rooms and all the evil that had resided within made her stomach tight. But those men had to eat and she was sure they had a healthy supply of food somewhere. William hadn't been carrying much with him, but he did have a bag over his shoulder.

The doorway didn't look as threatening as she remembered from this morning, but the eerie silence made the hairs on her neck stand up. She started off walking slowly, placing each foot ahead with the goal of making no sound at all. After creeping down three empty halls and finding the entrance to an open courtyard, she decided that this wasn't what she wanted. She should be noisy in case someone was left inside. The three brothers weren't a threat anymore and the guards had quickly abandoned the men, given a chance. But that didn't mean there wasn't still someone who would see her as an enemy. Or someone to fight with over any food she found.

"Okay, spirits. I kind of need you now. How about a little guidance?" She shuffled the gravel and started to whistle.

In spite of her bravado, the raven landing on the high wall brought a scream to her throat.

"Ca ca." He tilted his head and stared out at her with a beady black pellet of an eye.

"Are you my guide?" She turned around and looked at the three doors surrounding her. "Which one? Where's the food?"

He fluffed his feathers as if to rid himself of dust.

"You're no help." She looked down at her feet and noticed that one doorway had a worn path leading toward it. "Ahh, so that's what you were trying to tell me."

Like Sen-tshe tracking a deer, she followed the faint path in and out of hallways and doorways. She felt like she had walked around the whole complex twice when she finally found what she was looking for.

Dried meat. Not only that, but good dried meat in big hunks. Not squirrel or mouse. Vegetables as well. She filled her bag and stuffed a few pieces into her pouch, which was still strapped to her waist, surprisingly enough. In all the crazy running and fighting the leather thong had held. When she had taken as much as she could carry she wound her way out and set off down the wide road.

Martha had just rounded the first curve when she heard something behind her. Before she could turn toward the sound, something grabbed her hand. She screamed and yanked away, spinning around and grabbing the cane from her belt to strike whatever had touched her.

"Mar-tee-ya, I come with you."

"To-be-né! What are you doing here?" Martha dropped the cane and swept the girl up in her arms. Po-ko was here too, leaping up and licking Martha. Never had she been so happy to see living things.

"I come with you."

"Oh no, yes, I mean of course you come with me." It was clear that To-be-né had not stepped through the vortex with the others.

"Where were you?"

"When the dark clouds came and you went off to the sacred place, I followed. I hid in one of the dark rooms. I was scared of the warriors."

"When did you come out?"

"I think I fell asleep, Mar-tee-ya. When I woke up there was no one. I climbed up to the big mountain to see, to look far. That is when I saw you walking on the road."

Martha hugged the girl again, sorrow seeping in with the knowledge To-be-né had not gone to safety.

"Are we going home, Mar-tee-ya?"

"Yes, we are. We must go see Damé." Martha took the girl's hand and they set off down the road.

That night the two found a cluster of rocks to sleep in. Martha wasn't worried about cold or animals, but human predators might still be about. She was glad that Po-ko was with them. The dog would alert them to anyone approaching.

She didn't think she would sleep, but exhausted she curled next to To-be-né. She squeezed the raven fetish in her hand and pressed it to her chest. "Goodnight, my love," she whispered to the sky.

The sun was already over the mountains and warming the sleeping pair when Po-ko gave a happy woof. Martha opened her eyes and sat up quickly. Someone was coming. The dog waved her long tail, then started her wiggle of happiness. Martha's left hand went to the cane at her side, where it lay tucked under the blanket. She clutched the knife in her right.

Mosinobu came around the corner, reached out and patted the dog. "Po-ko, who is with you?"

Martha had forgotten all about him. He had been behind her on the ladder one minute and nowhere the next. She'd assumed he had gone through the vortex.

"Mosinobu, it's me, Martha. To-be-né is here too." Martha stood and rushed to him. She threw her arms around him in a hug. In spite of his previous stiff reception to any physical contact, he returned her hug, folding his big arms around her and squeezing.

"I wondered if everyone had gone through the swirling clouds."

"No, I wasn't meant to go and To-be-né fell asleep. What about you?"

"I was not meant to go either." He offered no further explanation.

"We're headed back home. We want to check on Damé."

"That is where I am headed as well."

Martha was glad to have Mosinobu, particularly since she doubted that either she or To-be-né could have remembered the way. The straight road part was fine, but there had been several branches and she hadn't really been paying attention to all those turns.

THIRTY-SEVEN

"**I** don't have a phone." Jack was tired of telling folks that he wasn't up to speed on the third arm everyone else carried around. Although he had spent years holding strong on his principles of not following the ebb and flow of social flux, using Mom's phone kind of ruined him for that particular stand. Dad hadn't been happy to learn that Jack had taken the phone, but that was the catch with auto-pay—Dad never looked at the bill and noticed the phone was in use. Jack's excuse that the family plan was the family plan didn't placate his father. Just when things had smoothed out between them.

Naomi and he both turned and looked at his mother's phone, lying in the basket atop the blue paint, the needles, the tweezers and the chewing gum. Naomi must have dusted them or something, because everything looked like it had just been placed there.

"I don't think you should take it back," she said.

"I know. It's what we agreed on, but it just seems so ridiculous." He frowned. "Don't get me wrong. I think she's going to wake up and I'm glad the ceremony brought her back for a minute."

"We were close, Jack. I felt it."

"I did too."

Mom lay without moving. Her breath was so soft it seemed she didn't draw any air at all. For a split second, Jack felt like his mother would be better off dead.

He shook the thought from his head and grabbed the basket. It had been a mistake to leave his journal here. What if someone read it? He glanced at Naomi. What if she read it?

"What's that?"

Relief flooded through him. "Just a notebook. I left it with Mom a while back."

"Have you checked it?"

"Checked it?"

She nodded. "If you left it here for her to write in…"

"You think she wrote in it?" Maybe the nurse had read it.

Naomi shrugged.

He looked down at the worn cover, licked his lips, then flipped to the back of the book. He used his thumb to fan through the blank pages, from back to front. He didn't want Naomi to see that the first half of the notebook was filled with his writing.

"What the—?" Someone had written in the book. On the page following his spontaneous message to Mom.

Jack, my love. Your words fill my heart with sorrow but they also open my eyes. I have been so wrong, I can't begin to explain because the words are mere excuses and excuses have no place between a mother and a son. I can only hope that a time will come when I can hold you and ask you to forgive me. I am so

The note stopped abruptly. Jack looked up at Naomi. "She…she wrote…when?" He shook his head, unable to form a clear thought.

"What does it say?" She reached out.

He closed the notebook and held it to his chest. "The thing is…this book, it has some things I wrote."

"Okay, so tell me what it says."

"She answered me. She read my stuff and answered me." He looked at his mother. "Could she be waking up at night or something?"

"I can't see how. There's staff, they check on her at night. Nothing is ever changed, Jack. The things in the basket aren't moved, they're always the same."

They sat in silence. Then Naomi leaned forward and pulled the sheet smooth.

"I think we should try again."

"There is no way you are going to get Clarice to go for that. Even with the whole spooky-arm-grab thing."

"I know. But we can do it, you and I."

"I thought we needed all that spiritual power and stuff."

"It's best. But she's so close, I think just a nudge would take care of it."

Naomi sat holding his mother's hand. Why did this nurse have such a strong attachment? Was she this way with her other patients?

It made him love her. Which was crazy because he didn't really know her at all. Sure, he spent most of the time he allotted for visiting Mom talking with Naomi. He had learned about her family, her education, her political leanings. He pushed his crush aside—that's what it was—and didn't ask her out or make a move, pretty sure that would ruin everything. If she wanted a ceremony, he would give her a ceremony.

"Sure," he said. "When?"

Naomi turned and looked straight into his eyes and for a moment he couldn't breathe. "Right now."

THIRTY-EIGHT

The threesome made good time, and it was only nine days later that they approached the canyon, their steps taking them quickly down the steep trail towards the village.

"Damé, Damé." Martha called out as she ran down the trail.

"I am here." She heard the soft voice just as she caught sight of the old man, wrapped in his worn gray cape, sitting on the stone near the fire pit.

There was another figure, bending over the fire, removing a cooking pot. It was Teji, the old cook, and here was Katudu. Martha was confused. She was sure that Katudu had been with the second group at the sacred place.

"Mar-tee-a, you have returned." Teji set down the pot on a flat rock and turned to her, a wide smile on her face.

"Me too, I am here." To-be-né hopped up and down.

Mosinobu had walked directly to Damé. He sat next to him, a brief nod the only show of emotion between the two men. He turned to the woman, "Do you have something for us to eat there, Teji? We are very hungry."

"Yes, yes. We have food."

Two other women joined Teji as she ladled a thin stew into bowls.

Soon others joined the group and Martha was surprised to see Dampo-nu. Surely the girl had wanted to join her mother? Why had she stayed behind? When Katudu walked to the girl's side and touched her arm, both young people breaking into the warm smile of love, Martha knew the answer. The two had stayed…to be together and to care for the elders.

Be-we and Teji approached, smiling and tittering. Martha was relieved that these women had continued to make the best of things. She was fighting the panic of uncertainty and could use some calm spirits around her.

"Mar-tee-a," Teji said. "Here is your food."

Be-we held out a bowl of stew. The bright blue paint shone in the afternoon light.

"My bowl." Martha reached for the clay dish. The blue paint was glowing in the last of the afternoon sunlight. Holding the pot made her smile. So many things had happened since she painted this and it was nice to think that something remained. While everything had changed, this bowl was just as she made it, the picture in her mind of how she would eat out of it fulfilled in this moment.

The stew was thin, but it tasted wonderful.

When they had finished eating, the two women picked up the bowls. "You rest, but don't tell what has happened until we return."

Martha settled back into her old spot, propped against the smooth stone. To-be-né settled on one side, while Po-ko took up her place on the other. Damé and Mosinobu lit up their pipes. It almost felt like old times, but there was no Sen-tshe behind her and no Wi-yen sleeping in her lap, no Kwe-in-ye clucking softly with her tongue as her busy hands repaired some basket or blanket.

There weren't enough people left to do the work needed. There was food hidden still, maybe enough for the small group to get through next winter, but Martha couldn't picture this frail band surviving the cold. If they spent the whole summer chopping wood and gathering food, they might have a chance. Of this group only Dam-po-nu and Katudu could make the journey to the big river for water. To-be-né and Martha could go too, but four people couldn't carry much water. Not enough for drinking, let alone crops or washing or anything else. They would have to make many trips.

Martha wished that Sen-tshe had insisted on staying. If he had not stepped through the vortex she would have a strong man by her side. To hunt, to carry water, to tell them what they needed to do. And what about her sense that Wi-yen was the key? That hadn't proved true at all. She had sent the two people she loved most through the portal. She imagined them in some other place. Maybe the next world of the legends or maybe just another time. A time without the evil brothers. A time with rains and farms and food for all.

Suddenly the image of another man—her husband—pushed away the thoughts of Sen-tshe and Wi-yen. Nearly a year had passed since she came to this world—it was mid-summer and it had been October when she had arrived. What was Glen doing? And her kids? She still didn't know if her disappearance meant that she no longer existed in the other world. Was she just gone? Was she still herself, going through each day and no one even knew she existed in two places? Had she died? What about the way things appeared, tucked into the skins or next to her in the morning? And Jack's letter. Martha hadn't looked at the journal for many days. She reached into her pouch, but it wasn't there. She tried to think of the last time she had felt it. It had been there at the sacred place. She remembered pushing it aside to grab the phone. Maybe it was with her other things, she reassured herself. It was false reassurance because she knew it was gone. Jack had been taken away again, just like everything else.

The old women returned and settled by the fire.

"Now we are ready to hear."

She wasn't ready to talk about what had happened. Instead she turned to Katudu. "How did you get here?"

"When the storms started we left, but we had been planning to leave anyway. We did not want to be slaves, to work on those roads for only a bit of food. We thought if we came back here we could gather enough to feed Damé and the others." Katudu looked at Dam-po-nu by his side. "And our baby."

A baby. Was that a wonderful thing now? Martha remembered the thin young women, losing their babies, and all the infants who had died, not enough milk from the mothers to keep them alive. *Life goes on.*

These people eagerly awaited her story. Not unlike the stories Damé told. It was their way to listen and remember the history. "Okay. I will tell you."

She told of her journey, of the arrival of the others, of the blessing and dancing the night before approaching the Man-With-Three-Spirits.

"He wasn't one man. He was three men…triplets…brothers all born at the same time. And they were from another time. Not my time, before that. They were greedy and hoped to be rich by using the people as slaves."

Damé nodded and Martha continued. "The storm produced many vortices, doorways to another place. The people entered them and they are gone now, I don't know where. I know it was a good place, because the spirit guides were there, at the doorways, helping the people through." To-be-né's eyes grew big as she listened to Martha.

"When it was my turn to step into the vortex, the spirit guide stopped me. She told me I could not." Martha took a breath as she remembered the last look of Sen-tshe, before he turned and left. "Just as the last of the people went through, the evil leaders decided that they would also go into the vortex. But the doorway closed and…one of them fell. He died."

"I slept through all this?" To-be-né asked.

Martha paused and looked to Damé and Mosinobu.

"The three evil men used parts of their own religion from a different time, to get the people to do what they wanted, to make them rich. I think they thought that somehow they could take our things with them to their time. Most of the rooms of the great storage house were empty, so it might have worked. There was some food, but not enough for all the people who had come to the sacred place. Pottery and turquoise, feathers and weapons, were still in some rooms, but there wasn't much. One of the men was gone already, although his brothers couldn't say where. It was probably he who had taken most of the beautiful objects the people worked so hard to create."

"And what of the other one, the one who was not killed?" Mosinobu leaned forward, his hands on his knees.

"He walked toward the setting sun, looking for a way to go back to his own time."

"Will he come here?" To-be-né's voice held a thin quaver.

"I don't think so. He didn't take any of the treasure with him. He only wanted to go back to his own time."

The group now turned to Mosinobu. "What did you see?"

All were quiet as Mosinobu's words followed Martha's. He told of watching the clouds, named the different spirits he recognized and talked of searching the empty rooms of the buildings. Mosinobu still didn't explain why he had not stepped through the vortex.

After the storytelling ended no one spoke or moved until Damé reached for his cane and struggled to his feet. Katudu jumped up to help him and the old man leaned on his arm as they made their way to Damé's room. Mosinobu rose and reached for To-be-né's hand.

"You come with me to my room. It is where you will sleep now."

Dam-po-nu stirred the fire and walked silently away. Katudu followed.

"Just you and me now." Martha stroked Po-ko's soft head. She couldn't go to the cave that she had shared with Sen-tshe. She should go to her old room, the one she had shared with Kwe-in-ye, but she stared into the last flames, tiny little flickers in the night. She tried to clear her head, all of the thoughts of the last few weeks pushing to the top of her consciousness and just below, like fish swimming beneath the surface of a stream, were thoughts of Glen and the kids. As she focused on her breathing, emptying her thoughts, her eyes slipped shut and she fell asleep.

"Mart-ee-a, please come."

"What?" Martha struggled to wake. What was so important that Damé was here just as the sun broke over the canyon wall?

He leaned over and reached out his hand. "We must tell the story of the people."

"Tell it to who?"

"Tell it to everyone."

She wondered if she were going to take his place as the next storyteller? Maybe he was taking her off to give her lessons. With so few people left, and really no children, he might have decided that she was the only choice.

He led her to the big cave where, after he set his cane to one side, he attempted to climb the wall. Martha watched as he carefully placed his twisted hands into the depressions and pulled his weight up. She stood below him and held out her arms, ready to catch him. She was comfortable climbing now but she had never returned and climbed up to this cave. She knew now that To-be-né should not have brought her here because it was a very special place, a kiva only for the very high leaders.

He didn't fall, but after about six feet he climbed down. His head hung low and he clenched and unclenched his hands. Finally he looked at her.

"Mar-tee-a, you will have to do this alone. Up in the cave there are many stories." He took three small stones out of the bag strapped to his hip. "Use these to draw the story of the cruel men and of the swirling clouds."

Martha nodded, slipped the stones into her pouch, and climbed the wall. She rested for a moment on the ledge, peering over to where the old man sat below. The memory of Sen-tshe and how he rescued her burned inside of her and she quickly climbed the rest of the way. She wouldn't let herself dwell on him.

When she reached the cave she walked around the edges, examining the walls. It was as he said. There were many stories here. She saw things she could recognize: the exodus of the families from the sacred place and the arrival of the three men. Many of the pictures were high on the walls and for a moment she wondered who had carved them into the rock. She followed the pictures around the wall and stopped in front of a blank spot, just at eye level. As if it was waiting for her to finish the story.

Where to start? She thought about the time she had spent in this world. She took one of the sharp stones and drew a circle. It didn't show and she had to grind away at the edges until she was satisfied with the depth. She added her hair, her eyes, mouth, a dress and stick legs. With a smile she added her sheepskin slippers. Laughing, she realized that her drawing was like those displayed on her refrigerator with magnets. Sara's stick families with big grins and arms akimbo, each sporting the requisite five fingers. Martha added a stick dog by her side.

Stepping to the right she drew three figures, long and thin, angry faces. Next to that she tried to draw a long line of people carrying things. Her figures became simplified as she continued. It would take forever to draw all the details and the other drawings in the cave appeared more symbolic than what she was trying to do. Not only that, the first stone was dull and she couldn't cut through the rock wall. She took out the second stone and added a mountain and a tree behind the people to give some perspective and make them look less like ants.

Now she drew Sen-tshe. She added herself next to him, both with kindergarten smiles. She stood on tip toes and reached high on the wall, carving a swooping tornado, curved lines coming down toward them.

Wi-yen. He hadn't figured into saving the people, in spite of all her premonitions. Simply a boy who had brought her great joy and then disappeared. She drew a tiny figure, Wi-yen being drawn up into the vortex. She added tears to the faces.

Tears flowed down her cheeks as well. She missed Sen-tshe. Why did she have to suffer so much heartbreak? She traced her finger across the floating Wi-yen. And the boy? She had been cheated not only out of those she loved but of knowing the answer to the puzzle she had lived with for nearly a year.

When she stepped back to look at her work, she snorted and shook her head. What a mess. This was nothing like the other drawings in the cave. She had started small and grown bigger, the whole thing expanding like a trumpet and sloping down as her arm grew tired. There was no sequence to this thing, just a bunch of random scribbles. She took the last stone from her pocket and drew squares around each part of her story, separating the events. It seemed a little better in her mind, but she wondered about a culture that wasn't used to reading left to right and people who had never seen a comic strip.

"It'll have to do. That's all there is to it." She leaned forward and kissed the stick man and climbed down.

Damé waited at the foot of the wall, dozing in the sun. She didn't want to startle him, so she sat next to him and coughed. The old man opened his eyes.

"You have finished?"

She nodded.

"Then let us go back."

Martha took his arm and helped him rise. He smiled his thanks and kept a grip on her as they started down the trail.

The sun filtered through the leaves, reflecting diamonds of sunlight on the world. Birds twittered and flitted from tree to tree and a woodpecker drilled away on a tall ponderosa. This was a day not much different than the first time To-be-né had brought her here to climb the endless wall.

Outwardly the same place. Inwardly, nothing was the same.

"Damé?"

"Yes?"

"In your stories, has anything like this ever happened before?"

"There have been hard times."

"But the spirits and the clouds with the vortices, these gates to another place. Do you know where they went?"

The old man drew a slow breath in through his nose, then let it out. "There have been gateways for the people. Long, long ago."

"Like the star people coming out of the darkness?"

"Yes."

"And now? Where did they go? Kwe-in-ye and Yo-en-u?" She paused. "Sen-tshe and Wi-yen? Will I ever see them again?"

He stopped and took her hand, then shook his head. Without a word he turned and continued down the trail. She didn't know if this meant she wouldn't see them or that he didn't know.

Martha's knee throbbed and she tossed and turned. The drawing, the fire, all following the quick journey home, left her melancholic. It was not enough to have Po-ko curled next to her. She needed Sen-tshe and Wi-yen. Her thoughts raced as she chased after sleep, as elusive as ever.

Why was she still here? What force had sucked her from her world with Glen and their children, her grandchildren, her spotless house, decorated with years of treasures purchased on family vacations? Each room held a special feeling for her. The kitchen where children had sat at the table working on homework, or pretending to work in Jack's case, the snacks she would set in front of them if they came straight home. Any later than three o'clock and supper was ruined, that was her rule. She loved washing the dishes, her hands soaking in the warm soapy water as she polished each of the special plates and gazed out the greenhouse window Glen had installed, past the old swing-set, in need of repair. Martha imagined looking over the back fence to the tiny sliver of trees along the river. Their "view" they always joked.

All this time, these months adjusting to this new life, she had expected that there would be an answer. One day something would happen that would explain everything. But now, with nearly everyone gone, she couldn't erase the image of William trudging off to the west, searching forever. She didn't want to be that person. She either had to know or she had to accept she would never know and move on with her life.

Kwe-in-ye had been correct in bringing her here to help the people, Martha knew that was true, but if that had been her purpose, why was she still here? Why hadn't the spirit woman let her go with those she loved? Was she destined to starve to death in this ancient world?

Or freeze, she thought as she pulled the skin tighter around her shoulders. This room was warm when there were people sleeping beside her, but the hard floor reminded her that she wasn't a young woman. Her shoulder ached nearly as much as her knee. She rolled the raven fetish in her hand. She slept with it every night although she was worried about losing the one thing she had from Sen-tshe.

That night, she dreamed of Wi-yen. It was one of those dreams where the baby was young at times, and suddenly old and spoke to her in a man's voice. She felt someone touch her, but she ignored it. She needed to stay in this dream because it was going to show her the answer to the puzzle.

"Tell me, Wi-yen. Tell me the answer."

"Mom?"

The voice was louder now. And insistent. The hand held hers and squeezed.

"Mom, it's me. Jack."

THIRTY-NINE

Martha fought the pull of wakefulness, intent on grabbing whatever rest she could. She was so tired. There were sounds all around her and they crept through the wall of sleep, as if something solid had become a gauzy curtain.

They were not the sounds of the canyon.

"Mom, don't leave again. Open your eyes."

She squeezed her eyes tight, but it was too late. She was awake.

"Come on Mom."

This dream was too hard, putting her back in the old world when she needed to think about what was next in this one. How would her people find enough to eat? Gather enough wood and water over the coming months to last them through the dry times and the cold times? How would they survive?

"Mom?"

She blinked and reached up to rub her face. Why did this dream keep such a grip on her? It must be all the events of yesterday, confusing her unconscious mind.

Rubbing her eyes didn't change anything. Jack's face was still right in front of her. She stared back at him, unsure of what to do.

He reached for her, placed his hands on her cheeks and stared directly into her eyes.

"Are you back?"

"Jack?" Her voice was croaky and her throat dry. With some effort, she cleared it. "Where am I?" Martha tried to push herself up into a sitting position, but her elbows bent under the strain and collapsed, sending her shoulders back onto the bed. She felt something sharp in her hand and rubbed her finger over it. She knew by the shape and size what it was.

Sen-tshe's raven fetish.

She tucked it neatly under her hip.

Jack looked over his shoulder and spoke to someone. "She's awake, we did it. You're a miracle worker."

Martha turned her head and watched as her son jumped up and hugged a young woman who was standing at the foot of the bed.

She shut her eyes, then opened them, daring the bed to go away. It was still there. Jack rushed back to her side and kissed her cheek.

"I can't believe it. I just can't believe…we need to call Dad."

She finally took a closer look at the young woman and gasped. She was looking into Wi-yen's eyes. "I…uh…" Her voice was stuck, the air huffing as she tried to make sense of this face.

"I'm Naomi. It's nice to meet you, Mrs. Grimson."

Her eyes might be Wi-yen, but her mouth, her voice, it was all Sen-tshe. Martha reached out for her hand.

"I know you."

"Yes, we've been together awhile now." Naomi held onto Martha's hand and sat on the edge of the bed.

"Who are you? Did you come from the other time?"

Jack and the young woman exchanged puzzled glances.

"I'm your nurse, Mrs. Grimson. You are in a care home. You have been in a…kind of a coma."

A kind of a coma? What did that mean? All this time she had been here and in the other world at the same time? But maybe no time had passed at all. "How long? How long have I been here?"

"Nine months."

The room was awhirl with activity that attacked her like a swarm of bees. Unbearable. She let her mind flee from the buzzing.

"Martha, don't close your eyes…please don't go away again." Glen held her hand.

"I don't think I am." She squinted. Glen had changed. His grasp was unfamiliar. "I'm just very tired."

He looked over his shoulder at the others, gathered in a cluster, staring at her. "When is Dr. Braundo going to get here? I don't want to lose her. I don't think we should let her sleep, it's too risky."

"When have the doctors ever been there for us?" Clarice paced anxiously. Martha wanted to reach out for her, but the electric charge that surrounded her daughter felt dangerous.

Everything felt a bit dangerous, so Martha stared up at the ceiling, trying to block out the noise. She didn't want to be here, yet she didn't really want to go back to the canyon without Sen-tshe and Wi-yen. But what about To-be-né? The girl was her responsibility.

According to her family—so happy to have her back, yet so anxious —it had all been a dream. There was no To-be-né. No Sen-tshe or cuddly little Wi-yen. She turned her head and looked at the nurse. Naomi, the girl had said. Martha had been with this woman for nine months and that was why she looked like Sen-tshe. Or rather Sen-tshe had looked like her. The things in this world, this sterile room, these curtains around the bed, the television perched up like a rock on a canyon wall, had all been the catalyst for her dreams.

Martha shook her head. "It wasn't a dream."

"Now honey, don't you worry about that. We're just going to hang in here with you until the doctor comes." Her husband squeezed her hand so tight it ached.

It was all coming back. How Glen was like a terrier when it came to an idea. She needed to come up with something to distract him. Something to get everyone out of the room and give her some quiet. She needed to think.

She needed to talk to Naomi. Alone.

She looked past Glen and found the nurse's almond eyes, shining at her. "Can I have a shower?"

"I don't see why not." Naomi turned to the others. "Maybe you all could go out to the community room? I think there's some coffee."

"Since when are you a doctor? I don't think you can make a decision like that." Clarice stepped in front of the nurse, as if to rescue Martha from a kidnapping.

"Absolutely not. I'm not leaving." Glen squeezed again and Martha struggled to break his death grip.

"It's okay," she said to him. "I'm not going away. I promise."

Doubt clouded his face and she saw his lips part as he started to protest, stopped himself, thought for a minute, and then nodded. Maybe he had learned something in those nine months without her.

"No, Mom. You can't do this. We have to wait for the doctor."

Had Clarice always been this angry? Her daughter glared at her, seemed to regret her words and turned to Naomi. "Think about it. Do you want to be responsible if anything happens?"

"It will be fine. It really will be." The nurse who looked like Sen-tshe had his smile and his soft tone. "Let me just get a wheelchair."

As Naomi pushed her to the shower down the hall, she wondered how they bathed an inert body. The nurse was correct in her assumption that Martha would have trouble standing. Her legs—so strong from all the activity in the canyon—were weak and thin. After a single attempt to pull herself up, she sank back into the bath chair provided and used the hand-held spray to clean her body.

Her hands shook as she rubbed the liquid bath soap over her chest, under her armpits, down her torso and worked to wash the parts sitting on the chair. She had to stand if she was going to do this. She used the metal bars and leaned against the fiberglass wall, plopping back into the seat after a three-second rinse.

"How are you doing? Don't try to stand."

"Okay," she called and turned off the water. Naomi stepped close with a large towel.

"Let me help. You're weak, but that's to be expected. I know you want to fight it—everyone does—but falling isn't the best thing right now."

Martha sighed and nodded. Naomi smelled of bleach and some sort of perfume. Martha inhaled. An image of Sen-tshe eating his mush of saltbush and the green lambsquarter—which stunk like an adolescent's unwashed gym clothes—flittered through her mind.

She grabbed Naomi's hands and brought them to her nose.

No, she was wrong. This odor was the soft combination of baby and the tough twigs used to relieve teething pain. A sharp, clear odor.

"Wi-yen."

The girl pulled her hands away. "What?"

"You smell like...the baby..." Martha stopped.

"Wi-yen?"

She nodded.

"This is the name of someone in the other world?"

This nurse believed her story.

"Yes. A baby...a toddler, really. He went away."

"Died?"

"No...it's a long story, but his father and I, we..." Martha stopped. Did she trust this woman not to spread tales to her family?

Naomi bent her knees so that she was face to face with Martha. "This name...my great-grandfather. His name was Wi-yen."

Martha did the math. Naomi was in her twenties. Subtract thirty years for each generation and it was still nowhere near the time she had been in the canyon. Nine hundred years is hundreds of generations. Thousands, actually. "Could it have been a family name? Passed down?"

"I guess. That was common during certain times, but I really don't know anything about that as far as my family goes."

It could be a crazy coincidence.

"Did you ever talk about him? Here? To me, I mean?"

"I don't think so."

Or maybe when Sen-tshe and Wi-yen stepped into the vortex they were carried to another time. The time of this girl's great-grandfather. Martha shivered.

"Let's get you dressed. We can talk about this later." Naomi helped her into a nightgown.

Martha didn't recognize it, but the flannel was soft and it felt wonderful on her clean skin and she smiled for a moment at the memory of Kwe-in-ye battling her for the flowered nightgown. That thought brought more memories streaming in which circled back to the fact that this girl smelled like the baby Martha had cuddled with each night.

She tried to shake the thought of Wi-yen grown and married and having a son, who then had a son, and on and on until she reached this girl, but she didn't want to leave it to later. "Where are you from?"

"I am from San Ildefonso." Naomi paused and looked at Martha. *"Po-Weh-Geh-Owingeh."*

Martha nodded. "Up above. Where the water cuts through. Could you…would you tell me…what is the history of your people? The ancient stories?" If she was right this girl was a descendant of the people of the canyon.

"Of course I will. But right now, your husband is probably ready to call in the swat team. Let's get you back to your room."

FORTY

Mosinobu awoke to a warm tongue licking his face, sliding down his cheek and curling into his ear.

"Po-ko, what are you doing here?"

Po-ko was a wise dog. She knew what every person needed. He often wondered whose spirit had decided to inhabit the animal rather than move on to the next world.

The dog probably came to find To-be-né. Mar-tee-a might claim ownership, in spite of being told there was no such thing, but everyone knew the animal's attachment was to the girl who was soon to be a woman. Mosinobu considered her as he rose and pulled on his leather moccasins. He could take the girl as his wife, but at his age there was no guarantee of a child. He must think about the future. There were few young men left and it was likely each would have to take more than one wife. Katudu would be a good choice for To-be-né.

The sun peeked over the ridge of the canyon and Mosinobu lifted his chin and stretched his neck and spine. He had been here for so long, looking forward. The future was held by something as thin as the thread of the spiderwebs that stretched across the trail, shimmering with the last of the morning dew. Yet these were strong webs and the spider was able to succeed in spite of the wind and the birds and the deer. His people could live on.

He thought about Mar-tee-a. How the strange woman had pushed them to the gateway of the spirit world. The others had moved on to something else by stepping into the swirling vortex. To what, he did not know. Better? Worse? Perhaps a vast nothingness was more comfortable than starving to death in the cold of winter. No one really knew what was on the other side. And the story kept changing. He had grown up believing in what he learned from his elders only to be told that the ideas were wrong and the new religion of the Kachinas was to be followed. Then the strange men had appeared and all the people had to pray to a different god. In his heart he yearned for the world of his past.

Mosinobu walked up the trail eager to talk to Mar-tee-a about what would come next. Yesterday, when she told the story of her confrontation with the Man-With-Three-Spirits to the others he felt a connection to this woman. If she were not beyond the age of having a baby he would take her for his wife. Maybe this would be a good idea anyway. The two of them would provide for the people with a balance of wisdom.

Once she quit grieving for Sen-tshe.

Po-ko ran ahead, sniffing, then hurried back to him. She was acting strange. If the dog was running around perhaps the woman was already out. Early mornings seemed to hold hands with age, and she was of his age.

"Mar-tee-a," he called. The hair on the back of his neck tingled. "*Ja pa.*"

The dog ran inside the room and back out. She whined and wagged her tail.

Mosinobu leaned into the doorway and rested his hands on his knees. He called out once more, but he could see the room was empty. He didn't need to search the canyon or look around because Po-ko had told him all he needed to know.

Mar-tee-a was gone.

FORTY-ONE

Clarice stood behind the chair her father had pulled close to Mom's bed. Her mother had initially insisted the family all listen to her story at the same time but Aunt Deborah couldn't get a flight until tomorrow. None of them wanted to wait another day. and Mom was eager to start, so she decided it would happen today and they wouldn't wait for her sister. Clarice wasn't happy she had been nominated to pick Aunt Deborah up at the airport at noon, the worst time for the drive. She would be stuck in the car explaining everything. But Dad wouldn't leave Mom's side, not for more than a quick break. He had brought the camper down to the hospital and took naps when one of them was here to relieve him.

"I'm fine now. I don't need to go to the hospital." Mom had insisted that she was ready to go home, but Dr. Braundo refused. So here they were, back at Magnolia General, although he promised the tests would happen right away and if nothing showed up, her mother could head on home. In the meantime she had physical therapy and a nutritionist and a respiratory therapist. Everyone but a mental health worker, which in Clarice's mind was the one thing her mother truly needed.

"The night after Dad and I toured the ruins, that night I had a strange dream. I was walking down a steep trail into the canyon. When I arrived at the bottom of the canyon there were people, but they were ancient people." Mom smiled. "They weren't ancient, but they lived a long time ago. One woman, Kwe-in-ye, could speak English, because she had a dream also and in her dream I was sent to save her people, for they faced terrible problems."

Mom's story took nearly two hours. Sandra recorded everything with her phone. The only pauses had been to give her mother sips of water. Clarice kept quiet and so did everyone else. They had agreed to let Mom talk uninterrupted because they didn't want to stress her.

"I fell asleep that night, Po-ko curled beside me. When I awoke I was here, with Jack touching my face and talking to me."

Clarice shifted and shook her head, looking at Vince. Dad squeezed Mom's hand and glanced at Sandra. Only Jack nodded, intent on the story.

Clarice decided not to discuss her thoughts with her father or brothers. She sought out the doctor instead. Past history of how every little decision turned into a giant family battle had taught her if she wanted something done she would have to bypass that snarl.

She caught up with Dr. Braundo in the hall. "What about her mental state? I mean, not the coma stuff, but this dream about another world? Should she have a psychiatrist working with her as well?"

"Let's give her a bit more time to recover. The world she describes is very real to her but as she spends more time back here with us, it will fade." The doctor didn't seem concerned about Mom's insistence that she had time traveled.

"I don't think so. She can't talk about anything else. When she gets home, I'm worried about that." Worried about Dad, really. He had felt so abandoned when Mom was unconscious, but at least being in a coma didn't have the lacerating impact of Mom choosing to be somewhere else. Her mother was animated when she talked about these characters, completely unaware that the last nine months had been hell for her family. These stories, this insistence that they needed to know these people, left them all feeling less-than-important.

"There will be an adjustment, my dear. Why don't you focus on the fact that your mother is awake...and as far as I can tell with no damage at all." The placating bastard shook his head. "No explanation, but a stroke of good luck, I would say."

"Sure. Great. A flippin' miracle, that's my mother."

Dr. Braundo kept Martha for three days. Tests and more tests.

"Dad, do you think he could be ordering things just because you have good insurance?" Clarice was sitting with her father beside the bed.

Mom pushed herself up to a sitting position. "I do. Take me home. I'm sure you can, dear. You know, like on those crime programs? The injured police officer who must get out to solve the crime? You just have to sign something saying I left against their advice. And Clarice, darling? Please don't talk about me as if I were still unconscious."

"Sorry." It was true. They had gotten so used to talking around her that if Mom had her eyes closed they forgot she could hear them.

"Now wait a minute. I trust that doctor. I'm not going to do anything until he gives the okay." Dad patted Clarice's hand, as if she were nine years old.

She was so sick of placatory men. Surrounded by them. The doctor, Dad, Vince...even at school. This semester hadn't produced one female instructor. And those young professors didn't seem to care that her mother had just come out of a coma...no pity for missing class at all. One had even had the gall to say "hire an aide," as if being a daughter didn't come with any emotional responsibility. Only Jack didn't talk down to her and that was mostly because he was off on some unique train of thought of his own.

"Where are my things?"

"Huh?" Mom's question brought Clarice back from her spiraling internal rant. "What things?"

"That basket that was in the other place. Naomi said they were the things I had asked for while I was..." Mom hesitated. Apparently she didn't know how to describe her state of absence either. Initially when they called it a coma, she corrected them and said it was a journey, but now she had resorted to vague implications. She was probably afraid they would never let her go home if she kept acting crazy.

No worries about that, dear mother. The doctor thinks you are perfectly sane.

"I think Jack took them to the house. Why?"

"I just wanted...I wanted to ask you about them. To tell you my version and to hear yours."

"I don't get it. You just mumbled 'needles' and then we brought them." She didn't tell her mother it was Vince who had insisted. The rest of them thought it was foolish.

"When?"

"When? Right after, well, the next day or so."

"No, when did you bring the needles? What month?"

Clarice shrugged. "Mom, I don't really remember. It was early on, I think." She turned to her Dad. "Do you know?"

Her father shook his head. "It was Vince. He brought the things. Sometimes we heard you, but more often it was Naomi telling us what you had requested."

"Except the first time. That was a shock. We thought..." Clarice paused. "We thought you had woken up. Come out of the coma. It was your birthday party. November 14."

Mom smiled. "You had a birthday party for me?"

"Of course we did." Dad spoke up. "Why wouldn't we?"

Mom laughed. "Because you never did before."

"That's not true," Clarice protested. She wished she could pull back those words when she saw the laughter die in her mother's eyes and she realized it was true. Mom had planned all her own parties. Dad hadn't done a thing and neither had any of the rest of them. They brought whatever Mom asked for, a casserole, a piñata, decks of cards for a Canasta tournament, but no one had ever been the one to come up with the ideas or organize the production. Now that Clarice thought about it, none of them knew what her mother liked. Or had even tried to figure it out.

"So tell us about your end. What was happening when you asked for the needles?"

The smile returned, although it was wan and her mother gazed past her. "I was learning to sew. They had cotton, you know. They didn't grow it, they traded for it. And dyed it as well. But the thread was from the yucca plant and it broke if I wasn't careful. Plus, those bone needles, you spent all your time threading and re-threading because they didn't fit through the beads."

"Say honey, maybe you would like a party when you come home? Not right away." Dad wasn't paying attention to the conversation. Clarice could see he was stuck on the guilt of her mother's claim he had never had a party for her.

Mom actually snorted.

The tension between her parents was like a thick sponge, sucking all love from the room. Clarice was torn. She didn't want her mother to keep talking about the dream world, but she needed to distract them. Maybe she could absorb everything that passed between them so that it never actually soaked the other with the unspoken accusations.

"So you sewed a lot there?"

"Not a lot. It was one of the things I learned. I didn't even use those needles much myself, but they increased my social status."

Clarice caught her father trying to get her attention. He was scowling and shaking his head.

What was his plan? Should she talk about the weather? Or maybe update Mom about what had happened in the real world while she lay unaware for months? Politics and how things hadn't improved with time? Or maybe an in-depth discussion of Clarice's online arranged dates and rapid escalation of intimacy followed by quick break ups?

It was possible her mother was the lucky one, escaping into this land, the canyon as she called it, where everything was new and it pretty much sounded like the people there made all decisions for her. Maybe listening to Mom and finding out what it was that made it seem like she wasn't happy to be back with them was the key to happiness.

"What was it like? Their social structure?"

Her mother looked surprised by her question. "It was different, but in many ways the same. They were somewhat settled by clan. Family and religion played a role in their lives which eventually divided them. Not just because of the three men, but because of their own evolution and changes."

"Where did you fit? In the hierarchy? They told you what to do all the time, right?"

"There were definitely those with higher status, but it had to do with knowledge and skill, not wealth or being a movie star. Like the medicine people. My history books always said it was the medicine man, but in truth it was both men and women. I was low only because I didn't know about things." Her mother shook her head. "Yet the expectations of what I could do for them also came into it. Anyway, it's true, the men were the hunters. Physical strength, I think. And women took care of the children. Except for—" Mom looked away, staring down into her lap. "Except for one man. His wife died and so he carried his son around on his back. But he was different."

Clarice watched her mother's eyes glaze over as she stared out the window. "Were you happy there?"

"Most of the people...they were happy. The drought had them worried and they were trying everything to make things work, to have enough food and to stay healthy. But day to day? They were still happy." Her mother had deftly avoided the question. "I guess when you have to keep doing the work, making the pots and the shoes and drying the food and planting the fields, you don't have time to feel sorry for yourself. No one was depressed."

Dad stared at Mom. "Is that it, Martha? Is that why you did this? Were you depressed?"

She shook her head without looking up. "I didn't *do* this Glen. It wasn't by choice."

"I know. I'm sorry. I didn't mean..." Her father struggled and Clarice was compelled to rescue him.

"I can't picture it. There had to be things that upset them, right? Didn't people die from accidents and stuff? Bear attacks?"

Her mother didn't answer. Simply stared at Dad and looked terribly sad.

FORTY-TWO

"What happened?" Martha stopped inside the front door of their house, shaking loose from Glen's firm grip on her elbow. He still acted like she couldn't walk, although the three days in the hospital had been plenty of time to regain her strength. She had been subject to walks every hour with one type of therapist or the next.

Her view of the living room was blocked by a wall. White, with the old Steven Lyman painting from Glen's mother hanging smack dab in the middle. She had never liked the stillness of the painting and kept it tucked out of sight in the hall. Martha stepped around the corner.

A double bed stood where her couch should have been. The open floor plan to the kitchen was closed in with another white wall, this one devoid of any decoration, hovering like a monolith.

And then Mandy was there.

"Mmm, arggg, mmm." The dog wiggled and whined and ran in circles around Martha. She stooped to pet her, letting the beagle jump up and lick her face.

"Somebody's happy to see you," Glen said.

Martha looked up at him as she rubbed Mandy's soft ears. "You remodeled?"

That was too kind of a word, but she was so shocked no others came to mind. She stood and walked into what had been the kitchen, expecting that her refrigerator and oven would be missing.

Instead there were new granite counters, a reddish brown, and the cabinets had been replaced with something that was trying hard to look Italian, but simply looked garish. She turned to Glen.

"What in the world have you done?"

The look on her husband's face was that of a dog who has just offered up a dead squirrel.

"Jack and I...we thought you would like to come home to a new kitchen."

"What happened to my living room?"

"The couch is in the den."

"Den?"

"Come on, I'll show you the rest."

"Just tell me why there is a bedroom here. Maybe Glen had thought she would never come out of that coma and he had taken in...who? A girlfriend with children?

She must be in the coma still, and this was just another crazy dream.

"We thought you might need...need to be here where we could take care of you when you came home." Glen shrugged.

Martha glanced down the hall. The doorways were all widened.

"Wheelchair access?" She spun and looked at Glen. "You were preparing for the worst?"

"No. The worst would have been you staying in that convalescent hospital. The best was that we would bring you home."

She couldn't have felt heavier if someone had attached a cement block to her waist and thrown her off a long pier.

"I need to rest." She walked down the hall. There had been changes in the master bedroom as well. The bed had been moved away from the wall that faced the window and stuck nearly into the doorway. The door to the bathroom was gone and the walls replaced with a strange glass block partition. She found her way to the toilet, complete with fat stainless steel grip bars on each side. There was a free-standing sink under a tiny mirror. She was determined not to think about what had happened to everything that was stored in the old cabinet and how anyone could think that having the toilet open to the bedroom was a good thing.

"Honey? Is everything okay?"

"Yes. Please, Glen. I just want a nap. And to pee in peace."

Martha tossed and turned, as if the bed had been replaced. It wasn't the fact everything was changed...nothing felt familiar to her anyway. She sank into the deep mattress and her neck bent at an awkward angle.

Sleep wouldn't save her. She couldn't fall back to the world where love and excitement and simplicity had surrounded her. She was here now and she had to accept that the canyon might have been only a dream after all.

She curled up on her side and tucked her hands under her head, palms together and knuckles pressed against her ear. For the first time in months she felt the need to make a list. How nice it had been to escape the constant mental and written tasks, lined down the page like the ladders she hadn't wanted to climb. Funny thing was, she hadn't noticed that they were missing. Contentment was like that—filling your day so completely you never had to think about anything else.

Number one: Glen. No, that was too much right now. How about number one: the house? It would be easy enough to insist the couch was returned to the living room but all those walls? And that hideous kitchen. Cooking like she had before her journey wasn't going to be easy...well, actually it probably was easier than grinding corn and building a fire, but it all depended on what was meant by easier. Maybe she could put in a fire pit in the back yard and keep on doing it the old way.

Old way. For her family it wasn't going to be the old way. It had been the new way for her in the canyon and this life, this was really her old way.

She stared at the wall six inches from her face. The bed really did have to be moved because while she hadn't minded sleeping in a tiny cave in the canyon she felt claustrophobic now. She closed her eyes and tried to imagine she wasn't in this house, she tried to smell the dust of the trails, the piñon pines, the rabbitbrush, and wild roses.

Number two, she thought. Find a way to go back.

"Martha?" The gentle hand on her shoulder squeezed and she swam up through the sludge of sleep and opened her eyes.

"I'm sorry. I know I should let you sleep, but you were gasping and you don't have your machine." Glen motioned across the bed. "It's on the other side. I can help you move over there."

She shook her head. "I'll get up now." She should have added *we need to talk.* Instead she pulled the blankets off her shoulders and stretched her cramped legs.

"Are you hungry?"

"Thirsty."

"How about some ice tea?"

She nodded, thinking about how good her old favorite would taste. She remembered the times hiking up from the big river carrying pots of water when she had imagined a tall raspberry ginger tea with a lime floating in it, tiny ice cubes clinking against the sides of the glass.

"You can wait here and I'll go get it."

"No, I'd like to see the yard."

He nodded and slipped away.

She swung her legs over the edge of the bed and stared at her feet, bare and pale. Not the feet of a woman who had walked in yucca sandals.

She had to stop. She would never adjust if she kept comparing everything with the past. With a sigh she walked to the closet and pulled out her flip flops. But this made her think of the sheepskin slippers Kwe-in-ye had stolen and that made her think of the vortex and To-be-né and Mosinobu and Damé.

"Stop, stop it, stop it." She pushed her palms firmly against the sides of her head as she hurried out of the bedroom. Maybe if she sat with Glen, kept her eyes open and looked at the house, the yard, the dishes, she would fill her mind with all these things and send these unwanted memories far away.

The trouble was they were not unwanted at all.

FORTY-THREE

"It's hard to put into words, this whole conflict the people had. It was a transition from working for what they needed to survive, taking care and respecting the earth, with everything shared, like a community that really took care of everyone. The new way, in that other valley, with the men from the future in control, was more materialistic and some of it leaked over into everyone. Those men were trying to store up things to trade, have things just for the sake of having things, not noticing—not caring, really—that people were starving and the crops weren't doing well."

"Mm...hmm." Glen was tired of listening to Martha. It had been a month and all she would talk about was "the people". Clarice mentioned that she had asked Dr. Braundo if Martha should go to therapy, but the doctor had recommended a little more time. His daughter thought he should insist on Martha seeing someone, but his relationship with his wife was too fragile. If he did anything that might upset her, she might shatter.

Martha was a changed person. He didn't expect her to be a slave to the house or anything, but she had trouble focusing on tasks. She spent her days painting and making pots while dishes piled up in the sink and the refrigerator sat empty.

Last month, on the day she came home from the hospital, it was a full day before she noticed that Jack was living in the house. She had thought he was just visiting.

"Oh, Jack is living here now? That's nice." This was not the old Martha, who had cut the enabling apron string long ago. This Martha spent hours on the porch swing, staring off at the two trees at the end of the lawn, as if she were looking into a deep forest, not at the redwood fence which separated their home from the culvert behind it.

"What do you think about moving?" Martha's voice broke through to Glen.

"Moving? Why?"

"To New Mexico."

"Martha, what would be the sense in that? It's not the place from this, this..." *What should he call her coma-dream?* "...world you have in your head."

"I know that, but it's what I feel. I don't want all these things around me, Glen. I want to follow the ways of these people, to understand what's important. It's not all this—" she waved her hands around her "—stuff. It's taking care of those we love, respecting the earth."

Glen realized Martha did want to be back in the physical spot. She explained to him that after talking with Naomi, she knew that the people of the pueblo had to be the descendants of the people from her dream world.

"Martha, I agree with those things and they are important. But the people we love are here, right here in Lindenville, not in New Mexico." He paused. Might as well get it over with. "And these stories, what do they even mean? Why is every element of our life reason for some ancient fairy tale?"

"They aren't fairy tales...they're lessons. I learned so much during my time there and I want to share it with you."

"I get that. But can you cut to the chase? Give it to me in a nutshell? Like, that one, the idea that the trees were taller closer to the water. Of course they were...it was a canyon, they had to reach for light above the rock walls. Nice story, but what does it have to do with us?"

She looked down at her hands and twisted her fingers together. When she lifted her eyes from her hands, she licked her lips. "I guess, I guess it's kind of like we're just as much the forest as we are the trees."

He shook his head. From fairy tales to proverbs and rock song lyrics. How could he ask her this without making her feel bad? "Can't you just say what you mean? Straight out? What do you need, honey? What's missing or different or…" He looked up at the ceiling and pressed his lips together.

She didn't answer, just retreated to the back yard. It was at that moment he knew he was wrong to think it could all go back to the way it was. She was different and deep inside he knew that the people he thought she loved, the children, but mostly him, were not those living here. They were in another place.

He finished washing the dishes and watched her through the window over the sink. He had to do something, but he really didn't know what. Mandy trotted over to Martha and she absently patted the beagle's head. His wife wasn't even satisfied with their dog anymore, comparing Mandy to some feral dream dog from her coma. A dog that bred with coyotes or some such thing. A dog that had a choice to be with her or to run through the forest. Was that her way of saying that was what she needed? While she had been in that hospital bed he had sworn he would do anything for her and he had wracked his brain for answers. Now that she was here, things weren't so simple.

That night, after Martha slipped out of the living room at 8:30, much too early for him to think about going to bed, he reconsidered his options. Before all of this, Martha had moved out of their bedroom, much to his dismay. She had claimed it was part of her insomnia treatment—she didn't want her machine to keep him awake, his snoring disturbed her, she needed fewer blankets than him—there had been a list of excuses. And while their sex life wasn't what it had been, it existed. His worry that her moving to the other room meant that part of his life was over hadn't panned out. Not completely, anyway. There had still been romantic evenings when she slipped into their bed. Although never for the whole night. They would make love, he would fall asleep and in the morning he would be alone.

Now Martha had gone back to sleeping in their room. She ignored the new room for a week, then insisted he turn her living room back into what it had been. He didn't point out that he was sleeping in that bed, Jack in the spare room, just agreed to do what she asked. He and Jack spent the weekend removing the walls and the bed was disassembled and stored in the garage.

At least his son recognized Glen didn't have a place to sleep now. "Hey Dad? Don't worry. I'll find a place soon. I can use the camp cot in Mom's sewing room and you take the spare room."

He knew if it were possible, Martha would have asked him for her old kitchen.

So, here was his wife, sleeping in the bed that had been his for the last three years. No discussion about it, just the clear expectation that he sleep somewhere else. What about those romantic nights? She'd had a month of recovery, so surely he could slip in beside her and hold her in his arms?

He stood in front of the closed bedroom door. The hum of the CPAP machine matched the rhythm of his breath. He pressed his palm against the thick oak door and listened. Maybe this was one of those things where both of them were unsure about what to do and no one was talking about it and they both wanted the same thing. Or maybe it wasn't.

He turned and walked down the hall.

FORTY-FOUR

Martha sat in the back yard and listened to her family talk about her. Apparently checking for open windows never entered their minds.

Clarice's voice came through the loudest. She must be standing at the sink. "Have you talked with Mom lately?"

"I was here last weekend. It's been busy, I'm trying to make up for lost time with Sandra and the kids. All this stuff with Mom, I've neglected them. I'm working some overtime when I can. Sandra and the kids…we…need a vacation this year. Something special, something to. …" Vince stopped midstream and for a moment Martha thought he must have noticed her or the open window or both.

"I get it. Something to take your mind off Mom."

Martha held her breath and listened.

"She may be awake, but she's still living in that other world of hers. I told Dad she needs therapy. I tried to make it easy for him, with the name and phone number of a woman who specializes in…in…people like Mom. People with blank spaces."

Naturally Clarice would be vocal about Martha's state of mind.

"Therapy? She seems okay. Kind of absorbed maybe."

What in the world did Vince mean by absorbed? She was distracted, yes. But she took care of things.

"Dad wants to wait with the therapy, but the longer we let her stay in this other place, the worse, I mean the harder it's going to be to get her out of it. I was hoping that you would talk to him. He respects what you say, well, more than anything Jack has to offer or I try to tell him."

"I could do that."

"Thanks, Vince."

They left the kitchen and Martha didn't know what they said next. Were they headed straight in to talk about her with Glen? She should get up, go in and make sure she had some sort of say in this discussion.

She leaned her head back on the chaise. The sun felt good today. She wouldn't think about what her kids were saying or about the sink filled with dishes or the sticky patch on the kitchen floor where Sam had spilled juice. She could hear the voices of her grandchildren, the steady buzz of the insects, feel the wind as it changed direction, blowing first one way, then the other, as it carried the scent of sage and cedar all the way across the country and into her mind.

Mandy crawled up on the chaise beside her and she felt the dog's warm breath against her thigh. She rubbed Mandy's head. "Don't you wish you were free, pup? You could chase rabbits, lay in the sun, sniff out mice. You could be with who you chose and it could change every day. Play with children, hunt with the men, or dig with the gardeners. You could comfort someone who is lonely, but I guess you are doing that, right girl?"

"Martha? You out there?" Glen slid the door open. "Can you join us please?"

"Yes, of course." She went into the restored living room where Vince sat on the couch, Sandra sat in Glen's recliner, and Clarice paced in front of the fireplace. No Jack today, he was at his new job. Well, not that new for him, but new for her. Everything about this time seemed new to her now. As if she had never lived here. She took a seat on the couch next to Vince, straightening the scattered newspaper as she did.

"Vince wants to talk with us about something."

"What is it? The kids? Your job?" She scrunched her eyebrows together in an attempt to look concerned. Best to use some sort of distraction technique to keep from looking guilty for eavesdropping.

"The kids are fine. It's about you."

"About me?"

"We're worried about you. You know how hard it is for us to understand this world you lived in. It's just...well...we're trying, but it's so different from anything that's real to us. The thing is, you're back here now, back in this life. Mom, this is your life, not that other world."

"I know that. I just miss the other life. I missed this life when I was there. I guess I wish I could have both."

"Mom, I think it would be a good idea if you went to see a therapist, someone who could help you adjust. It's been a big transition, like moving to another country or something."

Martha listened to her son try to come up with a rational reason that she should see a therapist.

"Are you saying you think I have some sort of mental disorder?"

"No, Mom, I don't think that. Frankly I don't really know what to think. But I do see you having a hard time adjusting. Things seem kind of…out of whack."

Martha knew that her story was unbelievable. Jack might believe but he was so non-committal these days, sitting next to her all the time and trying to start conversations. It was nice, actually. The two of them had some great discussions. They talked about the different ways of the canyon, about music and about his job. They hadn't talked about his notebook, but she would do it soon.

If only there was a way to make her family understand. She had even tried agreeing with them that it was all a dream, but she still needed to talk about it. Apparently that wasn't enough for them. Since when wasn't it okay to talk about dreams?

She turned to her husband. He was chewing his lower lip and he gazed past her, out the front window. "Glen, what do you think?"

"I think it might be a good idea." He hesitated and she watched him draw in a deep breath. For courage?

"You…it's just…there are things I don't think you're aware of. You stop right in the middle of doing something, to the point that you drop things, as if your hands don't work."

"I know I do. But that doesn't hurt anyone."

"What about the clock? You threw out the clock."

"We don't need to be controlled by mechanical things. It's so much healthier to eat when you're hungry and sleep when you're tired. That clock, its ugly face looking at me, commanding me, I didn't want it."

Guilt slipped in and out of her mind as she remembered how much she had relied on her watch.

"You don't eat when you're hungry." Glen stared at her. "Look how thin you are."

She just couldn't stomach the processed foods. Even the fresh vegetables and meat tasted dull to her. And when he microwaved a can of soup or made a bologna sandwich with pickles, it made her stomach heave. It had always been her job to cook a meal her husband enjoyed, but she couldn't bring herself to feel that way anymore.

She looked at the anxious faces, all staring at her, waiting for an answer. She wished she could think of something wise to say, something that would show them she wasn't crazy.

They never expected wisdom from her. Compliance, that's what they expected. She looked at Clarice, who had remained silent throughout, although she knew her daughter was the driving force behind this conversation. "What do you think?"

Clarice shook her head and clasped her hands in front of her stomach, as if the mere thought of telling her mother what she thought pained her. "Mom, I...you have to come back. We need you here."

They needed her.

Suddenly she saw the whole thing. Status quo. Back to the old ways. Keep everyone happy. She would be the invisible force who kept them fed, was there when they needed an ear or a ride or babysitting. She wasn't objecting to anything other than being ignored. Although that wasn't it, not exactly. She did want to be left alone about some things, yet she wanted them to listen to her. The real her, not the imagined wife, mother, sister, cook. The soul behind her words.

She looked at their faces and she thought about how Clarice and Glen would work to bring back the familiar Martha, how Vince had so much on his mind that she was just another problem to be checked off on his list and how her sister, during their infrequent phone calls, waited patiently and then changed the subject.

On her journey—which was not a dream—she felt things were being offered to her so that she could have a second chance. To-be-né was the little Clarice she had neglected by trying to control everything, Wi-yen the baby Jack she could cuddle, and Sen-tshe her chance for love. It was possible Kwe-in-ye was her sister, Deborah, complete with her bossy ways. Vince? She hadn't figured that one out yet. Mosinobu had wisdom. Maybe there was something in how her friend approached life that would help her see Vince.

She had come back and cast aside these lessons. Her family was right. She spent all her time thinking about the other world, wishing to go back and not thinking about the lessons she was meant to learn.

She could use the therapy sessions in the ways she wanted, not in the way the family clearly pictured. She desperately needed to bring what she had learned from the ancient people into this life, to make things better here and now. The therapist could help her with this, guide her in how to bring about these changes in spite of her family's resistance. Clearly they were not going to listen to her stories any more.

"Fine. I hear you. I'll try it." Martha listened to her own words. She wasn't going back to being the old Martha, giving in to pressure. This was her decision.

Later that night Martha sat on the couch next to Jack, as he extended his stomach and beat his hands on it like a drum. "Great dinner. As you can tell by the drum instead of a belly."

"No one forced you to overeat." She stopped herself before she told him that the people only ate when hungry or gave her own version of the starving-children-in-the-world story. "Can we talk about your poems?" His notebook wasn't in the basket and she thought about how she had lost it before she came home. Was it lost forever?

"I guess that would be okay." His voice was low and tight. He was being compliant with her request.

"I want things to be different. They are different, but one thing I would like is for you to say no to me when you need to. We don't have to talk about the poems if you don't want to."

"Mom, I'm sorry…"

Martha placed her hand over his. "Don't apologize. What I'm trying to say…"

She had thought about this conversation so many times before she came back. Hoped she would have another chance with Jack. She knew it wasn't going to be some miraculous fix of a lifetime of mistakes. "I'm not sure how to do this. But, Jack, I'm strong. I'm not who I was and I want to know who you are. I love you, but I don't know you. The poems helped. They gave me a preview. All I want is a chance to…I don't know how to put it. A fresh start."

Jack's eyes filled and he nodded "I saw what you wrote." He turned his hand over and clasped hers.

He must have got the book back. Yet he didn't seek an explanation about how or when she added her response to his journal. As she sat and studied him—the stubble on his cheeks, the unruly hair, his chameleon eyes—she felt a surge of love. It was followed by a wave of sorrow at the price she had paid to have a second chance with her son.

He was her baby once. She remembered how he resisted her arms, struggling to get away, happiest if left in his bouncy chair or lying on a blanket. He probably would have loved a cradleboard and swaddling.

"When did you get so smart?" She leaned over and kissed his stubbled cheek.

FORTY-FIVE

It was only the second visit to the therapist but Martha knew she wasn't coming back.

"So here is a card for Dr. Holcomb. She's the one I mentioned? I really do think you need to consult with her."

Chantice Darmo, an exotic sounding name for a plain woman, recommended Martha see a psychiatrist for a medication consult. The therapist's voice had joined the choir of those who thought she was crazy.

Why did I think she would be different? Martha had hoped there was some sort of therapists' creed that said they must believe the patient, but apparently there was no such thing.

She did need someone to talk to. Glen made it clear he didn't want to listen, Clarice had made herself scarce, and Vince only listened with half an ear during his duty visits. Twice a week, Tuesday afternoon and Friday morning, for twenty minutes.

Jack listened. They had discussions about how a person could make choices, about poetry, ritual, even his substance addictions. While she loved these conversations, she couldn't talk to him about everything. She couldn't talk to him about passion and love and sex. She couldn't talk to him about Glen and she couldn't talk to him about Sen-tshe.

One morning, after a particularly fitful night, when Glen had left for work and Jack had gone out for the day, Martha sat on the back deck with a cup of tea and Mandy by her side. At moments like these she allowed herself to slip back into the canyon. She imagined a lovely spring morning, sitting in a patch of sun. Wi-yen toddled nearby and Po-ko was chewing on a stick. Sen-tshe sat near her, repairing his tools. It was an ordinary day, filled with peace. Each of them was content to be near the other. No one demanded anything, no one expected anything, no one wanted anything. They were just happy to do what needed to be done.

Martha's daydream was interrupted by the phone.

"Hi, this is Naomi. I was just checking in to see how things are going. How are you feeling?"

Maybe it was a fantasy, but the girl's voice sounded so much like Sen-tshe's that for a moment Martha couldn't speak.

"Hello? This is Mrs. Grimson, right?"

"Sorry. I...I'm good." The instant the lie was past her lips she decided to take it back. "No, that's not true. I'm not good. In fact, do you think we could get together? Talk about...things? You did promise me that I would hear more about your family and the pueblo."

"Of course. When would you like to meet?" Naomi said.

"How about lunch?"

"Lunch sounds great. Will 11:00 work?"

"Perfect."

"Such a sweet dog." Naomi didn't seem to mind that Mandy needed to lean on her leg.

"She is a good dog, but I can't help but feel sorry for her."

Naomi raised a questioning eyebrow.

"I had a dog. In the canyon. Well, she wasn't my dog. Po-ko. She loved everyone. She spent time with To-be-né, a nine year old girl who loved adventures. She actually belonged to a man, Sen-tshe." Suddenly Martha was crying.

Naomi leaned over and took her hand. "You miss them. The people from the canyon."

Martha nodded and sobbed. Naomi held her hand and didn't pressure her to speak.

"I'm sorry. I can't imagine what came over me," Martha tried to say, but her words came out garbled as they caught in her throat.

"Don't talk."

So they sat, one woman crying and the other woman comforting. Finally Martha rubbed the tear trails from her cheeks with her sleeve.

"You can talk to me about it."

Martha nodded, thankful for Naomi's perception.

"It was so different there. I was scared and overwhelmed at first. Everything was strange and they, especially the old woman, I think she was my spirit guide, put so much pressure on me. I was supposed to save their whole world."

"Maybe you can start at the beginning?"

"That's right. You weren't there when I told everyone the whole story." Martha spent the next hour telling Naomi about the ancient Puebloans and the canyon and the time she had spent there. Then she told her how her family wasn't receptive to listening to her talk about what had happened.

"I think, dream or not, the purpose was for me to learn something. When I was there and it was happening I felt like I saw the messages. But now that I'm home—" Martha sighed. "I can't seem to mesh the two. Except for Jack. But Clarice is as angry as ever and Vince as busy and Glen…that's the hardest of all."

She glanced at Naomi and decided this was her chance. "The man I told you about, Sen-tshe?"

Naomi nodded.

"We were in love. I lived with him."

The air was still and Naomi didn't speak.

"I miss him so much and now, with Glen, I know I'm supposed to love him. I'm supposed to have learned what love was all about and brought that lesson back with me, but all I can do is think about Sen-tshe and how I want to be with him."

"There is a story my grandmother used to tell me. It is about a woman who loves someone other than her husband. About the choices she had to make. And how hard those choices can be."

"Will you tell me the story?"

Naomi glanced at her watch.

Martha jumped up. "I'm sorry. I didn't mean to make you stay here, to be my therapist. It's been hours and you probably have to sleep or something." She faltered. "Because of the night shifts?"

"Sit down, Mrs. Grimson. I'll let you know when I have to leave."

Martha sank back to the chair.

"The point of my grandmother's story was that we can't see the future. When we make choices we travel down the uncertain fork in the road and we can never go back and choose a different path. What if you are wrong in how you see things? Maybe you were simply there to save Sen-tshe's life? And Wi-yen." Naomi smiled. "I say this from a selfish perspective. What if I am the descendant of this man? If you hadn't saved him I wouldn't be here."

Martha understood what Naomi was trying to say, but she knew that wasn't enough. "I can't feel it, that the love I had with him was so trivial to be just a passing thing."

"Well, maybe something else? What you had there and what you have here, is there a way to make them closer to the same thing?"

"I've thought about that a lot. But every time, I just...I think about how what was there was better and everything here is dull and tarnished. It's hard for me to get moving at all. I don't have anything to say to my old friends, the speakers at the garden club and the quilt guild bore me, and the food tastes horrid."

"And you don't feel close to Glen?"

Funny how this young woman wouldn't let her get away with changing the subject.

"No. Not that we were all that close before. We hadn't been for a long time."

Naomi looked at her watch again. "This time I do have to go. But I'd love to come back and talk some more."

"Oh, you don't have to do that. I mean, thank you for coming. It has been wonderful. But I know you have a busy life and I'm not your patient."

"I'm not saying this to be polite, Mrs. Grimson. You and I? We have a connection and I want to explore that with you."

And so Naomi became a regular visitor. She taught Martha about the life on her pueblo and Martha talked about her time in the canyon and eventually they came around to something that worked toward a—well, if not satisfactory, then do-able—solution for Martha's confusion about her husband. She accepted that she was not going to see Sen-tshe again. Ever. And she should cherish the time she had and make an effort to find something, if not exactly like what she had, something better with Glen. She had loved him, did love him. There had been passion and excitement when they first met. Maybe if she had grown old in the canyon her relationship with Sen-tshe would have dulled and become routine, just like her marriage. It was up to her to change that.

One night, after a dinner of quinoa and venison, a meal closer to what Martha craved than most, she folded her napkin and looked at Glen.

"Maybe tonight, instead of standing outside my door, you might want to come in."

He blushed.

Martha smiled. "I hear you. I just want you to know, I'm ready now."

FORTY-SIX

"I slept with Glen."

Naomi set her mug on the table. "Slept as in shared a bed or slept as in made love."

"There was sex involved." What a funny phrase making love was. As if Martha could gather the ingredients and follow a recipe and love would be created as easily as chocolate chip cookies. "Maybe that's the secret? Maybe it is like chocolate chip cookies."

"Sex was like cookies? You lost me." Naomi shook her head.

"Oh my mind was just wandering. It was hard, sleeping with him and keeping my mind off Sen-tshe. It has been a long time. Not just the time I was gone, but before that."

"So where do cookies come in?"

"You used that phrase—making love. And I started thinking about what the recipe would be, you know. Like there really are special ingredients." Martha glanced at Naomi.

Naomi smiled and raised her chin. In that moment Martha saw Wi-yen. Of course, he was this woman's ancestor. How could she ever have doubted it?

Martha laughed.

"What's so funny?"

"It just came to me. Wi-yen was never the key to saving the people. That was my job. But he was the key to something important. He was the key to saving me." Martha reached out and took Naomi's hand. "It was you. You were the thing, the person who would save me."

"Wait a minute. I'm happy to help you but don't put that kind of responsibility on me." Naomi smiled as she spoke.

"You're a nurse. It's kind of your job."

"You got me there. Okay, back to your ingredients of love. Of course there are. Just the other day I read a book about pheromones and DNA. There's scientific proof now that you can actually smell the right mate. Biologically speaking."

"Interesting, but I was thinking more along the lines of things like respect and shared household duties. I think I'm past the biologically induced attraction." Martha walked to the sink and rinsed her mug. "More coffee?"

"Nope." Naomi finished the last bit and brought her mug to the sink. She stood next to Martha and they gazed out at the back yard.

"That was a lie." Martha pressed her palms against the edge of the sink and dropped her chin. Then she raised it and looked at Naomi. "With Sen-tshe it was about biology. I loved his taste, his looks, his smell. Every cell in my body was alive."

Naomi was silent and both women turned back to staring out the window.

Mandy was making her rounds, nose to the ground as she checked the fence line. The dog walked the perimeter constantly. Before her journey Martha had viewed it as responsible. Her watchdog checking the borders of the family's world, vigilant for threats.

Now Martha felt it was sorrowful. The beagle, limited by the six foot wooden fence, sniffing the edges in desperation to gather knowledge about the world outside the barricade. A world she could only imagine through smells and sounds.

"How was it with Glen?" Naomi didn't turn toward Martha as she spoke.

"Truthfully? It was really sad. I felt...he...I guess it felt like pity sex. Not an obligation, just a hand out because I feel so guilty about what I did. I cheated on my husband and I can't even confess because he thinks it's all in my imagination." Martha rinsed Naomi's mug. "Not only that but I miss Sen-tshe so much and every movement—how Glen kisses, how he touches me—I can't stop myself from comparing it to what I had with Sen-tshe."

Naomi stood very still, something Martha had come to recognize as a sign the young nurse was deep in problem-solving mode. It was best to wait when this was happening because the help this woman had given her over the past few weeks was incredible.

Mandy stopped in the back corner of the yard and buried her nose deep in the tulip bed. She prodded a half-buried bulb with her paw and picked it up in her mouth. Martha no longer cared if the dog dug up her flowers but she was worried about the toxicity of bulbs. She knocked on the window and Mandy dropped the bulb and ran back to the house.

Without a word, eyes still half closed, Naomi walked out to the deck. Martha followed her and the two sat down. Mandy wiggled with delight that company had joined her.

Naomi opened her eyes and turned to Martha. "Do you think you can list the ingredients for love? Take what you learned on your journey and apply it to this life?"

"The whole dream as a lesson thing?"

"Yes."

"I don't know if that would work. Sen-tshe and Glen are two very different people."

"But you? Aren't you the same person?"

Martha frowned. "I'm not sure what you mean?"

Naomi touched Martha's wrist. "You can only know yourself. Martha Grimson. That is your area of expertise. But Glen and Sen-tshe, they know themselves and they show you what they want you to see. You can't assume to know what is truly inside your husband. If you communicate with him, tell him what really matters, don't you think he would want to know that?" She paused. "And it would be wise to get to know him. Find out what really matters to him."

"The ingredients for love?"

"Exactly. And you will make the cookies together."

Martha waited two days before she brought up the ideas she and Naomi had discussed. The young woman was so wise. Was it the lessons of her ancestors? Martha liked to imagine Wi-yen growing into an adult who married and had children. In her mind he held them on his knee and told them the story of the strange woman who had come from the future and had cared for him as a baby. In reality, he had been so young it wasn't likely he remembered anything other than the stories his father told him. But the image made her smile.

She rehearsed what she would say to Glen over and over, a habit she knew wasn't helpful. In her imaginary conversations he said certain things and she prepared certain responses but in real life it never happened that way.

They had finished dinner—Chinese takeout because she had been too anxious to cook—and he was headed to the remote control.

"Glen? Can I talk to you about something?"

"Sure. What is it?" His look betrayed his true feelings: a grimace and lips pressed tight.

"Let's sit outside. It's nice out there."

"Uh oh. Must be serious." He tried to joke but Martha didn't return his smile.

"How about some tea?" Martha realized she was delaying things, but holding something in her hands would help calm her nerves.

"Sure."

When they were settled at the table on the deck, the bug zapper plugged in and Mandy chewing on her rawhide bone, Martha drew in a breath. "I know you don't think my journey was real, but real or dream, there were some things I learned and I need to share them with you."

"Is this homework from your therapist?"

"My therapist? No. I'm not going to her anymore."

Glen turned and scowled. "Since when?"

She wasn't going to lie about it. "I only went twice."

Glen's face was pale and fear grew in his eyes. Not what she wanted when she was attempting to get him to take her seriously.

"Where have you been going? You leave here every Tuesday at 6:00."

They were already off on another track and she hadn't even started talking about her recipe for love. "I've been going to a yoga class. It's

295

more helpful than that woman was. But listen, please. That's not what I want to discuss right now."

"You can't just brush off something this important."

"Okay. I promise I'll talk about it later. Right now I want to talk about something else. Can you please just listen? You never listen. This is hard enough without these tangents." Damn. Now she was throwing out accusations. That wasn't in the script at all.

"Hard?" Her husband leaned forward. "Why would it be hard to talk to me? What are you trying to say? Is that why you…you went away? Went into that coma or fake coma or whatever it was? I don't understand it. What have I ever done to make you afraid of me?"

Dear God. This was definitely not in the script. "Please. No. I wasn't unhappy and no, I'm not afraid of you. Things can be hard anyway, just because they're different. I'm simply trying to tell you about how I feel, that's all. And I didn't choose to go where I was, it just happened. It wasn't my fault and it wasn't your fault. I don't know what it was, a dream or an altered state or time travel. But what I want to say, what I keep trying to say, is that I learned something while I was there and I would like to share it with you."

"Oh, I see. Another story."

Martha drew in a huge breath and let it out slowly. "I know the stories frustrate you and this isn't another story. It's about you and me and our love and this day forward."

He leaned back with a sigh and rolled his hand in front of him. Continue, the gesture said.

"While I was there I met…" No, that was something she had decided in advance. She wasn't going to tell him about falling in love with Sen-tshe. "I found a way of believing in myself. There were expectations of me, but there was also respect for me. And that made me feel important. It made me feel worthwhile. I would like to feel that way here, in this world."

"So you have never felt worthwhile?"

"Please. Don't take this as criticism. My life was good, it really was. I wasn't lying to anyone, not even myself, when I said I was happy. It's just that there can be more. That's what I learned. Don't you agree that things can always be improved? Isn't that true in every aspect of the world? There can suddenly be a better way to design an engine or transport vegetables or...you know?" Martha tried to think of a way to show Glen what she was saying. "It's good that I'm back here with you. But there are things, new things I like."

"Are you talking about sex?" Glen turned and stared at her, eyebrows arched.

She blushed. "Well, I wasn't talking about that, but sure, even that. Think about it. When we first met, how everything was new, an adventure. During my time...away...I found things I liked to do. Hiking, exploring the outdoors, really looking at nature. Even the cooking...if you and I could cook together and explore the flavors and not just fall back into the you-cook-I-clean-up routine."

"I don't understand. I really don't. The way we cook is what will make you happy? I'm fine with that, but there are days when work just takes it all out of me, Martha."

She looked at her husband. His face was gray now. Very little color had returned during their conversation. The wrinkles around his eyes stretched down toward his ear lobes and his eyebrows were losing their deep color. He kept his hair cut very short, although she loved it when he let it grow to curls on the back of his neck. He used to do it when they were young. Had she ever even bothered to find out if he liked it too? Or had she just laughingly convinced him to do it for her?

This past year had been hard on him and while she had thought about that, had she really *thought* about it? Here she was, complaining that no one really saw her but did she really see him? She considered what Naomi had said, that you only really know yourself. One of the ingredients was trying to know the other person. And that went both ways.

Plus she was here. This was her life. She had to make it work.

"Oh, Glen. I'm not communicating what I want to tell you. I just... love you and I want everything to be perfect. That's all I'm asking. I want to listen to you, too. I want it to be perfect for both of us." Martha reached across the table and touched his hand.

Glen looked at her. There were tears in his eyes as he turned his hand over and clasped hers in his.

FORTY-SEVEN

Martha picked up Sara and Sam from school. Sandra had agreed to let the kids go on an outing today. There was a display of ancient pottery at the University museum. It just so happened that Sara's fourth grade class was studying native history and Martha wanted to show the kids the wonderful pots. Clarice had agreed to meet them during her lunch hour.

They sat outside the entrance, waiting for Clarice. Her daughter was running late, which didn't bother Martha, but the kids had only so much wait time in them. After all those years of changing her major and her mind, Clarice had finally found something she loved. Her daughter might not always travel the same path to get to a destination, but when she achieved what she was after it worked out for her. A PhD in environmental studies and a job working with an agency focused on taking care of this earth. And one that she could take time away from during the day. Martha was very pleased with her daughter's accomplishments.

"Sorry, Mom. Hey, my little peanuts, how you doing?" Clarice arrived in a flurry of pats and kisses. "So this is exciting, right? A show straight from New Mexico?"

It was a small display, but the moment Martha walked in she knew that this was a collection of the pottery from her canyon. She recognized the designs of Ta-kan and Momo. Sara pressed her face close to the glass display cases and Martha pointed out the different pots.

Sam was drawn to the next room, where an array of weapons was visible. "These are great, Grandma. But let's look in that room."

"Let me take him, Mom. I'll keep him busy while you show Sara the pottery."

"I'd like you to see it too." Martha didn't like the fact that neither Sam nor Clarice seemed very interested in the pottery. At least Sara was curious.

"It's okay. I can buzz through afterward." Clarice glanced at Sam. "Come on, my man. Let's see what they have over here."

Martha brushed off the wave of disappointment. She had resolved not to be bossy to Clarice and now was her opportunity. She took hold of Sara's hand and they walked to the next display.

"After the clay is brought from the special part of the riverbank, it is worked with the hands. There were no tables but there were plenty of big flat rocks. You didn't have to worry about making a mess either." Martha continued her explanation, talking Sara through the shaping, painting and firing of the pots.

"Each woman has her own design, her own way of making her bowls and pots."

"Did they put their names on them? I don't see the names? Mrs. Quimby makes us put our names on our things."

"No, they didn't put names. The people didn't think anyone should try to stand out above anyone else. They felt you should do your best job and be proud of it, without attention. They didn't have prizes or art shows or anything like that."

Sara thought about this. "I like it when Mom puts my pictures on the refrigerator. I can tell when people don't like it because they just say "Oh, how nice" and then they have a fake smile."

Martha laughed and hugged Sara. "You're so smart. I know just the smile you're talking about."

"Sometimes my dad asks a lot of questions like, is this a horse?" Sara wrinkled her nose. "That means he doesn't really like it."

"Do you like it?"

Sara nodded. "I get it, Grandma. It's good if you don't really care what anyone else thinks. If you like the picture then that's good. They teach us that all the time, but still…it really is better when my dad likes it."

"I'll let you in on a secret. When I was there, with these women, I wanted to remember which pots I made. I was just learning and I really wanted to know how they turned out after they were baked in the fire. I kind of thought that they might be so bad that the other women were hiding mine, telling me different ones were mine. So I signed them, but I did it in such a way that no one would know."

"What did you do?"

"I put my thumb print just on the bottom edge, the same spot each time, where the two designs met." Martha pointed to the black on white pot in front of them.

"That was smart, Grandma. Were your pots good?"

"They got better as I practiced. And when I had the blue paint everyone was amazed." She thought about what she had told Sara earlier. Martha had still needed recognition, not yet assimilated into the ways of the people. At the time, she had told herself it was to have something of greater value to help the people, but now she could see that their admiration and respect meant a lot to her.

Sara headed to the next display, while Martha took one last look at the familiar thick and thin lines intertwining around the bowl. She could feel Ta-kan's stern direction and picture the woman's deep concentration and steady hand as she painted her pottery.

"Grandma, come quick." Sara called.

"What is it?"

"Your pot. It's your pot!"

Martha looked to where Sara was pointing. The shards of the pot were in poor condition, but they had been put back together to form a partial bowl. The design and paint were faded, but it did seem like blue, rather than gray or black. She bent down to Sara's level, following her granddaughter's finger to the thumb print, just there, where the two designs met.

"I...I think you're right." Martha looked up to the placard which accompanied the display.

Archeologists have never found an explanation for the few pieces of blue pottery among the work of the area. No other blue pots were found during this time period. Analysis of the paint indicated a fact that has puzzled researchers. The only explanation is that at some time the site was infiltrated by some other source of pottery.

"Hey you two. Are you about done? We're ready for lunch." Clarice and Sam had returned.

"Look." Sara said to Clarice. "Grandma's pot is here."

"Grandma's pot?" Clarice frowned.

Martha turned to her daughter. "I know it seems strange, honey. I know you don't believe what happened to me. But this…this is my pot."

"What do you mean, your pot?"

"This is a pot I made when I lived in the canyon."

"Oh Mom. How could you think that? This pot is in ruins, broken and ancient. There are so many pieces in this show. Why would this one be yours?"

Sara bounced up and down. "It has her fingerprint."

Clarice finally quit arguing and actually looked at the display. Martha watched her daughter's face go from frustrated to confused. She turned to her mother and whispered "The blue paint."

When she got back to the house, Martha had to wait an hour before Glen got home from work. She felt like a eager child, rushing to greet him as he walked in the door.

"How was work?" She asked, as she kissed him and took his lunch pail.

"Wow! Front door service," he said. "It was good."

"My day was exciting."

"The museum? It went well?"

"More than well. Do you think you can take the day off work tomorrow to go there with me?"

"Not tomorrow, but I'd be happy to go see the exhibit on Saturday."

She couldn't wait until Saturday. "The thing is, Glen. It's unbelievable. There are pots there. Pots from my people and, I know it's crazy, but there is a pot that I made."

Something swept over his face and he looked away, unable to meet her eyes. After all this time she knew he was over his initial rejection of her story of living in the past, so what was he thinking?

"How did you know it was your pot?"

"I remember making it. It was my design, although it was faint from time passing. And the blue paint, it had my blue paint. And if that's not enough to convince you, it has my thumbprint on it."

She didn't wait for him to reply. "Clarice believes me now. Finally, after all these years. Although the shock was huge. She got a headache."

"Martha. I believe you. And there's something I need to show you."

Ten minutes later Martha was staring at the book on her lap. She couldn't believe that her cave drawings were shown in the old photograph. Why had Glen kept this from her? Things had been good between them. She loved her husband now. Admittedly not with the same electric passion she had felt for Sen-tshe, but there was more fire between them than there had been in years.

"If you had proof my story was true, why did you keep it to yourself? You put me through so much!"

"It couldn't be true, don't you see. I thought you had seen this book, or another one, in that museum and made up the story. I didn't want there to be more ridicule. People thought you were doing it all on purpose, don't you see? Manipulating things."

"People? What people?"

Glen took her hands. "Your family. But look, what's going to happen now? Do you actually want scientists to come in and check out the pot? Compare your thumbprint?" He shook his head. "Think about it. How disruptive it would be."

"I don't need to prove anything to anyone. I guess I understand why you didn't show this to the kids, but I'm mad about it, Glen. You'll have to give me some time to get used to knowing."

"I don't want you to be mad. I'm sorry, really sorry. Can you forgive me?"

"Of course." She kissed his cheek and stood. "But I'm still upset."

FORTY-EIGHT

Jack's truck was parked in the driveway, blocking the garage, so Glen pulled up in front of the house. He glanced at the bouquet of Dutch iris on the seat. So much for a romantic anniversary celebration.

"Hello?" he called to an empty house. Then he heard music coming from the yard.

It was one of the native melodies that had become the only thing Martha ever listened to. Glen had to sneak off into the garage when he needed a bit of country-western.

Once in the kitchen, Glen could see that Naomi was with Jack and Martha. His son was seated in one of the new chairs—Martha and he had gone last weekend to buy a new patio set, their anniversary present to themselves—and Naomi and Martha were dancing.

Dancing was one of the things his wife had carefully explained to him. After their agreement that they would set aside time each week on Thursday evenings to talk about those things that would lead to growth in their lives. After all these years he hadn't felt the need to be so formal, scheduling every Thursday at 6:30, but Martha insisted if they made it compulsory they wouldn't be tempted to skip it.

"I need to dance. It does something wonderful for me...like a moving meditation. You should try it. It takes you completely out of your head and lets you exist purely in the physical components...I'm in my hips, my spine, my neck."

"I'm sure it's good exercise." Glen hadn't been willing to go so far as to join her.

But now, apparently, she had convinced Jack and Naomi to jump in.

Martha's little blue speaker that projected music from her phone was sitting in the middle of the table. A haunting rhythm of drums and flutes was accompanied by violins. It was also accompanied by his son.

Jack held a polished native flute. He played along with the tune from the phone. His eyes were fixed on Naomi and his foot tapped to the beat of the drums. It was obvious to Glen that his son had been playing this instrument for a while.

Although their relationship had grown strong, he still didn't really know this man.

Naomi and Martha held small drums. They moved in time to the music, dipping and twisting as they struck the drums. Martha claimed that Naomi was the descendant of these dream people and she had been sent here to save her. Glen let his wife play out this drama, because Naomi truly had been a godsend to the family. Other than palliative care and her strange ceremony, she really hadn't saved Martha. Coincidence, he was sure.

He glanced at Jack. But she might just be saving his son.

Martha smiled, her eyes focused on a distant point. He knew the dancing took her back. Back to that world that had given her so much joy.

She spun and dipped, then suddenly her gaze landed on him.

"Glen! You're home." She didn't stop her fluid movements. "Flowers! You remembered. Can you put them in water?"

"Sure." He turned to the sink. As he placed the iris in a blue vase, he felt isolated. This world Martha was in, with Jack and Naomi clearly by her side, felt so distant from him.

He nearly dropped the vase when arms snaked around his waist.

"Come on. Come dance with us." Martha squeezed and spun around to his side, still dancing.

"You know I can't."

"Can't or won't?"

She looked so happy. Teasing him, moving back and forth, eyes sparkling. Had she ever looked this way before?

"Well, okay. I guess you're right."

"Hurray! Just remember, no one is watching you. Just leave your thoughts out of it. Enjoy the feeling."

It took three songs for Glen to relax. But when he finally let go, he suddenly knew what Martha was talking about.

"Hey, has anyone seen Mandy?" Martha walked into the kitchen, where Jack and Naomi sat with Glen, munching on the chips and guacamole Naomi had brought.

"She was there when we were dancing. I saw her sniffing around the back fence." Jack fished a broken corn chip out of the dip.

"She's not there now."

"Let me look." Glen wiped his hands on the cloth napkin Naomi had passed to him.

They all went out to the back yard to search for the missing dog.

"Here, come over here. She dug out." Jack had pushed aside the thick andromeda and Glen saw a spot he had not shored up with wire. The pile of freshly turned soil bordered a hole just big enough for a beagle to squeeze through. He turned to Martha.

"Don't worry. She won't have gone far."

"I'm not worried."

He turned and stared at his wife. She had a strange look on her face, gazing past them all at the gully behind the house.

"She's chasing something. Something that she has been hearing and smelling on the other side of that fence for years."

Glen wiped his hands on his pants. "That could well be. And when she's done, she'll come home."

He saw Naomi whisper something to Jack.

"Hey, Dad? I'll help look, but Naomi needs to be at work. I'll take her and come right back, okay?"

"Sure. That would be great. I'm just going to walk around to the trail and look out back." Glen headed into the house to change into his hiking boots. He had only made it to the hall when Jack's shout interrupted.

"Mom! Dad! She's here."

Sure enough. The panting beagle sat on the front porch. Waiting for someone to open the door and let her in.

FORTY-NINE

Vince shifted from his left foot to his right and back again as he waited by the baggage claim entrance. He squeezed Suki's soft hand in his, then turned and lifted her to his hip. His granddaughter was so much like Sara had been at this age: generous and curious.

"Hey Peanut, how're you doing?"

"Good, Grandpa. Does Auntie Clarice like cookies?"

"Cookies? I imagine she does. Why do you ask?"

Suki pointed over to the food counter, travelers lined up for coffee. The glass case was filled with pastries and cookies, eye level for Suki. "Maybe when she gets here she would like a cookie."

Vince laughed. Any other child and he would have suspected ulterior motives, but with Suki? Who knows? Sara had been greatly influenced by his mother. The two had spent many hours together, Sara always listening intently to "the way of the people," as his mother liked to call her value system. Suki was a good reflection of these values, transferred down through the generations. She always thought about others, even at the tender age of four.

"Why, I think we should just go pick out a cookie for Auntie Clarice. I'm sure she would love one. I'm kind of hungry, too. Maybe we should pick out some cookies for us?"

A few minutes later Suki held a white paper bag tightly. She refused to eat her cookie before Clarice arrived, and she insisted it would be a good idea if Vince waited also. "Unless you are really hungry, Grandpa, then you should eat it now."

"How is she?" Clarice and her small bag were tucked into the car, Suki strapped into her booster seat in the back. They all munched on the cookies, Suki pleased that her great-aunt was hungry right now.

Vince kept his eyes on the road. "She's weak. You know her heart was never quite the same after the coma-thing. Not damaged really, but just impacted somehow. It became her weak point. She never wanted to take any of the medication, insisting that nature would take its course."

"What about her mind?"

"She's good. She knows who we are, talks with us. She's quiet a lot. I suppose she's thinking about her other world. She likes it when Naomi comes to visit, or Sara. She always felt those two were the only ones who really believed her story."

"Grandpa?" Suki piped up from the back seat. "Are we going to see Mommy?"

"Thanks for reminding me," Vince called over his shoulder. Turning his attention back to Clarice, he asked her if she would like to stop and visit the Farmer's Market. "It's on the way, and since it's only one day a week, I thought you might like to see Sara's set up. Dylan should be there too."

"I'd like that. I haven't seen the kids in a long time."

Vince was able to find a parking space close to the entrance of the market. He held his sister's arm as she walked across the gravel lot with Suki's hand tucked into her great-aunt's other hand. Looking ahead to the white tented booth, tables set in a "u" shape covered with the fresh vegetables and fruits Sara and her husband grew on their organic farm, Vince saw Sara was holding a bunch of carrots, deep in discussion with a young couple. Dylan was weighing potatoes and collecting money.

"Mommy, we're here." Suki released Clarice's hand and ran forward, to wrap her arms around her mother's legs.

"Hurray, you're here." Sara bent and planted a kiss on the soft brown hair, tickling Suki under the arm.

"We had cookies."

"Oh, cookies, what a nice treat." Sara's eyes met with Vince's. She tried to get him to be easy on the treats, but didn't give him too bad a time when he caved to the charms of his granddaughter.

Sara hugged Clarice. "I'm so glad you came."

"This is quite something, isn't it?"

For a minute Vince thought his sister was talking about their mother's illness. Then he realized she was referring to the Farmer's Market.

Sara guided Clarice through the mini tour of the booth, inviting her to come see the farm later in the week. "How long are you planning on staying?"

"I don't really know. Your dad said that Mom..." Clarice choked a bit, stumbling for words. "...she might not...I thought I would plan on staying for a while."

"Jack and Dad will be glad for the company." Vince said. "Mom too, although..." It was true, his mother was fading fast. He hoped she would have some good days while Clarice was here to visit.

"Do they have room for me? I haven't ever been to Jack's house."

"Plenty of room. Four bedrooms. Jack did such a beautiful job building his place, you'll love it."

Vince was proud of his brother, taking on Martha and Glen when it became clear they were having some trouble living alone. "Mom loves it. There's a huge deck overlooking the creek. She spends most of her time out there, watching nature, as she puts it." His father had aged so slowly, no health issues, just a little slower each year. Really, for seventy-eight, his Dad was pretty darn healthy. His mother had become weak and distracted. Just the small chores of washing dishes and preparing food had been hard for months, and now she was bedridden.

Funny how Jack turned out, finding his calling as a builder. His brother was in high demand. The work he did was classified as home building, not construction, for he truly paid attention to all the details that made his designs amazing and comfortable. The home he had started years ago, picking a piece of land just outside of town on the edge of a regional park, had finally been completed. Jack and Naomi had moved in and the family joke had been how the two were going to fill all those bedrooms. Three kids later, people quit asking. It was only after the couple invited Mom and Dad to move in with them that Vince had noticed the wide doorways, the one area set off from the rest, its own little sitting room with a big window for a view. He was sure Jack had planned all along to ask his parents to move in, but they would have resisted if he insisted too early.

FIFTY

The old man slipped on the loose gravel and went down hard. He lay for a moment on the trail, staring up at the sun.

His son had told him not to come. "It is better to remember it with fondness and light in your heart," he had preached.

But the thought of her face, her touch, her smell was still as real to him as it had been so many years ago. Really, such a short time together, but the magic and love had sustained him through a lifetime of puzzles and trials and joys and sorrows.

He pushed up onto one elbow and looked down at his shriveled body. In his mind, he still wore the muscles of a young man. He ran through the trees and climbed these canyon walls as swiftly as a fox. Pulling himself up on the smooth white boulder, he continued down the steep path.

A walk back in time, he had imagined when he set out this morning. But it was not to be. As he looked down at the canyon he did not recognize anything. Not a tree, not the path of the creek, not the walls. Everything had changed.

No one lived here anymore. The beautiful paintings on the walls had faded, the clay bricks had crumbled, and the kivas were now holes in the ground. As he moved slowly through the ruins, he shook his head.

When he got to the wide spot, a place he did remember, he looked around. Surely this was where the rooms had been. Kwe-in-ye and her sister tucked into one, with Mar-tee-a insisting he move from his isolated cave to the room next to them and he refusing. She was adamant that Wi-yen grow up around other children, but he knew that she had never quit worrying that the boy would fall out of his cave and be crushed on the rocks below. Yet the cave had been such a sanctuary for him. Away from the angry stares of the people and close to her.

He sat on a stone and rubbed his bruised knee. The magic he had hoped for didn't exist, but he was not sad. He could close his eyes and feel her in these walls. He knew that he would see her soon.

FIFTY-ONE

"**M**om, how are you feeling today?" Clarice had brought fresh flowers for her mother's room. She pushed aside the glasses and notebook, making room for the vase.

"Okay. I was thinking about walking across that huge caldera. Those elk. I had decided not to eat meat, you know."

"Hmm." As usual, Clarice chose not to respond when her mother slipped back into that world. After that first year—post coma—her mother had seemed to return to normal. Oh, there were differences. She was much more definite in her opinions and she refused to attend the community church, switching to her own set of spiritual beliefs. She hadn't preached to the family, but she had tried to teach "the ways of the people" to all her grandchildren, starting with Sara and Sam. Of course Naomi and Jack had the whole native-spiritual thing going anyway, so not much impact from Martha there. And now Suki seemed to be carrying on the family tradition.

"I'm going to see him soon."

"See who?"

"Sen-tshe. I know that now." Martha coughed and waved toward the glass of water on the nightstand.

"What about Dad?" Clarice thought about her father. He had loved her mother so much. She never knew what happened all those years ago. He had changed. He carried some burden but no matter how hard she tried to get him to talk about it, he never would. She picked up the glass and held it to her mother's lips. Martha sipped and sank down into the pillow.

"Dad will be here soon. He and Jack went to the hardware store. They're going to fix that door so it stays open."

"I need something."

"What? What do you need?"

"In the basket. It's a small fetish. A little black bird."

Her mother had never changed the basket. Those strange things, the needles and the blue paint, they were always in her bedroom, even when she moved. No one else was ever allowed to inspect them, not even the beloved grandchildren. Clarice walked to the basket and rummaged through the dusty items. She found the little black bird at the bottom and took it to her mother.

"Mom?" She placed the fetish in her mother's palm. Mom tightened her fist around the bird and Clarice wrapped her hands around her mother's hand.

"Clarice, I love you."

Her mother tried to pull away but Clarice held on tight, grasping her mother's hand between both of hers. Her mother's eyes moved rapidly behind her lids, as they had so long ago when she was in the coma.

"Mom? Open your eyes. Mom?" Suddenly Clarice felt a great heat coming from her mother's hand. It filled her own hand, moving up her arms and into her chest. She was paralyzed by the heat, hypnotized.

Mom spoke. Or maybe she didn't speak in this room, but only in the vision that had moved into Clarice's mind.

"Do you see the path? Doesn't it feel good under your feet?"

Her mother led Clarice down the misty trail. The air swirled around them and there was a figure up ahead. It was a tall woman, wearing a beaded leather dress, which for some reason was green. Her hair was in a long shiny black braid. She smiled at Martha and Clarice, beckoning with a wave of her hand. Clarice looked past her. There were people walking towards them on the strange path. A short woman, also dressed in beaded native attire. Her hair was gray, long braids hanging over each shoulder. Behind her stood a man. As he came forward Clarice noticed that he looked like Naomi, those deep eyes never blinking. He smiled and stared only at her mother, trying to push past the old woman. The old woman put her arm out, holding him back.

The woman in green shook her head and held up her hand, like a crossing guard stopping cars. "Clarice, let go of your mother's hand. It isn't to be."

Clarice squeezed her mother's hand, then loosened her fingers and let go. Mom ran forward, first grabbing the old woman by the shoulders and planting a kiss squarely on her cheek, then pushing past and falling into the arms of the smiling man. They embraced and stood with arms around each other, staring into each other's eyes.

Clarice felt herself slipping back. The mist was fading as were the people standing on the trail. She turned her head and looked at the woman in green. The spirit woman reached out her hand and ran her fingers across Clarice's cheek. "Go back."

Glen's voice broke into Clarice's dream. "Martha? Clarice?" She opened her eyes and turned to where her father stood, on the other side of the bed, looking down at her mother. Naomi was by his side staring frankly at Clarice.

"She's gone."

The tears rolled down Clarice's cheeks, following the tracks of the brief touch of the tall woman in green.

ACKNOWLEDGEMENTS

It takes a village to write a book....and I want to thank everyone who helped. I am double checking and hoping and praying that I don't leave anyone out, but it took me six years to write this book and my memory... well...you know.

I thank all my alpha and beta readers for their amazing input.: Cindy Whitson, Marlene Koons, Chris Phipps, June Gillam, Alex Beldon, Sheila Myers, and Clare Travers. Thanks to my editor, Laura Buckner. And thanks to my proof-copy readers, Janet DeGras, Regan Sobaje-Pierce, Laura Boatman and Joli Roberts.

As always thanks to my muse and massage therapist, Barbara. She will recognize the death of the deer scene as coming from that hideous day when a man in fatigues, carrying a bow, pounded on the door during my massage. It messed up the relaxation, but it turned into a good scene.

Thanks to the rangers at the National Parks who answered all my questions. Thanks to my cousin George for hiking the canyons and calderas with me.

The biggest thanks goes to my husband, Dan, for putting up with my need to write and sending me off with a kiss each time I set out on another journey.

ABOUT THE AUTHOR

Robin Martinez Rice is a retired Educational Psychologist and Marriage Family Therapist taking advantage of her time off. Traveling in an old time RV—"The Bookmobile"—she writes in places with a view. Visit her website at www.robinmartinezrice.com for more information about her books.

www.ingramcontent.com/pod-product-compliance
Lightning Source LLC
Chambersburg PA
CBHW071230250626

47163CB00001B/125